THE SUMMER SEASON

Heartsease House is in desperate need of renovation. Its owner, widower Joel, is struggling with life as a single dad. Mum to twin girls, Lauren's life is a constant juggling act. When her ex, Troy turns up wanting to see his daughters, she's determined to keep her distance. Then guerilla gardener Kezzie bursts into their lives, with her infectious enthusiasm to restore the gardens. But who is Kezzie? And what is she running away from? As the warm days of summer draw on, Heartsease House and its garden are transformed. But will Joel, Kezzie and Lauren be able to restore their own hearts?

THE SUMMER SEASON

THE SUMMER SEASON

by

Julia Williams

Magna Large Print Books
Long Preston, North Yorkshire,
BD23 4ND, England.

British Library Cataloguing in Publication Data.

Williams, Julia
 The summer season.

 A catalogue record of this book is
 available from the British Library

 ISBN   978-0-7505-3773-5

First published in Great Britain in 2011 by Avon
A division of HarperCollins*Publishers*

Copyright © Julia Williams 2011

Cover illustration © Ilona Wellmann by arrangement with
Arcangel Images

Julia Williams asserts the moral right to be identified as the author of
this work.

Published in Large Print 2013 by arrangement with
HarperCollins Publishers

Magna Large Print is an imprint of Library Magna Books Ltd.

Printed and bound in Great Britain by
T.J. (International) Ltd., Cornwall, PL28 8RW

To the memory of

Alfred Thomas Clark 1890–1918
Ernest Ophir Clark 1896–1916
And Jemima Clark 1863–1944
who must have been so brave

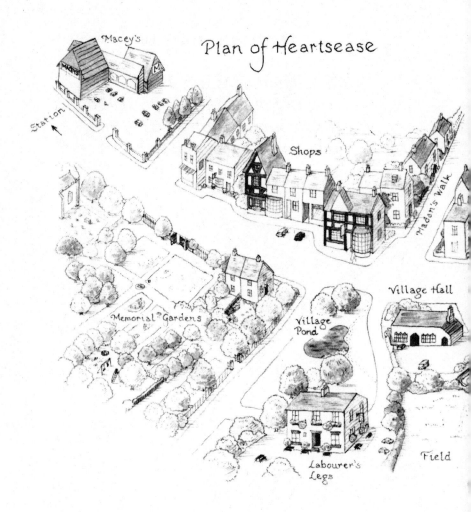

Plan of Heartsease

Macey's

Station

Shops

Madon's Walk

Memorial Gardens

Village Pond

Village Hall

Labourer's Legs

Field

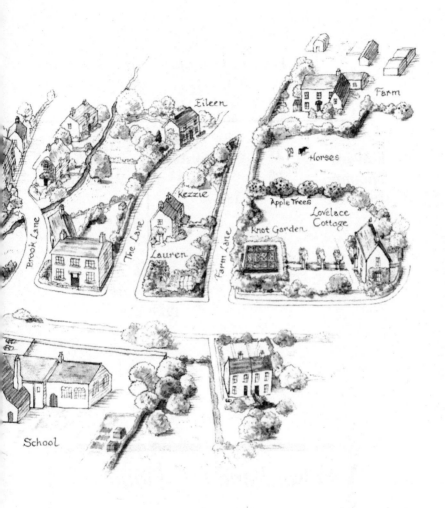

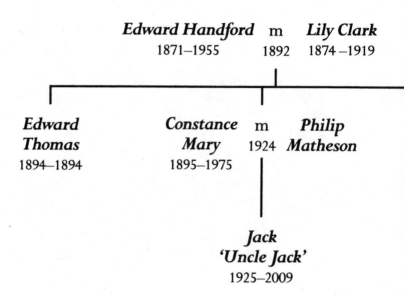

Edward Handford   m   Lily Clark
1871–1955   1892   1874–1919

Edward   Constance   m   Philip
Thomas   Mary   1924   Matheson
1894–1894   1895–1975

Jack
'Uncle Jack'
1925–2009

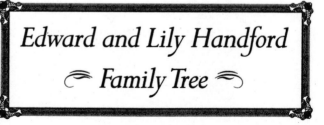

Edward and Lily Handford
Family Tree

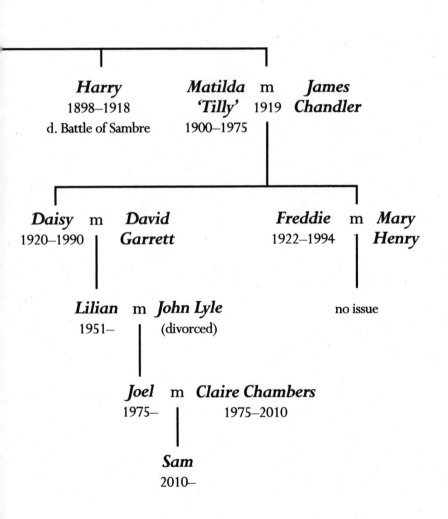

Harry
1898–1918
d. Battle of Sambre

Matilda m **James**
'**Tilly**' 1919 **Chandler**
1900–1975

Daisy m **David**
1920–1990 **Garrett**

Freddie m **Mary**
1922–1994 **Henry**

Lilian m **John Lyle**
1951– (divorced)

no issue

Joel m **Claire Chambers**
1975– 1975–2010

Sam
2010–

Edward

Edward dreams of Lily. She comes to him in the garden, holding a bunch of pansies. It is summer and she wears a sun hat, which falls down her back.

'Here, for you,' she proffers, 'to ease your heart.' She laughs, and her long, dark curls fly loose down her back in the summer breeze. It is always summer, with the Lily of his dreams.

He reaches out to touch her, to feel her, to know that she is once more real and dear to him, as she ever was. As he does so, she scatters petals to the wind, and her touch on his hand is as light and insubstantial as the breeze. As soon as he grasps her, she is gone away from him, to a place he knows he cannot reach.

Edward dreams of Lily, and awakes to a cold hearth, a lonely old age and tears forming on his face. One day soon, he knows he will join her. Why can't it be today?

Edward and Lily

1890–1892

In the spring a young man's fancy lightly turns to thoughts of love…
Alfred, Lord Tennyson, 'Locksley Hall'

'Edward, you never said you were coming!' His mother rose to greet him as Edward came into the garden; she was sitting entertaining as was her wont. He hadn't let her know and he had walked up from the station so as to surprise her. Now he was caught, left-footed, wanting to have her to himself, unwilling to share her with these strangers spilling out of the rose arbour on the veranda, which overlooked the garden, nonchalantly sipping tea, in the wilting summer heat.

'I wanted to surprise you,' he said. Her delight at seeing him was infectious, and he couldn't keep up his feelings of discontent for long. He was here, back where he belonged at Lovelace Cottage, a larger residence than its name suggested, nestling in roughly an acre of land on the Sussex, Downs where they bordered Surrey. The air always seemed better here, purer, away from the fetid smells of London where he was studying.

'Come, sit,' she said, linking her arm in his, 'you must eat, I insist.'

'Sorry to break up your party, ladies.' Edward bowed slightly, tipping his hat. He vaguely recognized some of his mother's companions, worthy women of the parish all, but there were one or two new to him; he had after all been away for several months.

'You haven't met Mrs Clark, have you?' his mother made the introduction. 'She's our new vicar's wife. And we're very pleased to have her. The church flowers have never looked more beautiful.'

'Oh, that's Lily's doing, not mine,' said Mrs Clark. 'My daughter has a way with flowers. Always had, ever since she was a little girl. She works magic in the garden at the rectory I tell you.'

'Then she has something in common with Edward,' said his mother. 'You know he studies Botany, don't you?'

Botany – a subject his late and unlamented father had been very sneering about. John Handford had wanted his son to follow him into the family business – as an importer of exotic goods from the colonies – it was a business that had made his father rich enough to buy this beautiful house and gardens. But like his casual acceptance of Edward's mother, his father hadn't appreciated what he'd had. The house and gardens were merely signs of his success, possessions to be gloated over, just as Edward's mother was. He'd never appreciated the beauty and the peace here, preferring the hurly-burly of city life that had always sustained him.

When he'd died five years previously, Edward's

father had left the house to Edward and the business jointly to Edward and his mother. Edward had sold his share of the business to his cousin Francis, who was more suited to it than he. His mother had retained her share, which provided an income on which she could live comfortably, while she ran the house in Edward's absence. They were both much the happier for it.

'Talking of Lily, where is she?' said Mrs Clark. 'It really is about time we were going.'

'I could sense she was getting bored with our conversation,' said Edward's mother, 'so I sent her down to the wood.'

The loosely styled 'wood' was an area of the garden that Edward had long wanted to change, but had so far lacked time and funds to do so. In the spring it was full of bluebells, but the trees were old and creaking, and overshadowed the house too much in Edward's opinion. He longed to cut them back and open up the space in the middle to make a more formal garden. It was his hope that after he had completed his studies, he would design gardens for the gentry, and he planned to start here.

'I'll go and fetch her,' offered Edward, happy to escape the clacking of the women for a moment. The veranda steps led down to a green lawn, which fell away from the house for nearly two hundred feet. In the bottom left-hand corner the offending trees stood in a dip, and Edward made his way down to it. He couldn't see any sign of anyone at first, so he strode through the trees to the clearing, where he caught sight of a tiny, dark-haired girl, framed in the sunshine. She was wearing a white muslin dress, and peering intently at the flowers in her lap. Long, brown curls tumbled down her back, and her sun hat was slung halfway down it. Her dress was covered in grass stains, and her hands looked rather grubby.

Edward's first impression was of a small, and no doubt tiresome, child, and he immediately regretted his offer to fetch her. Then she looked up at him and his preconceptions fell right away. Her green eyes opened wide and her perfect heart-shaped mouth formed an 'oh' of surprise at seeing him, and her slender hands flew to her mouth, as she blushed prettily with embarrassment. This was no child, but a girl on the verge of becoming a woman. Her radiant beauty was like nothing he had ever seen before, made more charming by her unconscious ignorance of it.

'Hallo,' she said, shaking the daisies from her lap, as she rose in some disarray. He could see that even standing she was small, but her petite frame couldn't hide her womanly figure. He swallowed hard again. 'Are you Edward?'

'Yes,' said Edward, still reeling from how wrong his first impression had been. 'How did you know who I was?'

'Oh, your mother talks about you all the time,' said Lily. 'It's Edward this and Edward that. How did you know my name?'

'Your mother sent me to fetch you,' Edward offered.

'Oh,' Lily pulled a face. 'I was enjoying it here. No doubt I shall be summoned back home to face Papa and be told off again for my hoydenish ways.'

19

She looked down ruefully at her stained skirt. A stray curl fell across her face and she absent-mindedly pulled it back, reminding him again of the child he had thought her to be.

'Are you often told off for being hoydenish?' Edward said, laughing. There was something so lively and disingenuous about her, it was impossible not to be enchanted.

'All the time,' said Lily, with an impish look on her face. 'I don't know how it happens but I was so interested in seeing the plants, I hadn't realized I had made such a mess of my clothes. Did you know you had heartsease growing in this wood? It seems such a shame to hide it. If it were my garden, I'd cut down some of these gloomy oaks and make a proper garden here, to show them off.'

'Oh, would you now?' Edward was caught between captivation and irritation. She really was the most enchanting creature he'd ever seen, but he rather resented her telling him what to do in his garden.

'Oh dear,' Lily looked stricken. 'I shouldn't have said that should I? Please forgive me; it's none of my business what you do in your garden. It's just that gardens are rather a passion of mine.'

'Are they?' said Edward with a smile. 'They're rather a passion of mine, too.'

'Have I drawn it properly?' Lily looked at him anxiously, as Edward came over to see how her work was progressing. In the six months since he'd left university, Edward had become used to having Lily for his assistant on his expeditions into the Sussex countryside to document the flora and fauna. Her mother, Lily confessed, had given up trying to keep her at home and teach her how to be ladylike. And though it was an unconventional career choice, learning about flowers was still an important part of Lily's education, so Mrs Clark had been easily persuaded to let Lily come on these trips with him, so long as Sarah the housemaid accompanied them as a chaperone. As it happened, Sarah was rather fat and lazy, so more often than not she'd accompany them as far as the first field, and sit down to await their return. It meant that Lily and Edward were spending more and more time together, and Edward for one was not sorry.

'It's perfect,' declared Edward, impressed by the delicacy of the poppy that Lily had painted. She had a natural affinity with plants, and a talent for drawing them technically. It was Edward's plan to put together the material he had collected to make a small book about the plants of Sussex, in the hope that not only could he earn some money in his own right, but also build up a reputation as a serious botanist. His desire was to go abroad, to visit far-flung corners of the globe and make his reputation by bringing back exotic plants the like of which the world had never seen.

'Hark at you,' teased Lily when he told her. 'Who do you think you are? A mighty explorer like Doctor Livingstone?'

'No,' said Edward, very serious – Lily's laughter made him realize just how intensely serious he could be sometimes, 'I just want to see the wonders that are out there. Imagine trekking through the Amazon, or scouring the deserts of the Sudan. There's such a huge world out there, I want to go out and explore it. I want to find something new and different. I'd bring it back for you.'

'Oh, would you, now,' said Lily, her laughter putting him in mind of silver bells. It was impossible for him not to feel cheerful when he was with Lily. It was as though she made the sun shine. 'Suppose I don't want your smelly plant. It might be poisonous for all I know. Besides, why do you want to search for the exotic, when we have perfectly good flowers of our own here?'

'I could take you with me,' he said. 'You could come as my assistant.'

'Shocking shocking, man,' she declared with a coquettish smile. 'I suppose Sarah would have to accompany us as my chaperone then. I don't think she'd make it past the first step into the jungle.'

Her pretty green eyes danced across her face, and her boisterous curls spilled out of the plait they were supposed to be in and tumbled down her back. Edward took her upturned chin in his hands and kissed her gently on the lips.

'You don't have to come as my assistant,' he said. 'You could come as my wife.'

A wife. *To have a wife.* That would be quite a thing. Edward turned the word over in his head. In a few short months Lily would be his, and nothing could ever take them away from one another. In the meantime, much to the amusement of his mother, he had finally started work on creating the garden he had always envisioned, but now with renewed purpose; it was to be a wedding present for Lily.

'Look at this!' he would cry every day, as he pored over plans and read books about the gardens of the past. He was transfixed by the idea of creating a knot garden in the Elizabethan style – a knot garden that would be a symbol of his love for Lily.

'Look at what, Edward?' his mother would retort with humour. She was pleased for him, he knew. She was very fond of Lily, and only desired her son's happiness.

'See here,' Edward would say, pointing out the patterns in the *Compleat Gardenes Practice*, a reference guide from the sixteenth century, which he was using to give him ideas to utilize and improve upon. 'The way they created geometric patterns and wove the plants together. I could do something similar. It will be a knot garden the like of which no one has seen. And Lily will love it forever.'

'I'm sure she will,' said his mother, smiling. 'With such a genius behind it, how could she not?'

Edward ignored his mother's gentle teasing, and concentrated on his plans. He designed the garden with careful precision. He would wall off the bottom part of the garden, where the old oak trees grew, and place the knot garden centrally, enclosed by gravel paths. From the edges of the paths to the wall would be flowerbeds full of perennials. For the knot garden itself he planned to use box with an interweaving of ivy and rosemary in heart shapes, the centrepiece to include the letters E and L. As was the current vogue he planned to fill up the gaps with bedding plants: heartsease, which was abundant in the area, forget me nots, gloxinia, but in each of the four corners, he left space to plant flowers for the children who would make their happiness complete. And so Edward toiled on his garden, planted in love with hope for the future; a garden he could be proud of forever.

'Where are you taking me?' Lily was clearly bursting with curiosity as he led her, blindfolded, down the garden.

'Shh, it's a surprise,' said Edward. He had worked hard to keep secret from Lily what he had been planning over these last few months, pretending that the trees at the bottom of the garden had become unsafe, as a way of keeping her away from the garden. He hoped that she would love his garden as much as he did, having poured his heart and soul into the project. He felt it was quite possibly his best work to date, and maybe the best he would ever do.

'I hate surprises,' said Lily, 'come on, please let me peep.'

'No,' said Edward firmly, 'the sooner you co-operate the sooner you can see it.'

He took her by the hand

'Watch out, there's a step here,' he said, as he led her down into the garden. He pushed open the wrought iron gate he'd had specially commissioned. 'Now you can see,' he pulled back her blindfold, which was the scarf that tied her summer hat on her head.

'Oh, Edward!' Lily clapped her hands over her mouth in delight as she gazed on the fruits of his labour, a garden set out in love and hope. A knot garden of hearts weaving rosemary, ivy, forget me nots, and gloxinia, with borders of the heartsease which gave their village its name.

'Do you like it?'

'Like it? I love it!' She danced excitedly down the paths. 'Did you do this for me?'

'Of course I did,' he said. 'It's a love knot garden, dedicated to my one true love.'

'Edward, I don't know what to say.' Lily came back to him and threw her arms around his neck.

'Just say you love me,' said Edward, with feeling.

'Always,' said Lily, 'always.'

He held Lily fast, and kissed her on the top of her head. Then he led her to the far end of the garden, where they sat on the wrought iron bench he had had specially made, with their initials on. Never had he felt more happy and content. This would always be their special place. A garden to represent their married life, a life that he knew, with Lily by his side, would be well worth the living.

Part One

Summer's Lease

Chapter One

'Come on, girls, time to get up! Important day today.' Lauren came softly into her twin daughters' bedroom, to watch two tousled heads sleepily awake and register their surroundings. Two brand new uniforms hung over the end of the identical pine beds, and her daughters slowly emerged from underneath their matching pink princess duvet covers. She drew the Cath Kidston inspired floral curtains, and looked out on the little garden that belonged to her rented cottage. It had a small patch of green for the lawn, and her pots of lobelia, geraniums, busy lizzies and alyssum were still flowering in a tumbledown fashion. It was homely and neat, pretty much the way she liked it. The warm, early morning sun belied the promise of the September day. It was going to be another hot one.

Lauren turned back to look at the girls and her heart contracted with a deep spasm of love. Four years old already and starting school for the first time. Where had all that time gone? It seemed only minutes since they'd been born three weeks prematurely, on a baking hot August day. Had they been born on their due date, she'd have had a whole extra year with them. As it was they were going to be among the youngest in their class.

'Come on, girls,' she said again, then went to sit on Izzie's bed and tickle her under the duvet.

Izzie was usually the slower of the sisters (and being asthmatic, the one who gave Lauren most cause for concern) and sure enough her giggles brought Immie immediately over to join in the fun. The three of them romped about on the bed for a bit, laughing, before Lauren said, mock sternly, 'Come on, time for school.'

By the time she'd helped them on with their clothes, and got them downstairs to the cosy kitchen, with its wooden pine table and cheerful mugs on mug racks, Joel had arrived with Sam – on time for once.

'Big day today, girls,' he said, as Izzie and Immie came to show off their school uniforms. They looked so sweet in matching grey pinafores (a size too big for them, to allow for plenty of growing room), crisp white shirts, and green cardigans. Their bright white socks were pulled high above their knees, their black Mary Jane shoes positively sparkled and their fair hair was tied up in identical ponytails, which by the end of the day Lauren was fairly sure would be coming undone.

They smiled shyly at Joel, as he popped Sam in the high chair, and watched them parade their brand new green book bags proudly in front of him.

'You wouldn't mind taking a photo of the three of us, would you?' said Lauren. 'Only, it would be nice to have a memento.'

'No problem,' said Joel, proceeding to snap away. 'Are you excited, girls?'

'Yes,' they chorused.

'I should say so,' said Lauren, 'I don't think

they slept a wink all night.'

'Ouch,' grimaced Joel. He looked at his watch. 'Is that the time? I'd really better dash.'

'Oh, of course.' Lauren clocked his sober grey suit, and kicked herself for forgetting what day it was. 'Good luck, today. Hope it's not too grim.' She touched him awkwardly on the arm, not quite sure whether the gesture would be appreciated. After Claire had died, their mutual grief had brought them very close. Too close she felt at times. Sometimes it had felt a little too intense, and now she tended to stand back more.

Joel gave her a tight, tense smile, his dark eyes brooding. His face was sombre and sad. 'It has to be done,' he said, before kissing Sam on the cheek. 'Have a great day, girls.'

Poor Joel. Thirty-five was far too young to be widowed. It was tough on him being alone with Sam, she knew that. That was why, in the main, Lauren cut him some slack when he took her for granted, which he invariably did. Lauren felt she owed it to Claire to look out for Joel; he needed support, and she was going to give it, even if he didn't always make it that easy. She felt a familiar spasm of grief for Claire too. A year on, and part of her still expected to see Claire pitch up at the cottage as she had done every day with Sam before her sudden and shocking death.

Lauren sent the twins up to brush their teeth, while she cleared up the breakfast things. She stacked the girls' matching Belle plates in the dishwasher, next to her favourite Cath Kidston mugs and bowl set (a present from Mum, Lauren could never have afforded them). She loved her

31

kitchen, which had been extended to make room for a dining table. It was cosy, and full of clutter. The children's toys – a magnetic easel, a plastic car and a small table and chairs set – competed for space with her pine table, washing machine, dishwasher and fridge freezer. Though Lauren didn't have quite as much work surface as she'd have liked, and what she had was crammed full of cookery books, this was her favourite room in the house – the real heart of her home.

Lauren lifted Sam out of the high chair, and put him into the buggy she kept here for him. She felt stupidly nervous for the girls, even though they had been going to the nursery part of the village school for nearly a year. But still. Proper school. True, being the youngest in the year, they were only part time to begin with. But before she knew it, they'd be gone all day. No longer would she have them to herself in the afternoon. If she didn't have Sam still to look after, the days could be long and lonely. Just like her nights...

A sense of melancholy came over her as she walked down the front path, with its familiar white picket fence, and creaky iron gate. The twins were holding on to either side of the buggy, chatting away nineteen to the dozen about what was going to happen in their day. They didn't seem nervous in the slightest. It was only Lauren who felt a vague sense of loss, with the realization that after today nothing would be quite the same again. She pushed the buggy down her road, waving hello to her neighbour Eileen, who was out walking her dog, and turned right onto the main road that led down the hill to the centre of Heartsease, where the girls were starting at the village school.

The September sun was still warm, and the day was shaping up to be one of those last blasts of summer lazy days, which you had to cherish before autumn took hold. But there were small signs of the approaching autumn. The trees were beginning to turn, the first conkers were beginning to ripen, and a gentle breeze blew a few leaves softly to the ground. It was days like these she remembered most from the period after Troy left her, and this time of year had remained bitter-sweet to her ever since. Just as she was getting used to the shock of motherhood, she'd had the bigger shock that she was going to be doing it alone. And now more then ever, sending her beautiful daughters off to school for the first time, she wished that it wasn't so.

Joel got in the car with a heavy heart, turned left out of Lauren's road, and drove back up the hill past his house and out of Heartsease across the Downs, towards the neighbouring town of Chiverton. He drove down a windy country road, arched with trees, their leaves beginning to shimmer with an autumn hue. He loved the countryside here and it was one of the many reasons, when his mum had inherited Lovelace Cottage and suggested he bought it from her, that he had. Even Claire, who'd at first been reluctant to leave London, and 'live in the sticks' as she'd put it, had agreed that when you came to the brow of the hill and looked out on the Sussex countryside, the views were stunning.

Claire. His heart contracted painfully. A year

ago today. Could it only really be a year? A year and a day ago he had been so happy. So rich and fulfilled. With everything in life he needed. But he didn't know it then, didn't appreciate it at times, maybe didn't even want it. It was only after he lost Claire, and his world came crashing down around him, that he belatedly realized how truly lucky he had been.

Today was going to be a painful and difficult day. Joel had promised to go with Claire's parents to her grave, in the cemetery on the other side of Chiverton, and then for lunch. He wasn't sure he was going to be able to get through another heartbreaking day with them. It wasn't that Marion and Colin were unkind or unsupportive, far from it. Although they lived over an hour away, they would help out with Sam at the drop of a hat, and they had been an immense source of strength to him. They had shown him compassion even though they were grieving too. No, it wasn't Marion and Colin who would make this day hard. It was Joel's guilt about what he'd done, and how he'd let Claire down.

Every day for the last year he had said sorry to her. Every day. And today, at the graveside, he would lay freesias, her favourite flowers (which he'd bought at great expense) and say sorry again. But it was never ever going to be enough.

Joel blinked back tears as he arrived at the graveyard. It was a bright, warm September day, unlike the day of Claire's funeral, which had been the bleakest, rainiest autumn day he could remember in his life. The church had been packed, and so many people had been so kind and thoughtful. But Joel had barely been able to acknowledge their kindness, responding like an automaton, feeling only a numbness that he now realized must have been deep jolt. The suddenness of Claire's death still shocked him, even now, a year later. How could someone as beautiful and alive and vibrant as Claire be there one day, and not the next? He'd be trying to make sense of that till the day he died.

Joel was pleased to see he had arrived earlier than Claire's parents. Selfishly, he wanted a bit of time on his own, for his own private grief. He walked up to her grave and felt again the sudden shock of seeing her name there:

Claire Harriet Lyle
1975–2010
Loving wife, mother and daughter
Taken from us too soon

He never got over the unreality of it. Nor, did he imagine, he would ever get used to it. Claire should be with him now, watching Sam learning to walk and talk, helping Joel restore the house and gardens as they had planned. She shouldn't be here, on this Sussex hillside, buried six feet under. He felt a sudden sharp bolt of anguish, the pain of it almost taking his breath away. Claire was lost to him, and there was no saying sorry now.

Kezzie sat in the middle of half-packed boxes, in her tiny lounge crying. She felt like she'd been sitting in the middle of boxes crying forever, ever since she'd made the decision that she had to leave. Only weeks ago, at the height of summer, she'd been excitedly packing up to move out of her small flat in Finsbury Park and move in with Richard. The gardening course she'd completed finished, the redundancy from her much hated job in web design accepted. A whole new life lay before them. She would design the gardens, Richard, the architecture. Together they would take Chelsea and Hampton Court by storm. And now that would never happen. The last month of her life had been the most painful, confusing and ridiculous time she'd ever known.

Should she ring Richard again? Kezzie sat on her heels in the chaos of her lounge and thought about it. She was sorely tempted. It had been nearly a week since their last painfully awkward conversation. Somehow she clung to the hope that maybe he could find it in himself to forgive her for what she'd done. She flinched as she saw the cold contempt in his eyes at their last meeting, heard him say over and over: 'You've let me down, Kezzie. I can't trust you.' That scene kept playing like it was on a hideous time loop, over and over in her brain. However much she tried to shut it out, there it was every time she closed her eyes. A reminder of what she had done, and what she had lost.

But all that ringing and texting Richard in vain were making her feel slightly unhinged, and even Flick, the kindest and most supportive of best friends, had gently pointed out she was losing dignity in trying to win him back.

'You have to give him time, Kez,' she said.

'You're going to lose him for sure this way.'

Kezzie knew she was right, but the temptation late at night to email him after a glass of red, or ring him, just to hear his voice, had proved too much for her time and time again. The last occasion had been so mortifyingly cringe-making – Richard had answered saying, 'Kezzie, I have my parents here, please don't make a scene' – that she'd hung up straight away. At that moment she decided she was losing the plot big time, and needed to escape, somewhere, anywhere, so she wouldn't chance running into Richard, and where she wouldn't be reminded of him, on every corner.

It was then that Aunt Jo had stepped in. Arriving on an unexpected flying visit to London, and seeing the state of her beloved niece, Jo had declared that Kezzie needed a bolt hole. 'And as luck would have it, hon, I can offer you my place.'

'What do you mean?' Kezzie had asked.

'I'm off round the world for a year with Mickey,' said Jo, referring to her latest toy boy. 'You remember him, don't you? We're going to *find* ourselves, and maybe get married in Thailand.' She giggled excitedly. 'You can stay at my cottage for as long as you want – stay all year if you need to, babe.'

'Really?' Kezzie gulped through her tears. It sounded like the best solution she could think of. She had to get away from London, from the car crash that had been the end of her relationship, and the mess she'd made of everything. She needed time and space to regroup, and sort herself out. Staying here moping after Richard was doing her no good whatsoever. He was never coming back to her, and all she was doing was prolonging the agony.

So here she was shoving things in boxes. Every little thing reminded her of the last two brilliant years with Richard, from the framed certificate stating she'd passed the Landscape Gardening Course she'd taken at his suggestion, to the picture of the two of them walking in the Lakes earlier in the year, when he'd asked her to move in with him. And then there were the gardening gloves he'd given her at Christmas, and the silver earrings, which had been a birthday present. In London, all she could think about was Richard. Escaping was the only chance she stood of getting over him.

She picked up her phone and rang Richard's number. This was the last time she'd do this. The very very last time.

His answer phone kicked in. 'Hi there, Richard isn't here right now, but leave a message and I'll get back to you later.' She kept doing this, just to hear his voice. She couldn't help it, even though she knew it didn't do any good. It was time she stopped and moved on.

Taking a deep breath, and trying to ignore the telltale wobble in her voice, she said, 'Hi, Richard. This is Kezzie. I'm leaving town. You won't hear from me again.'

She put the phone down, trembling, tears spilling over her cheeks. But it was done. Kezzie surveyed the mess of the room she was in, and slowly started to rationalize the boxes. There wasn't any other option. The summer was over, and autumn had begun.

Chapter Two

Different sounds. That was the most unusual thing about living in the country, Kezzie decided. It wasn't dead silent, as she'd always imagined. The previous evening, the birds had been making a right racket in the hedgerow at dusk, and she'd heard bats squeaking in the dark. This morning she'd been woken by a very early morning dawn chorus. It was still relatively light in the mornings, though approaching mid September, and having left London's gloomy weather, it had cheered her up no end to get up and watch a very pink sunrise give way to a bright and sunny September morning.

It had taken her all day to pack up her stuff in the van she'd hired, drive down to Jo's house in the pretty village of Heartsease on the Surrey/ Sussex border which she'd fallen in love with on previous visits, and unpack it all. Kezzie knew she could have asked Flick and the others to help but she was too proud. She'd told Flick about the split, of course she had, but she still felt sore and embarrassed about the reasons for it. She couldn't face actually telling anyone, let alone her best friend, what had really happened. And part of her need for escape was a need to re-evaluate every aspect of her life: her drinking and drug taking, and slight feeling of always living on the edge. Until she had met Richard that had been all she'd wanted, and she'd revelled in shocking him, and teasing him about being so straight-laced. But since their break-up, she'd become uncertain about her lifestyle and wondered whether she was right to always be so frenetic and spontaneous. It used to feel fun. Now she wasn't sure. And sadly, Flick and her friends were part of all that. Maybe if she was away she could unpick what and who she was, and work out where her life went from here. Maybe.

First things first though. Kezzie realized last night, before she fell into bed, that she'd forgotten to buy milk and teabags. Jo, a caring and thoughtful individual in many ways, hadn't thought to leave any groceries in the fridge. Mind you, as Jo appeared to have taken off on her voyage of self-discovery with one very small backpack, a few necessities, and had yet to email, perhaps that wasn't all that surprising.

Kezzie stretched and slowly got out of her aunt's big, cosy bed. Jo had modelled it on a Bedouin tent and built a frame above it to hang curtains from. Kezzie felt like she was emerging from a cocoon; it was the perfect bed to hide herself away in. She threw on a dressing gown and padded downstairs to the bathroom, which led off from the kitchen. Even on a warm day like today it felt chilly and slightly uninviting, with its flagstone floor and wooden door, which didn't quite reach the floor. That was going to be draughty in winter. The bathroom was the one room Jo hadn't got round to modernizing, and the shower was erratic to say the least, spewing out boiling water one second and icy cold the next. Kezzie spent the shortest time possible in there, got dressed quickly and left the cottage. On the way down the little lane she passed a middle-aged woman walking a Border Collie.

'Would you mind telling me where I could buy some teabags?' Kezzie asked.

'Turn right out of the Lane, go down the hill, and there's a little shop on the corner of Madans Avenue and the High Street. It's less than five minutes. Or if you have time, walk right to the end of the High Street, and you'll find a small local supermarket, Macey's, which has most things you need.'

'Thanks very much,' said Kezzie.

'You must be Jo's niece,' said the woman. 'Eileen Jones. I live across the road.'

'Oh, hi. Kezzie Andrews,' said Kezzie. 'Nice to meet you.'

She set off down to the shop, taking in the wide sweep of the road lined with broad oaks and beeches as it wound its way down to the picturesque little village at the bottom of the hill. It was indeed as Eileen said, only five minutes away. Ali's Emporium declared the sign above the door, though in truth it was more of a minimart than an emporium. Still, it sold tea and milk, though not the herbal variety.

'You must be Jo's niece,' smiled the man behind the counter, who was presumably Ali. 'Nice to meet you.'

'Yes, I am,' said Kezzie. 'Er, nice to meet you.'

She made her way home, shaking her head with amusement. She'd been here less than twenty-four hours and already said hello to more people

41

than she did on her street in London.

After a reviving cup of tea, Kezzie decided to go for a walk up to the Downs. She'd only been here a few times before, and remembered going for a lovely walk with Jo ages ago. She fancied a quick blow away of the cobwebs, before she got down to doing stuff she needed to, like getting on with unpacking, and sorting out her entire life. It was all very well living on her redundancy, but Kezzie knew she'd go mad with boredom if she didn't find something constructive to do soon. Much as she hated it, at least she still had enough contacts to get her some freelance web design work, if the gardening didn't take off straight away.

She turned right out of the house and made her way up the Lane, till she came to a fork in the road. Ahead of her was a farm, and to the left was a path which presumably led back down to the village. She struck off up to the right, figuring that would keep her walking in the right direction. She'd been walking for about five minutes up a tree-lined path, the trees laden with orange and yellow leaves, through which the sun shimmered and shone, when she came across an attractive, high, redbrick wall. Kezzie wondered idly what lay on the other side, and coming to where the wall turned a corner at the main road, she saw there was an old oak tree, with roots that were breaking up the bottom of the wall. It had a bough low enough to tempt her to swing up to see what was hidden behind the wall.

'Wow.' Kezzie was stunned. She had assumed it was going to be someone's back garden, but was taken aback by what she saw. It was a sunken garden, with steps and a metal gate at one end, a square in the middle, surrounded by gravel paths and a rusty old bench near to where she was. At one time it had clearly been well maintained; the ivy, rosemary and box that now straggled over the paths, still resembled some kind of pattern, but they were now so choked with weeds it was hard to make out what it was. She swung herself slowly down. What an amazing place. A proper secret garden. She walked a little further up the hill and followed the wall round a corner, to where she saw a large, derelict-looking redbrick house. Its high windows looked soulless and empty, the paint peeling off them, and the curtains faded and old. The front door was painted a dark green, and had a charming stained-glass pattern at the top, but several of the glass panes were cracked, and the privet bushes and wisteria planted in front of the two bay windows were crowding over the cracked garden path and obscuring the doorway. The house looked unlived in and neglected, much like the garden.

'What a shame,' said Kezzie out loud. 'Someone should do something about it.' Someone? Kezzie thought back to her early guerrilla gardening days, when she, Flick and Flick's boyfriend, Gavin had called themselves the Three Musketeers and taken it upon themselves to restore gardens that were uncared for. She'd been looking for something to do. She might just have found it.

Monday morning, and Joel was running late. It had been over a week since the painful graveside meeting with Claire's parents. As usual, their

43

kindness to him made him feel more fraudulent then ever, and he'd felt too guilty to take Marion up on her kind offer of babysitting at the weekend. Instead, he'd asked Eileen Jones to do it, and then felt guilty that he was depriving Marion of seeing her grandson. His evening out at the local pub, the Labourer's Legs, had gone a bit awry. In a moment of madness he'd agreed to go out for a drink with Suzanne Cawston, a cashier at Macey's, who clearly fancied him, as well as feeling sorry for him. Why he'd said yes he didn't know, but he found himself sitting in the pub with her, under Lauren's scornful eyes, as she poured him a pint. Though she had never said anything, Lauren seemed to him to be the only person who disapproved of him dating other women – or was it that looking at her reminded him of Claire?

Joel quickly established he and Suzanne had nothing in common – at twenty-two she was far too young for him – and not wanting to be rude, had drunk far more than was good for him. After that he ended up having an embarrassing fumble in the dark, outside the pub – Suzanne's comment 'We can't go home, my mum and dad are in,' reminding him how little he should be doing this – before he made his excuses and fled back home. He ignored her plaintive cry of, 'We will see each other again won't we?' as he made his way up the hill.

Sunday had been spent visiting his mum. He never mentioned these women to Mum. He suspected she guessed something of his private life but she never asked him, unless he brought it up

44

first. He'd taken her and Sam out for lunch in a cosy restaurant in nearby Chiverton, where she lived in a warden-assisted flat, and as usual, she'd cooed over her grandson. It was only towards the end of the meal, she'd tentatively asked, 'Joel, are you OK? Only you're very quiet. I know last week must have been so hard for you.'

'I'm fine,' he assured her. 'More than fine. It's been hard, but we're getting through it, aren't we, Sammy?' And he tickled Sam's chin, and ignored the hand Mum held out in front of him. He didn't refer to it again, till he dropped his mum home, gave her a kiss, and told her she worried too much.

But later when he got home, and put Sam to bed, he'd had a whole evening to brood. As he sat alone sipping a whisky, idly flicking through the TV channels in the lounge he'd started decorating just before Claire died, and had still not finished, he knew that his mum was right to worry about him.

The house weighed heavily on him – what had once seemed an exciting lifetime's project now felt like a burden. Without Claire to share the work with him, without her to give him something to aim for, restoring this old, falling down wreck of a house seemed a pointless exercise. His enthusiasm for restoring it had died with Claire. And as for the secret garden, which had excited him so much when he and Claire had first got here, he hadn't been in it for months. Even his great great grandfather's old writing desk (left to him with the house), which he'd started to strip down and lovingly planned to restore, sat aban-

45

doned and unfinished. He felt in limbo. Unable to go back, unable to move on. He was very very far from all right.

Matters didn't get any better the following morning. Sam wasn't being cooperative and he'd got porridge all down the top that Joel had just put him in. Joel had ended up shouting, and of course Sam burst into tears, which made him feel terrible. What kind of monstrous dad shouted at their seventeen-month-old? As ever the thought – what would Claire do? – floated in his head. He sighed, got Sam changed, and then himself when he realized that he was smeared with baby porridge. Seeing the time he raced to the car, strapped Sam in, and drove like the clappers down the hill to Lauren's house.

He got on well with Lauren, and she'd been a fantastic source of strength to him after Claire died. She had been one of the few people he could face being around in those early weeks. She didn't ask anything of him, or besiege him with questions about how he was doing, but was quietly supportive, and they had grieved for Claire together.

Their childcare arrangement (fortunately already in place before Claire died) was a good one, but he often felt wrong-footed when he was with Lauren. It was one thing to constantly be home late for an uncomplaining wife, quite another to face Lauren's wrath for the hundredth time, when he'd got stuck working late. He did his best, and for the most part the small charity where he worked accommodated him, but his life was now full of tense compromises between work and home. He was always joking that he was like the wife of the office, always the one rushing home early for the children. And only now was he beginning to realize quite how tough things had been for Claire when she first went back to work.

'Sorry I'm late,' he said, as he thrust Sam into Lauren's waiting arms. The twins peeped mischievously from behind her, already in their school uniforms. How did she do that? Joel wondered. She had two of them, it wasn't yet 8 a.m., and they were both spick and span and ready. Even after a year he still felt inadequate when it came to the domestic side of his life.

'No worries,' said Lauren lightly, but he knew her well enough to tell she was irritated. Though she generally showed him nothing but sympathy and kindness, Lauren wasn't above putting him in his place from time to time. She had pointed out on more than one occasion that she wasn't his slave, and he really needed to take more responsibility for things. She'd never quite said, 'Just because Claire put up with you, there's no reason why I should,' but Joel sometimes felt sure it must be on the tip of her tongue, and he knew he deserved it. He knew he should make more effort for Lauren. She was great with Sam, and filled the gap Claire left behind as well as she could. Joel never meant to take her for granted, but life was so overwhelming sometimes he leant on her a bit too heavily. Lauren loved Sam almost as much as he did. He was immensely lucky to have her.

Lauren sighed as she shut the door behind Joel.

He could be so frustrating at times, it nearly drove her demented. He appeared to have no concept of time at all, or appreciate that her life didn't just revolve around him and Sam. For the most part, Lauren felt really sorry for him – it was hard for him having to bring up a child alone, and she was sympathetic. But lately, she had also begun to feel resentful. She'd been left literally holding the babies and had had no choice but to get on with it. Everyone in Heartsease thought that Joel was an amazing dad and he was, but Lauren also knew from things Claire had let slip that he had been quite unhelpful when Sam was born. So while she was sympathetic to his situation, somehow she couldn't quite shift her feelings of irritation.

'It must be difficult for him, I guess,' Claire would say, to Lauren's annoyance. Much as Lauren had loved Claire, it drove her mad the way she constantly forgave Joel, when Lauren felt he was being so unsupportive. *Claire.* Lauren felt the loss of her friend keenly. The grief could still come suddenly like a deep punch to the stomach. Claire had put up with Joel's vagaries because she loved him, Lauren should probably try and do the same.

But Lauren had found it difficult to cope with the scandalously short time it had taken Joel to start dating other women. Claire had barely been in her grave, or so it seemed, when Lauren had spotted him with the first one in the Labourer's Legs, where she worked some evenings. True, on that occasion, Joel had been pounced on by Jenny Hunter, the village slapper, who'd been known to fell lesser men at five paces, so he didn't have much chance. But Jenny had been swiftly followed by Mary Stevens, the Year One teacher at the village school, and Kerry Adams, who ran the chemist's.

If she hadn't known better – Joel had cried on her shoulder more than once in the early weeks after Claire's death – Lauren might have thought he didn't care about Claire at all. Only the other Saturday – a few days after Claire's anniversary – Lauren had spotted him all over Suzanne Cawston. His behaviour exhausted her patience with him. If the boot had been on the other foot, Claire would never have done that, and Lauren felt indignant on her friend's behalf that Joel should apparently have replaced her so lightly. But she didn't want to fall out with him about it. Not only did she love looking after Sam, the bottom line was she needed the money.

And Joel was good to work for in many ways. He always compensated Lauren financially when he was late, but she resented the time taken away from her own girls, and hated the stress-inducing moments when the clock was ticking and she was going to be late (again) for the pub. It was like having all the disadvantages of marriage without the sex.

'Come on, Sammy, let's have a cuddle before we take the girls to school,' she said. Sam, she'd noticed, loved to be tickled and played with in the mornings. She wondered if it was because Joel didn't quite know how to – although for all her carping, Joel was clearly devoted to Sam, he just hadn't had much practice looking after him, and it showed.

'Maybe we should teach him, eh?' said Lauren, and she was rewarded with a great big smile as she tickled Sam's chin. 'Get that silly daddy to see what he's been missing.'

Chapter Three

It was dark, just the way she liked it. Kezzie had forgotten the sheer dizzying excitement of guerrilla gardening. She felt the familiar frisson of being out on a moonlit night, in the middle of nowhere. Ever since she'd stumbled across the decaying garden a couple of weeks earlier, she'd been determined to make a statement to whoever the owner of the garden was. Presumably *someone* must own it. Shocking, how such a beautiful place could be left so neglected. Whoever it belonged to, clearly didn't value it as they should.

She found the oak tree, from which vantage point she had peered into the garden last time she was here. She hooked herself up, heart pounding, before swinging her legs from the tree to the wall, and jumping down into the garden. She rummaged round in her bag for her torch, then decided she didn't need it. The moon was so bright she could clearly make out the contours of what had once been an orderly and well-managed garden. Overgrown with weeds it might be now, but it was obvious that once upon a time someone had lavished a lot of care and attention here.

On the far side was an ornate iron gate, with

steps leading down into the garden. There were borders running round the edges, which were full of weeds creeping over the paths, and in the square in the centre was a tangled mass of ivy and rosemary and box. She spotted the rusting iron bench near where she had landed, so she put her rucksack down on it while surveying the scene. An owl hooted nearby, startling her, and she could hear the sound of foxes fighting, not far away. It gave an added thrill to what she was doing. She felt like Rapunzel's dad, stealing lettuces in the dark. Any minute now an ugly witch would appear.

She opened her rucksack and pulled out the garden clippers, fork and trowel she'd brought with her. The garden was hideously overgrown, but she could make out an ancient hedge – box? Probably, it looked like it had been a border once – beneath the weeds. Taking her clippers, she started to hack back at the brambles and convolvulus threatening to strangle it. As she worked, she tried not to think about the night she'd done this in London – the night she'd met Richard, the night her life had changed forever. If she hadn't broken into the rough patch of ground by the posh gated community, where he lived in Clapham, and planted daffodils, she'd never have met him at all. He was on his way home and he'd accused her of vandalism, until she pointed out that you couldn't vandalize something you were trying to improve.

A couple of months later, when the daffodils were blooming and he'd found her admiring her handiwork, he'd grudgingly admitted that she was right and her efforts had transformed a scrubby patch of ground into a little haven of green in the city.

'You should do that for a living,' he said. 'You seem to have a way with plants.'

'I've got a job,' Kezzie had replied defiantly, not wanting to admit that designing logos for a company that advertised on the web wasn't really fulfilling her. It turned out that Richard was an architect specializing in garden design, and he encouraged her to train up in her spare time. One thing led to another, and before long she'd found herself agreeing to move in with him, and giving up her job, once she'd finished her course in landscape gardening. Of course, none of it had worked to plan, her job giving up on her, before she had a chance to resign, and then losing Richard before she'd moved in. Something she had simply never thought would happen...

Richard had been a revelation to her. He was completely unlike any of the boyfriends she'd had before. Kezzie had had the unfortunate habit of spending most of her teens and her early twenties attracted to the wrong kind of guy, and after a disastrous liaison with a small-time drugs dealer had forsworn men, until just before her thirtieth birthday when she'd met Richard.

For starters it was unusual for Kezzie to be dating someone with a job – let alone someone like Richard in his late thirties, with such a high-powered job. Not only that, with a failed marriage behind him ('She left me, sadly,' he'd explained to Kezzie that he'd have done anything to make the marriage work, but his ex had been equally determined to move on), Richard also had a fourteen-year-old daughter, Emily. Kezzie didn't even know anyone who had a baby, let alone a full grown teen. That aspect of things hadn't been ideal, Emily being as unkeen on Kezzie as Kezzie was on her, but Kezzie had been overawed by the trendy, open-plan loft living apartment Richard had owned near Clapham Junction and ashamed to take him back to her small rented flat in Finsbury Park. But Richard was totally unfazed by the differences between their lifestyles – or some of them at any rate, later on it would be all too clear that he disapproved of the drug taking and late night partying – but to begin with he'd said, 'We're not that different, you and I.'

'Really?' Kezzie was incredulous. She stared at his fair hair, public school boy good looks and his smart shirt and Armani suit. 'We inhabit different planets.'

'Maybe we do now,' said Richard, 'but I didn't always earn good money. And I might have gone to public school but my parents worked hard to get me there. My dad ran a pub you know. I spent most of my time at school pretending he owned a chain of hotels.'

Kezzie laughed, 'And I used to lie to people about which estate I grew up on.'

'See,' said Richard, with his crooked grin, which made her fold up and melt inside, 'not so different after all. I don't pay any attention to trappings. They don't mean anything. It's the person inside who counts.'

And of course, that was how it had all gone so

wrong. She had turned out to be different from the person he thought she was.

'That was then, this is now,' growled Kezzie to herself and continued with her work, while trying to put painful thoughts of Richard and what might have been behind her.

As she worked, she cleared away the brambles and began to see the box was really out of shape and ragged. Once upon a time, though, it had clearly formed a pattern, woven into which was rosemary and a kind of ivy she couldn't identify.

What was hidden in this wonderful place? Ever since the day she'd climbed up the oak tree and peeked over the wall, she'd fallen in love with this secret garden, and it looked like it was about to surrender some of its secrets to her.

The more she uncovered, the more excited she grew – the box, ivy and rosemary definitely formed an interconnecting pattern. Eventually she uncovered enough to see it was in the shape of a heart.

Suddenly, she realized what she was looking at; she'd studied this kind of design. 'It's a knot garden,' she said out loud. 'That's amazing.'

A security light flooded through the iron gate. She looked up and saw to her surprise there were lights on in the derelict house she'd seen the other week. A torch was bobbing its way down the garden. Shit. Although she'd imagined someone must own the house, it had looked so ramshackle, she'd assumed no one was living in it. She must have made a mistake. Gathering up her things, she ran to the corner of the wall and slung her bag over the top. She was scrambling up the wall, trying to grab for the branches of the oak tree, when–

'What the hell are you doing in my garden?' said a distinctly male and very attractive voice.

'Um–' Suddenly Kezzie felt very foolish. She had a feeling that guerrilla gardening might not quite have made it to this quiet corner of Sussex...

Joel shone his torch into the eyes of a petite woman – a very pretty woman he had to grudgingly admit. She had short, dark hair, and an elfin look and was dressed in oversized combat gear, which made her look like a little doll. She'd dropped back to the ground when he'd accosted her.

'I didn't realize it was your garden,' she said. 'I saw the high wall and was curious, so I climbed up the oak tree and discovered your garden. I thought it looked uncared for.'

'So you thought you'd care for it did you?' said Joel. 'Perhaps I prefer it this way.'

'How can you possibly like it like this? All your beautiful plants being strangled to death by convolvulus. It's criminal neglect. It deserves being brought back to life. If it were mine that's what I'd do.'

'Well it's not yours, is it?' said Joel, resenting this stranger telling him what he should or shouldn't do in his garden. 'So quite frankly it's none of your business, and I should ask you to leave.'

'No, it's not,' the stranger looked a bit sheepish. 'Sorry, I get carried away sometimes. I saw your garden and didn't think anyone lived in the house. It looked a bit neglected. I just wanted to help.'

Neglected. You could say that.

'Well, it's a work in progress,' said Joel.

'Doesn't look like there's much progress happening,' said the stranger.

'I'm a busy man,' Joel said defensively. 'I work full time, and I've got a young son I'm bringing up alone. There are only so many hours in the day. Not that that's any of your business either.'

What the hell was he doing even chatting to this girl? By rights he should call the police.

'Oh,' his strange intruder looked a bit dumbfounded for the first time since he'd met her. 'Sorry, I didn't know.'

'No, you didn't,' said Joel. 'Really it's nothing to do with you what I do or don't do with the garden. I'm going to ring the police.'

'No – don't,' she said quickly. 'It's not like I vandalized the place. Honestly, I know I shouldn't be here, but I only wanted to make it better. You could come and see what I've been doing if you like.'

Joel tried and failed to look authoritative. He could hardy call the police and say someone's broken into my garden and improved it, could he? Despite himself he was intrigued by this girl who seemed to have appeared out of nowhere.

'OK,' he said. 'Show me then.'

She produced a torch and shone it into the undergrowth in the furthest corner.

'Look,' she said. 'I've been cutting back the brambles and digging up the weeds, and look what I found.'

She pointed to a ragged edge of box, with rosemary and ivy intertwined.

'I think it must be part of a knot garden,' the girl said, her eyes shining. 'Did you know it was there?'

'Yes,' said Joel. 'This place belonged to my great great grandfather, Edward Handford, who was a semi-famous garden designer in the nineteenth century. I think, if memory serves me right, he created a knot garden for his wife, Lily, when they got married.'

'Edward Handford? I've heard of him,' she said. 'Wasn't he influenced by Gertrude Jekyll? I think there was a brief mention in a book I read about an Elizabethan knot garden he'd created. Is this it then?'

'I believe so,' said Joel, slightly stunned that a complete stranger would even know about his great great grandfather. He frowned. One of the things he'd meant to do when he moved in was ask his mum more about his family history. He'd been fascinated with what he'd dubbed the secret garden as a child, when he'd visited as a boy. But then Sam had come along, and Claire had died, and like so many things in his life, his interest had stalled. But his strange night-time visitor had piqued it again. He would ask Mum about Edward the next time he saw her.

'Oh, that's such a lovely story,' said the girl. 'And it's so sad that it's been destroyed. Wouldn't it be great to restore it?'

'And how do you propose doing that?' said Joel caught up in her infectious enthusiasm. 'What do you know about it?'

'I'm just setting up in business as a landscape gardener,' she said.

'Didn't anyone tell you that landscape gardeners normally work by day? Oh, and they tend to ask their clients first, before they start work,' said Joel.

'Yes, well, this is a bit on the side, as it were,' said the girl. 'I started off in London as a guerrilla gardener and someone persuaded me I should do it for a living.'

'What brings you down here?' Joel's curiosity got the better of him.

'Long and boring story, let's not go there,' she said. 'But listen, about your garden. I think it is really special. Seriously, you should do something with it.'

'I know,' said Joel. 'It is a pity that the garden should have fallen into such disrepair. I've been meaning to sort it out since I moved in.'

'So what's stopping you, then?' asked his unlikely gardener.

'Time and money, mainly,' said Joel, ignoring the voice that said, *You wanted to, remember?* 'I don't have enough of either.'

'Have you thought of applying for a grant to do it?' she asked. 'Someone like the National Trust or the RHS might sponsor you.'

'I hadn't thought about that,' admitted Joel. Haven't thought beyond the end of my nose since Claire died, he thought to himself with a jerk. All those dreams and hopes he'd had for the future of the house and garden. They'd all died with Claire.

'Why not?'

'Like you said, long story,' said Joel, taken a-
back by his sudden resurgence of interest in the
garden. 'The only person stopping me doing it is
me. Perhaps you're right, it *is* time to carry on.'

Lauren had put the children to bed and was busy
baking muffins in the kitchen, when there was a
knock on the door.

'Oh hi, Eileen, what can I do for you?' she said.

'Something smells good,' said Eileen, as she
followed Lauren into the kitchen.

'Muffins,' said Lauren. 'I love baking. I find it
so relaxing, and it's my special treat to myself
when the kids are in bed. Please,' she swept away
her mixing bowl, recently purchased from the
new Lakeland in Chiverton, and swiftly wiped
away the crumbs from the old pine table that she
loved to cook on. The kitchen was cosy, but the
table was the only work surface she had. 'Sit
down, I was just about to put some coffee on.'

Lauren got out her coffee percolator, and took
down her favourite Kenyan coffee while Eileen
settled herself down.

'I know it's a long way away,' said Eileen, 'but I
don't know if you'd heard, I've just been appointed by the Parish Council to sort out next
year's summer fete.'

'Go on,' Lauren was wary. When the girls were
at pre-school, she'd found herself practically
running the committee, and had had it up to here
with Christmas fairs, cake sales and the like by
the time they'd left. Izzie and Immie had only
been at school for five minutes, and already she
was having her arm twisted to join the PTA

committee. Somehow everyone assumed, because she was at home with small children, and didn't have what some people thought was a 'proper' job, Lauren must have loads of time to organize charitable events.

'I know you're really busy,' said Eileen, 'but I really do need some help. You see next year it's the 140th anniversary of Edward Handford's birth, and we want to celebrate it. He did such a lot for the village – from giving us the Memorial Gardens, to the village school, and we've got a lot of projects we want to fund. Quite frankly our last summer fete was a bit of a disaster, and the Parish Council is keen not to have a repeat.'

'Oh, you mean someone noticed the fact that Andy drank more Pimms than he served?' said Lauren with a grin. It had been a source of great amusement to her when her irritating boss from the pub had keeled over while holding court in front of half the village.

'That was only the half of it,' said Eileen. 'Thanks to Cynthia Green, we had that wretched bore from Radio Chiverton opening proceedings, and he gave the longest speech I have ever heard. Plus the stalls were so drab and uninteresting, and the weather was so lousy we hardly made any money. The problem is, everyone thinks so small. We need to make it more of an event if we want to make any serious money. So Tony Symonds, who's Chair of the Parish Council this year, has suggested we shake it all up a bit. And he asked for my help.'

'So where do I come in?' said Lauren. 'I don't have a lot of spare time.'

'I know you don't,' said Eileen, 'but we could do with some young blood, and as one of the restoration projects we've got in mind is the Memorial Gardens, particularly the play area, I thought a mum like you might be perfectly placed to tell us what's needed.'

'That's blackmail,' said Lauren, laughing.

'I know,' said Eileen, 'but could you help? It would be great if you could.'

'Oh go on,' said Lauren. 'And I'll try and see if I can get Joel Lyle involved. You know Edward Handford was his great great grandfather, don't you? Joel was planning to restore the garden at Lovelace Cottage when he and Claire moved in, but he's not got round to it yet.'

'How stupid of me,' said Eileen. 'I dabble a bit in local history, but I hadn't made the connection. I've always been fascinated by Edward's story – he created that garden for his wife, when they got married. I'd love to see it.'

'I've only seen it once, but it's a bit of a mess,' said Lauren. 'I think it needs a lot of work.'

'Hmm,' said Eileen, 'I wonder how Joel might feel if I suggested we helped him restore it.'

'I don't think he's much of a committee person,' said Lauren. 'And since Claire died, he seems to have lost heart a bit with the house. I'm not sure he's going to want to help, but there's no harm in asking.'

Chapter Four

Kezzie poked her head out of her bedroom window. The dawn chorus had woken her up again. She still couldn't get used to the fact that she could hear their chatter, which would have been drowned out in the noisy bustle of London. Apart from the sounds of wildlife, it was much quieter here though, and sometimes the stillness drove her a bit mad. But she loved the cottage, which like her aunt was quirky and homely, and full of trinkets Jo had acquired on her many travels abroad. She was grateful for Jo's impetuous generosity. It hadn't occurred to her to ask anyone for help, knowing she'd get none from her parents, who were in their own loved-up retirement cocoon in Spain.

But thanks to Jo, Kezzie now found herself buried in the Sussex countryside. The plus side was she did find the quiet soothing, and enjoyed living so close to nature. The downside was that she knew no one and the contacts she'd cultivated in London with the aim of setting up her own freelance gardening business, now seemed a long way away. The redundancy she'd willingly taken from her job at the website company was enough to tide her over for the time being, and she had some freelance web design work, so getting a gardening contract wasn't urgent. But she'd have to get a job soon, so her plan today was to get down to it, and start planning her future.

Kezzie got dressed and ate her breakfast in Jo's kitchen, looking out at the garden. She loved this room, which was dominated by a huge Aga, and decorated in muted yellows and oranges, which gave it a cosy, warm feeling. It felt very much the hub of the house, and Kezzie spent a lot of time here.

It was a beautiful, sunny October morning and the birds were running riot in the hawthorn bush that belonged to her neighbour. Kezzie hadn't spoken to her properly yet, though she had said hello once or twice to a rather frazzled looking young woman with long, fair hair, pushing a buggy accompanied by two little girls. Blimey. Three children and she barely looked out of school. Kezzie couldn't help but thank her lucky stars that she'd never made *that* mistake. It had been bad enough discovering that Richard had a daughter. Kezzie had had no desire to play step-mum to Emily, to Richard's evident disappointment.

'You have to grow up some time, Kez,' he'd said, and Kezzie had laughed and said, 'I don't see why I have to.' Now she wasn't so sure.

Breakfast over, she opened the back door and scraped the crumbs of her toast out on the bird table positioned right by the hedge for the birds who so noisily woke her, and went back inside to get her laptop. She had so much to do: pitches for commissions, putting the finishing touches to her website, sorting out a leaflet to go out with the local paper, but she ignored all that. Kezzie had been so intrigued by the garden she'd broken into last night, the first thing she had to do was find out more about it.

She typed in Lovelace Cottage, and got a few matches, but nothing very concrete. So she tried again, putting Edward Handford into the search engine. Immediately a Wikipedia entry popped up:

Edward Handford – 1871–1955, *Late Victorian landscape gardener and botanist of minor importance. Heavily influenced by the work of Gertrude Jekyll and Edward Lutyens, but using his own style…*

His most notable work was designing the garden of Hillcrest Manor, a stately home owned by the de Lacey family, in Nottinghamshire, but he is also known for the Elizabethan knot garden he created for his wife Lily, on the occasion of their marriage in 1892, although very little is known about it…

There was a bit more about his later work, and a mention that much of his youth had been spent hunting exotic plants in India, but nothing much about Joel's garden. To Kezzie's disappointment, there was no plan. Kezzie printed off what she'd found and filed it for later use. It wasn't much to go on if she was to restore the garden properly, but it was a start. Maybe Joel would have some more information about it. She'd have to ask him the next time she saw him.

'So have you met my new neighbour yet?' Lauren greeted Joel as he came to drop Sam off.

'What new neighbour?' he asked, yawning. He had found sleep hard to come by after his moonlit encounter the previous night.

'She's Jo Knight's niece. Just moved in,' said Lauren. 'She's very pretty. Just up your street.'

Joel at least had the grace to blush.

'I'm not that bad.'

'You so are,' said Lauren teasingly, to hide the fact that the details of Joel's love life made her feel uncomfortable.

'Poor lamb, left all alone up there in that big house, it's understandable he wants some company,' she'd heard someone say recently.

Lauren was slightly aggravated by this. The one and only time she'd disastrously dated John Townley, who worked in the village garage, she'd actually heard the word 'strumpet' bandied about in the local high street. 'And her with two little ones and all,' as if by dint of having two small children she was condemned to be a nun for the rest of her life. And secondly, it made her so mad on Claire's behalf. Lauren still missed Claire, who'd been a sane, calming influence on Lauren's often chaotic life, and for the life of her she couldn't see why Joel could apparently have forgotten her so easily. Or for that matter why local opinion seemed to think it was OK that he should. If it had been anyone else, Lauren would have thought he was a prize shit, but knowing as she did what a state he had been in after Claire had died, she knew the truth was more complicated than that.

'What does she look like?' he asked. 'Not that I'm interested or anything.'

'Well, she's a bit hippyish,' said Lauren. 'I was teasing, she's not really your type at all. She's

65

quite small – elfin looking – dark hair, brown eyes.'

'Oh–' Light dawned in Joel's eyes. 'It's the guerrilla gardener.'

'The what?'

'I found her in my garden last night,' explained Joel. 'She told me she was doing a spot of guerilla gardening and then had the cheek to have a go at me about leaving it to rack and ruin. She thinks I should restore it.'

'Well you should,' said Lauren. 'That was the plan, right?'

'Yeah, well, plans change,' Joel mumbled, and a look of such sadness shot across his face that Lauren felt her heart contract. Perhaps she was too hard on him. Her experience with Troy had left her a little too eager to be unforgiving with men. They weren't all selfish bastards.

A stab of protective tenderness came over Lauren and she touched his arm lightly. 'Maybe it's time they changed again?' she said. 'I was talking to Eileen Jones the other day, and she was saying the village want to honour Edward Handford next year for his 140th anniversary. I suggested she get in touch with you about restoring the garden. It might be just what you need and if your guerrilla gardener can help you...'

'Maybe.' Joel shook himself out of his reverie, looked at his watch and gave Sam a quick hug. 'I must dash, see you later.'

'Have a good day,' said Lauren.

He set off, leaving Lauren thinking that her new neighbour sounded intriguing. She'd never met anyone before who'd broken into gardens at night. Jo was a lot of fun, so maybe her niece would be too.

It wasn't long before Lauren got her opportunity to say hello properly. She'd just got back from the school run and was unclipping Sam from his buggy, when there was a knock on the door, and the small elfin girl she'd glimpsed through the garden hedge was standing there, looking very apologetic.

'I'm so sorry, you're going to think me very stupid, but I've managed to lock myself out. I know I left the back window open, and I've noticed there's a gap in your fence. I was wondering if I could shimmy through it and hop back in.'

'No need for that,' said Lauren, lifting Sam up. 'Come on in. Didn't your aunt tell you I had a spare key?'

She ushered Kezzie into the kitchen, where she kept all her keys in a little wooden box above her wooden spice rack.

'I'm Lauren Callan by the way,' she said. 'It's lovely to meet you at last.'

'Kezzie Andrews,' said Kezzie, looking embarrassed. 'I'm such a dope. Jo did mention it and I completely forgot.'

'Do you fancy a coffee?' said Lauren, who had only been planning to bake cookies with Sam. He was quite happy when she put him down, and he pottered about, putting magnetic letters on the fridge. Lauren knew that she'd be searching underneath the fridge for half of them.

'That would be lovely,' said her new neighbour, with a smile.

It would be nice to have someone young living

next door, thought Lauren.

'I've been meaning to come over and introduce myself properly, but I've been so busy sorting myself out since I got here, I haven't had a chance.'

'Yes, I gather,' said Lauren. 'Do you often break into people's gardens in the middle of the night?'

'Oh my God, how did you know about that?'

'Small place, Heartsease,' grinned Lauren, flicking on the kettle and getting her favourite Cath Kidston mugs from the cupboard. She motioned to Kezzie to sit down at the cosy kitchen table.

'Blimey,' said Kezzie, 'this country living is going to take some getting used to. I expect the whole village knows by now.'

Lauren took pity on her. 'Actually, I only know about it because Sam here is Joel's son.'

'Joel?' said the girl.

'The guy who owns the garden. He's quite discreet, I'm sure he won't tell anyone. I look after Sam for him. Here, have a muffin.'

She opened a Tupperware box and offered Kezzie one of the blueberry muffins she'd made a few days earlier.

'Don't mind if I do,' said Kezzie. 'So all those children I've seen you with don't belong to you then?'

'Just the two girls,' said Lauren, 'they're my terrible twins.'

'Twins. Must be a handful,' said Kezzie.

'Sure are,' said Lauren, 'particularly when you're on your own.'

'I take my hat off to you,' said Kezzie. 'I can barely look after myself, let alone twins. If you don't mind me saying, you're very young to have kids.'

Lauren grimaced. 'I was twenty-one, way too young. It's the old old story. I fell for the wrong guy at uni, who promised me the world and then left me literally holding the babies.'

'I'm sorry,' said Kezzie.

'Don't be,' said Lauren. 'We're well shot of him, and even though he doesn't pay anything towards their upkeep, I manage. I look after Sam for Joel, who's very generous, and then work in the pub a couple of evenings a week, while my mum looks after the girls. Luckily she lives nearby. Anyway, tell me about breaking into Joel's garden. I'd have loved to have seen his face!'

'I was walking past the bottom of the garden and out of curiosity climbed up in a tree to see what was hidden behind the wall. I thought it wasn't being cared for,' said Kezzie, 'so I went in for a spot of guerrilla gardening. I used to do it in London all the time, though admittedly there's less cause for it here. I hadn't realized that the garden belonged to the big house up the road. Joel should restore it. It's criminal that he doesn't.'

'That's what I keep telling him,' said Lauren. 'There's a lovely history attached to the garden. The guy who designed it created it for his wife on their wedding day.'

'I know,' said Kezzie, 'I looked it up on Wikipedia this morning. So I'm curious, why doesn't Joel do something about it?'

'He's had a really difficult time,' said Lauren. 'His wife died very suddenly last year. She had an undiagnosed heart condition that no one knew about. Joel was restoring the house and garden for her. I think he's lost a bit of hope with it now.'

'Oh, bugger,' said Kezzie, 'typical of me, I've gone and put my great clomping size 10s in it again. I told him he should restore it. God, I wish I'd known.'

'Well you didn't,' said Lauren, 'and I have been saying the same thing for months. Maybe it's time he started to do something about it.'

'I did offer to help him,' said Kezzie. 'I'm setting up a gardening business and maybe eventually planning to show a garden at Chelsea. If Joel would let me I'd love to recreate Edward Handford's knot garden.'

'That is a fantastic idea,' said Lauren. 'I think we should both work on him, don't you?'

Later that day Joel was at home, thinking about what Lauren had said earlier about his guerrilla gardener. He wrapped Sam up snugly and opened the back door, stepping out onto the patio. The last throes of a crimson sunset set the trees alight, and a shiver ran down Joel's spine as he stood looking out onto his garden properly for the first time since Claire's death. It was neglected and overrun. It wasn't just the sunken garden at the bottom that needed attention, the grass on the main lawn was too high, the flowerbeds that lined it were choked with brambles and ivy, and the bushes needed pruning badly. Even up here on the crumbling patio, where the remains of a little wall and some cracked steps bore the evidence of something previously much grander, the rose bushes that had once formed an arbour were wild and rambling, and could do with cutting back. Joel sighed. It was such a huge job. One more thing for him to think about, and one of many reasons not to tackle it. Everything had halted since Claire died. The house and gardens were frozen in a time warp of his grief. And yet, and yet...

Despite the neglect, and the thought of hard work, for the first time since Claire had died, Joel was suddenly reminded of the vision he'd had when he came here, and saw the legacy he'd been left. This had once been a beautiful home and gardens, but because Uncle Jack had lived alone for many years, both house and garden had suffered. Joel had wanted to restore both to their former glory when Claire was alive, and had lost heart. But as he held Sam, and watched him laughing at the bats that were swooping and diving over his head, Joel felt something stir inside him. He'd lost Claire but he still had Sam. Maybe it was time to start again.

Since Claire had died, Joel had barely spent any time in the garden, and only had half-hearted attempts at the DIY he'd started inside. The ancient scullery, which he'd stripped out, extended and thoroughly modernized, with the intention of making it the heart of a happy home, had been finished for over a year. But far from being a heart, it felt like an empty shell, with its expanse of gleaming surfaces, and cupboards filled with pots and pans that Joel hardly ever used. The lounge, which had French windows that opened onto the garden terrace, had still to be redecorated, and he hadn't had the heart to start on the dining room. When he and Claire had moved in, one of his first actions was to strip out the dark wooden panelling in the hall, which Claire had found gloomy. He hadn't got round to replacing them with lighter wood, nor had he carpeted the floor as he intended, so every day the bare floorboards of the hallway were just another reminder of how the house was in limbo. It was no wonder Kezzie had thought the place was empty, he realized, looking at the house through her eyes. The windows and front door needed painting, and the back guttering was looking fairly crazy. He'd have to sort that out soon with winter approaching.

Joel loved the view from the top of the garden, which sloped gradually away from the house for nearly two hundred feet. The sunken garden was in the left-hand corner of the plot and the main part of the garden ended at the bottom of a lane, which led straight on to a farm. When Sam was a bit bigger, he was going to enjoy seeing the horses in the farmer's field, which ate the apples from the apple tree next to the right side fence at the bottom of the garden.

The autumn sun cast a fiery light on the trees, as he stood with Sam watching the rooks cawing in the branches above them, and the sheep on the far side of the hill gently baaing. It was this view and the sunken garden, which had first captured his heart and convinced him that this was the home for them.

'Let's go and look at the secret garden, shall we, Sam?' he said, and carried his son down the slope towards the garden. He unlocked the gate and surveyed the ruin of what must once have been a magnificent display of plants. Joel remembered showing Claire this garden before they moved in and how she had been as inspired as him to restore it to its former glory. She'd been in the early stages of pregnancy then, and both of them had been looking forward to a wonderful future together. The reality of parenthood was still a long way off, and they had joked about working on the garden together in the summer, while the baby slept in its crib.

Of course, when the summer came and Sam was born, Claire was too exhausted to do much more than sit at the top end of the garden on the cracked patio, which was large enough to accommodate a table and chairs, bemoaning the loss of their tidy little London patch, while Joel had been so determined to get the house just right for her, he hadn't taken the time to sit out with his family in those precious, precious moments. He regretted that so deeply now.

Joel swallowed hard, and blinked a tear back. He couldn't go on like this, living in the past and never looking forward to the future. He no longer had a future with Claire, but he did have one with Sam. Maybe he should let Kezzie have her way and help him restore the garden. It would be something to look forward to, something to achieve. And maybe, just maybe, it could help him heal.

Edward and Lily

Summer 1892

Lily – how often Edward would later think of her as she was in those early days of their marriage at Lovelace Cottage, when they had shut the world out – his mother had gone on a trip to London – and they had sent the servants away, and lived for a blissful few days as if they were the only two people left on earth.

Lily, as she lay in their marriage bed, dark hair tumbling all about her, looking at him with those lazy, alluring come-hither eyes. He'd never even known what that meant until now.

Lily, waking up as he flung the shutters wide open to allow a bright summer morning to flood sunlight into their little kingdom.

Lily, protesting about him getting up and leaving the warmth and comfort of their marriage bed. Lily, wanting to always keep him to herself.

Always Lily, laughing, joyous, as they wallowed in the sensuous happiness of being together, alone, with no one but themselves to consider.

In his memory, the sun always shone on those early days of marriage. Every morning they would awaken, and walk down the lane at the end of the garden to fetch milk and eggs from the farmer. Then Lily would make breakfast on the stove, determined to show him that not all domestic skills were beyond her.

Often he sketched her, sitting in the garden, or lying on the grass, staring up at the bright summer sky.

'Come and join me,' she'd say. 'You see the world differently from here.'

And together they would lie and look up at the bright, white clouds scudding across the azure blue sky. Lily seeing all sorts of things in them he could never have imagined. Where he saw soft, rolling shapes, Lily saw castles, animals, witches and princesses. He loved the way she allowed her imagination to transport her somewhere completely different. She had an other-worldly quality that he found entrancing.

At other times they walked down the hill to the brook, and followed it to where it widened to a stream and then a river. There they would picnic underneath an old willow tree, delighting in the freedom of being unchaperoned, and leaning against each other, talking about their plans for the future.

'We shall have six children,' declared Lily, 'three boys and three girls.'

'When we come back from India,' promised Edward, who had arranged for them to go on a three-month expedition to Lahore in order to search for exotic plants. 'We can bring back plants for each of the children we are going to have. I shall build a greenhouse, so we can nurture them.'

'And plant them in the knot garden,' said Lily. 'It will be wonderful, you'll see.'

Those days seemed endless and gloriously heady, in Edward's memory, filled with laughter and fun and love. He wished the time could stretch out endlessly, but alas, honeymoons cannot last forever, and all too soon, real life intruded. Work must be done, Lily must become the lady of the house, though he hadn't quite realized how very ill-suited she was to the task, prone as she was to wandering off into the gardens to smell the roses when she was meant to be telling Cook what to prepare for dinner. Or helplessly looking to him for advice when it came to the servants' wages. Though she had been brought up to it, Lily simply didn't possess the right character for the ladylike genteel world she had to inhabit; her spirit was far too free for that. And with his mother away for several months, there was no one for Lily to ask. He knew she chafed at the constrictions of afternoon teas with the neighbours and visits to the poor of the parish. His wild and wandering Lily, tamed and hemmed in by domesticity. He should have known it would lead to trouble.

Chapter Five

Late. Late *again*. Joel hated clockwatching, particularly when he had to discuss painful decisions about funding cuts that a few months of coalition government was forcing the small charity he worked for to make. Redundancies he had reluctantly had to tell Dan Walters, the director, were going to be necessary. At the very least they'd have to have a job freeze, and this at a time when services were going to be more squeezed than ever.

When he and Claire had first mooted a move to the country, Joel had been tempted to jack in his job and retrain in carpentry – something that had been a slightly obsessive hobby in his pre-married life, but which had gone by the board in the years since he'd met Claire. But with a big mortgage, and a baby coming, both he and Claire had decided this wasn't the time. So the compromise had been that he joined the charity Look Up!, which catered for the needs of the blind, as a finance director. Up until now he'd enjoyed it, feeling at least he was working on something that made a difference to people's lives. But hearing the staff regaling stories of the difficulties encountered by various service users, who were finding it harder and harder to get the help they needed, had made him feel pretty depressed about the future.

The meeting broke up, to Joel's relief, but he felt gloomy as he left the room. In the main, people were supportive of his domestic situation. Most of them had families too, but everyone else worked hard and late in the office; Joel didn't like them to think he was being a slacker, but he knew he was already late for Lauren.

Finally – too late – he understood Claire's point of view. She'd frequently complained about the stress of leaving work early to get home for Lauren on the couple of days a week she'd worked (thank God they'd employed Lauren while Claire was still alive. It had ensured at least some stability for Sam). Joel hadn't understood.

Like so much else. Too late. He'd always been too late.

He felt his phone vibrate in his pocket.

'Can we review the situation in a month, Joel?' Dan said, calling Joel back in. 'Any chance you can get those figures I need by tomorrow?'

Joel surreptitiously looked at his text message. *Lauren.* Of course. *Where r u?* The message glowed at him, bristling with resentment. It was amazing how guilty Lauren could make him feel. But then he often felt racked with guilt these days.

'Sure thing,' said Joel, looking forward to another late night date with his laptop.

'Brilliant,' said Dan. 'On my desk, first thing?'

Joel had never been late yet delivering figures, but Dan always made him feel as if somehow he were likely to be.

'First thing,' he promised, and tried not to leg it out of the meeting room and to his office.

He rang Lauren as soon as he was back at his desk, rooting around for the information he needed to take home with him that night.

'Sorry, sorry, sorry,' he said. 'I'll be with you as quick as I can.'

Thank God he'd got a job not too far outside Chiverton. Switching jobs when they moved to Heartsease had felt risky at the time, but turned out to be a godsend. There was no way he could manage a job that involved a big commute now.

Ten minutes later he came flying up Lauren's path, his heart pounding, sweating like a pig, and feeling like he might be about to have a coronary any minute. Lauren already had the door open, Sam in her arms, bag ready, disapproval rippling from her every pore. He couldn't blame her. If life was tough for him, he knew it was equally hard for her. Lauren had told him snippets, and Claire had told him more, about Troy, the feckless father who'd left her in the labour ward, and on several occasions she'd confided in him how tough she found it being a single parent.

'I'm so sorry, Lauren,' said Joel. 'I was stuck in the meeting from hell.'

'It's not me you'll have to answer to, it's my mum,' said Lauren, her voice tight with evident frustration. 'I've just had to put up with twenty minutes of nagging about why I let you get away with it. Mum did offer to stay with Sam, but I don't like to leave him with anyone else.'

'I'm really sorry,' said Joel, again, feeling terrible. It was unusual for Lauren to actually say what she thought. 'I promise I'll do better next time.'

'You always say that,' said Lauren, but her tone was softening.

He took Sam from her. 'Thanks, Lauren,' he said. 'Look. I don't say it very often, and I should.'

'Should say what?' He could still feel some hostility.

'Thank you,' he said. 'Since – since Claire died, I don't know what we'd have done without you, Sam and I. You're always there for us, and I take you for granted.'

There was a silence and Joel felt more awkward than ever.

'And I am sorry,' he added.

'Oh stop,' he detected a wobble in Lauren's voice. 'You know I'd do anything for the pair of you. It's the least I can do for – for Claire.'

She turned away from him for a moment, and he thought maybe she'd wiped a tear away from her eye, but she looked back and added casually, 'Oh, by the way I had coffee with your guerrilla gardener. Her name's Kezzie and she thinks you should get back on with restoring your garden.'

'I gathered,' said Joel.

'I think it's a great idea,' said Lauren. 'I hope you don't mind, but I told her I thought you should.'

Kezzie stood outside Joel's house wondering whether she'd made a mistake. She felt absurdly nervous. Having rashly declared to Lauren that she was going to take on Joel's garden for him, she'd decided she should go round and just tell him that's what she was going to do. Logically she knew all that could happen was that Joel would say no. But somehow it mattered to her more than she thought possible that she restore the garden. Not only had the magic of the place infected her, but if she could do this, and do it well, she might be halfway to her dream of getting a show garden ready for Chelsea, just as she and Richard had always planned. And she did want to fulfil that dream. If only to show Richard what he was missing.

'Come on, Kezzie, are you a woman or mouse?' she said out loud, then pushed open the creaking gate, and walked up the cracked path. Now she was up close to the house, she could see there were evident signs of occupation – a pair of boots by the front door, a child's plastic scooter hidden in the privet bush that jammed its way up against the bay windows, a light faintly shining through the stained-glass window. But it had a sad, lonely air, as if it were a house that had been left to its own devices for a very long time. Even the wisteria bush which clung to the front of the house looked lost and untended.

Taking a deep breath, she knocked hard on the door. There was no reply, so she knocked again. Still no reply. Oh well, perhaps she should come back another day. She was about to leave when suddenly the door was opened and Joel was standing there. Taller than she remembered, with dark, floppy hair, and kind blue eyes. Her heart gave a little flip. He was more attractive than she'd realized on their previous encounter.

'Right, here's the thing,' she said, 'I want to restore your garden for you.'

'Sorry?' His voice wrapped itself round her like dark velvet. She hadn't noticed how warm and deep it was.

'It's me, Kezzie. I did tell you my name was Kezzie, didn't I? I've decided I want to restore your garden. May I come in?'

'Er. OK,' said Joel, looking and sounding bemused. 'If you just give me a minute. I've just put my son to bed, and I'd better just check he's settled down. Go on straight through to the kitchen.'

'No problem.'

Not that she was interested in Joel, but he was the only halfway decent male she'd met in the bruising months since Richard had ditched her. It had occurred to her she needed a nice uncomplicated fling to get Richard out of her system, but attractive as Joel seemed, she had a feeling he'd be very, very complicated.

She walked through the hall noticing the unfinished floors, and unpainted walls. It all felt so terribly sad. She was surprised when she turned left into the kitchen, that it was shiny and new, with the latest modern gadgets, and a dazzling array of equipment. It was a kitchen to die for, and yet somehow it seemed to lack soul. She sat down on a bar stool, which she found tucked under the breakfast bar, and sat at the kitchen window looking into the dark. What was she doing here? She didn't know this man from Adam. If Joel had wanted to do something about his garden he'd have done something about it by now. She was just interfering in something that she had no business interfering with. Kezzie sat there, irresolute, her heart churning, her palms sweating.

'Sorry about that,' said Joel, interrupting her thoughts as he came silently into the room. 'So what is it you want exactly?'

Kezzie took a deep breath. He hadn't told her to get lost, maybe this could work. It was worth a try at least. 'I know we didn't exactly get off to a good start, and you probably think I'm interfering, but I really would be interested in doing up your garden. I want to exhibit at Chelsea at some point and I think restoring your knot garden would be a fabulous project to work on. And Lauren said you always wanted to restore it...' her voice trailed away. 'Look, I'll understand if you say no, it's just an idea.'

'No, you're OK,' said Joel. 'I did – do – want to restore it. Life's got in the way a bit, that's all. I'd like you to do it, if you still want to.'

'Are you sure?' said Kezzie. 'I'd love to.'

'I can't pay you,' warned Joel, 'or not much. And I can't help except at weekends. I have to go to work.'

'I've some money put aside from my redundancy, and I've got some freelance work, so I can survive for a bit. Besides, it could be my showcase garden, and help me get other business. You would be doing me a favour. And I can look into the possibility of getting a grant to help restore if you like,' said Kezzie, unable to hide the excitement in her voice. 'Edward Handford is of historical significance, I'm sure someone would be prepared to help with the restoration. I really am keen. I've been looking into Edward's work. He adapted a lover's knot garden from an original Elizabethan design and made his own version, which was more in keeping with Victorian times. But that might seem a little over the top for modern tastes, so I thought I could stay true to the basic vision, but simplify it a bit, and have heartsease at the heart of the garden. It seems appropriate.'

'If you say so,' said Joel looking amused.

'Sorry, running away with myself again,' said Kezzie. 'Bad habit I have. But look, I've printed off some stuff that I thought might be interesting.'

She showed Joel everything she'd found so far along with a plan of an Elizabethan knot garden, which Edward had apparently used as a guide.

'This is amazing,' said Joel. 'I had no idea of any of this. You've really inspired me to start again with it.'

'I'm really frustrated that I haven't managed to track down Edward's actual design,' said Kezzie. 'Having that would be an enormous help.'

'You can just about see the shapes of the original,' Joel said. 'It has been semi maintained over the years I think. But in the latter years, poor old Uncle Jack couldn't cope any more and it fell into a complete state of disrepair. So now it's full of weeds as you've seen, and needs cutting back and starting again. I only got as far as trimming back the box hedge.'

'I think it was beautiful, what Edward Handford did for his wife,' said Kezzie. 'All that effort to create a garden that spelt a message of how much he loved her.'

'I don't really know an awful lot about Mum's side of the family,' said Joel, with a frown. 'My Uncle Jack – well not so much an uncle, more of a second cousin, we just called him Uncle Jack – lived here alone. I think his mother was one of Edward's children, but I'm not sure. I should ask Mum about it. She must know something.'

'So how did you end up with this place?' said Kezzie.

'By dint of being the only one left,' said Joel. 'My mum's got Parkinson's so though Uncle Jack left it to her, Claire and I did a deal where we took out a mortgage on this house, and bought Mum a warden-assisted flat in Chiverton. She always used to go on about the garden here, and I was intrigued. I came here a few times when I was a small child, and I remember breaking into the knot garden. It was like a secret place, all locked up. When Jack died there was no one else but Mum and me to leave it to. I fell in love with it immediately. Claire and I had so many plans...'

His voice trailed off wistfully, and Kezzie felt as if she'd walked in on some private grief. She wished she knew him well enough to give him a hug.

'Claire never liked it though,' he continued. 'She thought it was gloomy. I took out the heavy oak panelling in the hallway and made it lighter, but what with work and looking after Sam, I haven't really had time to finish what I started.'

He looked sad, as if something pained him.

'You're right about the garden of course, that was the one bit of the place Claire really liked. I should have got it sorted.'

'Well, now you've got me here, you can,' said Kezzie.

'Really?' Joel looked as if he couldn't quite believe what he was hearing.

'Really,' said Kezzie.

'It's masses of work,' said Joel, 'and I won't be able to help you much.'

'I know,' said Kezzie. 'But I think it would be amazing to restore it, a huge privilege. Please let me.'

Joel stood for a moment looking as if he were battling with some inner demon, then he gave Kezzie a huge, and charismatic grin.

'You're on,' said Joel, and it was all Kezzie could do to stop herself from punching the air in delight.

It was a quiet evening in the Labourer's Legs, only a few punters had wandered in. It was the middle of the month, so people were probably saving their money till pay day, there wasn't any football on and the darts match scheduled for the night had been cancelled, leaving the sandwiches that Sally the landlady had laid wilting on the bar.

'Go on, take them home with you at the end of your shift,' Sally said to Lauren, with a slightly patronizing, sympathetic tone, as if she'd never be so foolish as to have been left holding one baby, let alone two. She also seemed to assume because Lauren was young she couldn't do anything for herself. Lauren had to bite her tongue from saying that it was most unlikely that two four-year-olds would be interested in stale prawn sandwiches, let alone risk a tummy bug. It was a battle at the best of times to get them to eat anything other than chicken nuggets and chips.

The clock dragged slowly towards 8 p.m. Two hours into her shift and already Lauren was losing the will to live.

'Mind if I pop upstairs to put my feet up for a bit, love?' Sally's inevitable request came as it always did, early on in the shift. Then a bit later on she would wander down, and say, 'You're all OK for locking up, aren't you, love?' before disappearing again to leave Lauren cashing up alone.

Lauren's mother was always telling her to stand up for herself, but jobs for single mums didn't come easy in Heartsease and she couldn't afford to give it up, much as she frequently felt like telling Sally to stick her job.

Bored, she half-heartedly let her eyes settle on the TV screen in the corner, which was tuned in to Sky Sport, and began to clean the bar surface down.

Phil Machin, one of the regulars, walked up to the bar. 'Barrel's gone, love,' he said smiling cheerfully. So off she went down to the cellars to change it.

When she came back, she spotted a missed call on her phone, which she'd left at the bar. It wasn't a number she recognized. Odd. She wondered who it could be. It was probably a wrong number.

Around 9.30 the place started to fill up a bit. The lads from the cricket club were on a pub crawl, so it was nearly 11 p.m. before she spotted another two missed calls. Who on earth could be trying to contact her?

As it had got busy, Sally and her equally lazy partner, Andy, had made their way downstairs, and Lauren was relieved that for once they let her go at just after 11. At least she'd be on time for her mum.

As she walked back up the road home, the phone rang again.

'Who is this?' she said.

'Lauren? Is that you?'

Oh my God. Lauren stood stock still, her heart hammering wildly in her chest, as she heard a voice she hadn't heard in a very very long time. 'Troy?' she said incredulously.

Chapter Six

Lauren pushed Sam up the road on her way back from the school run. It was nearly half term, the weather had turned from bright autumn golden days, to a wet, windy drizzle which was doing little to lift her spirits. She was dog tired. The phone call from Troy had unsettled her to say the least. Troy had spectacularly left her in the labour ward, claiming that because he lost his mother to cancer when he was very young, he 'didn't do' hospitals, running out on her when she needed him the most. After which he had shown no interest whatsoever in meeting his daughters until he'd turned up out of the blue when they were eighteen months old. Lauren hadn't wanted to see him, all the more so when it was apparent he was only after somewhere to crash after he'd lost the latest in a string of jobs and had no money and nowhere else to go.

Looking back now, Lauren couldn't believe how naive she had been to be taken in again by Troy. But he had this trick when you were with him of making you think you were the only person in the world who mattered. It was terribly beguiling, and the months of loneliness without him had left her unprepared for the sheer animal magnetism of his presence. He had a sensuality about him that was hard to resist. She had told herself that it would be good for the twins if she let him move in. Lauren's parents had split up when she was young, and she'd been desperate for her own children to have a stable family life. Lauren couldn't admit to herself that she still had the hots for Troy, so had made the mistake of letting him stay a while. And if she was totally honest with herself, despite everything he'd done to her, she was still a little in love with him, even now.

It turned out to be an unmitigated disaster. The twins were unsettled by this strange man who sometimes wanted to play with them, but often shouted at them for no apparent reason. It was clear to Lauren, too, that he was quite happy to sponge off her, pay no maintenance, and had no intention of getting another job while his life was this cushy. In the end she'd had enough and chucked him out, and apart from the odd message via mutual friends, she hadn't heard from him since. The twins barely remembered him, and used as they were to Sam not having a mummy, didn't appear to find it odd that they didn't have a daddy. And now their daddy was back and apparently he wanted to see them.

She had played the phone call with Troy over and over in her head all night.

'Why?' Lauren demanded. 'Why now, after all this time? You can't just waltz back into our lives and expect to become a dad when it suits you. I have to protect them.'

'I know,' Troy had pleaded. For once he sounded really sincere. 'I've been useless, but I've changed, really I have. Look. There's been stuff going on in my life. Stuff that's made me realize

I want to be a proper dad to them. I know what I've been missing and I want to make it up to them and you.'

'I'll have to think about it,' said Lauren, 'I'm not about to let you turn the girls' lives upside down.'

'I'm their dad, I have a right to see them,' said Troy.

Lauren was silent. That was something she'd always promised herself. If Troy ever came back and wanted to see the girls, she'd let him. Whatever she thought of Troy, he *was* their dad.

'You've taken me by surprise,' she said eventually. 'You haven't seen the girls for over two years, and you've never paid a penny towards their upkeep. How can I be sure that you have changed?'

'Oh, but I have,' Troy said hurriedly. 'I know I've made mistakes in the past, but I want to put them right. Please let me.'

There was a pleading, desperate note in his voice that she'd never heard before. God knows, maybe he really did mean it.

'I'll think about it,' said Lauren.

Everyone deserved a second chance, didn't they? Troy had sounded sincere, and she didn't want her girls growing up not knowing their dad. But did a leopard really change its spots? Troy hadn't been reliable in the past, why would he be now?

Lauren was roused from her reverie when she noticed Eileen Jones walking towards her waving enthusiastically. She smiled. Lauren liked Eileen; not only was she kind and thoughtful, but she occasionally sat for the girls when her mum couldn't. Her husband Ted had, as Eileen put it, become a cliché and run off with his much younger secretary, leaving Eileen on her own at fifty-two. And on top of all that her youngest son, Jamie, was soon off to do a tour of Afghanistan.

Lauren had really hit it off with Eileen, despite the difference in their ages. While she'd been left holding the babies, Eileen had brought hers up, a devoted wife and mother, and still ended up alone. Although recently, Lauren had noticed, she was spending a lot of time with Tony Symonds, who was the new Chair of the Parish Council. Eileen had a real twinkle in her eye and Lauren was pleased to see her so happy.

'Lauren, I'm glad I caught you.'

'Don't tell me ... the fete?' said Lauren.

'How did you guess?' said Eileen.

'Something about the determined way you were making a beeline for me,' said Lauren, laughing.

'It's just to let you know we've got our pre-liminary meeting coming up in a couple of weeks, and I wondered if you'd had a chance to talk to Joel about it yet.'

'I did mention it to him,' Lauren said, 'but he was fairly noncommittal. I'll talk to him about it this evening.'

'That would be great,' said Eileen. 'It would be fantastic to have access to the house and gardens.'

'It would, wouldn't it?' said Lauren. 'I'll see what I can do.'

Kezzie was back on the internet researching more about Edward Handford. She was interested to learn that he'd been something of a philanthropist, creating a little park in the village for the children of the poor. Originally known as Heartsease Public Gardens, they were renamed the Memorial Gardens after the First World War. Edward also paid for the village school, now very small and barely surviving. Most of the local kids were bussed into the bigger primary in nearby Chiverton. Lauren, with whom Kezzie was fast becoming friends, was unusual apparently in having opted to put the twins into the village school, but as she'd explained to Kezzie, 'Some-one's got to support the local community and services, or we'll lose them. Besides, the twins are too small to go on the bus, and as I don't drive I don't have much choice.'

Having lived all her life in an urban setting, Kezzie was coming to appreciate the pleasure of living in a small community, even if it meant people knowing all your business. She'd been stunned when she walked into Ali's Emporium to be told by Ali how great it was that she was working on Joel's garden.

'That poor boy,' Ali said, with a cheerful smile. 'He needs something good in his life. It is wonderful what you are doing for him.'

Not wanting to point out that she wasn't exactly doing it for charity, Kezzie had muttered, 'Yes, it's great to be working on it,' and fled with her pint of milk and loaf of bread before she got the Spanish Inquisition.

Kezzie decided she'd done enough research for now. The one time she'd tried to visit the Memorial Gardens, they'd been locked and she'd only had a chance to glimpse through the gate. She wanted to take a closer look, as it might give her a better feel for the kind of vision Edward Handford had had. While wanting to give his garden a modern feel, Kezzie wanted to be faithful to that vision. Somehow, she felt that was important.

She walked down the hill into the centre of the village, as ever getting a little thrill as she turned the bend and saw Heartsease spread before her, nestling cosily in the lee of the hill. The broad tree-lined road that swept down into the village was now littered with fallen leaves, but there were still a few remaining on the branches, to brighten up the greyish day. Kezzie couldn't have felt further away from London if she'd tried.

When she got down to the High Street, Kezzie followed the signs to the Memorial Gardens, past the butcher's, Keef's Café where Kezzie had learnt you could purchase a mean latte, the tiny chemist's situated in the oldest building in Heartsease, and the baker's. Heartsease wasn't exactly big, but she'd not yet had time to explore it all. What she saw when she arrived at the Memorial Gardens was utterly depressing. A rusting, wrought iron gate, bearing the name Heartsease Memorial Gardens, screeched open onto a forlorn-looking patch of green. At the far end was a pavilion, which was in desperate need of repair. Raggedy bits of grass were covered in glass beer bottles and fag ends. Graffiti on the walls proclaimed that *Daz Loved Zoe 4 eva*. The rest of the village wasn't like this. A cracked path ran down the middle of the grass, ending in a circle in which stood an enormous concrete plinth, which was empty. Presumably, it had been home to a war memorial. Kezzie vaguely remembered reading that Edward had erected one after the war. So where was it?

'What a shame,' she said out loud.

'Yes, isn't it?' Eileen was out walking her dog. 'I'm really hoping we can persuade the Parish Council to restore it.'

'Why have they let it get into such a state?' said Kezzie.

'It's been a gradual thing,' explained Eileen. 'When my children were small we used to come here all the time, particularly in the summer. But then kids started to go on the bus to the school in Chiverton, so they stopped coming. And then the County Council built the big leisure centre in Chiverton and everyone went there, and before you knew it, the vandals and graffiti artists had moved in, so even if the locals still wanted to come they got pushed out. At least we don't get the drugs any more. We had a spate of that but it's stopped, fortunately.'

'What happened to the war memorial?' said Kezzie.

'The local council took it away for restoration,' snorted Eileen, 'and never thought to bring it back.'

'That's terrible,' said Kezzie.

'I know,' said Eileen. 'We always used to have our Remembrance Day parade here, but now the Heartsease British Legion have to go to Chiverton.'

'Someone should do something about it,' said Kezzie.

'Someone is,' said Eileen. 'Me. I've been writing to the County Council about it for months, and now my friend Tony is the Chair of the Parish Council I'm hoping I can get things moving a bit more. But we could always do with some new blood. Maybe you could help?'

'Maybe I could,' said Kezzie. 'But I've got a lot on at the moment, I'm going to help Joel Lyle restore his garden.'

'Lauren mentioned that,' said Eileen, 'and I think it's wonderful. Lauren was hoping to persuade Joel to help out at next year's summer fete, perhaps you could put in a word too?'

'I'll do my best,' said Kezzie, laughing.

Joel was playing with Sam in the lounge. Sam had recently discovered peekaboo and a significant part of the bedtime routine now involved Sam hiding and Joel pretending to try to find him. It was silly but fun, and Joel was starting to really look forward to these precious moments at the end of a long day at work. He had, he realized, lost the capacity to laugh spontaneously, but Sam was slowly beginning to tease it out of him.

'Two – two, Da-da,' Sam clapped his hands over his eyes, as Joel mentioned the dreaded 'b' word just before bedtime, and this was Sam's way of telling Joel it was time to play their hiding game.

'Daddy hide, or Sam hide?' asked Joel, tickling his son on his tummy.

'Sam, hide,' squealed Sam, delightedly, toddling off while Joel made a great show of shutting his eyes and counting to ten. Usually Sam's hiding places were very obvious – and Joel spotted him within seconds, but Joel realized, when he opened his eyes, that Sam had squeezed through the lounge door, which was a bit ominous. He could just about get upstairs now, but was still a bit wobbly, and not very safe. Joel went out into the hall, and was relieved to hear Sam talking to himself in the little study on his left, which faced out onto the front garden.

Sure enough, he found Sam playing with his favourite rabbit, underneath the desk, the game momentarily abandoned.

'Come on, tiddler,' said Joel, swooping his son up in his arms, 'time for bed, now.'

'Two, two?' Sam looked hopeful.

'No more two, two,' said Joel, 'time for bed and milk and a story.'

He took Sam up to bed, got him changed, and sat down with him and read *We're Going on a Bear Hunt,* which was one of Sam's favourites. Having tucked him into his cot with a bottle of milk, Joel went downstairs to check on the carnage Sam had left behind, before settling down to another lonely evening in front of the TV. It never failed to amaze him how much havoc one small boy could wreak, so he went back to the study, which he rarely used, to make sure Sam hadn't left anything else under the desk. Sure enough, he found a couple of bits of Duplo, a baby board book, and bizarrely two spoons, which he presumed Sam had managed to swipe from the kitchen. Laughing to himself, he picked everything up and went to take them away, when he suddenly stopped and stared at the desk. He'd not paid it any attention for so long, and it was gathering dust, but he was suddenly struck anew by what a beautiful object it was.

It had been a real labour of love working on that desk, but then Claire died, and like so many other things, Joel hadn't touched it for months. But since Kezzie's arrival, Joel had felt something shift slightly. For the first time, he could see the point in moving on, making things better, if not for him at least for Sam.

He ran his hand over the rolltop desk lid. It really was a stunning piece of furniture, made of walnut, with several drawers on either side. When he lifted the roll top up, there were several little compartments. Joel recalled Uncle Jack sitting at it, on one of the few occasions Joel had visited as a child, and Uncle Jack had seemed very old, though he probably hadn't been much more than sixty.

'There's a secret compartment in this desk, young man,' Jack had said, tapping the side of his nose.

'Show me! Show me!' Joel had begged, but then they were interrupted, by his mum probably, as it was time to go home. When they'd first got to Lovelace Cottage, Joel had tried and failed to find the secret compartment, and concluded that Jack had been teasing him. For some reason tonight he had a sudden compulsion to see if it was there. He put Sam's toys down, rolled the top back, and fiddled around in all the compartments, to no avail. Maybe there was something underneath?

He felt underneath the desk, but there was nothing. Then he opened all the drawers one by one. Still nothing. Oh well. He was about to turn and leave again, when a tiny, frayed edge of paper caught in the corner of the smallest compartment to the far right of the desk caught his eye. He tugged at it, and as he did so, realized that there was a slight indentation in the side of the desk, just small enough for him to get his fingers in. With growing excitement, he slid his fingers in, and found a knob, which he pressed. He was rewarded with a sudden click, and a small shelf swung out to greet him. On it was an old and dusty leather-bound book, the pages yellow with age.

He picked it up, and running his fingers slowly along the spine, he blew the dust off it. He opened it carefully and read: *Edward Handford. His personal diary.* A black and white sketch floated out to the floor. Joel picked it up and instantly recognized the girl in it, from her photographs. She was very young, very beautiful and laughing. *Lily, June 1892* was written by hand underneath it. How lovely. Edward must have drawn her. Joel felt a pang. He had no pictures like that of Claire, but plenty of photographs, sad, stolen records of a far happier time.

He carried on leafing through the book. This was incredible. Edward Handford's *actual* diary. A real connection with the past. For the first time in a long time, Joel felt excitement coursing through his veins. He sat down and read the first page, it was dated May 1893:

This is my last night in England, for tomorrow I leave Lovelace Cottage on a great adventure, he read. *I am only sorry that Lily will not accompany me on my journey to India, but Doctor Blake thinks it would be foolish for her to travel in her condition. I will of course miss her, and am apprehensive of the journey ahead, but I cannot help but be excited by thoughts of the plants I may yet discover...*

Wow. Edward travelled to India. How wonderful. Joel flicked through the diary to see if there was anything about the garden. He'd have to show this to Kezzie. Perhaps it could help her restore Edward's layouts. Joel put the book down and laughed out loud. Despite his initial reluctance, he was hooked. Finding out about Edward Handford and restoring the knot garden was too intriguing a proposition to ignore.

Chapter Seven

It was Kezzie's first morning working at Joel's. She'd set off early and it was only just light. She shivered in the chilly autumn morning; winter would soon be on its way. Still, the icy rain of the last few days appeared to have eased off, and she walked up the hill, crunching through the autumn leaves, watching the sky turn from blue to metallic grey, feeling relatively cheerful. A feeble sun was trying to peep through the clouds when she finally reached Joel's house. She pushed open the creaky front gate, and went to knock on the dilapidated front door.

'Hi.' Joel held Sam in his arms as he let Kezzie in. 'You're early. I'm impressed.'

'I like the early mornings,' said Kezzie, 'you can

get so much more done, particularly at this time of year when you lose the light so soon.'

'Shows how wrong you can be about people,' said Joel. 'I wouldn't have had you down as an early bird.'

'Cheeky bugger,' said Kezzie. 'I may not look the part, but you will get your money's worth out of me.'

'Sorry,' said Joel, looking embarrassed. 'Can you bear with me a minute as I sort Sam out?'

Kezzie was still in the process of drawing up plans, but she'd agreed with Joel she would make a start on tackling the weeds in the garden and find out what lay underneath. Given that winter was on its way, it seemed a good opportunity to try and tidy things up.

'Feel free to come in and have a cup of tea whenever you want,' Joel added, as he expertly changed his son's nappy. Gross, thought Kezzie. She'd been very grateful to discover that Richard's daughter was already fourteen. She couldn't have coped with a baby.

'Right, that's you done.' Joel tickled Sam's tummy and he giggled infectiously. OK, the nappies were gross, but Kezzie had to admit Sam was cute.

'You're very good with him,' Kezzie said, as she followed Joel, still carrying Sam, cosy and warm in his winter coat, into the garden.

In the short time Kezzie had been in Heartsease, the leaves had fallen from the trees and she was now crunching them on the ground. She loved being outside this time of year, but preferred to garden in spring with the hope of summer and all the glories that were to come.

Joel pulled a face and Sam immediately giggled.

'Do you think so? I feel fairly useless on the parenting front most of the time. Lauren is much better with him than I am. I used to leave it up to Claire, because she was so good at it. She was a natural mother right from the start, whereas I was all fingers and thumbs. Now she's not here, I muddle through, but I wouldn't say I was much cop at it.'

'He doesn't seem to be doing too badly,' said Kezzie, as Sam gurgled contentedly in his dad's arms. 'And you're probably doing better at it than I would. I've not got a maternal bone in my body. I wouldn't know where to start with a toddler.'

Joel smiled. 'It's nice of you to say so, but I'm sure that can't be true. Haven't any of your friends had babies?'

'A couple have,' said Kezzie, shuddering. 'But they've put me off for life.'

'Surely you don't mean that?' he said teasingly. 'I thought most women wanted children, underneath it all.'

'Well, *I* don't,' said Kezzie, firmly. 'This planet's overpopulated enough without me adding to the numbers. Besides, I'm far too selfish to become a mum. I like my freedom too much.'

Joel took Kezzie down the garden towards the shed.

'I think you'll find everything you need here,' he said. 'Uncle Jack did have a sort of layabout handyman, who occasionally cut the hedges back, but clearly he didn't know what he was doing, which is why the garden's such a mess. I did have a go at keeping the weeds under control, the first summer we were here, but then Claire died, and...' his voice trailed off. 'Well, let's say I've barely touched it since.'

'Well, I'm here now,' said Kezzie. 'And I can't wait to get going.'

'I'd better shoot off,' Joel said, anxiously looking at the time, 'or I'll be late dropping Sam off at Lauren's. Can I leave you to it? There's a spare key hanging up in the kitchen, if you need to go out. I'll get you a set cut so you don't have to come up so early next time.'

'It's no problem, really,' said Kezzie, which was true, it wasn't. She liked the feel of an early autumn morning, like this one, when the sun was beginning to peep through the mist, the crows were cawing mournfully in the trees and the air was crisp and clear.

As Joel left, she gathered together a fork, trowel, rake, spade, some garden shears, and bin bags and put them all in a wheelbarrow. She let out a deep sigh of satisfaction. She was going to enjoy this.

Lauren walked through her front door after the school run with the twins jabbering excitedly in her ear about their harvest festival, which was to take place the following week. Sam had fallen asleep in the buggy, so she left him in the tiny hallway that led into the kitchen. The girls were demanding to make cookies after lunch, which was often an afternoon treat for all of them. Lauren was on the point of agreeing, when she noticed her answer phone was flashing.

'Just give me a minute, girls,' she said, helping them off with their coats, which she hung up in the small understairs cupboard. 'Why don't you run upstairs and wash your hands while I get lunch ready?'

The girls thundered up the stairs, and Lauren clicked on the answer message while she took a bag of flour and a packet of chocolate chips out of the larder.

'Hey, babe.' Oh God, Lauren sat down quickly on one of her pine kitchen chairs, feeling her knees turning to jelly. Troy. *Again.* Lauren had still not decided what to do about him. She hadn't rung him back, nor had she discussed the situation with anyone else. Mum was out of the question, she'd have flipped her lid if she knew Troy was trying to get in touch again. Lauren didn't feel she knew Kezzie well enough to confide in her. That left Eileen, who was a reliable source of comfort, or Joel. When Claire was still alive, Lauren wouldn't have dreamt of confiding in Joel. He was her friend's husband, with whom she got on well, but it was Claire who knew all her secrets.

Lauren had met Claire out walking with Sam when he was a baby and the twins were two years old. The girls had been particularly lively that day, and Lauren had had another call from the CSA to say they hadn't heard from Troy, and she'd been up to her neck in debt. Somehow, over a coffee in Keef's Café, the whole story had come out. The two women had hit it off immediately. Claire was looking for someone to care for Sam when she went back to work, and somehow Lauren had come away agreeing to register as a childminder so she could look after him. Thereafter when she'd had a wobble about Troy or anything really, it was always Claire she'd turned to. Claire had been such a good friend to her, and Lauren felt a familiar gut-wrenching sense of loss, at the thought that she no longer had her friend for support. Claire had always been full of sound practical advice, and Lauren missed her wisdom. When she died, Lauren had on occasion found herself confiding in Joel, but it wasn't the same, and she wasn't sure if she should ask his advice on this.

She listened again to Troy's message. 'Have you thought any more about it, babe? I need to know soon. Call me.' She clicked the answer phone off. She couldn't face this right now.

Joel was so dog tired by the time he got home he'd completely forgotten Kezzie was there. For a moment, when he came in the kitchen and saw a half-drunk cup of tea on the drainer, and the kitchen door wide open, he'd had the sudden dizzying sensation that Claire was back, somehow returned to him. He'd had lots of those moments in the early months, but it had happened less often of late. He nearly called her name, but stopped himself in time, when a very dishevelled and rather muddy Kezzie appeared, divesting herself of her wellies as she went.

'Mind if I leave these here?' she said, putting them by the back door. 'It seems a bit silly taking them back and forth each day.'

'Yeah, no problem,' said Joel, as he put Sam down and let him potter around the kitchen.

'You look knackered, if you don't mind me saying,' said Kezzie. 'Fancy a cuppa?'

'That would be great,' Joel yawned. 'It's been a long day. But first I need to get munchkin here into his bath.'

'No rest for the wicked,' said Kezzie.

'None indeed,' said Joel, with feeling. 'Come on, Sammy boy, bathtime.'

'Ba, Ba!' Sam clapped his hands and giggled.

When Joel had first bathed Sam alone, he'd hated it. He worried about the slipperiness of a wriggly baby in water; he was scared the water was too cold or too scalding. Some of Joel's tension had seemed to affect Sam and bath times had been neurotic, miserable affairs.

But one time, knowing he was going to be late from work, Lauren had offered to bath Sam for him. When Joel had come to pick him up, he had discovered Sam happily sitting in the bath blowing bubbles and pouring water over his head.

Joel had immediately invested in a couple of plastic cups and bubble bath, and bath times had been a cinch ever since. It was the one point in the day he felt he could really relax with his son.

He was sitting on the floor, singing stupid songs while Sam put bubbles on his nose, when Kezzie came up with a cup of tea.

'That looks fun,' she said.

'Fun, fun,' burbled Sam.

'It is, actually,' said Joel, 'an unexpected but absurdly simple pleasure of fatherhood.'

'Are you hungry?' said Kezzie, 'only you look half starved. Do you ever eat?'

'I don't often cook for myself,' admitted Joel.

'Lauren feeds Sam most days, and while I don't mind cooking, there never seems much point for one.'

'Thought so,' said Kezzie. 'You stay there. I'll forage in your kitchen, and see if we can't get you a square meal for once.'

Half an hour later, with Sam happily ensconced in his cot, cuddling his favourite toy rabbit, Snuffles, Joel emerged downstairs to the smell of something delicious on the stove.

Tears prickled his eyes. It was a long time since anyone had cooked for him. He came into the kitchen to find Kezzie stirring a bubbling pot.

'I've rustled up some pasta,' she said, 'I hope that's OK.'

'That's more than OK,' said Joel. 'It's very generous of you.'

'Well, I like cooking,' said Kezzie, 'but you're right, there never seems much point for one. Sorry, you don't think I'm interfering do you?'

'To be honest,' said Joel, 'it's nice to be cooked for, for a change. I can cook – but I can't be bothered most of the time. I think I've got a bottle of red knocking about somewhere. Shall we open it and have a toast to the start of the garden project?'

'Perfect!' said Kezzie.

'Talking of which,' said Joel, 'how did you get on today?'

'It's hard work,' admitted Kezzie. 'Harder than I thought it would be. I have managed to clear a very small corner in one part of the pattern, and I think Edward wove the ivy and rosemary into heart shapes, but the plants are so old, they've

106

gone a bit scraggy and the trunks are too thick. I can't imagine it's actually how he designed it. I'd love to see his original plans. I'd like to put my own stamp on the garden of course, but I want to be as truthful to his vision as I could be.'

'Oh, that reminds me,' said Joel. 'I didn't have time to tell you this morning. Guess what I found last night?'

'No idea,' said Kezzie.

'Edward's diary,' said Joel.

'That's fantastic,' said Kezzie. 'Where was it?'

'There's an old desk in the study, which I was restoring. I was having another look at it last night, thinking I should get it finished,' said Joel. 'And then I found a secret compartment, and there it was ... Edward's diary.'

'How exciting,' said Kezzie. 'Wouldn't it be wonderful if Edward's plans were in it?'

'I flicked through it,' said Joel, 'but then Sam started crying, so I put it down and forgot all about it. Hang on a sec, I'll go and get it.'

He came back a few minutes later, and they carefully pored over the yellowing pages together. Although there was plenty about his daily life at Lovelace Cottage, the diary appeared to have been started after he'd created the garden, so there was precious little to help them with their task.

'Isn't it incredible to think that Edward was sitting at your desk writing all this down?' said Kezzie. 'And that picture of Lily is gorgeous. It's such a pity that there isn't anything more about the garden.'

'Couldn't you find anything out on the internet?' said Joel.

'I've found some fascinating information about Edward but not enough about the garden plans,' said Kezzie. 'Are there any books about him?'

'Nope. He gets mentioned a lot, but I don't think he was prominent enough to have a book all about him. I've found out about the gardens Edward designed for other people – presumably they were his commissions – but he didn't appear to share his plans for the knot garden. Do you know if there's anything in the family? You don't have a family archive do you? I mean, there might be other diaries.'

Joel laughed. 'Not as far as I know,' he said. 'We're not that grand. I'll ask my mum next time I see her. There *is* an old trunk up in the loft, which Claire and I always meant to look through properly, but somehow we never had the time. I have no idea what's in it.'

'Would you mind if I had a look?' asked Kezzie.

'Be my guest,' said Joel. 'I'll show you where it all is tomorrow, if you like.'

'It's a deal,' said Kezzie, chinking her glass against his.

Joel sat back in his chair, sipping his drink and feeling a slight stirring of excitement. First the diary, and then the contents of the trunk. Maybe together he and Kezzie could uncover the secrets of Edward's garden. For the first time since Claire died, he really felt like finding out.

Chapter Eight

Lauren was feeling frustrated with Joel. While she was sympathetic to his situation, she felt he took it for granted that she wouldn't get upset when he was late home from work, or wouldn't mind getting Sam ready for bed on the evenings when he absolutely had to stay for that last minute meeting. And it had been worse since Kezzie had been on the scene. Lauren really liked Kezzie, she was fun and refreshing to be around, but there was something about the way she and Joel were developing a really cosy relationship that was beginning to niggle her. Somehow she felt surplus to requirements now.

Often, though, she was cross when Joel arrived late to pick Sam up. He did at least offer the chance for some adult conversation at the end of the day, which Lauren sorely needed after a day spent with small children. And recently she'd almost felt like opening up to him about the phone calls from Troy, but the moment never seemed right. But since Kezzie had started working on the garden, he always seemed in a dead hurry to get home to see what progress she'd made. On more than one occasion, he'd let slip that she'd stayed for dinner, which irked Lauren for some reason. And now, she'd found herself roped into helping out at the weekend while he and Kezzie rummaged around in the attic looking for bits of paper about Edward Hand-ford, which may or may not be of use to Kezzie's garden design. 'It's a Saturday, Joel,' she'd said. 'Remember, I don't work weekends.'

'I know, and I wouldn't ask you normally,' said Joel, putting on that slightly helpless Joel face, which was simultaneously endearing and irritating, 'but Claire's mum's away, and I really can't sort this stuff out with Sam running around downstairs. It's a one-off, I promise. I'll make it worth your while.'

That had swung it for her. Lauren wasn't so proud to pretend she didn't need the money. So she had bitten her lip and agreed to do it. 'Just this once though,' she'd said. 'Don't go getting ideas that I'll be doing it every week.'

Lauren arrived with the girls at Joel's at 10.30 as arranged. It wasn't as if she got the chance to lie in on Saturdays, but somehow the rigorous routine of the week slipped and she found herself unable to retain any normal standard of time-keeping. So she'd ignored Joel's suggestion to come round for 9 a.m.

Kezzie, it transpired, had got up there early to work on the garden.

'She likes getting up early,' marvelled Joel, as he ushered Lauren in. 'If I didn't have Sam, I would savour those lie-ins for as long as possible!'

For a moment there was a conspiratorial feeling between them, as the two parents remembered a semi-forgotten life where small children didn't get you up before dawn.

Lauren's world consisted of two gorgeous little girls who regarded 6 a.m. as the time when the day absolutely, definitely, had to begin. The notion of having any time early in the morning, without their chattering presence, seemed impossibly weird to Lauren. She liked Kezzie, but couldn't help feeling they inhabited different planets.

'Lauren, you are an angel,' said Joel. 'Thanks so much for doing this. I hope you don't mind, but I thought I'd pop out and see how Kezzie's doing in the garden, before we get going on the attic.'

Lauren *did* mind, although she couldn't quite pinpoint why.

Kezzie was out in the fresh air digging. The sun shone and a curious robin had perched on the end of her spade. Life really didn't get better than this. For the first time since Richard had broken up with her, she felt something approximating contentment. She was finding the process of discovery in this garden so exciting. So far she'd managed to dig out the weeds from the flowerbed furthest from the gate and uncovered the ramshackle remains of the original knot garden, which was about 60m square and stood in the centre, surrounded by a gravel path that needed replacing. The ivy had so completely overtaken the rosemary and box though, she felt it might need to be dug up and replanted. Hence her desire to find Edward's original plans. At the moment she had a rough idea of how he'd designed it – in a succession of interwoven hearts with the letters E and L interwoven in the middle – but what she was left with was such a poor and ragged substitute for the garden

Edward had planned, she felt it would be better to start again.

'I come bearing gifts.' Joel arrived with steaming cups of tea. 'How's it going?'

'Slow, but steady,' said Kezzie, stopping for a moment to survey her handiwork. 'I've cleared nearly a quarter of the garden, but it's a long way from the former glory of how it looked in Edward's time.'

'Lauren's happy to sit with Sam for a couple of hours, so I can help if you like.'

'It would be nice to have another pair of hands,' Kezzie admitted. 'Are you sure Lauren won't mind? We said we'd be checking out the loft, not digging up the garden.'

'Nah, she's cool,' said Joel. 'And there is a lot of digging. I won't have a chance to help you if I don't do some now.'

'I hate to say it,' said Kezzie with a grin, 'but your digging skills will come in handy too.'

'Is that what you call facultative feminism?' said Joel, with a grin.

'Probably,' said Kezzie. 'But I'm not proud.'

Progress with two was definitely better than with one, and in no time at all they'd cleared about a quarter of the undergrowth. Now it was getting a bit clearer to see where the original patterns had grown, but both the ivy and rosemary had grown too thick, and it was going to be a hard job reshaping them.

'You know, I hate to say this, Joel,' said Kezzie, 'but I think we're going to need to dig this all over and start again. I'm not sure it's going to be possible to get it back to its original shape. I do hope we can find Edward's plans. It would certainly help.'

Joel surveyed their handiwork.

'You're probably right,' he said. 'I can't work out what I'm looking at.'

'You see this here,' Kezzie pointed at a strand of ivy, 'it's interwoven with the rosemary. If the stems were thinner you could see it's the shape of a heart, but it's become misshapen. Come on, let's have a break from this for now. I'm dying to see what the attic holds.'

They put the tools away and walked up to the house. Lauren was in the kitchen feeding Sam, while the twins were watching TV in the lounge.

'Oh, lord, is it his lunchtime already?' said Joel. 'I'm so sorry, I hadn't realized the time. Do you want me to take over?'

Lauren rolled her eyes.

'No, it's OK,' she said, with evident sarcasm. 'You carry on, I'll be fine here. I've only got to feed the girls and put Sam down, so I may as well make you both some sarnies. I notice you've got bacon in the fridge.'

'Are you sure?' Kezzie felt uneasy, aware there were uncomfortable ripples beneath the surface. She had asked Joel if he was sure that Lauren didn't mind helping out and he had waved her concerns away with an airy, 'Oh Lauren's fine,' which Kezzie felt was a little glib. But Lauren seemed to recover her good humour and said it was no problem, while Joel had clearly managed to overcome any spasms of guilt quite quickly, and was already heading up the stairs to the top landing. He unhooked a trapdoor, which opened

113

to reveal a wooden set of stairs that took them up into the loft.

'Come on then, Gunga Din,' Joel said, 'let's see what we can find.'

The loft was dark and full of spiders, but Joel managed to remember where the light switch was. Light came through from the rafters. No wonder the house was so darned cold. With winter coming on, it was about time he put some insulation in. And investigated the state of the roof. Another thing to add to his To Do list.

Right. He stepped over the packing cases he and Claire had dumped up there, so long ago. Detritus of their former life, when they'd lived in London, and been poor and happy.

'I think the stuff belonging to Uncle Jack is over in the corner. We started going through it once, but never really had time to do it properly.'

'Ooh, this is just like *Cash in the Attic*,' said Kezzie, with contagious enthusiasm. 'I wonder what we'll find.'

Joel began rooting around in the ancient crates and boxes, picking through stacks of old Christmas cards, Uncle Jack's school reports, and Connie's photo albums. He was not quite sure what he was looking for, but he had a growing feeling of excitement. Since Kezzie had arrived and he'd found Edward's diary, Joel's long-submerged curiosity about his long-dead ancestor was being rewoken. Suddenly it really mattered to him as much as it clearly did to Kezzie that they find out something about Edward and his garden.

'Oh, wow, look at these,' he said excitedly, as he

found some old pictures rolled up together tucked under the eaves. Carefully, he unrolled them. There appeared to be several more of Lily, like the first one he'd found, and one with her holding a newborn baby.

'That's strange,' said Kezzie peeking over his shoulder, 'she looks sad for someone with a baby. What else is there?'

'Look at these,' said Joel, as he leafed through and discovered some delicate watercolours of different flowers and birds, drawn by a different hand, 'aren't they lovely?'

'Hey, look,' said Kezzie, pointing at a picture of a robin, perched on a step, 'I'm sure that's in the garden – see the gate behind it? Did Lily draw these, do you think?'

Joel squinted at the tiny signature in the corner of the painting. 'I think it says LH,' he said.

Carefully he rolled the pictures up again, and they carried on looking for a while longer, until Joel said, 'Here, this looks promising,' as he stumbled across a dusty old trunk in the corner. He carefully opened the trunk and caught his breath as he saw it contained books and papers, and letters all neatly stacked up inside. There was writing on the inside of the lid. He shone his torch on it: *Harry Handford, Lovelace Cottage, Heartsease* bore the inscription.

'So who's he?' said Kezzie.

'No idea,' said Joel. 'I've never heard of him, but he must be some relation, I guess. Mum would know.'

'Look at all these letters,' whispered Kezzie, her eyes shining. 'It's like we're touching history.'

'It is, isn't it?' agreed Joel. His excitement was growing now. This was fascinating, he'd had no idea any of this was here.

They started flicking through the bundles of letters, some addressed to Mr and Mrs Handford, some to Lily, some to Harry Handford. And several from Edward to Connie, talking about the work she was doing as V.A.D. in France.

'Oh look,' said Kezzie, 'this is from Edward to Lily.' She picked up the letter and began to read.

Lahore, June 1893

My dearest Lily,
Every day I am away from you, I feel my heart ache just that little bit more. I cannot tell you how much I long to see you again. I wish you had after all been here at my side. The work here is long and arduous, particularly in the heat, and the man they have given me as an assistant is by no means as diligent and attentive as you. It is of some satisfaction to me that I will be able, I hope, to bring home some new species of plants that will be of interest to Kew.

Edward went into a lot more detail about the exhibition he'd been on, before ending, *But however much pleasure I get from my work, not a day goes by, my darling, without my wishing to come home to you, and our beautiful garden. To think that in less than a year we will have a new family, is a joy beyond measure. With all my love to you as ever, my darling,*
Your Loving
Edward.

My dearest Edward,
The worst has happened and you are away from me.
The dark days of winter draw in, and I cannot sum-
mon the strength to raise a smile, now I know there
will be no happy event in the spring.
Mother tells me it is God's Will. I daresay she is
right, but do you think it very wicked of me to
question why God should have willed that our baby
should have died before it even saw life?
I think of nothing else but what might have been. I
fear your mother thinks I am overindulgent in my
grief, but how can I not be? Our future has been stolen
from us. I feel my heart has broken and you so far
from home. Hurry back to me, my love,
Your Lily

'Oh and look at this.' Kezzie had uncovered a
diary, which was lying underneath the batch of
letters she'd been reading through. Joel peered
over her shoulder and shone the torch on the
spidery handwriting. 'I think this is Lily's diary.'

October 1893
Today is a better day. The best in a very long time.
Edward is home, come back to me at last. Together we
have mourned our baby. I feel stronger and able to
stand it now he is once more by my side. He took me
out in the garden and he promised he'd plant some-
thing in memory of the baby we have lost, once the
spring is here. And he took my hands and whispered,

117

'*Do not fret, there will be more babies*' and he is right. My future hasn't been stolen from me. Just postponed for a while.

'Oh, how very sad!' exclaimed Kezzie. 'Just think of them having that lovely garden, and hoping to plant flowers in it to celebrate the births of their children and then they lost a baby.'

'Tragic,' agreed Joel. 'I have a feeling they had a lot of tragedy. I think Lily might have died quite young, but I'm not sure. I should ask Mum.' He felt a sudden odd surge of kinship with Edward, who'd clearly known heartache too.

'This is amazing,' Kezzie said, 'real social history. You must show Eileen – you know, who lives on our road. She's interested in all this stuff, and wants your help on the committee. I reckon a gardening museum would be interested in this. It's fascinating.'

'And it's taking up an awful lot of our time,' said Joel. 'I think we'd better get this trunk downstairs and look through it at our leisure.'

By the time they emerged from the loft, blinking in the sunlight and covered in dust, Lauren had fed the children, put Sam down for his nap, and produced a monster pile of bacon sandwiches. She was sitting in the lounge watching *CBeebies* with the twins.

Joel popped his head round the door with a plateful of sandwiches, while Kezzie went to freshen up.

'Thanks for this,' said Joel, 'you didn't have to.'

'No, I didn't,' snapped Lauren waspishly.

'Oh, no. Sorry.' Joel felt wrongfooted, but then

Lauren's tone softened as she said, 'So did you find anything interesting?'

'Yes, it was incredible,' said Joel, who was really feeling fired up by the morning's discoveries. 'There was a trunk with loads of letters in, and Lily's diaries – that's Edward's wife – and pictures they'd both done, but no sign of any plans yet.'

'That's a shame,' said Lauren, but she didn't really seem interested. 'Come on girls, it's time to go.'

'Oh, do you have to go so soon?' said Joel. 'I was hoping to get back in the garden for a bit this afternoon.'

'Well, you'll have to hope won't you,' said Lauren, with exasperation. 'I do have other things to do, you know.'

'Yes, of course,' Joel ploughed on. 'Sorry. I thought maybe the money could be useful...'

'The money is always useful,' exploded Lauren. 'That's not the bloody point. I've got to walk the girls to their granny's for a sleepover so I can work a late shift in the pub. I don't have much of a life, but not all of it revolves around you and Sam.'

'Oh,' said Joel, 'I'm really sorry, I didn't think–'

'No, that's the problem,' said Lauren. 'You never do. Come on, girls, time we were off.'

'Oh,' said Kezzie, looking embarrassed, as Lauren swept past her. 'What was all that about?'

'Me putting my size elevens in it again,' groaned Joel.

'Well, you do treat that poor girl like she's a bit of furniture, sometimes,' said Kezzie.

Joel looked a bit rueful.

'I know,' he sighed. 'I don't mean to. She's so

much better with Sam than I am.'

'Not better, necessarily,' said Kezzie. 'Just different. I think you need to spend a bit more time concentrating on being a dad and not letting other people do it for you.'

'So you wouldn't help me by getting Sam up from his nap then?' said Joel as a telltale sound of gentle wailing proclaimed Sam was waking up.

'Nope,' said Kezzie. 'I'm nobody's nursemaid. Least of all *yours.*'

Edward and Lily

1893

Lovelace Cottage
Heartsease
February 1894

My darling Edward,
I trust this letter finds you well. I wish I could be by your side drawing all your discoveries, as I used to when we went on our country rambles, here in Sussex. I cannot imagine how you manage in such a hot climate, with only poor Mr Salter to help you. He doesn't sound as though he is the best or most interesting of companions!

I long to see you, and hope that you will be back in Heartsease in the summer when our son – I am sure it is a son, he kicks so lustily! – will be born. Won't it be lovely to have a baby in the summer, sitting out in our beautiful garden? I cannot wait to see him or you.

Hurry home to me soon, my love, we both grow impatient!

Your loving wife
Lily

Delhi
March 1894

Dearest Lily,
You are quite right, Mr Salter is a poor companion compared with you. He suffers badly in this heat, poor chap, constantly takes snuff and I suspect from the way his hand shakes in the morning he secretly drinks. He tries very hard, but his skills in drawing are nothing like yours, but I don't have the heart to tell him so. Besides if I got rid of him, I'm not sure who would help me.

I hope to be finished with my expedition towards the end of the month, and am aiming to be back in Heartsease in June, just in time for the baby to be born.

The days cannot pass quickly enough till we meet again.

Your ever loving
Edward

Lovelace Cottage
Heartsease
May 1894

My dearest Edward,
I am sorry to write with sad news, but Lily's baby

121

arrived too soon. The doctor did all he could, but your son was born with the cord wrapped round his neck. He died soon after he was born. Lily is distraught and has not risen from her bed since. I cannot persuade her that her grief is too much and she should be more restrained. She is like a wild child when I try to calm her. The doctor has been and prescribed laudanum, but I fear for her wits if she carries on like this.

I hope you will be able to return soon, Lily needs you.

Your ever loving Mother

Delhi
May 1894

My dear Mother,
Thank you for you letter. I write to you with a heavy heart. I am sorry to be away once again, when Lily has need of me. I know you will look after her as I would. She is too fragile sometimes for this world, I fear, and bears her sorrows more keenly than others do. I am sure God will see fit to bless us with a child soon. I wish Lily could share this hope, but sadly she does not.

I hope to be home as soon as I can. Until then I remain,
Your ever loving son,
Edward

Lily Handford's diary, June 1894
The summer blooms bright and strong out there in the garden. Edward's garden. I hear the sounds of the

birds and part of me wants to join the joyful song. But I cannot. I feel trapped here in this dark room, but the dark is like a warm shroud that comforts me. I cannot abide the windows being opened. I do not want to let the light in. There is precious little light in my life now. I cannot believe we will ever hold a baby that breathes and lives long enough to laugh.

At least this time I was able to hold my baby boy for a short time, even if he didn't have the strength to suckle.

They say he died in sin. There was no time to baptize him. Father will not even allow him to be buried in the churchyard. My poor innocent little boy. How could he have sinned? How could God have let him die?

No, there is no light in my life, and none in my heart. Nor do I think there can ever be again.

Edward Handford came home to a very different wife. The household was cold and bare. There was no joy any more. The Lily he remembered only two short years ago, laughing with him by the willow tree, the Lily who had had so many hopes and plans for the future – that Lily had gone. In her place was a silent, pale ghost who barely moved from her bed. She stared blankly into space, her skin translucent against the pillow, her lips pale and bluish. Sometimes he feared she was dying; her hands were so cold; she lay so still.

Many an evening, he sat at his writing desk, recording his thoughts in his diary. *Lily is not like other women,* he wrote in November of 1894, *she is more fragile than they are, less able to deal with the loss of her baby. Where other women accept it as God's will, Lily rages against Him, in ways her parents both*

123

find blasphemous. Perhaps I should, but I cannot. Lily feels things more than others do. I cannot condemn her for it.

There were times when Edward had to stand up for Lily to his whole family – as the months wore on and still she seemed more and more enshrouded in her gloom, and less able to engage in the outside world, he even found himself quarrelling with his mother.

'I will not hear of it,' he said, when his mother suggested that he should have Lily committed because her behaviour was too extreme, too feverish, too hysterical. 'Lily will stay here with me, and she will get better.' Edward recalled with horror an aged aunt who had been locked in a sanatorium, and he had no desire for his beloved wife to be sent to one, however scattered her wits.

Later he wrote, *Perhaps it is wrong of me to have had Mother live with us. She, who is so strong and steady, cannot understand the pressures the world brings to one such as Lily who flourishes in its light, but is bowed under by the dark. I know Lily will get better. She needs tender nurturing to take her through the winter of her pain. One day it will be spring, and she will smile again.*

So Edward persevered that whole long dark winter, refusing her family's demands to have Lily sent away, gently encouraging her day by day to re-enter the world once more. Until a day came, in the spring, when he was able to persuade her to join him in the garden to show her the agapanthus he'd planted in memory of Edward James, the son who had lived a mere six hours.

Lily cried in his arms then, and he rocked and cherished her and promised there would be other babies, and that he would never leave her again.

Chapter Nine

After Lauren left, Joel and Kezzie dragged the trunk, paperwork and pictures down the stairs.

'You should really give Eileen a ring about some of this,' said Kezzie, 'I'm sure she'd love to have a look through it.'

'Good idea,' said Joel. 'Lauren's been nagging me about getting involved in the summer fete. I have to confess, it's not my kind of thing really, but I'm beginning to change my mind. The more I find out about Edward Handford, the more I think the world needs to know about him.'

'I think there's enough here to mount an exhibition,' said Kezzie. 'Wouldn't that be a wonderful thing to do in his anniversary year?'

'Just look at all this stuff,' said Joel. Now they had it in the light, they could see just exactly what was there.

There were boxes and boxes of letters, files, paperwork and photos piled higgledy-piggledy into the trunk. They were loosely organized into piles of letters with neat handwriting, saying Lily to Edward/Edward to Lily, Connie to Edward, and so on.

'I wonder who organized all this,' said Kezzie. 'Someone must have pulled all this stuff together.'

'Hmm, I wonder...' Joel picked up some of the packets of letters and compared the handwriting. 'I think it may have been Connie – see this letter here from her to Edward, the writing looks the same.'

'Remind me who Connie was again,' said Kezzie.

'Edward's daughter, I think, which makes her my great great aunt,' said Joel. 'I think she died just before I was born and Uncle Jack inherited the house from her. I can't believe how much stuff there is here, it's going to take forever to sort out.'

'Where's your sense of adventure?' said Kezzie. 'I don't mind having a look through it, I bet Eileen will be interested in it as well. I'll call in on her on my way home.'

Before she left, Kezzie turned to him and said, 'By the way, you are going to apologize to Lauren, aren't you? I know it's not my business, but I think she deserves better.'

'I know,' said Joel with a sigh. 'Claire always said I was a bit thick about other people's feelings. I'll apologize next time I see her.'

As he waved Kezzie off, Joel decided he'd have to try and make it up to Lauren sometime. Kezzie was right, he could be casual with Lauren, and it wasn't fair. He appreciated what she did for him and Sam, and he barely ever said so.

'You stupid sod, haven't you learnt anything?' he said out loud.

He thought back to that last catastrophic night with Claire, and how they'd argued because she felt he'd let her down and now here he was doing

126

the same thing to Lauren. In the morning he'd go round with some flowers and apologize. It was too late to make it up to Claire, but it wasn't too late to put things right with Lauren.

Lauren flew home in absolute fury with Joel. She snapped at the children, who trotted by her side like such frightened little mice till she got them home and hugged them, she felt terrible. It wasn't their fault Joel could be such an insensitive sod. Lauren felt immensely guilty that she'd taken her bad mood out on the twins, and made it up to them by giving them a cookie each. Lauren wasn't sure what had annoyed her most, the casual way Joel had let her make everyone lunch, the fact that he'd assumed she'd be able to drop everything to stay and help him out, or the way that Joel and Kezzie made her feel so left out.

'Serves you right for being such a soft touch,' she murmured. This was the problem of course. She did have a soft spot for Joel. Partly because of Claire – Lauren felt she should help him for her friend's sake – partly because of the situation he was in, and partly because it was impossible to stay cross with Joel for long. So by the time Lauren had walked the girls to her mum's, had a moan about Joel and got home again, she was feeling better. She decided that what she needed was to chill out before work and banish all thoughts of Joel and Sam from her mind. She walked back home fantasizing about a nice hot soak in the bathtub.

But as she got home, all her previous irritations paled into insignificance. She approached the house and to her surprise saw someone was waiting on the doorstep. As she drew closer, she saw to her horror it wasn't just anyone – *Troy* was lounging nonchalantly on her doorstep, smoking a roll-up. Her heart thudded in her chest and she felt slightly sick as she took in his sensuous good looks, the piercing blue eyes, the mane of slightly dishevelled hair, and incredibly sexy, unshaven look. She had forgotten just how good looking he was.

'What the hell are you doing here?' she said. 'I didn't say I wanted to see you.'

'Well, that's a nice greeting.' Troy got up laconically, stretching his long limbs in a languorous sensual movement. He'd always reminded her of a predator – a lion perhaps – and she recognized that look in his eye. Bastard thought it would be a cinch. He was still so sure of his power over her.

'Troy, I haven't seen you in over two years,' she said. 'You've only seen your children once since they were born, and never paid me any maintenance. Why should I give you a nice greeting?'

'Because you know, despite it all, you and me are made for each other.'

He leant over to touch her cheek, but she pushed him away, her heart pounding with a combination of anger and attraction. The knowledge that the attraction was there made her angrier than ever.

'When did you have this revelation? The last time I saw you, I seem to remember you saying you were a free spirit, made to wander, not cut out for domestic life.'

'Yeah, well. I may have got that a bit wrong,' said Troy.

'Latest floozy kicked you out?' said Lauren. 'Think I've been there before.'

'There isn't a latest floozy,' said Troy. 'I've just been through some stuff lately that's got me thinking. I realize I've not been a good dad–'

'You've not *been* a dad at all,' snorted Lauren.

'–and I've treated you badly. But I would like to get to know the girls properly. And you know I've always had feelings for you. I still do.'

'Stop!' said Lauren. 'You don't get to wander back into my life, declaring undying love and move straight back in again. You just don't. And while I'm delighted you're at last showing an interest in your daughters, they're older now. I want you to have a proper relationship with them. You can't wander in and out at will. You've got to be here for the duration.'

'I can be,' said Troy. 'I want to be. Can I see them?'

'They're not here,' said Lauren. 'They're at Mum's for the night. And I have to go to work now, so please just go.'

'Please, don't shut me out of their lives,' said Troy. He looked so woebegone, she softened. Damn his beautiful blue eyes. They were her Achilles' heel. 'I really do mean it this time.'

Lauren sighed. After her irritating morning at Joel's, Troy was the last thing she wanted to be dealing with.

'Why?' she said. 'Why are you here, after all this time? And how can I possibly trust you?'

For the first time Troy looked slightly less sure

of himself.

'There's been some stuff going on in my personal life,' he mumbled.

'Stuff? What stuff?' To Lauren's knowledge Troy didn't 'do' personal problems.

'It's to do with my dad,' said Troy, in a manner that suggested every word he was saying was torture. Which for him, it probably was. Troy's dad was among a number of subjects that Lauren had quickly discovered were taboo. For him to even mention his dad must mean something was up. Lauren took a deep breath. Perhaps she should give him a chance, but she wasn't going to make it easy for him.

'What about your dad?' she said.

'He's – he's been in touch,' said Troy. 'He's not well at all, and wanted to meet me. I've been to see him, but it's too late. He's done nothing for me my whole life, I just don't want to know now. And it made me realize what I'm missing. Please. I really do mean it; I would like to see the girls.'

He looked at her so plaintively she felt like slapping him. Arrogant Troy was far more attractive than this pleading version.

'OK. I'll think about it,' said Lauren. 'I would like the girls to know their dad, but if you let them down I'll crucify you – understand?'

'Got it,' Troy said. 'But this time I promise I won't.'

Kezzie spent the afternoon poring over some of the letters and diaries that she and Joel had found. It was fascinating stuff, full of the minutiae of other people's lives. She'd been particularly taken with the letters Edward had written Lily when he was abroad in India. Astonishing to think of the journeys they'd made in those days, and all so Edward could collect exotic plants – apparently there was at least one rhododendron at Kew named after him. Kezzie had also been excited to discover a black and white photo in one of the piles of letters. It was obviously out of place, as it was dated 1905 and pictured the original opening of the Memorial Gardens, when it was still known as Heartsease Public Gardens. Edward and Lily were standing in front of the garden's iron gates in the middle of a group of people, looking very stiff and formal, but maybe that was just the way photographs were done in those days. All the women wore light summer dresses with high lace collars and trim waistlines, and the men were in suits. Although the print was faded, it looked as though they were all squinting, so presumably it had been a sunny day. Kezzie liked the fact that Edward had done something for his community, it made her feel connected to him in some small way. She was beginning to feel connected in Heartsease, too.

When Kezzie had first moved in to Jo's cottage, she'd imagined she'd be bored rigid living in the country. Flick would have laughed in her face had she known, but to her surprise, despite missing her friends in town, Kezzie was slowly getting used to village life, and being here was certainly making her feel more rational about the whole Richard situation. Yes, she'd been an idiot. He'd been right to be angry with her, she could see that now, where before she'd thought he was overreacting.

But he had been cruel. When she'd tried to make it up to him, Richard had reacted in such a coldly furious way that Kezzie had felt almost as though she didn't know him. But then she thought back to his teasing comments in their early days together about her being a 'Greenham' and a dropout, when she'd thought he could be quite priggish and fuddy duddy. Kezzie had always felt their differences had made their relationship stronger, but perhaps she'd been wrong about that. Maybe they were just too different, and her actions had just highlighted the fact that they should never have been together in the first place.

Kezzie sighed, and put everything away. She wasn't so over Richard that the thought of an evening on her own in the cottage, brooding about him, was at all appealing. There wasn't much on TV and although she still had to respond to Jo's last email, and had lots to do on her new website, she wasn't in the mood for sitting at home. She decided to go down the pub. Lauren had said she was working that night, and it might do her good to get to know some other people in Heartsease.

After a quick bite to eat, Kezzie set off down the hill and made her way to the village pub. The Labourer's Legs was near the small village green, which formed the heart of the village. It backed onto the local pond where they drowned witches in medieval times, if the books in the little ethnic shop just off the High Street were to be believed. Now it was home to some ducks, a few moor hens and a pair of very bad-tempered swans.

She walked into the pub, which was quite small and cosy with its little nooks and crannies and an oak beamed ceiling. A large fire was crackling in the far corner, and she immediately spotted Lauren behind the bar, polishing glasses.

'Oh Lauren, am I glad to see you,' confessed Kezzie. 'I couldn't face the thought of an evening at home alone, but I was a bit nervous about coming in here on my own.'

'No need to worry,' said Lauren, 'the natives are quite friendly. I'll introduce you to some. What are you having?'

'Lager, thanks,' said Kezzie.

Several lagers and some introductions later, Kezzie found herself in the middle of a lively group of locals, including John Townley (whom Lauren had whispered she should avoid like the plague), the eponymous Keith of the café fame, who was an ex-fashion designer and full of out-rageous stories about some of the rich and famous he'd encountered in his previous line of work, and a couple of cheery builders who tried it on, but cheerfully accepted the knockback Kezzie gave them. She'd have felt awkward being the only woman, but luckily Eileen arrived with a man called Tony. They seemed to know everyone, so Kezzie soon felt accepted into the crowd. She had a fun and raucous evening, and felt fairly sozzled by the time she left at the end of Lauren's shift, which somehow carried on until gone mid-night.

'What time were you supposed to finish?' Kez-zie asked Lauren as they walked up the hill to-gether.

'Eleven,' said Lauren, 'but Andy and Sally are good at disappearing when I need them. They

133

only made an appearance at the end because it got so busy.'

'You shouldn't put up with it,' said Kezzie. 'You're far too nice. I told Joel so today. He takes advantage of you.'

'Oh, you didn't!' Lauren looked mortified.

'Well, he was out of order,' said Kezzie. 'I felt so embarrassed when I realized you'd made all those sandwiches for us. There was no need.'

'Habit,' said Lauren. 'I was pissed off, I don't deny it. The trouble with Joel is, he can be so hopeless sometimes it's easy to fall into the habit of looking after him.'

'Oh, is it now?' said Kezzie, resolving never to do the same. 'Well you shouldn't; you should stick up for yourself more.'

'I know,' said Lauren. 'Easier said than done, though.'

Kezzie thought back to how pathetic she'd become around Richard. 'True,' she said. 'We should be women, not wimps.'

'Yeah, right!' said Lauren, laughing at Kezzie as she fumbled for her keys and brought out her lipstick by mistake. 'Come on, let me help you inside.'

Kezzie giggled her head off as she and Lauren sorted out her keys. It reminded her of being out for the night with Flick. She said good night to Lauren and let herself in the cottage. For the first time since she'd been here, she didn't feel quite so lonely.

Chapter Ten

Lauren was still smiling when she let herself in. As she absentmindedly tidied up toys in the lounge before going to bed, she thought to herself how much she had enjoyed Kezzie's company. She realized with a jolt that apart from Eileen, she didn't have many girlfriends. Those she'd made at uni had faded away after the twins were born, and her friends from home had all moved on. Despite the age difference between them, Claire had been a fantastic friend to her in the short time they'd known each other. It wasn't just that they'd bonded over their children, Claire had been like the big sister Lauren had never had. But Claire was gone and had left a huge hole in Lauren's life. No one could replace Claire of course, but Lauren hoped that she could become mates with Kezzie. It would be nice to have someone to share things with again.

Though it was late when Lauren went to bed, she felt unable to sleep. It felt strange without the twins in the house. It didn't happen very often, but when her mum had the girls overnight Lauren missed them dreadfully. Added to which, whenever she shut her eyes a picture of Troy swam before her. To her annoyance, she realized half-forgotten desires were stirring. She'd put Troy firmly out of her mind for so long now, she'd convinced herself she was over him. But, dammit, there was a residual – who was she kidding – a strong attraction still. They had chemistry, always had. And it was that whole free-spirit nonsense that had attracted her in the first place. Of course, Lauren thought she'd be the one to tame him. And of course she'd been wrong. But maybe this time he really had changed. He did seem more grown up somehow. But then again, did the leopard change its spots?

She slept late in the morning, luxuriating in a rare opportunity to lie in, and enjoying the comfort of her double bed with its fresh linen and bright flowery bedspread. One of the luxuries of living without a man was that Lauren revelled in having a girlie bedroom, which made her feel relaxed and homely. The rest of the house was the same. Though there was the inevitable clutter that came from having small children in the house, Lauren had paid a lot of attention to having the house decorated brightly, with cheerful curtains and comfy rugs on the floors. Even though it was a rented house, and she didn't have much money, Lauren wanted her home to be bright and homely, and for the most part she felt it was.

Lauren made herself a cup of tea, and went upstairs to have a shower. She had just turned it on, when the doorbell rang. Thinking it was her mum bringing the girls home, she threw a towel around her and leapt down the stairs.

'Hi, Mum,' she said, flinging the door wide open. Then, 'Oh–'

On the doorstep stood Troy with a bunch of flowers, and closely following behind, walking up the garden path, was Joel with Sam under one arm, and another bunch of flowers under the other.

'Blimey. You wait all your life for men to bring you bunches of flowers, then two arrive at once,' she said weakly.

'Who's he?' they said simultaneously.

'Joel, this is Troy, the girls' dad. Troy, this is Joel, I look after his son, Sam,' said Lauren, feeling surreal. And then because she couldn't think of anything else to say, added, 'Would you both like a cup of tea.'

'No, I'd best be off,' said Joel, looking awkward. 'I don't want to disturb you when you've got guests.'

'Troy's not a guest,' said Lauren automatically.

'I just wanted to say sorry for being such a selfish sod yesterday. Here, take these, I hope you like them.'

Lauren leant forward to take the flowers. She was slightly staggered but pleasantly surprised that Joel had at least acknowledged he'd been a twat. As she did so, her towel came undone.

'Oh, shit!' she said, as she exposed herself to everyone in the Lane.

'Nothing I haven't seen before,' said Troy, with a familiar look in his eye.

'Now I really had better go,' said Joel, looking mortified. Lauren pulled the towel tightly around herself again in confusion.

'I knew you couldn't resist me,' continued Troy, as Joel walked away. 'Is that cup of tea still on?'

'Yes, I suppose so,' said Lauren. 'But I really am only offering tea.'

Joel, feeling like a total idiot after his botched attempt at apologizing to Lauren, went round to see Kezzie. She opened the door looking bleary eyed.

'Mind if we come in?' he said. 'I just called on Lauren, only it seems she's got – er – company.'

'Who would that be, then?' said Kezzie, frowning. 'I saw her at the pub last night and we walked home together. She didn't mention that anyone was coming round today. I didn't think Lauren had a boyfriend.'

'I don't think she does,' said Joel. 'It was her ex.'

Kezzie whistled, 'What, the one who left her in the labour ward?'

'The very same,' said Joel, unsure why he felt quite so uneasy about the sudden reappearance of Troy, or why the sight of Lauren's naked body was making him feel all hot and bothered. From everything Joel had heard about Troy from Lauren, it seemed he could only be bad news, and the thought of him hurting Lauren again made Joel feel strangely uncomfortable.

'Ouch,' said Kezzie. 'I hope she's careful.'

'Me too,' said Joel, with feeling. 'I went round to apologize for yesterday. You were right, I was out of order – and there he was in front of me. I could see I wasn't wanted, so I thought I'd better scarper over here. Hope you don't mind.'

'No worries,' said Kezzie. 'I was just having breakfast. Coffee?'

'That would be nice,' said Joel.

He followed her into the small kitchen at the back of the house. It looked out onto a pretty garden with a patio, a small lawn and a green-house at the end. Though autumn was turning into winter, the pots were still overflowing with petunias, busy lizzies and pansies.

'The garden looks great,' he exclaimed, feeling really pleased that he'd got Kezzie involved in restoring Edward's. 'Your handiwork, I presume?'

'Well, my aunt had the basics here. I've just had a go at making it a bit more homely. I'd take you out there, but these autumn mornings are a bit too chilly for sitting out.'

Sam was tottering about in the kitchen, and picked up a bottle of beer.

'Oops,' said Kezzie. 'My house isn't very toddler proof, sorry.'

'It doesn't need to be,' said Joel, scooping Sam up as his son made a bid for the door and the tantalizing but lethal-looking stairs. 'Sorry, we're not going to get much peace and quiet. Sam is a bit too much of a wrigglepot.'

As if to prove his point, Sam wriggled out of Joel's arms and headed for the vegetable rack. He proceeded to cause chaos by throwing all Kezzie's weekly veg on the floor. Joel picked him up and took him away and he started to howl loudly. Joel shrugged his shoulders helplessly. He felt that sometimes with toddlers it was just easier to stay at home.

'I see what you mean,' said Kezzie. 'Why don't we go out for a bit? I'd like to see the Memorial Gardens again. Eileen's got me involved in their restoration too, and I need to have a look at them again before I get going.'

'That sounds a great idea,' said Joel, feeling

hugely relieved. 'I'm sorry, Sam can be a one toddler destruction machine in a small space.'

'Don't worry,' said Kezzie. 'I'm not used to being around small children, and I keep forgetting the cottage isn't really geared up for kids.'

Joel went to his car to pick up the buggy, and they walked down the hill, chatting away about the garden and the difficulties of dealing with toddlers. It was a cold, clear day, and Heartsease, with its pretty little shops, redbrick buildings and lovely nooks and crannies, spread before them looking so attractive, Joel had a sudden shot of pleasure that he'd chosen to make this his home. When they got to the park, Joel got Sam out of his buggy and he went toddling down the paths, while Kezzie looked around at the scrubby flowers and tried to work out what would be best for the borders.

'Dadda, Dadda,' Sam was shouting and laughing with his arms outstretched towards Joel, who ran towards him and swung him up into his arms. His son. His gorgeous son. The best present Claire could have given him.

'Has no one tried to do anything about this before?' Kezzie said to Joel as they surveyed the sad ruin of Edward Handford's vision. The gardens were small, comprising a gated green enclave at the end of the High Street. From her research, Kezzie had learnt that it had originally been intended for the people of Heartsease for recreational purposes, and was only renamed the Memorial Gardens after the First World War. The presence of paths, laid-out borders and lawn were evidence of a previously well-tended garden. Now it looked abandoned and derelict, the empty plinth in the middle standing in lonely defiance.

'That's where the war memorial should be,' said Kezzie. 'Isn't it a shame people always feel they have to graffiti things?'

'I would have thought you'd be into graffiti,' said Joel, 'isn't it art?'

'Some of it is,' said Kezzie, 'but writing rude things about people you don't like isn't. And it seems disrespectful too. My granddad was in the war, so I always wear a poppy for him.'

'I agree with you on that one,' said Joel. 'Do you know, I hadn't even realized there was a war memorial till you mentioned it. I don't come here that often.'

'Not even to take Sam to the swings?' said Kezzie.

Joel shrugged. 'Have you seen them?'

Kezzie followed him down the furthest path, that led from behind the plinth towards some overgrown bushes. Behind the bushes there was a tatty play area, with an ancient rusty roundabout, two creaky swings and a slide that looked as though it might topple over if anyone actually tried to use it.

'This is ridiculous,' said Kezzie. 'Don't you guys *want* somewhere for the kids to come and play?'

'I hadn't really given it much thought,' said Joel. 'Until recently, Sam's been a bit small to take to the playground, and I've got plenty of room at home. I think Lauren comes down here, though.'

'I bet she'd like a clean, safe place for the twins

141

to play,' said Kezzie. 'Right. That's it. I'm going to get on to Eileen about this the minute I get back. It's time we shook this village up.'

Good as her word, once Kezzie was home, had said goodbye to Joel and grabbed a bite to eat, she was straight round to Eileen's.

'You're absolutely right,' she said, sweeping in. 'Oh, you've got company.'

'Just my son and family, and you've met Tony,' said Eileen, smiling. 'You can come and join us if you like.'

Kezzie felt wrongfooted. Until last night, when she'd seen Eileen out with Tony, Kezzie had pictured Eileen as a sad singleton. Here she was having a much livelier time than Kezzie, who spent Sunday evenings on her own.

'Oh I couldn't–'

'Of course you could,' said Eileen. 'Pull up a chair, grab a glass of wine. This is my new neighbour, Kezzie. Kezzie, meet my son Niall, his wife, Jan, and my two scamps of grandsons: Harry and Freddy.'

Before long, Kezzie found herself telling them all everything she'd discovered about Edward Handford.

'That's fascinating,' said Eileen. 'I've not been able to find out a lot about Edward's family, though I do know his son died in the war.'

'Maybe that's why Edward paid for the memorial,' said Kezzie.

'Could be,' said Eileen. 'It's still sitting locked up in some council warehouse somewhere.'

'Shocking,' whistled Niall. 'Was that the old memorial we used to play on in the park?'

'The very same. We always used to attend the Remembrance Sunday parade with your dad and granddad. Do you remember?'

'Yes, I remember,' said Niall, 'I can't believe they've not put it back.'

'Neither can I,' said Tony. 'I hadn't realized it was an issue till Eileen raised it at a Parish Council meeting.'

'What happens on Remembrance Sunday now?' Kezzie asked.

'Everyone goes into Chiverton,' said Eileen. 'They've still got their memorial. It's a shame, I'd love us to have our own Remembrance Day parade here again. Particularly with Jamie going to Afghanistan after Christmas.'

'Jamie?' Kezzie said. She knew Eileen had a daughter, Christine, but hadn't realized there was another son.

'My youngest son, he's in the marines,' said Eileen proudly, holding out a picture of a handsome young man in uniform. He looked impossibly young to be going to war.

'That must be scary,' said Kezzie.

'I try not to think about it, if I can,' said Eileen. 'Otherwise I'll go mad with the worry of it. But he's one of the reasons I want to restore the war memorial, to remind people it still goes on.'

'Time to get ours back then,' said Niall.

'The summer fete next year is all in aid of restoring the garden and play area,' said Eileen. 'And we're trying to pressurize the council to give us our memorial back. They say they haven't got the money to restore it, so we're trying to shame them into it.'

'Surely we don't have to wait for them to start tidying up the garden though?' said Kezzie. 'We should get cracking and dig over the beds before the winter sets in and it's too cold.'

'Oh, if I know the Parish Council, they'll be still debating that next spring, won't they, Tony?' said Eileen.

'Sad, but true,' said Tony with a grin.

'Time we took matters into our own hands then, isn't it?' said Kezzie, grinning. 'Just as well I've had practice breaking and entering.'

Chapter Eleven

'So?' said Troy, as Lauren came downstairs after she'd got dressed.

'So what?' said Lauren, as she put the kettle on, her embarrassment making her tetchy.

'Have you thought any more about me seeing the girls?'

'I've thought about nothing else since last night,' said Lauren. 'Look, you can meet them, but not yet. I need to sit down and talk to them about you. And we need to take it slowly. You can't expect them to welcome you with open arms.'

'Why? What have you said about me?'

'Don't flatter yourself,' said Lauren. 'I don't talk about you *that* often. They know they've got a dad, but that you're not around. Some of their friends are in the same situation and they know Sam hasn't got a mummy, so they don't ask a lot about you. But they're likely to be shy, so don't expect too much.'

'So when can I see them?'

'I'll let you know,' said Lauren, determined that if this was going to happen, it was going to be on her terms. 'They're going to be back soon, and I don't want them to see you without any warning. So push off now, and I'll give you a ring when you can come back.'

Troy got up slowly, as if reluctant to leave. He positively oozed charm and sexuality and Lauren had to fight very hard to counteract the strong feelings of desire that were stirring within her.

'And us?'

'What about us?' said Lauren. 'There is no *us*. You made that quite clear four years ago.'

'So I can't hope for anything?' He moved closer towards her. She could smell his aftershave; a musky smell that reminded her of the tangled beds, and lusty afternoons, they'd spent together in the heady days in her second term at university when they'd first known each other. *Don't. Don't think of that.* She forced herself to concentrate on something else, but Troy wasn't making it easy for her.

He brushed his lips across hers, and the touch of his hands on her shoulders was enough to make her want to give in and pull him straight towards her. But looking over his shoulder and seeing the picture Joel had taken of the twins on their first day at school, brought her to her senses. A sudden vision of herself in a hospital bed, unable to move after a caesarean with two screaming babies in cots beside her, swam before

Lauren's eyes. What was she thinking letting him worm his way in here again? She had to be stronger than that.

'No,' she said, pushing him away firmly. 'You can't. You had your chance and you blew it.'

'We'll see,' said Troy, blowing her a kiss as she bundled him out of the door. 'I can be very persuasive.'

Lauren shut the door behind him and leant back against it, her heart pounding.

Joel came to pick Sam up after work, and for once he was not late. He was exhausted though; it had been a long and harrowing day as people had started to get wind of the planned cuts to services. Everyone was on edge, not just about their jobs, but about the people they were going to have to let down. Joel had heard countless stories about vulnerable people being left without services they needed that day, and it was heartbreaking to have to tell people the cuts were going to have to come from somewhere. Sadly it didn't look like they were coming out of the Chief Executive's salary. As usual Joel had been in a hurry that morning, which had meant that there had been no time for either him or Lauren to mention the awkward scene from the previous day. He wasn't sure who had been more embarrassed, Lauren or him, by their last encounter, so he decided the decent thing was to pretend it hadn't happened.

'Has Kezzie mentioned she wants to do up the Memorial Gardens?' he said by way of conversation, as he watched Lauren change Sam's nappy for the last time.

'She did say something about it,' said Lauren. 'There, all lovely and clean, Sammy boy.' She tickled his tummy and he giggled. Joel felt a spasm of envy. Lauren made it look so easy, but Joel still felt out of his depth when Sam was having a tantrum. He wished more than anything that Claire was here to tell him what to do.

'We were talking about the playground as well,' said Joel. 'I hadn't realized what a state it's in. We think we should try and get that renovated too.'

'Now that is a good idea,' said Lauren. 'The kids need a proper play area. I'll have a chat with Eileen about it next time I see her.'

'Great,' said Joel. He looked closely at Lauren; she seemed a bit pale and withdrawn.

'Everything all right?' he asked.

'Why wouldn't it be?' said Lauren, though she didn't look great. There were dark circles round her eyes and she looked tired.

'You look a bit worn out, if you don't mind me saying,' said Joel. 'If it's anything to do with what happened yesterday, I've forgotten it already.'

'Oh, that,' said Lauren, blushing puce. 'No it's not that. I just haven't slept well for the last two nights.'

'Are you sure you're OK?' said Joel. 'I imagine yesterday was a bit of a shock for you what with Troy turning up out of the blue.'

'Ah yes, the return of my wonderful ex, no I'm probably not OK, but I just have to work out how to deal with him,' Lauren sighed.

'I hope you sent him packing. He doesn't deserve you,' then, embarrassed, 'Sorry, I've probably said too much.'

Lauren gave a sad smile.

'No, you're right,' she sighed. 'It's not as easy as that though, is it? He wants to see the girls.'

'Don't let him,' said Joel. 'Why should he suddenly arrive and expect everything to be the way he wants it?'

'I've spent the last two nights lying awake thinking the same thing,' said Lauren. 'But despite everything he *is* their dad, and they have a right to know him too.'

'But he could let them down again,' argued Joel, thinking privately that on past performance he was bound to.

'He says he's changed, and that he really wants to make it up to them. What if he has turned over a new leaf, and I send him away? I couldn't do that to the girls. They deserve a chance to get to know their dad, however useless he may be,' Lauren said.

'Well, I think you're being very generous to him,' said Joel. 'But make sure you call the shots. I really would hate to see you hurt.'

'I'm a big girl, I can take care of myself,' said Lauren, but her smile didn't quite reach her eyes.

'Well if you need anything...' Joel said awkwardly, picking Sam up and heading for the door.

'...I know where you are,' said Lauren with a half smile.

But as he got in the car, he turned to see her, looking lost and forlorn standing on the step. He had the uneasy feeling that Troy's arrival was going to change everything for the worse.

'So I hope you're not going to let Troy see the girls?'

It had taken Lauren nearly a week to pluck up the courage to tell her mum that Troy had made contact, and now she was on the warpath. Their phone conversation had already lasted half an hour and was going around in ever decreasing circles. 'When I think about what that man put you through, I could commit murder, I really could.'

'Mum,' warned Lauren. 'Whatever you think of him, he is still the girls' father. I just want to do what's best for them.'

'Hmpph!' snorted her mum. 'Letting them see Troy useless Farrell isn't what I regard as best for them.'

'Well, it's not up to you, is it?' said Lauren. 'In fact, I'm not sure it's up to me. I think I should explain it to the girls and see what they want to do.'

Lauren had spent the last week mulling over what to do, and she had decided this was the fairest conclusion. Troy had been ringing her incessantly all week, to the point where she'd switched off her phone, and was ignoring him. Her plan was to tell the girls at the weekend, and if they wanted to see him, invite him over.

'So long as you don't let him worm his way back in,' said Mum. 'That man is about as trustworthy as a snake. Don't say I didn't warn you.'

'I won't,' said Lauren. 'But I will let him see the girls if they want to see him. For their sakes, not his.'

She put the phone down and started to get Sam

149

ready to go and pick the girls up from school. Maybe she should tell them now, and get it over and done with. They had to know sometime.

So on the way back from school, she suggested they go to Keef's Café on the High Street for lunch, something she could rarely afford, but she thought the girls deserved a treat if they were going to find out about their dad. Smiling at Keith, who leant over and tickled the girls under their chins, she ordered the drinks and then went to find somewhere to sit.

'I've got something special to tell you, girls,' Lauren said, once she'd got Sam in his high chair and the twins had divested themselves of hats, coats, gloves and scarves. They perched on the high bar stools by the window, so they could see who was walking up and down the High Street, while they ate their lunch. Her lovely twins, so gorgeous, so vulnerable. Lauren hoped she was doing the right thing telling them about their dad.

'What is it?' asked Immie excitedly.

'Is it good special?' said Izzie, looking a bit anxious.

'Of course it's good, special,' said Lauren smiling bravely.

'Tell us, tell us!' the twins were wriggling with anticipation.

'Well,' began Lauren, 'you know a long time ago your daddy had to go away.'

'We don't have a daddy,' said Immie.

'Yes you do,' said Lauren.

'No we don't,' said Izzie, banging her glass down on the table. 'He doesn't *ever* see us. He *never* gives us presents. We don't have a *real* daddy.'

150

Lauren swallowed hard, this was going to be more difficult than she thought.

'You do have a daddy,' she said. 'I know he hasn't seen you very much, but you do have a daddy who has always thought about you. And now he's come back, and he really, really, wants to meet you.'

The twins looked at each other and then suspiciously at Lauren.

'Will he bring us presents?' said Izzie.

'What if we don't like him?' said Immie.

'I'm not sure if he'll bring you presents,' said Lauren, 'but I'm sure you'll like him. He's your daddy and he loves you very very much.'

She crossed her fingers behind her back as she said this, hoping against hope she'd told her beautiful daughters the truth.

'Hi, Mum,' said Joel, as he went to pick her up from her small flat in Chiverton, where as usual, she was waiting outside for him. It was a blessing that she'd been able to find it when she had, given the rapidity with which her Parkinson's had deteriorated. When Uncle Jack had died, he had left Lovelace Cottage to her in his will, 'On account of the kindness you showed my mother in her latter years,' he'd written. 'Oh, stuff and nonsense,' Joel's mum had said to him when he'd asked her about it. 'Aunt Connie had a sad and troubled life, no wonder she was so prickly. I just visited her a bit when she was old, that was all.'

But when it came to moving in, his mum had invited Joel and Claire round for lunch, and then said, 'I have a proposition. This house is too

151

much for me. I really couldn't manage it. I'd much rather you two had it and turned it into a proper family home.'

So it was decided that, despite Claire's initial reluctance, Joel and Claire would sell up their small flat in London and buy Lovelace Cottage off Joel's mum, who moved into a warden-assisted flat in Chiverton. It was near enough to the town that she could walk there to get what she needed, and small enough for her to manage easily. Joel was grateful that they had managed to find such a good solution for the ever growing concern about his mother's situation, and was only sorry that it wasn't in Heartsease, but Mum had insisted that she needed her independence, and they needed their space. He would have loved to be able to be nearer her so he could help her as much as she helped him. Since Claire died Mum had been a tower of strength, always available to listen when he wanted to talk, and just be there when he didn't.

'Lovely to see you both,' said his mum, kissing Joel on the cheek and giving Sam a cuddle. 'What do you want to do today?'

'I thought I'd take you for a drive and a country pub lunch,' said Joel. 'If that's OK?'

'Sounds perfect,' said his mum. 'The weather's been so wretched this week, I've hardly been out at all. I could do with a breath of fresh air.'

Joel drove them out of Chiverton, and up a winding country lane to the top of Chiverton Hill. The pub sat at the top of the hill, and the views were extraordinary, particularly as the trees had lost their leaves, which opened up vistas hidden in summer. The sun was shining for the first time in a week, and the hillside showed a stunning array of greens, blues and greys.

Joel parked the car in the car park, popped Sam in his pushchair, helped his mum and her stick out of the car, and they walked to the viewpoint to look out across the county. In the very, very far distance they could make out a strip of grey blue.

'Do you know, I think that's the sea?' said Joel. 'They say on a clear day you can see it.'

'What's that spire?' his mum said, pointing out a church in the near distance.

'Not sure,' said Joel, consulting the viewpoint. 'Oh, it's probably the Church of St Barnaby at Burnham Heath.'

He stared at the different locations indicated on the viewpoint.

'Oh look, it's even got Heartsease on it. Five miles to the Heartsease Memorial Gardens. I'm not sure why they'd mention that, they're not much cop now.'

'Presumably they were more of a feature once,' said his mum. 'Are they in a very bad way? I seem to remember, when I was a child, they were beautiful.'

'It's a shame,' said Joel, as they walked back towards the pub. 'You can see they used to be magnificent, but they've gone to rack and ruin now. Kezzie, the girl who's restoring the garden for me, wants to have a go at sorting them out too. They even want me on the village committee.'

'It might do you good,' said his mum. 'Give you something to focus on.'

'That's what Kezzie said,' said Joel. 'It turns out

next year is the 140th anniversary of Edward Handford's birth, and the Parish Council want to celebrate, and they seem keen to have a member of his family involved.'

'And do you want to?'

'I didn't,' admitted Joel. 'I thought at first it wasn't quite my thing, but since Kezzie and I found all the stuff in the attic – I did tell you about that didn't I?'

'You did,' said his mum with a smile, 'several times.'

'Oh,' said Joel, a little crestfallen, 'sorry, I've probably been a bit overexcited about it.'

'It's lovely to see you so enthusiastic about something,' said Mum. 'Really, I'm pleased. And I'd love to see what you find out.'

'So far, we've read some of the diaries and letters, and it looks as though before Connie was born, Edward and Lily lost a couple of babies. Which was very sad. And from what we can tell, Lily seems to have died fairly young. Do you know what she died of?'

'I'm not sure,' said Mum. 'My mother said her parents never spoke of it. I asked Connie once, and she went very quiet and said something about some things being better left alone. I'm amazed that you found all that paperwork. I wonder why she kept it.'

'I really feel for Edward,' said Joel. 'It sounds daft, but he was left all alone in that big, old house, just like I've been. I really want to bring both the house and garden back to life.'

'Well then,' said his mum, 'I think you should, don't you?'

154

Kezzie was on a train to London. She was still debating the wisdom of this, but she'd felt so lonely on Friday night, she found herself looking up all her friends on Facebook. She'd deliberately kept off it since she'd been in Heartsease, but once she had logged on, there were so many messages from people she felt quite teary.

Kez, where are you???? Flick had posted on her wall over a month ago, and then again, *KEZ what's up? No one's seen you. Please don't be dead.*

Kezzie hadn't been able to resist, responding:

Hi Flick. No. Not dead. Having some time out.

Where are you? came the instant response.

Do you live on FB? typed Kezzie. *Why don't you go out and get a real life?*

Cos my virtual one's such fun, retorted Flick. *But seriously. Where are you? How are you? Am worried, honx*

I'm fine, typed Kezzie. *But I do miss you.*

Well, what are you waiting for? wrote Flick. *Come and see us. What are you doing tomorrow night? There's a band on at the Liberty and a crowd of us going. Why don't you come? You could crash with us.*

I'll think about it, wrote Kezzie, but she knew she didn't have to think about it at all. She was enjoying her new life in Heartsease, but she missed her old life in London. And it wasn't just Richard she was missing; she was missing her friends too.

So Saturday morning found her on a train up to London. Her decision was so spontaneous, she hadn't got round to telling anyone where she was going. Although, who would she tell, apart from Lauren or Joel? She didn't know anyone else.

155

It seemed weird coming up to London after all these weeks away. She watched the countryside gradually flee away as the train sped through Sussex villages, and gradually raced towards more built up urban centres. After weeks of seeing hills, and trees, and sheep, it was a sudden shock to be rattling through council estates, back gardens, and fox cubs playing by the railway side. London seemed dirtier than she remembered, as the train crept slowly into Waterloo and the station itself seemed frantic and busy. Did people always rush this much in London? Had she, when she lived here? It was nice, she realized, taking things a little more slowly.

It took an hour and a half to get over to Flick and Gavin's flat in Walthamstow. The flat itself was lovely and cosy. But the road it was on was grim, with a towering estate looming ominously on the other side of the road. Kezzie grinned. She had fond memories of that estate. She, Flick and Gavin had started out planting a few bedding plants there, and although at first the local kids had pulled them up, in the end some of them had got interested in what Kezzie and her friends were doing. With some help and enthusiasm from their local community centre, the kids had ended up creating their own little garden. Kezzie still felt proud of that.

'Kez! You're here.' Flick threw her arms round Kezzie, and gave her an enormous hug. 'Tell me, where have you been? What's been going on?'

'It was just London, Richard, everything,' said Kezzie. 'I needed to get away.'

'But you could have told me where you were

going,' scolded Flick.

'I know, I'm sorry,' said Kezzie. 'Things all felt a bit mad here, and then my Aunt Jo offered me a place to stay in the country, and it seemed like the right thing to do.'

'You're living in the country?' Flick roared with laughter. 'What a hoot. Did you hear that, Gav?'

'I think most of London heard it,' said Gavin, who was also known as Space Cadet on account of him being not very with it a lot of the time. He was sitting at their rackety kitchen table, rolling a joint. 'Hey, Kez, great to see you. There's a whole crowd of us going out tonight. Should be a blast.'

And it was. After a bite to eat, the three of them strolled down the road to the local pub, the Three Compasses, where Kezzie had spent many a happy evening. She soon slipped back into things. Flick and Gavin had gathered a crowd together, some of whom she knew, Tom who'd come on lots of night-time expeditions with them, and Karen and Dan who lived down the road, as well as several she didn't. It was fun, and Kezzie was enjoying herself so much by the time they got to the gig, she allowed herself to be persuaded to have a puff of Gavin's spliff.

'I shouldn't really,' she said. 'I decided to give it up.'

'Oh, come on, don't be a party pooper,' said Flick, who was well away by now, 'what harm can one little puff do?'

'A lot,' said Kezzie, with feeling.

'What do you mean?' asked Flick. Overwhelmed suddenly at being with people she loved, who

157

loved her, and who knew Richard, Kezzie couldn't contain herself any longer. She'd spent so long hugging her secret to herself, the words came spilling out of her.

'The thing is, oh God, Flick, I've been such an idiot,' she said. 'I knew Rich hated me smoking dope. One of the few things we used to argue about was that he thought I could be feckless sometimes, incapable of taking responsibility. I wanted to prove him wrong, but instead I stuffed up big time.'

'Woah,' said Flick, raising her hand. 'Slow down. What on earth did you do?'

Kezzie put her head in her hands, and then sat up and looked straight ahead.

'You know we were going to move in together?' she said.

'Yes, so?' said Flick.

'Well, I offered to have Emily at my place for the afternoon, when Richard was going to be late at work. I knew he was worried about how we got on and that Emily was a bit wary of me, and I thought we could get to know each other a bit better. Stupidly, I thought we might bond a bit better away from Richard's flat.'

'And?'

'It was a disaster,' said Kezzie. 'Emily was bitchy to me from the minute she arrived. I tried to engage her in polite conversation, I tried to find out what she was interested in, and she was so bloody rude. In the end, I just left her watching TV and went into my room to work on some designs I was doing for one of Richard's clients, and we ignored each other till Richard came home. Which was when all hell broke loose.'

'Why?'

'He found Emily lying on the floor giggling hysterically, drunk and high as a kite, and blamed me for plying her with dope. I tried to tell him I hadn't – I didn't even have any dope in the house but he was so angry he wouldn't listen and the little cow told him I had given her some of my magic muffins.'

'Oh my God – were those the ones we made together?' Flick suddenly twigged what had happened.

'The very same. I'd planned to share them with you and Gav next time we were out gardening. Emily must have helped herself. Plus, she'd found some of my vodka and drunk that. I told Richard I hadn't given it to her but he wouldn't believe me. We had a row, and that was it, he wouldn't see me again.'

'Oh, Kez,' said Flick, giving her friend a hug. 'The silly sod. He must have known you'd never do a thing like that.'

'I don't think he's that rational as far as Emily's concerned,' said Kezzie. 'Emily told her mum, who blamed Richard, and stopped Emily seeing him for a bit, which made things worse for me and him of course. I accused Emily of doing it on purpose to split us up, and that was it. Richard stopped taking my calls, and refused to have anything to do with me. And it's my own stupid fault. I should never have had those muffins in the house where a teenager could get their hands on them. And it proved to Richard once and for all how irresponsible I was.'

'And do you think he's right?' said Flick with sympathy.

'Yes. No. I don't know,' said Kezzie. 'It's all been so muddled up in my head. I think the main thing is we both realized how different we are, how different our lifestyles are. I don't think we can be together any more.'

'Well, then,' said Flick. 'If that's the case, one spliff can't hurt can it?'

'I'm not sure,' said Kezzie, but she was weakening.

'After all, you don't have to please Richard any more,' continued Flick.

'Oh, go on, then,' said Kezzie.

Hours later, after a really brilliant evening, where she'd danced wildly, sung herself hoarse, and drunk far too much, Kezzie found herself rollickingly staggering back down the road with Flick and Gavin, and ordering a curry.

'I do love you two guys, you know,' she said. 'I've missed you.'

'I've missed you, too,' said Flick. 'Don't go away. Stay here.'

'Got to,' said Kezzie. 'Got a commission to restore a garden.'

'Sounds good,' said Flick.

'It is.' Kezzie told them all about Edward Handford and Lovelace Cottage, and she realized that it *was* good, and she was beginning to really like it in Heartsease. 'You could come and help me. We're trying to restore a community garden, too, do you remember that project we worked on over in Hackney? Only a bit posher.'

'You're on,' said Flick. 'Tell us where and when.

Oh, and if you're not coming back, take something from Spike home with you to keep you cheerful over the winter.'

Spike was the name Flick had given to the original cannabis plant she'd grown. Over the years Spike had produced much fruit as it were, and Kezzie grinned as she accepted the small plastic bag Flick offered her.

'Thanks guys,' she said. 'You're the best,' and sat back in her chair and relaxed. With the winter coming on she'd been feeling very lost and lonely, despite her burgeoning friendship with Lauren. Coming back to see her friends had reminded her of who and what she was. Suddenly she didn't feel quite so lonely any more.

Chapter Twelve

'Girls, do you remember who I said was visiting today?' Lauren sat down with Izzie and Immie over breakfast. She'd told Troy that he could come around and meet them, but she still wasn't sure she was doing the right thing. She looked from one to the other, so alike, and yet so different as they sat munching their toast in the homely kitchen. She'd worked so hard to make their home a haven for them, to make up for not having two parents. And in the main, she felt she'd succeeded. Was she about to destroy all that by letting him back into their lives?

In the last couple of weeks she'd gradually

161

introduced the idea of Troy coming back, but she wasn't sure how much the girls had understood about it, or whether they were upset at all. Having them actually meet him was a big step.

'You know I told you that Daddy had come back after being away for a long time?' said Lauren.

'Ye-es,' the girls chorused a bit doubtfully.

'Daddy's coming to see you today, isn't that lovely?'

'Oh,' the girls looked blankly at her.

'Where has he been?' Izzie wanted to know.

'I thought we might be getting a treat,' said Immie looking disappointed.

This wasn't going exactly to plan, but Lauren persevered.

'Daddy had to work a long way away from here,' she lied. She didn't like lying to the girls, but how did you tell two four-year-olds their dad hadn't wanted to know? 'So he couldn't come and see you before. But now he's back and he really wants to meet you.'

'I don't want to meet him,' said Izzie. 'Silly Daddy.'

'Yes, silly Daddy,' agreed Immie.

Very silly, Lauren silently concurred, looking at her daughters and wondering how anyone in their right mind could have ever abandoned them.

'That's a shame,' said Lauren, 'because I'm sure you'd like him.'

'Will he like us?' Izzie looked at Lauren so anxiously her heart melted.

'Of course he will,' she said feeling her throat constricting. This was so bloody hard. 'Come on,

I'll give him a ring now and ask him to come round. And if you don't like him, we'll send him away again. What do you think?'

The girls mulled it over for a few minutes, before tentatively smiling at each other and saying, 'OK. Can we watch *CBeebies* now?'

'Off you go,' said Lauren, with relief. She picked up her phone and rang Troy.

Half an hour later she was ushering Troy into the lounge. His slightly scruffy appearance looked out of place in her calm and tidy lounge, with its comfy sofa, plumped up cushions and bright, breezy curtains with tie backs. Troy stood there, slightly uneasily, as if he were finding it difficult. He couldn't have looked more awkward if he'd tried. The twins looked up at him, startled, as Lauren said, 'Izzie, Immie, I want you to meet someone very special.'

'Who's that man?' asked Izzie, pointing at Troy. It took all Lauren's resolve not to clap her daughter instead of scolding her. She could see it all too clearly from Izzie's point of view.

'Don't be rude, darling,' said Lauren, very carefully. 'This is your daddy.'

'He's not our daddy!' said Izzie.

'We don't have a daddy!' said Immie.

No you don't, thought Lauren, your daddy wasn't there to see you born, hasn't acknowledged a single birthday, and has only seen you once. What kind of a daddy is that?

'No girls, you do have a daddy,' said Lauren. 'Remember I explained it to you, Daddy was a bit busy and had to go away, and couldn't see you. But now he's back and he'll be able to spend lots of time with you. Won't you, Daddy?'

She shot Troy a warning look.

'Yes, that's right, girls,' said Troy, his voice thick with emotion. 'I'm going to stay around here and we can all get to know each other. Now which one of you is Izzie, and which one is Immie?'

Lauren winced. He couldn't even tell them apart. This was never going to work.

'We're Izzie and Immie,' the girls said defiantly.

'Right, so let me guess – you're Immie?'

'No, I'm Izzie,' Immie said, 'that's Immie.'

'Girls,' said Lauren warningly. 'They're teasing you. It's their favourite party trick. That's Izzie and that's Immie. You can tell the difference by their partings.'

'OK,' said Troy, looking a bit shell-shocked, 'so you're Immie and you're Izzie?'

'Yes,' they said in unison.

'And what do you like doing best?' said Troy.

'Park,' said Immie.

'Picnic,' said Izzie.

'That sounds a great idea,' said Troy. 'Why don't we all go out for lunch?'

'Don't want to,' said Immie.

'Not with you,' said Izzie.

'Izzie,' said Lauren, in a warning tone. She could only cut them so much slack. 'Maybe that's a bit ambitious for today,' she said. 'But we could go to the park if you like.'

The girls grudgingly capitulated, and she sent them to get their coats.

Troy said, 'That was hard work. Do you think they'll always be this hostile?'

'What the bloody hell did you expect?' Lauren

stared at him in disbelief. 'Actually that went quite well. They have been known to blank people they don't like completely.'

'Oh,' said Troy. 'Seems I've got a lot to learn.'

'Yes,' said Lauren, 'you do. Let's just take things one day at a time, shall we? You've got a lot of making up to do.'

Kezzie got off the train in Heartsease, and walked up the hill with a renewed sense of purpose. She took lungfuls of deep, fresh air, breathing in the country air gratefully. It felt great to be back, away from the fetid smells of London. While it had done her a power of good to see Flick and the others again, she'd forgotten the sheer madness and filth of the place. And although she'd had a fun evening, her sore head was a reminder that sometimes you could have too much of a good thing.

Kezzie turned out of the station and walked up the High Street, noting with pleasure the pretty redbrick cottages that lined the road leading up to the shops, and noticing anew the interesting variety of little shops, from the little black and white house from which Agnes Mayhew sold her crystals and witchy artefacts, to the sparkling, bright butcher's shop where she'd taken to buying her bacon. There was Keef's Café, where she regularly enjoyed a caffè latte, and the vintage dress shop, which sold all manner of gorgeous clothes, and the bakery, which was a daily temptation. She sighed with pleasure. It had been a good move coming here, and after Christmas Flick had promised her that she and Gavin would come over

165

one weekend and help out with the Memorial Gardens.

As she was walking up the hill, Kezzie met Lauren and the girls walking down the hill with a rather attractive-looking man. The girls were holding tightly on to Lauren's hands, and Lauren looked distinctly ill at ease.

'Hi,' said Kezzie, trying not to look as if she was dying with curiosity. This presumably was the ex boyfriend. 'Where are you off to?'

'The Memorial Gardens,' said Lauren. She looked embarrassed, as if she'd been caught out at something. 'By the way, Kezzie, this is Troy.'

'Pleased to meet you,' said Kezzie, holding out a hand and shaking the one that had been laconically handed to her. Troy looked at her with a penetrating stare and gave her a dazzling smile. 'Kezzie, lovely to meet you. Any friend of Lauren's is a friend of mine.'

He had a lovely, deep voice, and Kezzie had to admit there was something rather seductive about him. She could certainly see the attraction.

'Mum-eee, I want to go to the park,' Izzie was tugging her mother's hand, and Immie looked equally impatient.

'Nice to meet you, Troy,' said Kezzie, with a grin. 'See you all later.'

She made her way up the hill, wondering what was going on with Lauren and Troy. She assumed Lauren had the sense not to have just jumped back into bed with him so soon, but you never knew. Perhaps she really loved the guy, despite what he'd done. Kezzie knew that if Richard turned up suddenly wanting to see her, she wouldn't have the strength to resist, despite some of the hateful things he'd said to her.

She let herself into the cottage, taking in with pleasure the ethnic throws on Jo's rickety sofa, the kilims on the wooden floors and the African masks from Jo's many trips abroad. Kezzie tried to focus on the here and now, on the life she was leading, not the one she'd lost, but she couldn't stop herself from remembering that last awful meeting they'd had. Richard, her lovely kind Richard, had been so cold and haughty.

'How could you, Kez?' He'd looked at her as if she were beneath contempt. 'I thought I knew you... I was so wrong.'

Kezzie had been unable to say anything. What was the point in arguing about something that was true? She had let Richard down, and she'd let herself down. And in doing so, she'd lost everything she held dear to her. She deserved it, she knew, but Richard had been so cruel, so unkind – she wasn't quite as wicked as he painted. Yet even with the painful memories of that last time together, she knew she'd still have him back. Which was all very well, but Richard wasn't showing any signs of rushing to be by her side. He hadn't contacted Flick or any of Kezzie's other friends, and even though she hadn't been looking on Facebook much, he'd made no attempt to contact her there. He couldn't email or phone, as she'd changed both her address and number, but if he wanted to, he could get in touch. She knew she hadn't made it easy for him to find her, but the fact that he hadn't bothered, hurt most of all.

This was no good. Having had a nice weekend,

she was about to descend into gloom. Kezzie would normally have popped in to see Lauren, but she was clearly otherwise engaged. She knew Joel was still likely to be out to lunch with his mum, so she'd just decided to sit down with a coffee and a cheery DVD when the phone rang. It was Eileen.

'Hi Kezzie, just wondering if you were free,' she said. 'Only I thought it would be nice to come and have a chat with you about the Edward Handford exhibition and see what sort of material you've got.'

'It's mainly at Joel's,' said Kezzie. 'Why don't I give him a ring later and suggest we go and look through it? I know he's keen to get involved, I'm sure he won't mind.'

Joel hadn't been long in from visiting his mum when he got the phone call from Kezzie announcing she and Eileen were going to come up and look through some of the extraordinary finds he and Kezzie had made.

Sam was watching *Peppa Pig,* and Joel had only planned to sit down with a beer and flick through Edward's diary anyway, so he wasn't sorry for the company. The evenings were starting to draw in, and the prospect of long, lonely winter nights was not a pleasant one. It would be good to have some company on a Sunday afternoon for a change. The weekends could often seem like the longest part of the week.

'So, let's have a look at all this material you've got,' said Eileen, as Joel ushered her into the dining room, where he'd been keeping the trunk and its contents out of Sam's way. He was conscious suddenly of how shabby it looked. He hardly had visitors any more, apart from Kezzie. Maybe he should start thinking about redecorating again. 'It sounds really fascinating.'

'I know it is,' admitted Joel. 'Every time we look at the letters and papers it's like a treasure-trove and we find something new. I had little idea of who Edward Handford was, apart from the fact that he built the knot garden, until Kezzie started digging. Now I can't think about anything else. From what I've read so far he and Lily had such a lot to contend with – they lost two babies before their eldest, Connie, was born – and I had no idea of any of it. He's a fascinating character.'

'Not many people do know much about him,' said Eileen. 'Personally, I think he's one of those overlooked characters whose work was far more influential than gardening history lets on. He worked on so many famous gardens: Chatsworth, Hatfield, Sissinghurst. You name it, he's designed a garden out there somewhere. He was massively in demand until the end of the First World War, and then he seems to have withdrawn from public life.'

'That's strange. Do you know why?' said Joel.

'Nobody knows for sure,' said Eileen. 'But I know his son died in the war, which is probably why he built the war memorial here. His wife died a year later, I believe. He devoted the rest of his life to philanthropic works – he built the village school you know – but he didn't design any gardens after that. He seems to have become a bit of a recluse after his wife's death. And the world changed so much after the First World War, and he wasn't part of it. So he faded into obscurity.'

'Let me show you what we've discovered,' said Joel. The trunk with all the paperwork in now inhabited the dining room, which was strictly out of bounds to Sam because it had an open log fire, and was therefore the safest place from sticky fingers.

They sifted through some of the letters that Joel and Kezzie had already read, and then Kezzie exclaimed in delight. 'Oh my God, it's here, I've found it!'

'Found what?' It was impossible not to get caught up by Kezzie's enthusiasm.

'Look,' she said, carefully unfolding a large, brittle piece of yellowing paper. 'This is Edward's original design for his knot garden. I can't believe it. See – here are his plans, he drew the patterns out geometrically, and here are his notes about the plants. This is so incredible. A real find.'

'I can't quite make out his writing,' Joel said, squinting a bit. The writing was very faded.

'It says the borders are to have begonias, petunias, busy lizzies, and heartsease I think,' said Eileen. 'I hadn't realized the original garden had quite that many flowers, I thought it would be simpler than that.'

'Those borders round the outside of the knot garden itself are a bit fussy for our tastes today,' said Kezzie, 'but the Victorians did like their bedding plants. I think I'm going to need to simplify it a bit and mainly use heartsease for the beds, but I would like to find all the plants he used to commemorate the births of his children. It was such a lovely idea.'

'Oh look, this must be Edward and Lily with their firstborn,' said Eileen, finding a black and white picture of a stiff-looking couple. Lily was holding an infant in her arms and looking blankly into the camera; Edward looked proud and a black Labrador sat at their feet.

'Yes, I think it must be,' said Joel. 'I'm guessing the baby is Connie, my great great aunt. Her sister Tilly was Mum's grandmother. Hang on a sec,' he rooted around in the bottom of the trunk and pulled out an old book, 'I thought I'd seen it in here. This is the family Bible, I think it's got all the births written in it.'

He opened the cover carefully. It was a version of the King James Bible, dated 1881.

To darling Lily, on the occasion of your 7th birthday, your ever loving Grandmother, was written in the flyleaf. Underneath it, Lily had written in childish scrawl, *Lily Clark, her first Bible,* and then below in a stronger, more adult hand:

Lily Clark b. August 10th 1874 married Edward Handford b. February 22nd 1871, 9th July, 1892

Edward James Handford b. 20th May, 1894 d. 20th May, 1894

Constance Mary Handford b. 24th April, 1895

Harry Edward Handford b. 14th May, 1898

Matilda Harriet Handford b. 12th July, 1900

'Isn't that amazing,' said Kezzie. 'What a fantastic find.'

'I know, I can't believe all this was sitting up in the loft and I never found any of it before,' said Joel, grinning. He turned back to look at the

171

photo. 'They don't look very happy do they? Or maybe that's just Victorian photography.'

'Who knows?' said Kezzie. 'From reading her diaries, Lily had a very tough time. She lost at least two babies: it was really sad.'

'That's how things were then,' said Eileen tenderly. 'Thanks for letting me look through all of this, Joel. I think we can make a fascinating exhibition of Edward's life.'

'Thank *you* for the interest,' said Joel. 'Without you and Kezzie I would know very little about my own family, and I'm thoroughly hooked.'

'So can we count on you to help with the preparations for next year's summer fete then?' said Eileen, slyly. 'Our first proper meeting is coming up after Christmas.'

'Oh go on,' said Joel. 'I don't suppose I have a choice, do I?' But he smiled when he said it, and when he'd said goodbye to Eileen and Kezzie, given Sam his tea and put him to bed, Joel found himself drawn back to the trunk and its contents, and started to idly flick through Edward's diary once more. He'd got the bit between his teeth now; he was fascinated by the story of his ancestor, and he was desperate to find out more.

Edward and Lily

1895–1898

Edward Handford's diary, April 1895
The day draws near for Lily's confinement, and we are
both very anxious now. She is so afraid that this baby
will not survive, and I cannot comfort her, because she
may be right. What if it does not live? And how will
Lily bear it if this baby dies? I try to cheer her up by
spending time in the garden with her, to keep her mind
from morbid thoughts. It is so beautiful here at this
time of year, with the spring bulbs bursting with life,
and the newborn lambs baaing in Mr Carruthers'
farm. I cannot let myself believe that we will be un-
lucky again, not at this time of year, not when the
whole world is bursting forth with new life...

'Congratulations, Mr Handford, you have a
beautiful baby daughter.' Doctor Blake came out
from Edward and Lily's bedroom looking tired
but triumphant. 'I'm pleased to report that both
mother and baby are doing well.'

It was a hot, sultry evening in April, and Edward felt exhausted from the tumultuous events
of the last twenty-four hours when Lily had
informed him that the baby was coming. He had
wanted to stay with her, to help give her the
strength to go on, but convention and the doctor
forbade it. Though Edward had been inclined for

173

once to hang convention, when Lily asked him to leave, he could not resist her. He had spent an anxious afternoon pacing up and down, first in the garden, and then outside the bedroom door. The ear-piercing screams that she'd emitted had been harrowing, and it had taken all his resolve not to rush into the room to be by her side. But thank God, it was over.

Finally a child. A baby. Please God, she survived. He didn't know what it would do to Lily – to them – if they lost this one too. He had longed and longed to take the sadness from her eyes. Now, maybe this baby would finally do it.

'May I see them?' Edward said.

'Of course, but Lily is very tired. She needs rest.'

Edward entered their bedroom. Lily lay in their bed, her black hair straggled behind her, her face pale and pinched. She looked exhausted, but a brief smile crossed her face when she saw Edward. He went to embrace her, and then turned to the midwife, who was wrapping the baby in a shawl, before presenting her to them.

'Lily, she's beautiful.' Edward felt an unfamiliar spasm in his heart as he held the crumpled bundle in his arms. The baby gurgled contentedly, before reaching out and grabbing his finger. He marvelled at the size of that finger next to his own. He felt clumsy, awkward; like a giant holding a beautiful porcelain doll. He knew he would never forget this day, this moment, this meeting, for the first time of the child their love had created.

'What shall we call her?' Edward said.

'I don't know,' Lily turned away, as if she

couldn't bear to look at her, 'but I want her christened quickly, just in case.'

'Lily, the baby is fine,' said Edward. 'Look at her. She's a beautiful, healthy baby.'

'But what if she isn't?' whispered Lily. 'What if she dies like the others?'

'Lily, please don't talk like that,' said Edward in distress. 'You're tired, overwrought. You need some rest.'

'But first, the baby needs feeding,' the midwife said.

Lily looked at her daughter properly for the first time.

'I'm not sure I can,' she whispered.

'Nonsense, every mother can feed her child,' said the midwife. 'There's nothing to it, you'll see.'

Edward got up to go.

'I'll leave you for now,' he said, 'and I'll come back later, I promise.'

At Lily's insistence, her father was called and Constance Mary Handford was christened within three hours of her birth. But that didn't seem to satisfy Lily, who was anxious and peevish, and despite her best efforts, totally unable to feed Constance, or Connie as Edward had affectionately named her. Edward sat with them through several long nights, when the baby mewled for lack of food. She was growing weaker daily, and Lily had a set look on her face, sure she was right, and the baby would fail to thrive.

On the third day an exhausted Edward sent out for a wet-nurse, and took over the organization of the care of his daughter; Lily was clearly unable to. He had lost his wife. She had retreated somewhere into a haze of unhappiness and seemed unable to comprehend that she had a living child who needed her attention.

Edward, though, was enchanted with their daughter. As she grew stronger daily, she learnt to smile and laugh and she brought much needed joy back into the house. He was filled with a fierce, protective love that surprised him with its ferocity. But Lily he couldn't reach. She was so frightened of losing her daughter it appeared she couldn't learn to love her. All Edward could wish for was time to heal her wounded soul.

As time passed, Connie grew into a lively little girl, who smiled and played and ran everywhere. True to his promise to Lily to plant flowers to mark the births of their children, he'd planted snowdrops in the four corners of the knot garden, for Connie, as a symbol of hope. Lily slowly recovered from her post-birth torpor, and began to engage with the world again. She was often to be found in the garden, picking the heartsease that grew there abundantly and filling in the gaps when plants were lost. But to Edward's regret, she rarely played with their daughter.

It's as if she cannot bring herself to love Connie, he recorded in his diary. *She is afraid to love her for fear of losing her. So I must love our daughter for both of us.*

It was Edward to whom Connie came running when he returned home, when he'd been working away on one of the many gardens he'd been commissioned to landscape. To Edward, that she went crying or calling with her troubles. It was

Edward who helped her take her first tottering steps, and listened to her lisp her first words.

Connie rarely bothers her mother, instinctively knowing she is unlikely to look up from the flowers she often draws in the garden and take notice of her. I know that Lily cares for Connie, of course she does, but somehow she cannot manage her in the way that I can. It is as if Lily regards Connie as an exotic creature, somewhat different and distant from herself. I pray in time that will change. But gradually, slowly, my Lily is returning to me. She comes with me regularly into the garden now, and draws plants again, as she once did. Every now and again she laughs at my foibles, and I am reminded of the joy we shared when first we were married, and I am grateful for that at least...

Lily's diary, May 1898
At last. We have a son. A beautiful, healthy, baby boy. I feel so different this time. When Connie was born, I looked at her little, scrumpled, red face, and my heart was torn in two, so sure was I that she was not long for this world. But despite my fears, she has thrived, is thriving now, and God has seen fit to bless us with a brother for her. A gift that I had not dared hope for. I shall call him Harry after his grandfather. Now I feel my life is complete. After the years of pain and heartache, at last Edward and I have our family, and I can sit in the sunken garden Edward made for me and not feel the need to weep. The sun is shining, summer is here, and my future has been restored to me.

Part Two

Spring Fever

Chapter Thirteen

'The girls go to bed at 7 p.m. sharp,' said Lauren nervously. It was a month since Christmas, Eileen's first proper meeting about the summer fete, and the first time she'd allowed Troy to babysit. Over the last few weeks, Lauren had allowed Troy to regularly make the half an hour trip from Crawley, to visit the twins. Lauren had even included him in a very awkward and un-comfortable Christmas lunch with Lauren's mum (who'd just about been able to keep her thoughts about Troy to herself) and the girls were gradually getting used to their dad being on the scene. Lauren might never have been ready for Troy to take charge for an evening, if her mum hadn't gone away for some winter sun, leaving her without a babysitter. Troy had been adamant she had nothing to worry about, and Lauren was hoping that her negative thoughts would prove unfounded. If she was going to let Troy back into her children's lives he had to be alone with them sometime. 'They really must go to bed then, or they'll be too tired for school tomorrow.'

'I know you think I'm useless,' said Troy, 'but I think I can manage to get two four-year-olds to bed.'

'I don't think you're useless – well not entirely,' said Lauren, 'but you aren't used to four-year-olds, and I've never left them with anyone but

181

Mum and Eileen before.'

'I'm their dad,' said Troy, 'and I'm going to prove to you that I'm worthy of them and you. You've got to learn to trust me.'

Despite herself, Lauren had to smile. It was quite funny seeing Troy being so keen to please her, and rather charming in a way. It had always been the other way round before. And Troy was right, if he was going to play a part in the kids' lives, she had to learn to trust him.

The doorbell rang. It was Kezzie.

'All ready then?' she said.

'Yup,' said Lauren, firing last minute instructions until Troy pushed her out of the door.

'You know when you were telling me about Troy, before he pitched up again, you never once mentioned how good looking he was,' said Kezzie teasingly.

'Didn't I? It must have slipped my mind,' said Lauren. 'Part of the charm of course. Give me an ugly man any day of the week.'

'So you're not planning to get back together?'

'Absolutely not,' said Lauren. 'I've let him stay over a couple of times when he's come to see the girls, because it's a long way for him to get back to Crawley, but that's it. He keeps threatening to get a job and move over here, but I'll believe it when I see it.'

'I know he came for Christmas lunch,' said Kezzie, 'so I couldn't help wondering, and we haven't had a chance to catch up since.' Kezzie had disappeared to Spain to see her parents for a fortnight, and had come back looking bronzed and disgustingly healthy.

'Don't worry, I'm sure I'd have been just as nosy if it was the other way round,' said Lauren. 'Christmas was only just about bearable. I was treading on eggshells between Troy and Mum and hoping the girls didn't pick up on it. I don't think I could cope with a relationship with him. I'm glad Troy's back for the girls' sake, but it's early days, and I'm still not sure it's going to work.'

They walked down the hill towards the Parish Hall.

'So is this going to be dreadfully stuffy and dull?' said Kezzie.

'Probably,' said Lauren. 'But you never know, we might get them to perk up their ideas a bit.'

Eileen was already there when they arrived.

'Let me introduce you to some people.' She reeled off a list of names – Lauren knew most of them, having helped out at village fetes before – but Kezzie was clearly slightly overwhelmed by the number of people involved.

'Is there anyone here under the age of sixty?' she whispered. 'We're the youngest here by centuries.'

'Wonderful, some new blood. Just what we need,' declared Tony Symonds, who was a retired bank clerk and chaired the Parish Council with scary efficiency. 'We really do need to get something done about the Memorial Gardens. Eileen's been nagging me about it for ages. It's great that you're all on board.'

The meeting started late. Several people wandered in noisily at around a quarter to eight, mumbling apologies to Tony, who harrumphed before proceeding to talk about the fete.

'So this year we've decided that the proceeds of

the village fete will go to restoring the Heartsease Memorial Garden, in honour of Edward Handford's 140th anniversary. And we're delighted to have Edward Handford's great great grandson, Joel Lyle here. Not only has he promised to open up the knot garden Edward Handford designed at Lovelace Cottage for the day of the fete, I believe he is also going to provide some wonderful and fascinating material for a Handford exhibition on the day.'

Joel, who'd snuck in among the latecomers, looked mortified to have been picked out, but smiled graciously anyway.

'All right, to business,' said Tony. 'Has anyone got any ideas about how the summer fete should be run this year?'

'The same way we always run it,' said Cynthia Green, the grumpiest woman in Heartsease. 'It works, so why change it?'

'Well, I was hoping we could do a few things differently,' said Tony, 'given that we're celebrating Edward Handford's 140th anniversary. I think we need to make it more of an event, shake it up a bit. Eileen, I believe you have some ideas?'

'I do,' said Eileen, looking a little pink and flustered. 'I think we could be a bit more ambitious. In fact, a lot more. Rather than just have a fete for the village, why not widen its appeal and call it a Summer Fest like Chiverton does? We could make it an all day event. By all means let's have the normal stalls, but why not close off the High Street, have street entertainers, get some music going, have a farmers' market. Let's really show people what Heartsease is all about.'

'It will never work,' sniffed Cynthia.

'Why not?' said Eileen. 'We won't know until we try.'

'And we should have a celebrity to open proceedings,' said Kezzie.

'The charity I work for has some contacts with celebrities,' said Joel. 'I could always fish around a bit if you like, and see if we can get someone to open the fete for us.'

'Celebrities!' snorted Cynthia. 'We don't need nonsense like that.'

'I think it's a great idea,' said Tony. 'It will bring in the young people. Joel, if you're prepared to find out about it for us that would be fantastic.'

'We could run a competition for the best design for the play area,' suggested Lauren.

'And we could start planting out now, try and tidy it up,' chipped in Kezzie.

'What about Health and Safety?' objected a little pinched woman sitting next to Cynthia. 'There are those old oak trees in the Memorial Gardens that are a real menace. They should come down.'

'So get a tree feller,' said Kezzie. 'I know a couple.'

'Hmm, I'm not sure,' interjected a small man who was clearly attached like a limpet to the pinched-looking woman. 'It seems like a lot of extra work.'

'Well, that's not a priority for now,' said Tony. 'Sorry, Kezzie, we'll get to it later I'm sure. Now let's move on to considering the kinds of stalls we want.'

A good-tempered and long-winded discussion about the pros and cons of homemade ice cream ensued. Lauren caught Joel yawning and grinned. She knew there was a good reason why she'd resisted joining the committee.

'Can you believe that?' Kezzie was incandescent with rage. 'They talked about the price of ice creams for half an hour. And no one made any decisions about the Memorial Gardens. I can't believe we can't just go and tidy it up.'

'Welcome to village life,' grinned Lauren. 'At least we got through the idea of making the event bigger, thanks to Eileen.'

'True,' said Kezzie grudgingly. 'I think we should show them what can be done though. Anyone up for a spot of guerrilla gardening?'

'What, *now*?' said Joel. 'It's dark, cold, and if you hadn't noticed we're still in the thick of winter.'

'Yes now,' said Kezzie. She opened the rucksack she was carrying and revealed some small forks and trowels and winter bedding plants. 'Like a good boy scout, I always come prepared. Besides, spring is on the way. The snowdrops are already out, and you've got crocuses coming up in your garden you know. I'm up for it, if you are.'

'I really have to get back and make sure everything's OK with Troy and the girls,' said Lauren, turning to go. 'Sorry. Another time maybe.'

'And I should get back to Sam,' said Joel, looking at his watch. 'Eileen's daughter is babysitting for me.'

'Oh go on, live a little,' said Kezzie. 'It's only eight thirty, what time will she be expecting you? I'm sure Christine won't mind. This won't take long. I've already dug over the bit of ground I want to plant these winter pansies in. At least it will give some colour till the spring.'

'When did you start digging in the Memorial Gardens?' said Joel.

'I went out a couple of mornings last week,' said Kezzie. 'I couldn't sleep and so I thought I may as well do something useful.'

'Oh,' said Joel.

'Come on then, what are we waiting for?' Kezzie strode purposefully towards the playground, while Joel stood slightly irresolute behind her.

'Oh OK,' he said, 'but only for a bit.'

'That'll do,' said Kezzie, with a grin.

It was early in February, and the evening air was still cold. The gardens were in pitch darkness when they arrived. The rusting iron gates were padlocked and looked forbidding and unfriendly. For a moment even Kezzie felt a little daunted.

'So how do we get in then?' demanded Joel.

'Oh ye of little faith,' said Kezzie. 'We get in the same way as whoever's vandalizing the playground does. If you follow me round the corner, you will observe that there is a gap in the fence.'

Joel shook his head in amusement.

'Does nothing faze you?'

'Not much,' said Kezzie, as she squeezed through the gap. 'Careful, it is a bit narrow.'

Once in, she marched towards one of the beds to the side of the plinth.

'This shouldn't take long,' she said. 'We've got some plants to bed in.'

In fact they were hard at it for nearly an hour, but by the time they'd finished they'd transformed a bed that had been full of weeds into a vibrant patch of colour. Or that's what Kezzie had assured Joel it *would* look like in the morning. It was difficult to tell in the dark.

'Well done, partner,' said Kezzie with a grin, and slapped him on the back. 'How does it feel to inflict criminal damage in a public place?'

'Fun,' admitted Joel, who had been unprepared for the illicit thrill he'd got from their activities. Kezzie was amazing. And she was having a transformative effect on his life. Ever since she'd arrived in Heartsease, he felt that he was being propelled out of his grief-induced torpor to face up to life in the real world once more. She'd made him look at his house and garden, and reminded him what he'd planned before life had dealt him such a body blow. And learning about Edward and the history of the place had piqued Joel's interest. Despite himself, he was finding he was beginning to engage in life again. He had to admit, it felt good.

'You've got mud on your nose,' he said. 'Here, let me.' Gently, he wiped it away with a hankie.

Kezzie looked at him with a slightly wistful expression on her face, and for a heartbeat he thought she might kiss him. But then she said, 'Time to go,' and started packing up her things.

'Best get home,' she added, as if by way of explanation. 'I have work in the morning and I have a *very* demanding boss.'

'Yeah, right,' said Joel. 'I think you could change that to soft-touch boss, who goes along with your crazy schemes.'

'Does my soft-touch boss require a nightcap

before heading home?' Kezzie said, when they reached her cottage.

Joel looked at his watch – not quite 9.30 p.m.– 'Oh, go on then,' he said, and followed her into the cottage.

Kezzie went to the fridge in the compact but cosy kitchen. 'Red or white?' she asked. 'I have both. Or beer.'

'I'll have a beer actually,' said Joel, while Kezzie poured herself a generous glug of white wine.

'Go easy on that, otherwise the boss might have to be very tough with you in the morning.'

'Do you mind if I have a smoke?' said Kezzie.

'It's your house,' said Joel. 'Do what you want.' He wasn't keen on women who smoked, but he had always had a live and let live attitude about that kind of thing.

Kezzie, it appeared, rolled her own, but it was only when she lit up that he realized what she was smoking.

'Kezzie!' Why was he surprised she smoked dope? It fitted in with everything else about her.

'What?' said Kezzie. 'I did ask you. And like *you* said, it's my house.'

'Sorry,' said Joel, 'I'm just not really used to this kind of thing.'

'What kind of thing?' said Kezzie. 'It's a spliff, not crack cocaine. Where's the harm? I find it relaxing. I don't do it very often; it's not like I'm addicted. Alcohol's a worse drug.'

'I guess,' said Joel, but he felt faintly disturbed. Kezzie was a mystery, an exciting, mercurial, volatile mystery.

Chapter Fourteen

'So, you're going to trust me with the girls again?' Troy asked Lauren the next time he came round to see the twins.

'I expect so,' Lauren had to reluctantly concede. She had been pleasantly surprised at the lack of chaos when she'd got home two nights previously. The girls were asleep, and later reported that they'd had 'lots of fun with Daddy', the house was tidy and Troy was sitting watching TV, looking completely relaxed. It seemed, despite her fears, he *could* be trusted to look after the girls.

'Oh come on, Lauren, that's a bit hard,' said Troy. 'I think I did a bit better than OK.'

Laughing despite herself – annoying how he could still make her do that – Lauren was forced to agree that Troy had passed his first babysitting stint with flying colours.

'So I really think it's time you let me have them for the day,' said Troy. 'I could take them out on Saturday. Give you a break.'

'I'm not sure,' began Lauren, when the girls came running in from the other room. 'Daddy said he's taking us out to the cinema on Saturday, please can we go, please!'

'You sneaky sod!' whispered Lauren. He'd already asked the girls, knowing she wouldn't be able to refuse them.

'I didn't want you to say no,' said Troy, 'please

let me have them.'

'Please, Mummy,' said Izzie.

'We'll be good,' said Immie.

'It's not you I'm worried about,' muttered Lauren to herself. She looked at the pair of them, so eager and excited. It was the first time they'd asked to do anything with their dad, she couldn't say no.

'OK,' she agreed.

'Thanks,' said Troy, giving her an unexpected hug, which she resisted stiffly, trying not to inhale his intoxicating scent of tobacco and aftershave. 'You won't regret it.'

But come Saturday, of course, she did regret it. Troy arrived bright and early to take the girls away, promising to be back around five, and suddenly she was left with a long lonely day and nothing to do. She spent the first couple of hours scrubbing the house from top to bottom. Though she worked very hard at trying to keep the house clean and tidy, with two four-year-olds the reality was that there were usually toys in the wrong places, dirty clothes on the bedroom floor, towels put back crookedly, toothpaste smeared all over the sink and any number of gunky deposits on the kitchen floor. It satisfied her inner housewife to get the place up to scratch, and smelling all lemony and fresh.

Once that was done, and trying not to clock watch, Lauren did a serious amount of baking, always her refuge in moments of stress. By the time another couple of hours had passed she'd made muffins, cupcakes, scones and shortbread and her cake tins were bursting full. Really, she should start a business doing this, Lauren thought. It was satisfying, enjoyable, and something she appeared to be really really good at. Having used up nearly all her baking ingredients and it still only being lunchtime, Lauren decided to see if Kezzie was in, as she fancied lunch in Keef's Café. But Kezzie was out, and much as she loved the eccentricity of the place, Lauren couldn't face lunchtime there on her own. She settled instead for homemade soup, a muffin, and a catch-up with a book her mum had given her for Christmas.

The afternoon passed in a desultory fashion, and by four thirty Lauren was restless, and anxiously waiting for Troy to ring her. She tried calling him, but he'd turned his phone off. The minutes ticked away, and as dusk started to fall, she realized to her horror that he was late. Half an hour more went past, and still Troy wasn't back. Lauren was teetering between frantic worry, and telling herself off for being so stupid. Where was he? He'd been gone for hours. Was he about to do another bunk? Had he just wormed his way into her affections, only to take off again? And this time with the children? After all that guff about how much he'd changed. Lauren couldn't bear to think about it. She tried to phone his mobile again, but still there was no reply. She'd been an idiot to trust him, an absolute idiot.

Lauren was pacing the floor, on the verge of ringing the police, when Troy calmly strolled up the front path with two overexcited children.

'Where the hell have you been?' she yelled, as she opened the door, anxiety manifesting itself as anger. 'I was worried sick.'

'I didn't know you cared,' said Troy with a grin.

'I wasn't worried about you,' snapped Lauren. 'I was worried about the girls.'

'Why?' said Troy. 'They're fine.'

'You're late, and your phone was switched off,' said Lauren.

'Ah, sorry, we stopped off for a McDonald's, and I forgot to charge my phone,' said Troy. 'We're only just over half an hour late. What on earth did you think had happened?'

'I – oh – it's stupid but I thought you'd taken them,' muttered Lauren when the girls were out of earshot.

'I can't believe you would think such a thing of me!' It was Troy's turn to be furious. 'Why on earth would I take the girls away from you?'

'Because you left so early, and you were gone so long. And I didn't know what to think,' she finished lamely.

'I'm sorry,' said Troy. 'I thought it would be nice to have a good day out with my daughters. I didn't realize you'd be clockwatching. Jeez, there's no pleasing you is there?'

'Oh,' said Lauren, feeling foolish. 'I'm sorry. It's just on past performance...'

'How many times do I need to tell you I've changed?' said Troy, with a heavy sigh, and Lauren had the unusual experience of feeling guilty that she'd underestimated him. She changed the subject.

'How did you get on then?' she asked, attempting to sound more cheery.

'We had a great day, didn't we, girls?' said Troy.

The twins, who'd been anxiously watching their parents during the previous exchange, burst into ready smiles.

'Daddy took us to McDonald's,' said Immie.

'And we saw *Tangled*,' said Izzie. 'It was fun.'

'That's lovely, darlings,' said Lauren, as she hugged both girls really tightly. 'I was just being silly, I missed you both so much. I'll just pop a DVD on for you, while Daddy and I talk.'

When Lauren settled the children, she came back into the kitchen and looked at Troy directly and said, 'Troy, what is it you really want? Why are you here?'

'I know you might find this hard to accept, but I do want to get to know my girls,' said Troy.

'But why after all this time?' persisted Lauren.

'You know all that stuff I told you about my dad?' said Troy.

'What about it?' said Lauren.

'It's made me realize I don't want to be the kind of dad he was,' said Troy. 'I want to be there for the girls, I really do. And to prove it to you, I've found somewhere to live in Heartsease, and I've got a job working in the pub. It's only a stopgap, till I get something better, and can afford to pay you some maintenance.'

'Oh,' said Lauren, not sure quite how she felt about that.

'Please, Lauren, give me a chance,' said Troy. 'I know I can't do much about the past, but I can change the future, if you'll let me.'

'Well, that's good then,' said Lauren, patting his arm awkwardly, before withdrawing her hand. 'And it *is* what I've always wanted for the girls.

194

Our new family life starts from here.'

Kezzie spent the weekend immersed in garden plans, and by Monday morning she was raring to go. She'd been so excited since she and Joel had found Edward's original designs, she'd barely been away from the computer, trying to work out how she could incorporate the old with the new. She'd also wangled a grant from a small horticultural charity, which meant both she and Joel could really afford to go ahead with the project without worrying about the financial implications.

They had managed to rotavate the majority of the garden just before Christmas, before the ground had got too hard, so now Kezzie was able to start planning out. She was hoping to get the plants in by the early part of the spring, weather permitting. It felt good to be back in Heartsease organizing things, after spending Christmas with Flick, followed by a trip to visit her parents in Spain. As usual she had got a lot of flak about not being like her little sister, who was married and settled in a nice home with her 2.4 children, so it was a relief to get back to her real life. Although it had been nice to have a holiday, Kezzie couldn't help feeling it was more restful here.

Some of Edward's choices of plants for the borders felt overfussy for today's garden; she wasn't sure she wanted them to be such a hotchpotch of perennials for example, but she'd got the list of plants he'd placed in the gaps intended for his children. In each of the four corners, he'd planted agapanthus (representing immortality) in memory of the babies who had died in childbirth (the

195

name of one poignantly written in the margin), but gone on to plant snowdrops (symbolizing hope) for his daughter Connie, white carnations (good luck) to mark the birth of Harry, and finally peonies (for healing and a happy life) for his youngest daughter, Tilly.

Harry, it appeared from Lily's diaries, was very much the favoured son. Connie barely got a mention, but Tilly, as the youngest, was clearly doted on. Kezzie sniffed disparagingly. Having always suspected her parents liked her younger sister more, Kezzie felt an instinctive fellow feeling for Connie. Although it also seemed, from Edward's numerous and affectionate letters to his eldest daughter, that he had compensated somewhat for her mother's lack of interest. Kezzie hoped so. She was getting so immersed in the stories of these long-dead people, they were becoming more real to her than people she knew in real life.

Kezzie finished the design on her computer with a feeling of satisfaction. She'd looked up the entry requirements for Hampton Court, and she wouldn't have time to apply this year, but she could probably apply for Chelsea in the autumn, if she got her website up and running in time. She laughed to herself, thinking of the time she, Flick and Gavin had entered the Alternative Chelsea Flower Show and won with an eco-friendly garden designed for the twenty-first century. Richard had fallen about when she'd described how she'd snuck up and taken discarded stems that no one else had used. He'd been semi horrified of course, till she'd pointed out the waste. 'It's like those people who forage for food in bins,' she'd explained, 'only with flowers instead.'

Richard. A stab of longing for him came over her. What was he doing? How was he coping without her? She had a sudden desire to hear his voice, stupid as she knew it was. She'd left London months ago, and he'd made no effort to contact her, even at Christmas. Not that she had made it easy for him. She'd changed her mobile, moved house, and the only people who knew where she was were her parents and Flick. Richard had never met Jo, and associated Kezzie with town – she'd always proudly proclaimed her urban heritage – he would never look for her here. Always supposing he was looking.

Kezzie picked up her phone and played with it a while. Richard's number wasn't on it. She'd deliberately left it off, just as she'd deleted his email address from the computer to reduce the risk of repeating those awful, embarrassing, late night drunken texts and emails in the aftermath of their break-up. But she knew the number by heart.

She was stronger now though. Perhaps she could stand to listen to his voice. Tentatively, her fingers shaking, Kezzie rang his mobile number. Her heart was in her mouth, what did she think she was doing? What if he answered it? What if he didn't? It rang several times. Good. He wasn't answering. Any minute it would go to voicemail–

'Richard's phone.'

A woman? A woman had answered Richard's phone and it definitely wasn't Emily. Kezzie nearly screamed with shock.

'Who is this please?'

Kezzie turned off her phone. She was shaking

like a leaf, and felt vaguely sick.

What on earth did she think she was doing? She should leave Richard in the past where he belonged. Unsettled by what had happened, and feeling unable to stay in the house a moment longer, Kezzie decided to pop out for some fresh air. Without really thinking where she was going, she wandered into Heartsease and was meandering aimlessly past the shops, when she bumped into Lauren and Sam.

'Hey, Lauren, what are you up to?' said Kezzie, loath to go back home, and hoping she was free.

'Not a lot,' said Lauren. 'Going home and putting my shopping away, mainly. I lead an exciting life.'

'Do you fancy a coffee then?' said Kezzie, who was unwilling to go back home.

'Coffee sounds great,' said Lauren, and the pair of them ambled towards Keef's. 'What will it be, lovely ladies?' Keith asked, his eyes twinkling. 'I've got a new lemon-flavoured frappucino that is to die for.'

One of Keith's many eccentricities was introducing weird and wonderful flavours into the coffee. Kezzie had made the mistake of trying out his cherry-flavoured frappucino once, so hastily asked for a latte, while Lauren settled for a hot chocolate.

'I'm glad we bumped into one another,' said Kezzie. 'I've been meaning to pick your brains about the playground. I know it's really shabby but it's going to cost a bit to do it up...'

'First off, the kids need space,' said Lauren, counting on her fingers, 'that play area is ridiculously cramped. Second, they need new, clean, safe equipment with spongy surfaces so the kids don't hurt themselves when they fall.'

'Plain old concrete not good enough any more?' said Kezzie, jokingly, remembering scratched knees and elbows received from jumping off swings and roundabouts that were going too fast.

'Not in this day and age, no. It needs to be bright, friendly, have some areas of shade, benches for the mums to sit on, and stuff for kids to crawl, climb and swing on.'

'Anything else?'

'You should look at turning that derelict patch at the back into an area for teens. Give them a baseball court and skateboard park so they've got something to do. It might stop them taking over the baby playground.'

'Blimey, that's a list and a half,' said Kezzie. 'The fete's going to need to raise a whole load of dosh to do all that.'

'I think we should encourage Eileen in her aim of making it more of an event,' said Lauren. 'It's always very low key, the summer fete. I think they could make an awful lot more of it than they do.'

'Do you fancy going up against Cynthia at the next meeting?' said Kezzie, and they both giggled at the thought. Kezzie sipped her latte. She was still feeling shaken up about the phone call and felt she had to talk to someone about it.

'I did something really dumb today,' she said.

'Which was?'

'I rang Richard up. My ex.'

'And?' said Lauren.

'And a woman answered the phone,' said Kezzie. 'I felt so stupid. I can't believe he's found someone else already.'

'How do you know it was a girlfriend?'

'She answered his mobile.'

'So? She might be someone he works with.'

'I know everyone he works with,' said Kezzie, 'and I didn't recognize her voice. Besides, I rang him at nine thirty. He's never in the office that early. He must have been at home.'

'There might be another explanation,' said Lauren.

'I can't think of one,' said Kezzie. 'So, anyway. I've decided. It's high time I moved on. So that's what I plan to do.'

Joel was sitting at Edward's writing desk, reading his diary. The study was smaller than the other rooms in the house, and had a nice cosy feel. So of an evening, Joel had taken to sitting in there with his laptop after he had put Sam to bed. Since he'd discovered Edward's diary, he'd also found himself obsessively reading about his ancestor's trials and tribulations. It certainly put his own life into perspective. He was glad to read that after the children had been born there was a period of relative calm, when Lily and Edward seemed to have been happy again. He noticed with wry pleasure that the family often went for picnics by the river.

When Claire was alive they had gone on frequent walks on the Downs. There was one walk in particular, that went down into a valley and near a river, where there was the most beautiful willow tree, which had been a particular favourite. Joel found himself often retracing that walk when he wanted to think about Claire, and he liked the fact that it had clearly been a favourite spot of Edward's too. Sometimes, the river made him feel peaceful. At others, he came home feeling melancholy. The previous day he'd taken Sam out in the backpack, but being a cold and gloomy day, it had had the latter effect. And even Sam's giggling in the bath hadn't been enough to cheer him up. His mood hadn't improved after a hard day's work, when every decision that had to be made seemed to be a painful one. And when he'd got back with Sam that evening, Kezzie wasn't there. He'd forgotten that she had told him she was going to be working at home that day. The house felt cold and empty; the prospect of another lonely evening in front of the TV, bleak. He'd got used to Kezzie's cheerful presence around the place, and found himself missing her joie de vivre.

He poured himself a glass of whisky and stared out at the darkening front garden. He had a sudden longing for Claire. These feelings lurched on him without warning, knocking him for six and making him gasp with the hideousness of the pain. He could remember an evening in early summer, just after they'd moved in, when they'd sat outside on the old wooden bench on the crumbling patio and looked at their overgrown garden. He'd had one arm around her, and one hand on her stomach, feeling the thrill, when Sam – then only known as the Bump – had kicked. He'd do anything to go back to that moment – one of the last moments, he sometimes felt, when they'd been truly happy together.

Joel hadn't meant to let Claire down, but he knew he had. When Sam was born, Claire had taken to motherhood like a duck to water, breast-feeding through the night with seeming contentment, creating a bond with their son that he simply could not share. Joel had known it was petty and pathetic of him, but he felt pushed out – it was as though Claire didn't need him any longer. She had her baby, his needs came first, and Joel was superfluous to requirements. He'd tried to explain how he felt, and she'd just snapped at him and told him he was being ridiculous. 'Sam's a *baby*,' she said. 'He needs me. It won't be forever.'

But as the early weeks of parenthood dragged on, and Claire's obsession with their newborn son had continued to grow, Joel found himself making excuses as to why he was late home, or when he was there, finding projects that needed his urgent attention. There had always been plenty of those.

Looking back, he could see how Claire must have been puzzled and hurt by his distance and behaviour, but at the time he'd justified it by telling her that he was doing all of it for her.

'Yes, I *really* want to spend all of Saturday with a baby, while you knock walls down upstairs,' she'd said. 'There's nothing I love more than a house full of dust.'

And then inevitably there'd be a row, with all the usual tears and recriminations. And he'd been so resentful. So angry with her. If only he'd been able to see the future. How differently he would have reacted. He'd have taken her into his arms and kissed her and told her she was right. If only.

This feeling of guilt was something he was going to have to live with for the rest of his life. Joel closed his eyes and took another sip of whisky.

Chapter Fifteen

'So you think you've got New Horizons?' said Eileen, at the start of the next Summer Fest meeting (now the official name, despite Cynthia's objections), towards the beginning of March. 'Excellent.'

'Well, I hope so,' said Joel, whose search for suitable celebrities had included the glamorous ex wife of a jaded popstar, a washed-up alcoholic actor, and an ex soapstar, before eventually persuading New Horizons to show up. As the hottest boy band around, who were still new enough to need all the publicity they could get, they would definitely draw a crowd. 'They seem pretty keen.'

'Hmph,' said Cynthia sniffily. 'I don't know why we can't have Alan Marshcroft, as we've always done.'

'New ideas, remember?' said Tony Symonds, gently. 'I think that's brilliant news, Joel, well done.'

'You'll certainly have every little girl from miles around coming,' said Kezzie. 'And they *should* bring their parents.'

'How are we getting on with the other entertainments?' Tony asked.

'Fine,' replied Henry Clevedon, a retired judge.

He peered over the top of his spectacles at a list he was holding. 'We have morris dancing lined up, a choir singing madrigals, and the vicar's kindly opened the church for the bell ringing practice. He's also going to charge to visit the top of the tower. There are very fine views of the Downs from there, you know. On a clear day you can even see the sea.'

'Marvellous,' said Tony. 'Now, we've arranged for the High Street to be closed, and a number of people have booked stalls already. George Anderson from the butcher's is doing a hog roast for us in the field, and in the evening we're going to have music and fireworks.'

'Any joy sorting a venue out for the Edward Handford exhibition?' said Kezzie. 'Only Joel and I have uncovered lots of interesting material, and plenty of family photos. Edward Handford did such a lot for this village; it would be brilliant if we could celebrate his anniversary properly.'

'Why don't we use Lovelace Cottage?' suggested Eileen. 'Joel, would you mind?'

'Er,' Joel was taken aback. He was unsure whether anyone would want to visit his house, the state it was in, but he supposed it made sense to use Edward's house as the base for the exhibition. 'I suppose so, if everyone else thinks it's a good idea.'

'I think that's a great idea,' said Kezzie, and the rest of the committee seemed to agree.

'Well, that's settled then,' said Eileen. 'I've managed to track down the war memorial from the Memorial Gardens, by the way. If you remember, the County Council removed it a few years ago, intending to restore it, and the project foundered. I've spoken to the lady in charge, and she's put me on to the War Memorial Fund, which give grants to help restore memorials to their former glory. Apparently, we could get the memorial back and do a rededication ceremony if we so wish. But it is going to cost us a lot of money.'

'Do you think we can get some money out of New Horizons?' said Kezzie.

'I doubt it,' said Joel, who had already explored that avenue. 'I think they have a very tight contract as to who they can and can't support charity wise, but we could try and raise our profile a bit more by getting some famous garden people to visit the garden and exhibition, couldn't we?'

'Great idea,' said Eileen. 'Kezzie, you know about gardens, can you make that your priority?'

'Thanks very much,' Kezzie said to Joel slightly crossly, at the end of the meeting. 'Any gardening contacts I have are via Richard. I can hardly go and ask him.'

'Why not?' said Joel, puzzled. 'I know you've split up, but what's the big deal about approaching him on a professional basis?'

'Let's just say that I am not Richard's favourite person, right now,' said Kezzie, 'and I think he'd be very unlikely to help.'

'Shame,' said Joel, who still couldn't quite see what the problem was. 'We'll have to find another way. Do you fancy a lift home?'

'That would be great,' said Kezzie. 'Thanks.'

Lauren was working behind the bar at the Labourer's Legs, and so, for the first time, was

Troy. She'd been very nervous to start with, spilling drinks, and pouring duff pints, but as the evening wore on, she grew more relaxed in Troy's presence. To her surprise, he didn't try anything on and was gently solicitous with her all evening. He cracked jokes, helped her change the barrel, fended off the more leery of the pub goers, and in short made her session behind the bar far more interesting and fun than normal. He even noticed how much Sally took her for granted.

'You should stand up to them,' he said. 'You're too dedicated. They take advantage of your good nature.'

'Yeah, well I need the job,' said Lauren drily, and he had the grace to look embarrassed.

When they got rid of the last customer at 11.20, Troy persuaded her to sit down with a drink while he cleared up. As Lauren often didn't get away beyond midnight, she let herself be persuaded. It felt relaxing to be sitting in a pub with Troy again. She was reminded of the early days in their relationship, when Troy seemed like the most exciting thing that had ever happened to her. She remembered the thrill of his presence, and the way just a touch of his hand used to send chills up her spine. Troy would come round and take her dancing at midnight, or get her out of bed to drive to the seaside, just for the day.

Those days had been heady and giddy with love and desire. She had never met anyone like Troy, and no one had ever made her feel the way he did. She was dizzy with love, and nothing else had mattered except being with him. The years of responsibility with the twins had changed her, she realized with a jolt. It was a long time since she'd done anything just for her. And she missed the freedom she had had. Despite her reservations about being with Troy, she felt easy in his company, and allowed him to buy her another spritzer, though she insisted that she had to be home for midnight.

'I've got to get up in the morning, don't forget,' she said, taking a sip of her drink.

'I could stay over and look after Sam for you,' said Troy.

'I don't *think* that's a good idea,' said Lauren. 'You don't get back in that easy.'

'It's worth a try,' said Troy with a grin, and Lauren looked away, feeling uncomfortable. It was all very well sitting here having a drink with him, but she didn't want to encourage him.

'Stop flirting with me,' she said.

'I'm not flirting,' he said. 'Why, do you want me to?'

'No!' said Lauren. 'I'm happy as I am.'

'Are you? Really?' Troy leant over and touched her hand.

A tingle went up her spine. Dammit. She couldn't believe he could still have that effect on her. She snatched her hand away.

'I'm fine. More than fine. Blissfully happy in fact.'

'Ah well, if you say so,' said Troy in disbelieving tones.

'I do say so,' said Lauren. 'And even if I weren't, it wouldn't mean I'd be coming back to you.'

'Shame,' said Troy.

'Cut it out,' said Lauren. 'I'm pleased you're

back, for the girls' sake. I'm grateful for your help tonight, but you and me – it's just not going to happen. So get used to it.'

'If you say so,' Troy said again.

'I do,' said Lauren firmly. 'And now I'm going home. Be seeing you.'

She got up, annoyed that she'd been so rattled by him. Because he was right. Tonight, being with Troy had reminded her of why she had fallen for him in the first place. Feelings she thought long dead were resurfacing. She couldn't afford them to, and nor was she going to let them. Getting back with Troy was a foolish pipe dream and she would never let it happen.

Kezzie hesitated as Joel drew up outside her cottage.

'Have you got time – would you like to come in for coffee?'

Joel looked at his watch.

'I promise no dope this time,' she said.

'Oh go on, just a quick one,' he said. 'I've got Claire's mum sitting tonight, so I don't want to be late for her.'

'Do you see a lot of Claire's parents?' said Kezzie, as she opened the front door and led him into the kitchen.

'Not as much as I'd like,' said Joel, taking his coat off, and slinging it over a chair. 'They've been great. They live about an hour away, and they come over when they can. My mum's got Parkinson's, so unfortunately she can't help me as much as she'd like; it's been brilliant having the back-up.'

Kezzie turned on the kettle, and grabbed two

cups from the cupboard. 'You don't take sugar do you?'

Joel shook his head.

'It must be really hard for them,' Kezzie continued. 'I mean, I'm not saying it's been easy for you, but losing a child – that must be terrible.'

'I know,' said Joel. 'So it makes me really happy to see how much pleasure Marion gets when she's with Sam. He's kept us all going really.'

He looked so sad when he said this that Kezzie instinctively leant over and touched his arm.

'It will get better, eventually,' she said, knowing she was mouthing platitudes.

'Will it?' Joel looked bleak. 'There are days when I think I'll never get over losing Claire. And then I think I deserve that.'

'What makes you say that?' Kezzie was shocked.

Joel leant against the kitchen table with his head in his hands.

'The truth is, Kezzie, and I've never told anyone this – not even Lauren – I'm a fraud. Everyone feels sorry for me, the poor widower, bringing up his son alone. But I don't really deserve their pity.'

Kezzie gave Joel his coffee, and sat down next to him, putting a consoling arm round his shoulder.

'Don't be daft,' she said, 'of course you do. You're coping really well with a rotten situation.'

'I deserve it,' said Joel.

'No one deserves something like this to happen to them,' said Kezzie firmly, squeezing his arm.

'No?' said Joel. 'I was a lousy husband to Claire, and a useless dad to Sam. There isn't a day goes by when I wish I'd done things differently.'

'What did you do that was so bad?'

'I wasn't there for Claire when she needed me,' said Joel. 'I can see that now. But at the time I thought Claire wasn't interested. She was so wrapped up in the baby it was as if I didn't exist. It's pathetic for a grown man to admit, but I was jealous.' He laughed hollowly. 'How crap is that. Being jealous of a baby?'

'Isn't that quite common?' said Kezzie. 'I know Richard said the same when his daughter was born, but he got over it and you would have. You didn't know Claire was going to die.'

'But she did die, and every day I'm left with this terrible guilt, that I let her down and she never really knew how much I loved – love her.'

He looked so desolate Kezzie leant over and pecked him on the cheek. The poor bloke. What an awful thing to happen to anyone.

'You're way too hard on yourself,' she said. 'From where I'm sitting, you're doing a great job with Sam. And I can't imagine you being such a bastard as all that. Sounds a bit like Claire wasn't always sympathetic to your needs.'

'I've never thought of it like that before,' said Joel.

'Well, you should,' said Kezzie, sipping her coffee. 'I've had friends with baby brain, and they go off the planet for months, obsessed with the way their little darlings are behaving. It's infuriating for a friend, so I can imagine how frustrating it is for a partner. Point is they get over it and Claire would have done. You were just unlucky, that's all.'

'I suppose you're right.' Joel toyed with the cup in his hands. He only looked half convinced.

'I am,' said Kezzie. 'Do you think Claire would really want you to go through the rest of your life moping? What's done is done. Learn by it and move on.'

Joel looked up at her and smiled, as if something had suddenly dawned on him.

'You are amazing, Kezzie,' he said. 'I've never known anyone like you.'

She felt a little thrill when he said that. It felt like a long time since a man had paid her a compliment and she was flattered. She gave him a quick hug as a thank you, and then pulled away, feeling shy and awkward, but Joel pulled her back. It was a long time since she'd been held by anyone and it felt warm and comforting, and right. The months of aching empty loneliness seemed to fade away as she looked up into Joel's eyes. She was aware of the stubble where he hadn't shaved, and the heavy musky scent of him. She had the sudden heady feeling that she wanted him very badly. So when he leant over and brushed his lips against hers it seemed natural to respond, and suddenly they were kissing with a passion that she'd forgotten she was capable of.

For a few moments Kezzie was lost in the kiss, without thinking about the consequences, but as she withdrew, panting slightly, it dawned on her this was a mistake.

Stupid. Stupid. Stupid. Not that it wasn't nice. Or that Joel wasn't lovely, because both were true. Joel was the first man she'd kissed since Richard, and it was good to know that all the parts were still in working order. But it couldn't work between them. They were too different.

211

Kissing Joel was a big mistake.

Joel must have clearly thought the same, because he broke away from her abruptly.

'Sorry, I shouldn't have done that,' he said. He grabbed his coat and rushed out of the house, leaving Kezzie spinning.

Chapter Sixteen

Kezzie timed her arrival at work the next day for after Joel had left. She felt on the whole it would be better to ignore the events of the night before. It had been stupid and naive of her to invite him in for coffee, but she'd come to think of him as a mate, and really hadn't factored on him thinking of her differently. It was just loneliness and boredom that had led them both to cling to one another. Much as she liked Joel she didn't think they were right for each other. And she doubted that he was thinking of her as anything other than one of his many conquests. From what Lauren had told her, Joel had spent the last year going out with half the women in the village, and she was probably just the latest.

'Way too much baggage,' she said out loud, as she wheeled a laden barrow down the path.

Now that Kezzie had gone through all Edward's designs, she had been able to work out her own, and today she planned to peg it out, so that she could finally start planting out the pattern that she'd designed on graph paper. The garden wouldn't be properly established for the Summer Fest, it would take several years for that, but at least people would be able to get a flavour of what Edward's garden had looked like.

It was a windy warm spring day. The daffodils, which had popped up unexpectedly in the corners of the borders, were looking slightly flattened, and the buds on the fruit trees, which clustered around the bottom of Joel's garden, were looking slightly frazzled. But the birds were singing lustily; Kezzie had already identified a cuckoo and there was evidence that blue tits were nesting in the oak tree she'd climbed up the first time she'd seen the garden. Spring was definitely in the air, and putting aside her confused emotions about Joel, Kezzie felt a thrill of excitement that she could start working on and reproducing Edward's garden.

Kezzie had followed Edward's basic design of interweaving ivy and rosemary, with a heart shape in the middle incorporating the letters E and L. In the four corners she'd also replicated the shapes of crossover hearts, the middle of which was for the flowers that Edward had planted for each of his children: agapanthus, snowdrops, white carnations and peonies. For Lily and Edward she'd combined blue hyacinths (constancy – which she felt was appropriate for Edward) and white lilies (purity – for Lily). She also wanted to plant a pink rose bush to symbolize their married love. Round the borders she planned to plant forget me nots and gloxinia, just as Edward had done, but for now she had planted heartsease, so at least there was some colour.

Kezzie had been glad to discover that Lily and Edward had finally managed to have children. It was clear from Lily's diaries the pain that being childless had caused. Though Kezzie had never had any desire to have children of her own, it would have taken a heart of stone not to have felt the pain of Lily's loss.

As she worked, Kezzie took photographs to chart her progress. Once she'd got the plants in, the garden would really take shape. Kezzie smiled, pleased at her hard work. It had been a labour of love to get this far, but she knew it would be worth it.

Despite the wind, the work soon made her warm, and she quickly shed her fleece. After several gloomy days the sun had managed to put in a pale appearance, despite the clouds scudding fast across it. It was probably as pale as she was. Richard had always teased her about being a pale ghost, (which with her dark hair and fair skin was not surprising), putting it down to all her night-time gardening activities.

Richard. Kezzie sat back on her haunches. If anything, last night had proved to her how far she had to go with Project Get Over Richard. It had been nice kissing Joel, and he wasn't at all un-attractive, but he *wasn't* Richard, and as soon as she'd kissed Joel, Kezzie realized how much she was missing Richard – still. Richard was someone she couldn't forget in a hurry.

When they'd first met she'd thought he was a terrible snob – but she soon realized that what appeared to be diffidence was actually shyness. Once she got to know him she'd discovered that despite a tendency to stuffiness, he had a great sense of fun, and was also immensely kind.

Kezzie sighed, and dug her fork into the ground, and carried on turning over the soil. Richard was in her past. She needed to accept it and get over him. Joel wasn't the right person to do that with, clearly, but waiting for Richard to come back to her wasn't an option either. Spring. Time for a fresh start for the garden. And for her.

'You don't have to do this,' Lauren protested for the hundredth time.

'I know,' said Troy. 'I want to.'

Having discovered that Lauren's lack of car meant she never got to a supermarket, but relied on daily shopping in Heartsease, Troy had insisted he take her to the new out of town super-market, three miles away.

Lauren protested at first – she did actually like buying locally – but it wasn't cheap. And a trip to the supermarket meant an opportunity to stock up on some necessities.

She'd asked Joel if she could borrow Sam's car seat, and once the girls were at school, she loaded Sam into Troy's car and off they went. She felt slightly nervous. This was one of the few times she and Troy had been properly alone, – Sam didn't really count – since he'd moved to Heartsease, and she was conscious that too long in his company awoke familiar and unwelcome feelings.

'So how are you finding it here?' said Lauren, more out of a desire to fill any awkward silence, than because she really wanted to know.

'Do you know, I'm loving it,' said Troy. 'I've

always felt so rootless before, but I like Hearts-ease. I could really see myself here in twenty years' time.'

'What, *you?*' said Lauren, laughing. 'I thought you were the eternal wanderer. Wherever I lay my hat and all that.'

'Yes, well. Wandering can lose its charm,' said Troy. 'I've learnt my lesson there.'

'What happened to your last girlfriend?' Lauren couldn't help but ask. Troy was the kind of guy who was never on his own for very long. She was quite surprised he hadn't hooked up with some-one in Heartsease already, given that she'd made it clear that she wasn't having him back.

'Lisa? We drifted apart,' mumbled Troy.

'You mean you got bored and ditched her,' said Lauren.

'No, actually,' Troy looked faintly embarrassed. 'She ditched me. For ... for a *toyboy*. Can you believe that?'

Lauren burst out laughing.

'Now that's what I call poetic justice. Don't worry, studmuffin, I'm sure there are plenty of people who'll be foolish enough to fall for your charms. Just please don't break the heart of any-one I know.'

'I wasn't planning to,' said Troy. 'The thing is, what with Lisa ditching me and Dad showing up at the same time, I began to realize what I was missing.'

'Oh, and what's that?' Lauren said lightly, as she put two packets of Coco Pops in her trolley and tickled Sam's chin.

'You,' said Troy simply. 'I've realized I've been

missing you.'

Joel was grateful that Kezzie hadn't turned up early. He wasn't sure he could face her that morning. Idiot. What did he think he'd been doing kissing her?

There had been a few women since Claire, but they'd been fairly meaningless encounters to fulfil a physical need, and make him feel less lonely. But as soon as anyone had tried to get close, he'd made polite excuses and moved on.

But this, with Kezzie – in a moment of weakness, he'd let her get too close and it wouldn't do. It made for an incredibly awkward situation. She was in his house such a lot. He liked her but he wasn't sure he was ready to entrust his heart to anyone yet. He didn't know if he would be able to ever again. He'd try and tactfully tell Kezzie when he got home.

But when he got back from work that night Kezzie wasn't there. She clearly had been, as a cup and plate were neatly stacked on the drainer, and her boots were sitting outside the back door. She must be as mortified about last night as he was. Damn, he'd have to try and speak to her tomorrow.

But the following day it was the same. Kezzie arrived after he left, and was gone before his return. The only sign of her having been there was the daily progress on the garden, which was finally beginning to take shape. Joel was impressed with what Kezzie was doing; the patterns did look like hearts, and she'd cleverly woven the initials E and L into the centre, just as on the original plans. It was going to be fantastic. He should tell her so, if he ever got the chance to speak to her again that is.

On Friday he found his moment, as he arrived back slightly earlier than usual. He came home to change first, before picking Sam up, and encountered Kezzie walking up the garden with all her equipment, clearly on her way to tidy up.

'I was beginning to think you were avoiding me,' said Joel, feeling embarrassed.

'Well I am,' said Kezzie. That was Kezzie, nothing if not direct.

'I hope it's – look, Kezzie, I'm sorry about the other night. I wouldn't want you to get the wrong idea.'

'What wrong idea?' Kezzie looked blankly at him, suspicious.

'You know, because I kissed you,' said Joel, beginning to sweat profusely. 'I'm sorry, it was a mistake.'

'You mean you're *not* going to whisk me off my feet and ask me to have your babies?' said Kezzie.

Oh God. He'd really cocked this up. This was going to take some recovering from.

'Er – no.'

'Thank God for that,' said Kezzie with a grin, 'because I don't want to have anyone's babies, least of all yours.'

'That's a bit deflating.'

'Would you rather I told you, you'd broken my heart?' said Kezzie.

'No.'

'Well then,' said Kezzie. 'Let's stick at being friends shall we? I think we'd be better at that.'

Joel felt a weight slide off his shoulders. He enjoyed Kezzie's company and hated to think of things becoming awkward between them.

'Are you sure?' he said. 'I'd hate to think I'd upset you.'

'It's not that I don't like you,' explained Kezzie, 'I do, a lot. But the other night made me realize that I really am not over Richard, and I don't think you're over Claire. We've both got far too much stuff to sort out.'

'You're right,' said Joel with relief. 'Thanks, I've been really fretting about it.'

'Don't,' said Kezzie. 'Let's just enjoy being friends. I think romance is overrated, don't you?'

'Possibly,' said Joel. 'But don't you think you're stopping yourself getting over Richard? Hiding yourself down here, never seeing him? It's like you're running away. I think you should use Summer Fest as an excuse to try and contact him and pump him for gardening contacts. That way you might get a feel for how the land lies.'

'Hmm,' said Kezzie. 'Suppose he doesn't want to talk to me?'

'And suppose he's been waiting for your call?' argued Joel. 'You won't know until you try, will you? I know if it was me and Claire, I wouldn't think twice.'

He sighed, and looked away.

'At least you still have a chance,' he said. 'What have you got to lose?'

Edward and Lily

1900–1914

The years passed, and the children grew. In time another sister came to join the family.

Our new baby is called Matilda, Edward wrote in his diary, in the summer of 1900. *I have planted peonies for her in the knot garden. She is a plump and smiling child, and Lily dotes on her. I feel so blessed that despite our early heartache we have such a perfect family. And Lily I love more than ever. Tending the knot garden together, with the children playing around us, is the greatest of joys. My only sadness is that Lily still seems unable to love Connie the way that I do. I try to make it up to her, by loving her for both of us...*

Edward grew wealthy from his many clients around the country, but the more time passed, the less inclined he felt like travelling from the place where he felt happiest. He was content mainly to spend his spare time pottering in the garden with Lily and the children, or taking them on long walks in the countryside. In summer it was their favourite pastime to picnic under the old willow tree by the river and watch the children play.

While all his children delighted him, Edward couldn't help but reserve a special place in his heart for Connie, trying to make up for Lily's lack of interest in her as best he could. Lily doted on Harry and the baby, and barely seemed to notice Connie at times, but if it bothered Connie she never said.

Connie was so different from her mother, quiet and studious, and even as a child she was incredibly stoical in the face of pain. There was a day Edward remembered well when she came in with a thorn deep in her thumb, which clearly pained her, yet she shed not a single tear when Edward tenderly pulled it out. Even Lily had marvelled at her courage.

The years passed, the children grew, and Edward found himself more involved in philanthropy than gardening, the wealth he had accrued from designing gardens for the great and good, allowing him to do charitable works nearer to home.

I have decided to design a garden for the village, he wrote in his diary in 1904, *the people of Heartsease need a place to go for recreation, and I will willingly share my expertise.*

So in summer of 1905, Lily proudly opened the Heartsease Public Gardens for the first time. There was a grand party, and the whole village turned out. They had bunting and flags, and a village fete. Lily, Edward and the children – the girls dressed in white muslin dresses, Harry in a sailor suit – were photographed with the villagers in front of the gates of the new park. It was one of those languorous long summer days that seemed to go on forever. The sun shone, the village band played, and Edward felt blessed to live in a place like Heartsease. He watched with pride as the village children ran joyously in the gardens he'd created for them. *After the knot garden,* he wrote in his diary, *the Heartsease Public Gardens are my greatest achievement.*

'I'm so proud of you,' Lily said, as they returned home that night, the children full of sticky cakes and buns, and exhausted from running wild with the village children. 'You do so much good for everyone.'

She kissed him lightly on the cheek, and that evening, when the children were in bed, she and Edward sat on the veranda, watching the sun go down behind the hills, and listened to the bats screeching in the dusk. They held hands and celebrated their good fortune.

Later, looking back to that time, it seemed to Edward that the sun had always shone, and the summers seemed endless, full of joy and laughter as his children tumbled up in a happy family time.

Lily's diary, July 1905
Today I opened Edward's gardens. It is such a noble and good thing he has done for the people of Heartsease. Now all the villagers have somewhere to go, and judging by the children today, the gardens are an instant success.

I am so proud of Edward, so lucky to have married him. I looked at our beautiful children tonight, as they slept, and thanked God that I have been so fortunate. After all that early heartache I have my heart's desire right here, with Edward in Lovelace Cottage. I feel I will never want for anything again.

Chapter Seventeen

Kezzie spent several days mulling over what Joel had said. Maybe he was right. If she got in touch with Richard again, she could know one way or another if it was definitely over. It had been nearly six months now, and no word from him, but then she hadn't made it easy for him to get in touch with her. Perhaps, as Joel had suggested, Richard had been trying to.

But then again, if he'd been trying to find her surely Richard would have got in touch with her via Flick? She didn't hold out much hope for him finding her through Facebook, as Richard didn't even have an account. While he embraced modern technology for business, he was less keen on social networking in his personal life, claiming he'd rather speak to people face to face than online.

After some internal debate, she decided that rather than ringing him up again – she wasn't yet ready for the humiliation of having him slam the phone down on her, or hearing that other woman on the phone again – her best bet would be to use the excuse of the Summer Fest as a reason for getting in touch, and to do it by email.

After much deliberation Kezzie sat down at Jo's rickety desk with a glass of wine to write an email to Richard.

To: Richard.Lacey@L&GGardendesigns.com
From: Kezzie@hotmail.com

Dear Richard, she wrote. And then got stuck. What to say next? *I hope you're missing me as madly as I'm missing you?*

I know you said you never wanted to hear from me again last time we spoke but I thought I'd email anyway?

I think we've made a huge mistake?

No, she couldn't say any of that. It was way too personal.

She started again.

To Richard? Too formal.

Hi, Richard? Too friendly.

In the end she went with,

Richard,

Kezzie here. Just wanting to pick your brains about a community gardening project I'm working on. We're planning to overhaul a local park, and we need to raise a considerable sum of money. I know it's cheeky of me after all this time, but I was wondering if you could think of anyone I could contact who might be able to offer their services.

Hope you're keeping well,

Kezzie

She felt like she had been reasonably casual, and not too intense, while managing to maintain a friendly air. She read the email over several times, and took a great big gulp of wine.

'Nothing ventured, nothing gained,' she said, her finger hovering over the keyboard for a minute, before she decided she may as well just go for it, and pressed send. The minute the email had gone she regretted it, but it was too late now. Oh well. She'd have to deal with the fallout tomorrow. As she went to turn the computer off, an email pinged straight back into her inbox. Kezzie swallowed hard. She'd assumed Richard would have gone home for the evening, and hadn't imagined he'd still be sitting at his desk. It was tantalizing to think of them connected by their computer screens. So close, and yet so far away.

From: Richard.Lacey@L&GGardendesigns.com
To: Kezzie@hotmail.com
Kezzie,
If you want help with your gardening project your best bet is to contact the RoseThyme Agency who have a lot of gardening celebs on their books.
I recall from our last conversation I said I didn't want to see you any more. That hasn't changed. I think it advisable for you not to contact me again.
Richard

Kezzie felt as if a cold bucket of water had been thrown over her head. Seeing the words there so starkly in front of her was even more hurtful than it had been all those months ago. She let out a howl of anguish. Part of her wanted to launch a tirade at him, telling him how wrong he was, begging him to forgive her, but she was too proud. All that would do would make him hate her even more. Instead, she responded with a curt, *I only contacted you for the information you gave me. Thanks for that. You won't hear from me again.* And then she deleted her hotmail account. It was one she didn't

225

use very often, but she couldn't bear the thought of any more correspondence like that from Richard. Better if he didn't know how to contact her. And now she'd opened the correspondence, better if she wasn't tempted to contact him again.

Kezzie switched off the computer and stared out into the gathering gloom. Finally she had to face it, after all these months of pretending. It really was over. Richard was never going to take her back.

Lauren was having the opposite problem. After years of thinking Troy didn't want her, she was being faced with the prospect that now, all of a sudden he actually genuinely did.

Lauren had been stunned by Troy's revelation that he was missing her. It was what she'd wanted to hear for a long time. And yet now he'd finally recognized the error of his ways, she wasn't convinced she wanted him to. She'd got used to it being just her and the girls. They'd been doing fine till Troy came along. And if she wanted a man in her life, she wasn't sure it would be Troy she was after.

A picture of Joel swam unbidden in front of her eyes. Now that was ridiculous. He was good looking, it was true; you'd have to be a blind, hormonally challenged hermit not to notice that. But there was so much emotional confusion tied up in Lauren's feelings for Joel. First, as Claire's friend, she felt guilty for even thinking Joel attractive. She hadn't paid any attention to Joel's good looks when Claire was alive, but increasingly of late, Lauren had been aware that he was very, very, attractive. But she couldn't possibly think about it because Claire had been her friend. Besides, Claire had painted a very warts and all picture of her husband, so Lauren was fully aware of all Joel's faults. Claire had been running round like a headless chicken while Joel had ostensibly been doing up the house, but as far as Lauren could see, it was just an excuse not to be there at bath time. Joel probably wasn't much of a better bet than Troy. Having a man in the house wasn't a guarantee of support.

Lauren made her way reluctantly to the pub, knowing that tonight she was sharing another shift with Troy. Despite her anxiety, the sight of a new family of ducklings frantically swimming after their proud mother made her smile. Spring was definitely in the air.

Lauren sighed, enviously looking at the few stalwart smokers who were sitting under the patio heaters on the benches outside the pub. She would much, much, rather be drinking with them, but Sally had called and wheedled her into coming in this evening. 'I know it's short notice,' Sally had said, 'but I really can't get anyone else tonight, and you're always so reliable.' For which read, I know you need the money. Which was true. Lauren always needed the money, and never felt she could turn an offer of work down. Mum couldn't babysit, so Kezzie had stepped in, and now Lauren was hotfooting it – late – to the pub.

'You're late,' Sally was on her case the minute she walked in the pub. Who was helping who out of a jam here?

'Sorry,' said Lauren, 'you didn't exactly give me

much notice.'

Sally looked as though she was about to launch into a tirade, but Troy appeared like magic from his side of the bar, and said, 'Oh, come on, Sal, you know that's not fair, at least Loz has turned up.'

Loz. She liked the way he called her that. No one else ever did.

Sal was immediately flattered by Troy's attention; you could almost hear her purr, and within seconds she'd forgotten that she wanted to bawl Lauren out, and was being persuaded that she needed to go upstairs and put her feet up in front of the TV, which was precisely the reason Lauren had been called in at the last moment.

'Thanks for that,' said Lauren.

'No worries,' said Troy, giving her a wink. 'I won't have you being bullied like that.'

Lauren forced down the little thrill that shot through her as he said that. Troy was being Troy. He was trying to get her back, and would use any means at his disposal to do so, she had to remember that.

As it happened, he didn't try anything at all for the rest of the evening. It was a fairly slow night and only three or four of the regulars were in, so Lauren and he chatted amicably behind the bar for most of the night. To her surprise, Lauren found they had a lot to talk about. They argued about the football, Lauren supported the local third division club, while Troy (naturally) supported Man U, and couldn't work out why Lauren would be interested in a bunch of losers. They read the headlines in the tabloids left at the bar, and laughed at the shenanigans that low grade celebs were getting up to if the redtops were to be believed. And in between, Troy talked about the girls.

'I just can't get over how great they are,' he said. 'You've done a good job with them, Loz.'

Lauren felt a little glow of pride. It wasn't as if being a mum came with a yearly appraisal. It felt nice to get some recognition that she was getting it right.

'Thanks,' she said. 'Most of the time I feel like I'm just about coping.'

'I think you do more than cope,' said Troy. 'In fact I think you're rather magnificent.'

Lauren blushed, and turned away. Why did he have to be so nice now? If only he could have felt like this four years ago.

'Well, that's easy for you to say,' she said. 'You come in after all the hard work's done and think by complimenting me that makes it all right.'

Troy had the grace to look embarrassed.

'Sorry, that came out wrong,' he said. 'You're absolutely right. It is easy for me to say, but I know now what a tosser I've been. I should never have left you in the lurch like that, and I wish I hadn't.'

'Too right you shouldn't,' said Lauren.

'I do want to make it up to you,' he said, 'more than anything.'

Lauren sighed, 'It's not that easy to wipe out four years of hurt, Troy. Let's just leave it that we get to know each other again as friends, and you concentrate on being the girls' dad. Take one step at a time, eh?'

She touched his arm lightly, then went to clear up the empties and wipe down tables. When she looked up, she caught Troy looking at her when he thought she wasn't watching. He looked rather sad and thoughtful. She wondered, for the first time since he was back, if he really meant everything he said. Perhaps this time, he had changed, and for the better.

Joel was at home lovingly working on Edward's desk. He'd decided that if he was going to open the house for the Edward Handford exhibition, he needed to get on and renovate. Thanks to Kezzie having wangled some grant money for the garden from a small gardening charity, he'd had to spend less on the restoration than he'd budgeted for. Which meant he felt able to splash out on a decorator, and had managed to get the dining room and lounge finished. The hallway was next on the list, and in the meantime Joel had resumed work on the desk. As the only bit of furniture still surviving from Edward's day, Joel wanted it to form pride of place in the exhibition.

He finally finished stripping off the old layers of polish and lacquer, layers and layers of it, which he'd spent weeks doing when Sam was small, before Claire had died. But now he had attacked it with renewed vigour, and he was rewarded for his efforts by being able to see the original walnut in all its beauty. He took a piece of sandpaper to it, and started to sand it down gently. This was such a beautiful piece of furniture. It gave him a thrill to think of Edward sitting here, writing at it, looking out of the front of the house, just as he did. The more he read Edward's diaries, and looked through the other material he and Kezzie had found, the greater his affinity with his great great grandfather, who had moved into the house in the first throes of love, and created a garden in memory of that love.

For Joel too, it was love that had brought him here, though to begin with it was the garden that had attracted him – he clearly remembered as a child the excitement of coming to visit Uncle Jack, and finding it locked, sneaking into it in much the same way as Kezzie had. He could still remember the thrill, as he swung himself over the wall, and dropped down into the garden.

Back then it had been half tended – Uncle Jack had employed a curmudgeonly old handyman, whom Joel had instinctively avoided – but rarely visited, so the borders had been a jumble of weeds and plants. He particularly remembered there was a lot of heartsease, but then you found a lot of that growing round here. But he could also make out the patterns of the knot garden, just about being kept in shape, although he hadn't really appreciated what he was looking at. The bushes round the side of the garden had been very overgrown and Joel had spent a lovely half hour having adventures in them before he'd been called indoors. Forever after, the secret garden had held a magical place in his heart. When his mum told him about Uncle Jack's will it had been a no brainer to come here.

Realistically, though, when he saw the house he should have known it wouldn't be to Claire's taste. It hadn't, if he were honest, been altogether to his. He had taken her to Lovelace Cottage as a surprise, but their first view of the place had been hardly propitious. Uncle Jack had been a bachelor, with no children, and precious little money. So the house had fallen into a state of disrepair, and was in desperate need of modernization. What Joel remembered as romantic and exotic from his childhood had turned into a decaying lost paradise, and even he had balked a little as he opened the creaking iron gate, and led Claire by the hand up the path.

The crazy paving was broken and cracked, leaving the surface uneven. The grass was growing long and wild, and the flowerbeds were a riot of weeds, with the odd snapdragon and forget me not poking out. The scent of the wisteria over the front door was strong, but the plant itself had, triffid-like, taken over the whole of the front of the house and needed cutting back. Claire had blinked in the May sunlight. The sun played upon her face, and she raised her hand to shield herself from its glare. Her fair hair was tied in a high ponytail, and her face was alive and laughing.

'Um, it's a bit overgrown,' she said. 'And who in their right mind would plant a privet hedge so close to the house? It must be hideously dark inside.'

'I don't suppose it was like that originally,' he said. 'Nobody's done anything here forever. I'm sure we can trim that back so it's not so overgrown. Come on, let's go in.'

He opened the front door with some trepidation. Uncle Jack was a cantankerous old soul, and from his childhood memories the place had never been clean. Claire was used to the spick and span modernity of their flat in town; would she be able to cope with the amount of work needed here? Even Joel, who loved the idea of restoring an old house like this, felt a little daunted.

They had walked into a house trapped in time. There was dust everywhere, mote beams danced in the green, red and blue shadows cast by sunlight pouring through the stained-glass window of the front door, but the overall impression was of gloomy darkness. The stairway in the hall, though impressive, was made of dark mahogany, and matched the wood panelling up the walls. The parquet floor was partially covered in a faded red and white rug, which had seen better days, and pictures of various aged relatives stared vacantly out of ancient photographs.

'Who's this?' Claire chanced upon a family photo of a stiff-looking Edwardian family: the parents sitting down, the mother with her hair in a bun, looking terribly severe, the father sitting rigid and squinting into the sun, the children solemn and serious, two girls and a boy dressed in their Sunday best. They didn't look a happy bunch.

'I think it's my great great grandfather Edward Handford, who designed the gardens here,' said Joel. He looked around him, trying to picture what the place could look like without the dust, and the oppressive darkness. The rooms had high ceilings, and there was masses of space. This could be turned into an amazing house, but he could sense Claire's lack of enthusiasm. 'I know it's dark and old fashioned, Claire, but I'm sure if we took away the panelling and opened up the stairway the place would seem lighter. See that window halfway up the hall? If we made that bigger, it would bring in more light. Come on, let's look upstairs.'

Claire followed him upstairs, pursing her lips as they went through room after room that looked tatty and worn, as if nothing had been touched here for centuries.

'I feel like I'm in Miss Havisham's house,' said Claire, as they walked out of one particularly cobwebby room. 'How on earth do you think your uncle managed living here?'

'I have no idea,' said Joel. 'Look, I know it's a lot of work, but can you really resist those views?'

He pointed to the back window. The back garden, as overgrown as the front, stretched down a hill before them, and gave way at the bottom to views of the South Downs. Joel drew the curtains back, and threw open the casement window. Light came pouring in. Suddenly the dark, poky little bedroom they were in was transformed into something much brighter. The sprig-like wallpaper, now faded, had been pretty once. It was possible to see that the room could be bright and pretty again.

'This could make a lovely nursery,' Joel cajoled Claire. 'I know it doesn't look much now, but really there's bags of potential. And where else are we going to get so much space for the money?'

Although they were planning to take out a mortgage to buy the house from Joel's mum, she had generously given them a good price, one they couldn't really afford to turn down.

'I suppose,' said Claire reluctantly.

He looked out of the window and out towards

the bottom of the garden. There was a faint sound of sheep in the background, and the birds were singing.

'You don't get sounds like that in London,' he said.

'True...' said Claire, still uncertain.

'You don't like it?' Joel had been so certain she would be brought round, once she'd seen the potential of the house. He'd only visited here a few times in his life, but there was something about the mystery and romance of this place that had intrigued him. He couldn't wait to get going on the restoration.

'It's not that exactly,' said Claire, rubbing her stomach, 'it's just such a big move. With Junior on the way, and all the work here, I don't know how we'll manage.'

Joel took her hands in his. 'It will be fine, I promise,' he said. 'I am going to make this house perfect for the three of us, and for however many of Junior's brothers and sisters who come along. It's going to be fabulous, you'll see.'

And that's what he'd done. The first six months they'd been in the house, they'd put in central heating and Joel had worked as hard as he could to strip out the dark wood, bring in more windows, and open the old house to the light. He'd wanted to bring love and laughter back into the house. And now Claire was gone, and the work that had gone into their home seemed wasted and fruitless. He wondered if Edward had felt the same in the end about the garden. Why else had he let it go to rack and ruin? It all seemed such a waste.

Chapter Eighteen

Lauren couldn't stop thinking about Troy, as she pushed Sam down the hill to the park. It was one of those sharp, cold days you get in early March, but at least the sun was out, so she thought they both needed some fresh air. Over and over she repeated back their last conversation. Troy seemed to be hell bent on showing her he'd turned over a new leaf – he'd even started to pay her a bit of maintenance – and she felt that maybe, just maybe, he actually was.

Her mum was not as convinced, though, and every time Troy's name came up in conversation, she did her level best to make Lauren 'see sense' as she put it. 'That lad is never going to do right by you,' she said. 'He hasn't got it in him. Don't let him pull you down.'

Part of Lauren agreed with her mum. It was still early days, and while Troy seemed to be getting on with the kids, and enjoying their company, who was to say when the novelty would wear off? Lauren knew she should keep her wits about her, and remain wary, and yet, and yet...

As she turned into the playground she gasped in horror, all thoughts of Troy driven from her mind. Someone had clearly been having a party. The remains of an impromptu barbecue smouldered in a corner, and bottles, some of them broken, were scattered all over the ground. And yet again, someone had sprayed graffiti over the swings.

'Oh, this is the pits!' Lauren said to no one in particular.

'Isn't it?' Another mum Lauren vaguely recognized, came up behind her. 'We should get on to the council.'

'What are they going to do?' said Lauren. 'I've tried that before. All that happens is someone comes down here, paints over the graffiti, and then goes away again. Nobody actually *does* anything.'

'Well, what can we do?' said the mum, introducing herself as Rose Carmichael. 'The police never come down here. Nothing will ever change.'

'That's a bit defeatist, don't you think?' said Lauren. 'I'm not sure it's as bad as all that. If we *all* did something, maybe we could change things.'

'I suppose,' the mum looked unconvinced. 'Have you got any big ideas about what you could do?'

'Not exactly,' said Lauren, 'but at least I'm willing to try. I think it's time we took matters into our own hands and reclaimed the playground for families.'

She took out her mobile and rang Eileen.

'Eileen, have you got a moment to come down to the playground? It's in a terrible state – worse than normal. I really think we should start sorting it out. We can't wait forever for the Parish Council to do something about it.'

'I'm only on the High Street,' said Eileen. 'I'll be with you in a minute.'

Lauren put Sam into the swing and pushed him half heartedly while the other mum did the same with her little boy.

'I just don't get why anyone would do this,' she said. 'It's so mindless.'

'I know,' said Rose. 'Were you serious about doing something about it?'

'Absolutely,' said Lauren.

'Well, if you're prepared to do something about it, I'm in,' said Rose. 'What did you have in mind?'

'I don't know,' said Lauren, 'but I'm sure my friend here can help.'

Eileen was striding up to them with a horrified look on her face.

'This is awful,' she said. 'I keep bringing this to the attention of the Parish Council but so far they've done nothing. Even with Tony as Chair now, it takes so much to get them to change anything. So I wouldn't hold your breath and imagine this will make any difference.'

'I'm not,' said Lauren, 'which is why I want your help spearheading a clean-up campaign. Maybe if we prove to the council how much we need this place, they'll sit up and take notice.'

'So now you're running the Save Our Playground campaign, as well as being on the Summer Fest committee and the PTA?' Kezzie grinned when Lauren told her what had happened. 'Well, good for you. I think one committee is enough to send me potty.'

'Yes, well, someone needs to do *something*,' said Lauren. 'Otherwise the situation will just get worse. I think we should catch the little scrotes who did this and make *them* repaint the playground.'

'Quite the community policewoman, aren't we?' said Kezzie.

'Well, someone needs to be,' said Lauren. 'I can't help thinking if the place were spruced a bit more, the vandals might be put off.'

'They might,' said Kezzie. 'I really ought to get out there and start planting properly. Sod waiting for the Parish Council's approval – I may just do it anyway!'

'Oh, I think we can make enough fuss to ensure that,' said Lauren. 'I don't think the Parish Council can turn a blind eye any longer. I'm going on Radio Sussex to talk about it and I've already spoken to the *Heartsease Gazette* and the *Chiverton Post*. I've got a petition going, too, and thanks to mums in the playground and a Facebook page I started, I've got a hundred signatures already.'

'Blimey, that's impressive,' said Kezzie. 'Tell you what, I'll see if I can persuade some of my guerrilla gardening pals to come down for a few days. I did ask them if they would when I saw them last. They're pretty good at turning a barren patch of land into something that looks halfway decent.'

'And we should really start Neighbourhood Watch patrols,' said Lauren. 'The local police aren't going to do anything.'

'I bet it's bored kids,' said Kezzie. 'They probably just need something to do. When I was younger I used to get a buzz out of breaking into parks at night. Me and my mates didn't cause much damage, but we caused enough. I got tired of being so destructive, but enjoyed the buzz of breaking in. So I became a guerrilla gardener instead.'

'And now you're a landscape gardener. How did that happen?'

Kezzie paused. She still felt uncomfortable talking about the reasons why she'd come here. And now that Richard appeared to have completely closed the door on their relationship, she was even more reluctant to come clean. She liked Lauren, and didn't want her to think badly of her.

'Richard persuaded me that I had a God-given talent that could be put to better use. I was pretty disillusioned with my job at the time, and then I got made redundant, so it seemed like a good idea.'

'Why did you split up? If you don't mind me asking.'

Kezzie pulled a face. As ever, when she thought about her last meeting with Richard she felt sick to the pit of her stomach. How could a moment of such stupidity have caused such a catastrophe? If she could have one wish in life it would be for that evening to replay differently, for her not to have had Emily that day, for Emily not to have done what she did, for Richard to still be in love with her.

'I – well, let's just say I cocked up big time,' said Kezzie. 'I did something really stupid and now Richard doesn't want to see me any more.'

'What on earth did you do?' said Lauren. 'It can't have been that bad.'

'It was in his eyes,' said Kezzie, blinking back tears. 'Sorry, I shouldn't be so wobbly about it after all this time. It drives me nuts that I still am.'

Lauren reached over and gave her a hug. 'Come

on, Kezzie, we're mates. Talk to me about it, it looks like you need to get it off your chest.'

So reluctantly, Kezzie told Lauren the story she'd told Flick. With Flick she had been fairly sure that she wouldn't be judged, but Kezzie had heard Lauren go on about how much she hated drugs; she wasn't sure Lauren wouldn't be offended.

To her relief, when she'd finished Lauren snorted, 'Is that all?'

'What, you mean you wouldn't have been cross if I let the twins eat magic muffins?'

'They're four years old,' said Lauren. 'That's different. You know I don't agree with drugs. But it wasn't as if you told Emily to help herself. She shouldn't have just assumed she could eat whatever she wanted without your permission. And frankly, she does sound quite obnoxious. Which is fair enough, she's a teenage girl. I hated one of my dad's girlfriends so much, that I put pepper in her tea. It wouldn't surprise me at all if Emily knew exactly what she was doing and ate those muffins just to cause trouble between you and Richard.'

This was more or less what Kezzie had thought. 'Do you really think so?' She felt hugely relieved that her friend was being so supportive.

'I sure do,' said Lauren. 'And if you ask me, Richard's an idiot, letting his teenage daughter dictate his love life like that. I mean, he could have cut you some slack, couldn't he?'

'Do you know, you're right,' said Kezzie, wiping away her tears. 'He damned well could have. He doesn't deserve me.'

'No he doesn't,' said Lauren. 'Sorry, I hope you didn't think I was interfering.'

'Not at all, you've made me feel much better about it,' said Kezzie, in control of herself again. 'So come on, how are we going to go about patrolling the playground?'

'Patrolling the playground?' Joel said, when he came to pick Sam up. 'Yeah, I'm up for that, so long as I can get a sitter.'

'I can always have Sam overnight when it's your shift, if you want,' said Lauren. 'From what we can tell, a lot of the damage occurs around 10 p.m. That does make it rather late.'

'That would make life easier,' admitted Joel. 'Have you got many other takers?'

'Quite a few,' said Lauren. 'I've even persuaded Sally and Andy behind the bar to do a stint, by promising to do a couple of extra shifts for them.'

'And don't forget, I'm doing one.' Troy emerged from the kitchen, holding a spanner and looking very dishevelled.

'How could I?' said Lauren drily. 'Joel, you remember Troy?'

'Of course,' said Joel. What was he doing here? For some reason, Joel felt put out. He knew Troy visited the girls, but Lauren had been very specific about the fact that he only came to see them, not her. He hadn't realized that Lauren had started asking Troy for help around the house. He had no right to let it bother him, but he couldn't help it, it did.

Troy was rubbing the spanner with a cloth.

'That's all fixed for you, Lauren,' he said. 'You

shouldn't have any problems with that pipe now. I don't think it will leak again.'

'Thanks, Troy, that's brilliant,' said Lauren. 'That leak has been driving me mad for ages, and my landlady keeps promising to do something about it, and never does.'

Joel had no idea that Lauren had had a problem with a leaky tap. In fact, he realized he had very little idea of any problems Lauren might have. She never confided in him any more. He suddenly wished she would.

'You should have said, Lauren,' he said. 'I'd have fixed that for you.'

'Would you?' Lauren looked at him in surprise. 'It never occurred to me to ask.'

'No job is too small,' he said, wondering why he was so determined to prove his usefulness to her.

It was something about the way that Troy was arrogantly strutting around the place that he found frustrating. Troy had dumped Lauren in it, left her to it, and now seemed to have slotted straight back into her life, as if nothing had happened. It didn't seem right, and Joel liked and respected Lauren too much to want to see her being hurt again.

Who are *you* to judge? a little voice in his head said. You were no better with Claire.

But at least I stayed, he thought.

'It's OK, mate,' said Troy, whispering in a conspiratorial manner as Lauren busied herself getting Sam's things ready. 'Now I'm back on the scene, I can do all Lauren's little jobs for her. I appreciate your concern for her, but you don't need to worry about Lauren any more, she's got me to help her now.'

'I think Lauren's managed pretty well on her own so far,' said Joel bluntly. 'You're not the only one looking out for her, *mate.*'

He took Sam from Lauren's arms, feeling more furious than he could remember ever feeling before in his life.

'Thanks, Lauren,' he said. 'Please don't feel you can't ask me for help, you always can, you know.'

'Bye, mate.' Troy sat down on the sofa and picked up the paper. He really was making himself at home. Joel was seething when he got in the car. Who did he bloody well think he was? Lauren deserved so much better. But, depressingly, it was clear which way the land lay and Joel couldn't understand why that made him feel so edgy.

Chapter Nineteen

'Right, buckets and mops at the ready,' said Lauren to the crowd who had gathered outside the Memorial Gardens as they posed for a photo for the local paper. She had been amazed at how easy it had been to get people galvanized to come and clean up the mess that the vandals had made. She'd put the word out with the school-run mums, and once the jungle drums began to roll everyone was keen to get involved. Lauren felt a renewed sense of vigour and optimism as she looked at the number of people who'd come to help. Even the newly appointed local MP, who had a young family of his own and a keen eye for good PR, was eager to be seen at the playground. This was great from Lauren's point of view as it brought the added bonus of the local TV covering the story.

'We could do with more of this sort of community spirit in Chiverton, where I live,' the MP was saying. 'It's exactly the sort of thing the government want to promote.'

He was so enthusiastic he was even prepared to take the mop and bucket he'd used for his photocall and put it to use. His minders had to persuade him to stop scrubbing before getting him to his next appointment.

'Well, look at you,' said Kezzie, who was taking a break from working on her website to offer her services. 'Hobnobbing with MPs and appearing on national telly.'

'Hardly national,' said Lauren, 'we'll be lucky if we get a minute on the local news bulletin.'

'Whatever. I'll make a campaigner out of you yet!'

Lauren grinned.

'Do you know, I'm enjoying all this. It feels like the first time I've properly used my brain since the girls were born.'

'You've certainly gathered a willing workforce,' said Kezzie, looking around as Lauren's friends swept up glass, scrubbed off graffiti and disposed of chip wrappers.

'They've been great,' said Lauren. 'Do you know Rose Carmichael?' She pointed at a small, rotund woman, who was laughing and joking while she swept up. 'Her husband works for B&Q in Chiverton and he got us a whole load of paint so we can make the playground look better until we get a new one sorted.'

'Brilliant,' said Kezzie. 'And I've got some more good news for you. A gang of my mates are coming down in a few weeks to help plant out the borders that Joel and I dug over. In no time at all we'll have the place looking fantastic.'

'I just hope we can keep the vandals away,' said Lauren. 'Locking the gardens at night doesn't seem to deter them.'

'Well, a locked gate has never deterred me,' said Kezzie, 'but if we surprise them by being *in* the gardens, they might think again.'

'What if they're six feet tall and wielding an axe?' said Lauren, wondering if she'd bitten off more than she could chew.

'I'll run like hell,' said Kezzie. 'But I reckon they're just kids, and if we could only get them on our side, we might be able to turn it round and persuade them to help us make things better.'

'You're optimistic.'

'Well, you never know,' said Kezzie cheerfully. 'I've never done anything like this before, but there's always a first time.'

Kezzie and Joel sat in the park drinking a flask of tea. It was a chilly spring evening in March and they were both wearing warm fleeces and scarves. As arranged with Lauren, Sam was staying there for the night.

'Do you really think anyone will come?' said Joel. 'After all there's been a lot of publicity.

246

They'll probably go and find somewhere else to deface.'

'I do think it's likely to be kids,' said Kezzie. 'I feel quite sorry for them. They haven't got anything to do or anywhere to go, so they're bored and destructive. Heartsease could do with a community centre for teens. We should bring it to the attention of the committee.'

'Can you imagine what Cynthia will say?' snorted Joel.

'"Ai really don't think it is necessary. We are not some inner London housing estate,"' Kezzie mimicked Cynthia's modulated tones perfectly.

'Still, I'm not that sympathetic with them,' said Joel. 'I was frequently bored as a teenager and I didn't graffiti things.'

'I did,' admitted Kezzie. 'The estate where I grew up was like that. You started drinking at thirteen, hung around with your mates, and knocked things down for fun. It was either that, or get into knife crime.'

'So how did you get out of it then?' said Joel. 'I mean, you didn't turn into a hardened criminal, did you?'

'I was lucky,' said Kezzie. 'I had a couple of good teachers who spotted I was good at art, and encouraged me to go into design. Then I fell in with a bunch of guerrilla gardeners when I was at college, and realized what I really liked doing was gardening. But I needed to work, so I got a job in web design, but I never really liked it. I'd probably still be there now if it weren't for Richard...'

Kezzie paused. There was something about the two of them being here, after dark, that seemed to encourage intimacy. A sudden memory of the kiss they shared made her flush in the dark. She hoped that Joel wasn't thinking about it too.

'Why?' said Joel.

'He persuaded me to retrain and do gardening properly. He's a garden architect, and we were planning to go into business together.' Kezzie sighed. It had been such a great dream. She was going to design a winning garden for Chelsea, and he was going to create the structures to go inside. Together she knew they could have been a winning team. That was never going to happen now.

'What happened?'

'I was a bloody idiot's what happened,' said Kezzie. She shivered, and thought about her chat with Lauren. Richard was in the past. Time to let go. 'Never mind. He made it clear from that email he sent me. It's over now, and I'm here, and here's where I plan to stay.'

'So you wouldn't go back to London?' said Joel.

A bleak look crossed Kezzie's face.

'Nothing to go back for,' she muttered.

There was a rustling in the bushes. Kezzie shone her torch, and disturbed a fox, which looked quizzically at them.

'False alarm,' she said.

'I think we might have frightened the vandals off,' said Joel.

'With any luck,' said Kezzie. 'I'd hate to see all Lauren's hard work go to waste. The paint's barely dry on the swings.'

They sat in companionable silence for another half an hour. It was nearly eleven.

'I doubt anyone's going to break in now,' said

Joel. 'If it is kids, they should all be tucked up in bed by now.'

'I never was,' said Kezzie with a grin.

'What a rebel,' said Joel. 'You clearly had more of a chequered youth than me.'

'If you knew the half of it,' said Kezzie.

'So none of the patrols have spotted anyone at night. That's great.' Lauren was chairing a meeting at her house to update everyone on the progress of the clean-up operation so far. They'd been running the patrols for nearly a month, and it was now midway through April. Whoever had been causing the damage appeared to have been scared away. Which was something; though Joel privately thought the minute they stopped watching out for the vandals, they would be back.

'I think our next plan should be to renovate the pavilion and see if we can't turn it into some kind of community hall. I'm looking into seeing if we can get any lottery funds for it. I think if we can set up somewhere for teens to go, then we might not have such a huge vandalism problem.'

'Great idea,' said Rose Carmichael. 'I know my lot get really bored of a summer's evening. I'd love it if they could find something constructive to do.'

'But who would run it?' said Joel, thinking practically. 'Presumably we'd need to get CRB checked, and there will definitely be things like insurance to consider.'

'That's true,' said Kezzie, 'but surely as a community we can all pull together.'

'I've been a youth worker,' put in Troy, much to Joel's annoyance. He seemed to be everywhere

Lauren was these days, and now it looked as if he could actually be useful, which was even more galling. Joel chided himself for being so petty minded, but he couldn't help it. As far as Troy was concerned, everything annoyed him.

'You? Really?' Lauren looked at him in disbelief. Good, at least Lauren wasn't totally blinded.

'Yeah, me,' said Troy. 'I retrained last year and worked on an estate in Southampton. It was challenging and rewarding, and I'd love to do something like that here.'

'I didn't think you'd want to stay that long.' Lauren gave Troy a look that was impossible to misinterpret, and Joel felt his heart sink. Blinded enough, though. She was going to end up back with the worthless sap, and had clearly fallen for that I've-changed malarkey. A sudden stabbing sensation of jealousy shot through him. Jealousy? Why should he feel jealous of Troy? It wasn't as though he had even thought about Lauren in that way. But since Troy had been on the scene, Joel felt like he barely saw her. He missed the chats they used to have when he came to pick Sam up in the evening. If Lauren and Troy became an item, Joel would see her even less. Joel was used to Lauren being there, framing every day for him. She'd been his steady support system since Claire died. He couldn't bear to think of that changing.

Troy said, 'I told you I wanted to stay here.' But to Joel his words were loaded with significance. Troy was using Lauren again, getting involved with her, trying to impress her. It was so damned obvious, but she clearly couldn't see it.

'Well, we can certainly look into that,' said

250

Lauren, 'but I think to get things really up and running we need to put all this before the Parish Council, and we need to restore the pavilion first. It's a mess. In the meantime, anyone keen to help Kezzie on Saturday, please come along to the Memorial Gardens at around 10 a.m. We're going to need people with green fingers.'

'And depending on how much we get done,' said Kezzie, 'it's all back to mine for drinks afterwards.'

'I like the sound of that,' said Troy.

'You would,' said Lauren, and shoved him.

'Careful,' he said, and shoved her back.

The warmth of their banter was not lost on Joel. Lauren was going back to Troy, he was certain. And there was nothing at all he could do about it.

Chapter Twenty

'OK you guys, let's get cracking.'

It was early on an April Saturday morning, and Joel, finding that Sam had already woken and they were both unable to sleep, had come down to the Memorial Gardens to see if Kezzie and her friends needed any help.

They were an ill-assorted mob, who'd arrived in a battered old minibus. Kezzie introduced Flick, a standard vegan kind of anarchist, who fitted the stereotype so neatly. Joel was convinced she was a lesbian, till she planted a kiss on the lips of a tall and scary-looking individual, who was covered in so many tattoos and piercings he wouldn't have looked out of place in the *Guinness Book of Records*. Kezzie introduced him as Gavin, known as Space Cadet, who was an amiable giant ('and hugely clever' according to Kezzie), who had earned his moniker from the way he'd get distracted by his fascination in all things botanical.

'Did you know the botanical name for weed is *cannabis sativa?*' he was saying. 'You can grow it anywhere, you know.'

'Well, we're not growing it here,' said Kezzie firmly.

There were also two elderly ladies called June and Flo, who despite looking as though they belonged in the WI, possessed filthy laughs, a dirty sense of humour, and were veterans of Greenham Common, according to Kezzie. Joel was somewhat stunned to discover it was they who were the lesbians.

The party was completed by Tom, a morose young man who barely spoke, except when he was waxing forth about the state of the planet and giving gloomy predictions that global warming was accelerating at a speed beyond which the world had been told.

'It's a cover-up, I tell you,' he was earnestly discussing Wikileaks with Gavin, 'they're all in it together.'

'You think everything is a cover-up,' said Kezzie, with fondness. 'There aren't enough conspiracy theories in the world to satisfy you.'

Kezzie clearly treated Tom like a daft little brother, but from the adoration that Joel was amused to see in his eyes, he was evidently besotted with her.

They might have been a motley crew, but Joel quickly realized they worked well as a team. Kezzie and Flick concentrated on hacking down bushes and carrying rubbish away, while Tom and Gavin put their not inconsiderable muscles to use, digging over the ground. Flo and June dug in the compost, or where there was already space for them, put in some bedding plants which the Parish Council had supplied. And as more people slowly joined in, Kezzie, Flick and Gavin soon got them helping out in the most efficient ways. Before his eyes, the gardens were being slowly transformed.

Joel helped with the digging in between attending to Sam, who fortunately seemed quite happy gurgling in his buggy and watching proceedings.

By mid morning one complete bed had been cleared and Flo and June were readying themselves to fill it with bizzie lizzies, verbena, pansies and geraniums.

They spent most of the time in raucous fits of laughter, and Joel soon found it was infectious. It was impossible not to laugh with them, and Joel felt a sudden zestful feeling about the glory of being alive on such a wonderful day, doing something so useful. He looked over to where Sam was chewing contentedly on his buggy book, and was filled with an overwhelming joy of being with his son, shot through with sadness that Claire wasn't here to share the moment. But for once the joy seemed stronger than the sadness. He'd lost Sam's mother, but Sam gave him a lot to live for. And over the last few months he'd really begun to feel life was worth living again.

In the end Sam started getting fractious, so Joel said to Kezzie, 'Sorry, I think that's my lot. I'll come down again tomorrow if you like.'

'Not to worry, we've got reinforcements coming,' said Kezzie, as Lauren and Troy approached, with the twins dancing between them. 'Do you fancy coming back to mine later and having a drink with us all? We usually crack open a bottle when we've been working together. I'll ask Lauren too. You can bring Sam if you like. I should think we'll all be too knackered to be too raucous.'

'Sounds great,' said Joel. 'I'll see you there.'

'Hi Lauren, Troy.' He felt forced to acknowledge Troy's presence, but felt like punching the guy on the nose. He had such a self-satisfied air about him, and seemed to be almost proprietorial about Lauren, touching her arm constantly, as if he somehow had some claim over her. Why couldn't she see it?

'So how's it going?' Flick said, as she and Kezzie transported another load of branches to the skip the council had provided.

'The garden?' said Kezzie. 'It's fantastic. I'll ask Joel if we can go and look at it later, if you like.'

'Durr!' said Flick. 'Not the garden, dummy. I'm talking about Richard. Have you heard from him at all?'

'Oh,' said Kezzie, heaving a particularly heavy branch into the skip. 'Richard.'

'Well?'

'Well, nothing,' said Kezzie. 'I emailed him to

ask for some advice about contacting gardening celebrities, which he did, but he also made it clear he doesn't want any more contact. End of story. It's over.'

'Oh, Kez, I'm so sorry.' Flick came over and gave Kezzie a huge hug.

'Don't,' said Kezzie, her lip wobbling, 'otherwise, I'm going to be a puddle.'

'OK, OK,' said Flick, backing off. 'Did you at least get any contacts out of it?'

'I'm working on it,' said Kezzie, as they wandered back to pick up more garden rubbish. 'Couldn't find anyone to help us with the Memorial Gardens, but I have been talking to Anthony Grantham's agent – you know the guy who presents *Dig It!* – and he may do a piece on Edward's garden at the Summer Fest.'

'See,' Flick dug Kezzie in the ribs, 'there's always a silver lining.'

'I suppose,' said Kezzie, dragging a massive branch back to the skip. 'I just need to work out a way of getting over Richard permanently.'

'What you need is to get out there again,' said Flick. 'Surely there must be someone interesting here.'

'In Heartsease? I don't think so!' said Kezzie.

'What about Joel?' argued Flick. 'He seems nice.'

Kezzie sighed, 'Been there, done that, realized it wouldn't work. Joel's great, but we're friends, nothing more.'

'What about him?' Flick pointed over to Troy, who was helping Gavin dig up a flowerbed. He'd taken his top off to reveal a sixpack which was both toned and tanned to perfection.

'Troy? Puh-lease!' snorted Kezzie. 'He's Lauren's ex, and very very bad news. Wouldn't touch him with a barge pole.'

'So what are you going to do?'

'Nothing,' said Kezzie. 'I'm just going to wait till I'm over Richard. It has to happen sometime.'

Lauren had had a great day. To begin with she'd been helping Flo and June planting the bedding plants with the twins. The girls had enjoyed digging and got thoroughly muddy. Flo and June had been immensely patient with them, and let them help plant the bedding plants, while not appearing to mind too much that a lot of the flowers had been decapitated by the time they went in.

'Oh well, saves us dead-heading them,' Flo had twinkled. 'And they're so enthusiastic, the pets, I wouldn't like to stop them helping.'

Enthusiastic. That was *one* way to describe the way both girls threw themselves wholeheartedly into every activity, whatever their ability.

Later on Lauren had worked with Kezzie and Flick cutting down bushes, and enjoyed some rare girlie chat, most of which centred around Flick and Gavin's athletic sex life.

'You did what?' giggled Lauren. 'How on earth did you manage that?' as Flick described one particularly gymnastic kind of manoeuvre.

'Well, what can I say?' grinned Flick. 'That man is an animal.'

'Grrr, tiger, watch him roar,' said Kezzie, and they all collapsed in fits of laughter.

'What's so funny?' Gavin wanted to know.

'Oh, nothing,' Flick said innocently.

'Grr,' said Kezzie, and the three of them laughed some more.

'Honestly,' said Lauren, tears streaming down her face, as Gavin walked away puzzled. 'I don't know when I last laughed like that.'

She wiped the tears away.

'You've got a smudge now,' said Kezzie. 'Really, Lauren, you need to get out more.'

'Well it's not that easy,' said Lauren.

'I know,' said Kezzie. 'But now he's here, why don't you make more use of Troy? If he means what he says, he should take a bit more responsibility for the girls.'

'That's true,' said Lauren, 'but it is still early days. I want him to get to know the girls better before I start leaving them with him too often. That's why I got him to come along today.'

'Doesn't look like he's doing too badly,' said Flick. They watched Troy take a break from digging and play around with the girls, taking it in turns to throw each one over his shoulder.

'It doesn't, does it?' said Lauren with a smile. Maybe Troy would be here for the duration after all. She was beginning to allow herself the small smidgeon of hope that he would. And in her weaker moments the flame of attraction that she had felt when he first showed up was growing stronger. She was wondering if she shouldn't perhaps fan it some more.

'You are coming round to mine tonight, aren't you?' said Kezzie, over fish and chips, which Gavin and Flick had gone to get for lunch.

'I'm not sure,' said Lauren. 'I haven't got a sitter.'

'Bring the girls,' said Kezzie. 'It's only informal drinks. I told Joel to bring Sam.'

'You won't be smoking anything funny, will you?' said Lauren. She'd recently spotted the little plastic bag that Flick had given Kezzie on the kitchen window sill and clearly disapproved.

'*No.* Cross my heart and hope to die,' said Kezzie. 'I know what I told you about Emily, but really, I wouldn't do that round kids. Come on. It'll be a laugh. It won't be the same without you.'

'Oh go on then,' said Lauren, 'you've twisted my arm.'

'It will do you good to have some fun for once,' said Kezzie.

Lauren sat back in the sunshine munching her chips, watching the twins running around with Troy. Kezzie was right, it would do her good to get out. Today had been great fun, and the evening should round it off nicely.

Edward and Lily

1916–1917

Lily's diary, October 1916
Life has changed for us since this terrible war started. No one talks any longer of it being over soon. We were naive, I think, to imagine it could ever be over by Christmas.

Edward takes the train every day to work at the

Ministry of Agriculture, and Connie and I help out at Chiverton Hospital. It is hard work, and often distressing. I find I am not very well suited to bandaging the men's wounds; Connie has the stomach much more than I. But I can sit and listen to their stories. Many of them suffer terribly with their nerves. I understand their pain very much, even if I cannot imagine their experiences. At first I thought I could be no good to them, but happily I find I can help.

When war had come Edward was grateful that Harry was still too young to fight. He had hoped, initially, that the war would be over before he was old enough to join up, but since he'd turned eighteen, Harry had been desperate to go and do his bit, but Lily kept begging him to stay. And the stories that came back from the Front were growing ever more desperate. Though Edward wanted Harry to do his duty for his country, he was under no illusion as to what that might involve. And when Connie brought home George Forrester, one of the convalescent soldiers whom she'd met in Chiverton, Edward fretted for her future happiness.

It is clear to me that Connie is very much in love with George, who is a fine and upstanding young man, whom on discovering his own parents are dead, we have happily taken under our wing, he wrote in his diary. In former times, this would have been a source of great happiness to me. Loath as I am to lose my daughter, I can only rejoice if she has found a man who can make her as happy as Lily makes me. But I fear her happiness may be shortlived. George will soon return to the Front, and who is to say what will hap-

pen then?

But seeing how Connie flourished and sparkled in George's presence, his love bringing her a confidence and happiness he had never before seen in her, Edward could not deny his daughter. When, one sunny evening, the young lovers emerged, radiant and shining from a tryst in the sunken garden, Edward immediately knew the question George was going to pose him, as well as the answer he would give.

'George is returning to the Front shortly,' said Connie, 'so we will wait until his return to marry. After all, the war cannot go on forever. He'll soon come back to us.'

His brave, pragmatic, sensible daughter. How little any one of them understood how necessary those qualities would be in the coming months.

Edward was sitting at his writing desk, looking out of the window one sunny day in July, when he espied a small figure toiling up the hill on a bicycle. As the figure grew nearer, he recognized the boy who delivered telegrams and his stomach plummeted.

At first, he recorded in his diary, *I thought the telegram might not be for us, but then the boy climbed off his bicycle and turned down our path. I knew the telegram would be for Connie. I couldn't bear to think of her going through the heartache so many other families had endured. I leapt to my feet to get to the door before Connie did, but I was too late.*

Edward flung open the door of his study to see Connie standing pale and motionless, the door still held open for the boy, who was now making his way back down the path. She clutched the telegram to her breast. Her breathing was laboured, but she stood so still, she might have been a statue. Seeing her father, she mutely held the telegram towards him.

'George?' he said gently.

'Missing, presumed dead it says,' said Connie, a slight tremble in her voice the only sign of emotion. 'That means he might still be alive.'

'Of course,' soothed Edward, privately thinking it very unlikely, as he held his daughter in his arms. 'We mustn't give up hope.'

Lily came in from the garden just then, holding a spray of freesias she'd picked. Seeing Connie in her father's arms, she gave a slight scream of 'No!' Lily had come to love George as another son, but Edward suspected the fears she'd had for his safety were somehow bound up in her fear that Harry, too, would ultimately go off to fight.

Connie laid herself against Edward's chest, not saying anything, and Lily came over and hugged her daughter close, in an uncommon sign of affection. She looked at Edward with tears in her eyes. 'Why?' she said. 'Why poor George? Why poor Connie?'

But Edward had no answer for that. He wished he could wipe away Connie's pain, the way he had wiped tears, and patched up wounds, when she was a child. Now there was nothing he could do, and he watched helplessly as Connie moved away from him and stayed, staring mutely out of the window all that day and the next. She couldn't be persuaded to eat, or sleep.

'Why doesn't she cry?' Lily said. 'I couldn't

stand to be so silent and still. I don't think I could bear it, if it were me and you. And if anything ever happened to Harry...'

Her voice broke off and she looked away. Edward, knowing how real and vivid the fear of losing Harry was to her, took her hands and caressed them. 'Harry will be fine,' he soothed, 'and Connie is grieving in her own way. We should let her be.'

But even he was astonished when, on the third day after receiving the telegram, Connie rose as normal, and started to write letters to anyone and everyone who might possibly know what had happened to her beloved George. As the weeks went by and George's name had still not turned up on the prisoners' lists, Edward tried to prepare his daughter for the worst. But stubbornly she wouldn't listen, staying up late at night, wearing herself to the bone, reading and writing letters till she was hollow-eyed and quite thin. Edward worried that she was making herself ill, but if he tried to tell her to ease off, she would look at him blankly and say, 'I have to do this, for George. Until I know for sure.'

And the day eventually arrived when she finally heard from George's commanding officer.

Dear Miss Handford, the letter read,
In response to your request for further information in regard to George Forrester I can now be sure of the following.
On the night of --- July the ---- Platoon were engaged with the enemy for the duration of twelve hours. During this time several men witnessed George

in the thick of the action, but no one reported any sighting of him after 0600 hours. It was said that he fought with exceptional bravery.

In the course of the battle we were heavily out-numbered, and the retreat was sounded. But half the platoon was caught behind enemy lines, and of those we know, a substantial number to have been captured. For the rest we must assume the worst.

After nightfall a daring group was able to make a hazardous escape over the river. But sadly, George was not of their number.

Although George's body was never found, I have to conclude that he perished in that battle in the early hours of the morning of June --- Rest assured that he died a hero.

Yours...

Connie put the letter down, and for the first time in months her facade crumbled.

Lily and Edward both caught her as she fell, and Lily gently took her up to bed.

This wretched war, Edward wrote in his diary, *when will it ever end? I fear so badly for Harry. He keeps saying he wants to enlist, and though I know it will break Lily's heart, I also know he wants to do his duty. How can I stop him from doing what he believes to be right?*

Lily's diary, September 1917
Today Harry left for the Front. He looked so noble in his uniform; I declare he was the most handsome young man there. But oh! He looked so young. Too young to be going off to fight. I cannot bear it. He was

so cheerful and jolly as he left, giving me a hug and a kiss and promising to write soon. He thinks it is all one big adventure. His father and I know so different. And as I waved him off, trying to fight back the tears so he could not see them, I was overcome with a cold terror. I feel as I did all those years ago when I lost my babies. I have let something precious slip through my fingers. What will I do if I never see my beloved boy again?

Chapter Twenty-One

The party was in full swing by the time Lauren got there. Kezzie had invited several of the committee, and Eileen was talking enthusiastically about the work that had been done.

'Have you seen what these young people have achieved?' she was saying. 'The gardens haven't looked this good in years.'

Lauren took the girls' hands and wandered through the throng to find Kezzie pouring drinks in the kitchen and talking nineteen to the dozen. She seemed a bit merry already when Lauren said hello, but soon composed herself and pointed Lauren in the direction of the garden so the girls could run around.

Lauren got drinks for the girls and headed outside. Kezzie had lit up the garden with fairy lights, strategically placed among the bushes, and set her garden chairs out on the patio in between the planters, which Kezzie had recently planted up with heartsease, primula and a few petunias. It looked lovely.

'Ooh pretty,' said the girls, clapping their hands in delight. They were pleased to find Sam toddling outside, watched by an eagle-eyed Joel. She was pleased to see him too. Too often these days their exchanges were fleeting.

'Where's Troy?'

'I've no idea,' said Lauren, feeling put out that that should be the first thing Joel asked. It felt like she'd not seen Joel for ages, and she'd been looking forward to a proper chat. 'Why should I?'

'Oh. I thought you'd have come with him,' said Joel.

'Why would I do that?' said Lauren, slightly puzzled. What on earth was Joel getting at?

'It's just that you seem joined at the hip these days,' said Joel.

'What?' Now Lauren was really bewildered.

'Just— I thought—' Joel's voice trailed off. 'Never mind what I thought.'

'Oh my God. You think Troy and I are back together,' said Lauren, the penny dropping. She felt furious that Joel would assume such a thing, conveniently forgetting that in moments of weakness this didn't seem such a bad idea. 'Well, I can assure you categorically that we're not.'

'He just seems to be around such a lot,' said Joel. 'I was worried about you. And I just assumed...'

'Well don't,' said Lauren. 'Don't assume.'

There was an angry silence. Lauren was infuriated that Joel of all people should be interfering in her life.

'I can look after myself you know,' said Lauren.

265

'I'm not saying you can't,' said Joel. 'I was just worried that given your past with Troy, he might muck you around again. I care about you, Lauren – as a friend. I'd hate to see that.'

'Well, a) Troy is the father of my children, so of course I will be seeing a lot of him,' said Lauren, 'and b) it is possible for a person to change you know, and c) it's none of your damned business.'

'I'm sorry,' said Joel, looking wretched. 'I only want to help. I'm not sure that Troy is all that good for you.'

Lauren's fury erupted. 'You're not *jealous,* are you? My God. I actually think you are. Come on girls, we're going home.'

'But we want to play with Sam,' said the girls.

'Five minutes,' said Lauren. 'And then we have to go.'

She glared at Joel, who looked back at her, unhappily. Why did he have to go and ruin things?

At 9 p.m. Joel decided to call it a day. Sam had crashed in his buggy and Lauren, the only person he really wanted to talk to, had long since gone. He'd tried to apologize again, but she wouldn't have it. He was aware that in his misery, he'd probably had a bit too much to drink. Whoops. Drunk in charge of a toddler. At least he'd had the sense to walk; he should be able to make it home in one piece.

Joel was usually so circumspect with his drinking, worrying ever since Claire had died that if he got in the habit of drinking heavily he would be in trouble. But Lauren had rattled him tonight. It was as though a veil had been drawn from his

266

eyes. Lauren was right. He was, he realized, very jealous. While Kezzie had come along like a catalyst, to open up his eyes to the fact that he could start to live again, he suddenly understood that all along there'd been someone special right under his nose.

Lauren was the one person who'd been there for him more than anyone else since Claire died. She'd loved Claire too, and in the early days she had patiently listened to him talking endlessly about her. She had been great with Sam too, treating him like one of her own children. How could he have been so blind? All this time he'd had lots of short and unfulfilling flings, and there had been the possibility of happiness there, right under his nose. He wondered if it was too late to persuade Lauren that what she needed right now in her life was him.

'What do you think I should do, Sammy boy?' he said to his sleeping son, as he squeezed the buggy past the street lights outside Lauren's house. The lights in Lauren's house were still on; Troy was still at the party. Sam dozed contentedly in the buggy.

'You're right, I should tell her,' said Joel. 'Faint heart, never won fair lady.' Taking a deep breath, he rang the doorbell.

Lauren came to the door.

'Oh. It's you.'

This wasn't exactly the answer he was hoping for.

'May I come in?' said Joel. 'I won't be long. I've got to get Sam off to bed.'

'All right,' said Lauren.

267

'I'm sorry about earlier,' he said. 'You're right. What you and Troy get up to is none of my business.'

'Too right it's not,' said Lauren.

'It's just – well – you were also right about something else.'

'Oh?'

'Yes.' Joel felt his palms sweating. Lauren's body language was hostile to say the least. She didn't exactly seem enthusiastic about him being there, but he ploughed on.

'I am jealous. I've been a bloody idiot and never seen it before. But, Lauren, you're lovely. You've been wonderful to me and Sam. And I think I'm in love with you.'

To his dismay, Lauren burst out laughing.

'Now I've heard it all,' she said. 'You mean, you're in love with the idea of me being a mum to Sam and looking after you. Go home, Joel. You've had too much to drink. I'll see you on Monday and we'll forget this conversation ever took place.'

'Relight my fire!' Kezzie was warbling with Flick. She was having a great time. She'd forgotten how much fun she'd had with her mates, and how much she missed them. She'd discussed the Richard situation with Flick endlessly, and they'd agreed there was probably no way back now; the thought made her feel bleak and lonely.

'May I steal my lovely girlfriend?' Gavin appeared by her side and whisked Flick away to dance.

Kezzie sighed. Much as she loved Gavin and

Flick it was tough being around such happy couples when your own love life was so disastrous, no matter how much you loved them. She'd even seen Eileen and Tony, who were rather coy about their friendship, disappear off together.

Feeling sorry for herself, and hit by a sudden low, she wandered out to the garden to roll herself a joint. She'd promised Lauren she wouldn't smoke around the kids, but they'd gone home some time ago. One couldn't hurt, and it would soothe her fractious nerves. Kezzie sat down on the bench and rolled herself a spliff. She took a deep puff and sat back with her eyes shut, before exhaling slowly. Oh the glory of that first puff. Immediately she felt her worries recede and a calmness coming over her.

'Mind if I join you?' Troy appeared silently by her side.

Oh God, that was all she needed. What was he doing here?

'I didn't want to smoke inside,' he said by way of explanation, taking out a light.

He glanced sneakily across at her. 'Is that what I think it is?'

'Might be,' she said, touching her nose.

He gave her a long, sensuous look, which to her surprise made her shiver inside. He really did scrub up quite well. The thought made her giggle.

'Care to share the joke?'

'That's for me to know and you to find out,' Kezzie winked at him and took another puff. Suddenly the world seemed a happier place. She was at one with everything and feeling more relaxed than she had done all evening. She didn't even mind that Troy was here. She'd thought him good looking when she first met him, but hadn't realized quite how attractive he was.

'It'll cost you,' she said with a grin.

'Cost me what?' he said softly, moving in slightly closer to her.

'That depends...' Kezzie was feeling reckless, she had a sudden impulsive feeling that anything was possible right now.

'Are you flirting with me?' Troy asked mock accusingly, leaning towards her in a highly suggestive way.

'Might be,' said Kezzie, leaning towards him in response. She felt a small tingle of excitement. He really was very sexy. She pushed the thought away, guiltily, remembering his past history with Lauren. Lauren was her mate, she really shouldn't go there. 'This is good stuff. Care to share?'

They shared the rest of the joint and Kezzie felt the world and her troubles disappear to a faraway shore.

She and Troy talked and talked. A rambling disconnected kind of conversation that seemed somehow effortlessly sublime and meaningful, as if they'd plumbed the depths of the universe. She was dimly aware that she felt quite pleasantly sleepy and Troy's shoulder was very comfy. She came to with someone – Troy? – shaking her hard and saying, 'You really need to go to bed.'

'Bed. What a good idea.' Kezzie suddenly woke up a little and giggled.

Lips on hers. A stubbly chin. A not unpleasant sensation. Hang on, what was going on? Oh. *That* was going on.

'Troy, what are you doing?' she said, but her words sounded far away, and she felt she was stuck in a tunnel, watching from a long distance as Troy took another Kezzie upstairs and laid her gently on the bed. The other Kezzie seemed out for the count. Sleep. An even better idea. Her vision slewed down to a single dot. 'Night, night,' she mumbled, and then everything went black.

Chapter Twenty-Two

'Ouch, my head hurts.' Kezzie woke to find sun pouring through her bedroom window, and the realization that she was lying on top of her duvet dressed in her t-shirt and knickers. How had she got there?

She blinked. Her throat felt dry and rough, her head ached and she thought that if she moved too fast she might just throw up. She had no memory of getting undressed. No memory of coming to bed. Shit, shit and double shit. What had she done?

She vaguely remembered smoking a joint in the garden, drinking like it was going out of fashion, and staggering up the stairs snogging – oh no–

'Oh my God, Troy!' She sat bolt upright on the bed. Had she really been snogging Troy? What on earth must she have been thinking? Well, that was the problem of course. Rational thought hadn't come into anything. Otherwise she wouldn't have ended up all over Lauren's ex, who hitherto hadn't impressed her in the slightest. Though she did vaguely recall an alcohol-hazed attraction.

And where on earth was Troy now? Please God nothing worse had happened.

Gingerly, she got out of bed, threw some clothes on, and went downstairs to see what carnage awaited her. 'Urgh,' she said, surveying the scene. The place looked hideous. There was something to be said for Richard's methodical approach to life. He'd have had everything tidied in bin bags and put away the previous night, rather than be left with the fag ends, beer cans, spilt wine and empty crisp packets that greeted Kezzie. 'Double urgh.' Someone had left a whole can of Special Brew, another person hadn't quite finished their vodka. It was too early in the morning to even think about alcohol, let alone smell the remains of someone's leftovers. Someone was curled up in a sleeping bag under the dining room table. Someone rolled over and sat up. Oh my God, Troy. What was he still doing there?

'Well, hi there, sexy,' said Troy. 'Why don't you come and snuggle down with me?'

'I don't think that's a good idea,' said Kezzie.

'You seemed so keen last night.' Troy actually winked at her.

Kezzie felt like she wanted to throw up.

'Last night should never have happened,' said Kezzie firmly, wishing she knew exactly what *had* happened.

'And you and me were *so* good together,' said Troy.

'Oh my God we didn't?' Kezzie swallowed. She hadn't felt so mortified since her student days, when she'd woken up after an all nighter next to the right-wing president of the Student Conservative Society.

'No,' admitted Troy, 'sadly not. But not from want of trying. You know it's not very good for a guy's ego when his latest conquest collapses in a drunken heap on the bed.'

'Sorry,' said Kezzie, awkwardly. 'Actually, what do I mean? I'm not sorry. I didn't mean to lead you on. I was drunk and I was stoned. Under normal circumstances I wouldn't have touched you with a bargepole.'

'That's flattering,' said Troy.

'But true,' said Kezzie. 'You. Me. It's a car crash waiting to happen. But if it makes you feel better, it's not you, it's me.'

'It never is,' said Troy.

'In this case, it really is,' said Kezzie. 'I'm not over my ex, and I'm a complete mess relationship-wise. You really would be better off without me.'

'It's OK,' said Troy. 'Spare me the remorse. I'm not *that* into you.'

Now it was her turn to feel deflated, and more embarrassed than she thought it was possible to be, Kezzie escaped into the kitchen to make herself a cup of tea.

'Hair of the dog?' Gavin emerged from the lounge where he and Flick had kipped.

'I think I might just throw up,' said Kezzie.

'What you need is a nice fry-up and some fresh air,' announced Flick, who had followed him out, looking disgustingly chipper. 'Is there a decent café round here?'

'There's a good one on the High Street,' said Kezzie. 'Anything's got to be better than clearing up this mess.' She could almost hear Richard tut under his breath, and say *You'll only have to do it later.*

'Bugger off out of my head, Richard,' she muttered. 'It's my life, not yours.'

Joel, too, awoke with a hangover. But unlike Kezzie, he didn't have the luxury of sleeping it off. He was woken by a screaming Sam at 6 a.m. A late night hadn't affected his internal alarm clock at all. Reluctantly Joel got himself out of bed, sorted Sam out, and then poured himself a cup of strong, black coffee. It was 7 a.m. and the day stretched ahead of him – one when he was also going to have to drive over to Chiverton to take his mum out for lunch. It was, Joel felt, going to be a very long day.

By nine o'clock, he and Sam were all played out, and Sam was clamouring for the park. So he got the buggy out, strapped Sam into it, and set off down the hill. He paused at the end of Lauren's road, wondering if she'd welcome him coming round with another apology, and decided that would make matters worse, and more embarrassing all round. He was kicking himself for first, allowing himself to get drunk, and second, letting go of his inhibitions enough for him to have made a complete fool of himself. He was never going to be able to face Lauren again.

At the Memorial Gardens, he found Tom working on the flowerbeds alone. Apparently he was the only one without a hangover, and had got up early to make the most of the day. Sam was happy in his buggy for a bit, so Joel helped Tom start on a bed they hadn't touched the previous day. Gradually, the others appeared: Flo and June arriving first, laughing raucously at the state of them. 'You youngsters!' June said. 'No staying power.'

'In our day we'd dance all night and get up and do a day's work in the factory,' said Flo. 'No stamina, this lot.'

Eventually Kezzie appeared looking rather green, followed by Gavin and Flick, who didn't, and they all started working again in a desultory fashion.

'Good night?' grinned Joel, taking the opportunity to down tools and get ready to go to his mum's.

'Not really,' said Kezzie. 'I drank too much and made a total prat of myself.'

'Ditto,' said Joel.

'Why? What did you do that's worse than snogging Troy?' said Kezzie.

'Bloody hell,' said Joel, who felt quite shocked. He'd been so sure that Troy was going to make a move on Lauren. What a two-faced bastard he was. 'How on earth did you let that happen? I didn't think you were keen on Troy.'

'I'm not,' said Kezzie, 'and I know, I know, Lauren's my friend, and I should have definitely not gone there. I feel really bad about it. But he does have a certain seedy charm, and he was certainly more appealing through an alcoholic haze. I really am getting too old for this kind of thing. I think I may never drink again.'

'You're not the only one,' said Joel with feeling.

275

He cringed internally as he remembered the look on Lauren's face.

'So what did you do then?' said Kezzie. 'It can't be as bad as that.'

Joel sighed. He couldn't believe how cut up he was feeling about Lauren's rejection of him, or what a fool he was for recognizing his feelings for her too late.

'After I left the party I went round to Lauren's and told her I was jealous of Troy and that I was in love with her,' said Joel.

'About time too,' said Kezzie. 'You two are made for each other.'

'Unfortunately, Lauren doesn't agree with you,' said Joel, with a grimace.

'Ah,' said Kezzie.

'In fact, she laughed in my face,' said Joel, with a groan. 'How humiliating is that?'

'OK, you win on the humiliation front,' said Kezzie. 'How did you leave things?'

'It is never to be spoken of again,' said Joel. 'What about you?'

'Well, I was incredibly mature and ran out of the house,' said Kezzie. 'But basically I'm following the same idea as you.'

'We're pathetic,' said Joel. 'Lonely Hearts Club, eat your heart out.'

'Oh well. At least *we're* mates,' said Kezzie. 'And nothing can go wrong with *that*.'

Lauren didn't have a hangover. But she'd had a bad night's sleep nonetheless.

What on earth had Joel been thinking, coming on to her like that? OK it was obvious that the drink was talking, but really. She'd watched him seduce half the village. Why did he think he could get the better of her and that she'd fall for the charms that had broken hearts for miles around? Maybe it was her previous form with losers that made her seem like an easy target. If that was the case, then she was really cross. It implied Joel thought she was a pushover. And she wasn't. Not any more.

Although ... she had to admit. Despite her better judgement, Troy was beginning to win her round. He was kind and considerate whenever she worked in the pub, he had not missed a single day with the girls, who were really enjoying having him around, and she had to admit she'd been impressed by his plans for a community centre. Maybe he'd finally grown up and was preparing to settle down at last. If he was... Lauren allowed herself a brief wild daydream of them getting back together. All she'd ever wanted was the girls to have their dad, and Troy to want her again the way he'd wanted her when they first met.

The doorbell rang and Lauren immediately revised her opinion of Troy's grown-up status.

'You look a right mess,' she said, surveying him with dismay. He hadn't shaved, he was still in the clothes he was wearing the previous day, and he stank of beer and fags. She didn't want the kids seeing him like this.

'That's a nice welcome,' said Troy.

'Well, it's true,' said Lauren in exasperation. 'Have you looked in a mirror lately?'

'Haven't dared,' said Troy. 'Any chance of a cuppa?'

'Not until you've had a shower,' said Lauren, 'you stink.'

'But you love me really,' said Troy, with a cheeky grin. 'Care to join me?'

'Don't push your luck,' said Lauren. She put the kettle on while Troy showered, feeling all at sea. Joel had unsettled her last night with his declaration of undying love. She was sure he didn't mean it really, it was the booze talking, but now, holding him in the light against Troy, she felt confused. Lauren had been on the verge of letting Troy back into her life, but seeing him like this had put her off again. And while she didn't think she wanted Joel either, there was a part of her that didn't know *what* she wanted.

Troy emerged twenty minutes later looking much better, though he hadn't shaved, and his stubble made him seem that bit more attractive.

'Good night was it?' Lauren kept her tone light to cover up her inner turmoil. Why did Troy make her feel like this? If only it was as straightforward as saying, he's no good, I don't fancy him.

'So good, I crashed next door,' said Troy.

'Who's the unlucky lady?' said Lauren.

'Why do you assume there has to be a lady?' said Troy in plaintive tones.

'Because you're a predictable tosser,' said Lauren. Despite herself, she felt disappointed. She'd thought Troy was on the verge of changing and becoming responsible, she'd clearly thought wrong.

'I found a sleeping bag which seemed spare and crashed on the floor if you must know.'

'Yeah, right,' said Lauren. 'I so believe that.'

'It happens to be true.' Troy looked quite hurt

that she didn't believe him.

'Whatever,' said Lauren, trying not to show her relief, 'it's none of my business. Where's everyone else?'

'They're all back at the Memorial Gardens,' said Troy. 'I just thought with it being a sunny day, you and the girls might like to go for a picnic. If you get everything ready, I'll pop home and come back and pick you up in half an hour.'

Though irritated with his assumption that she would prepare the picnic, Lauren couldn't help being pleased that Troy had asked. It was worth it to see the girls' faces as well.

'OK, then,' she said. 'Lucky for you, I went shopping yesterday.'

'I'll be back soon,' said Troy. 'Don't you go anywhere, now.'

'And where would I go in Heartsease?' said Lauren, laughing. 'Go on, we'll see you later.'

Chapter Twenty-Three

'Come on, Sam,' said Joel. 'Here's Nanny. We're going to take her out for the day.'

His mother was waiting outside her flat, leaning on her stick. He always told her not to do that, but she nearly always insisted on being ready at least half an hour before he arrived, 'just in case.' She never explained in case of what, and in vain Joel tried to persuade her it wouldn't be much good if she tripped over, but she dismissed him with a 'Don't be daft, I can still get out of the house on my own, you know.'

'Nana!' said Sam, clapping his hands as Joel helped his mother to the car.

'Who's my beautiful boy?' Joel's mum kissed her grandson.

'You do realize he's actually saying banana, don't you, Mum?' teased Joel. 'It's his favourite fruit.'

'Shh,' said his mother. 'He knows his beautiful nana when he sees her, don't you, darling?'

'Nana, Nana!' Sam said again.

'See,' said his mum with a smug smile, 'he does know it's me.'

When they'd got to the old country pub Joel had chosen for lunch, he produced a folder with some of the documents he and Kezzie had found.

'Oh, Mum, I thought you might be interested in looking at some of the stuff Kezzie and I have found out about Edward Handford,' said Joel. 'We're going to put together an exhibition for the Heartsease Summer Fete. Or rather Kezzie is. She seems to be pretty good at that kind of thing.'

'That's wonderful,' said his mum. 'And how's the garden getting on?'

'Brilliant,' said Joel. 'Kezzie's done a great job. Next time, I'll bring you over to have a look. Anyway, we're a bit stuck with some of the photos, I'm not sure who everyone is and I wondered if you'd know.'

'Show me,' said his mother, as she put her reading glasses on.

'Ah, now, that,' she said, pointing out a picture of the family in the garden, 'that picture I remember.

My grandmother had a copy on her wall. She was Lily's youngest daughter, you know. Her name was Tilly. That's her, there,' Joel's mother pointed to a young woman who looked very sombre, 'and that's Connie, the eldest, and Harry the son. Very sad, that. He's the one who died in the First World War. Edward and Lily are sitting down.'

'Do you know who this is?' Joel pointed to a young man in military uniform, standing next to Connie.

'Oh, that must be Connie's fiancé,' said Mum.

'I thought Connie married a bank manager,' said Joel.

'Oh, she did eventually. Uncle Phillip,' said Mum. 'But she lost her first fiancé at the Somme. Very tragic.'

'Why didn't we have anything to do with them and the house?' said Joel.

'I'm not really sure, to be honest,' said Mum. 'Connie and Tilly fell out. Something to do with Tilly's husband, my granddad – whether Connie was in love with him or not, I don't know. But anyway, Connie stayed looking after Edward here, on her own, and later when she married, Uncle Phillip moved in too. We only came to visit Edward a couple of times when I was small, and both times Connie was out.'

Her face looked dreamy. 'I remember going as a child once, and meeting Edward for the first time. I thought he'd be very stern and old, but he was sweet and rather sad. He could never get my name right. He always called me Lily.'

'Maybe you reminded him of her,' said Joel. 'That's sad in a way.'

'Yes,' said Mum. 'My mother always said he never got over Lily's death. They were very much in love I believe. Look here, you can see it from their wedding photos.'

It was true. Mum had found a very faded sepia photo in the folder, of Lily and Edward in formal wedding garb. Despite the severity of the photo style, you could see the sense of fun in Lily's eyes, and the pleasure in Edward's face, bubbling out of the photo.

'The last time I saw Edward, I'll never forget it. He was confined to his bedroom by then, and Connie had locked up the garden. I broke into it once – it was like a secret garden, but so sad and neglected. Only Edward used to ask after it, and no one would tell him how ruined it was. So I promised him I'd look after it. Hark at me. Only five, I was.' She patted Joel's hand. 'I'm so glad you're restoring the garden,' she said. 'It's good for you to have a focus again. Give you something to think about.'

'Yes,' said Joel, acknowledging the unexpected truth of this. 'It is.'

Lauren found she couldn't feel irritated with Troy for long. He'd provided salmon and champagne as his contribution to the picnic. An extravagant, but not unwelcome gesture. It was such a novelty to have him spend any money on her, she couldn't help but be pleased.

'You clearly haven't done picnics with small people before,' she laughed, as she produced sandwiches, grapes, tomatoes, cucumbers, mini sausages and crisps for the girls.

They'd come to a high spot on the Downs where there was a glorious view of the county. It looked stunning on this wonderfully sunny April day. The grass was high already and waving in the breeze, the fields were full of gorse and heather, and there were catkins on the chestnut trees. Swallows were swooping in the azure blue sky and chaffinches were chirping in the hedgerows.

The girls were having a great time running around, picking daisies, playing with a bat and ball, and imagining fairies in the undergrowth.

Troy turned out to be particularly adept at going along with that game, somewhat to Lauren's surprise. She was doubly impressed, knowing how rough he must be feeling. But she was finding it restful watching them running and playing around together. It was as if she'd had a glimpse of an alternative life – one where they were a proper family.

'Enough. Enough. You two have worn me out,' said Troy laughing, as he came down and flopped next to her. The girls were still happily catching fairies.

'How's the hangover?' said Lauren.

'All the better for running around with my daughters,' he said. 'And one glass of champagne has done wonders to clear my head.'

'So long as you make it just the one glass,' said Lauren.

'Of course,' said Troy. 'I'd never drink and drive with the girls in the car. You know I'd never do anything to hurt them.'

'I know,' said Lauren. And she did know. Troy may have made mistakes in his past, but he was making up for it now.

'And what about you?' said Troy. He gently laced his fingers round hers, and she didn't pull away. 'Do you still think I would hurt you?'

Lauren swallowed. The champagne had gone to her head, giving her a pleasant fizzing feeling. The setting and the moment felt suitably romantic, and she felt herself weaken. But then she thought about Joel, and how confused he'd made her feel. And what a mess Troy had been only that morning. Was she ready to trust him again? Could they really let go of their past and give it another go?

'I don't know,' she said. 'I want to believe you won't, but you let me down so badly before.'

'I know,' he said, and tucked a stray bit of hair behind her ear. 'I was wrong. Very wrong. I'm so afraid of the responsibility, you see. I've realized now I shouldn't run away. Seeing some of those kids in Southampton, and how much it affects them not having their dads about was another thing that made me see I had to be here for the girls. I won't let them down again. I promise you. You do know that, don't you?'

She looked into his eyes and saw only sincerity. Lauren hated herself for doubting him. Troy clearly thought he'd changed, and at least he was trying. Perhaps she should give him another chance. Throwing caution to the wind she leant over and kissed him full on the lips.

'The past is the past,' she said. 'Let's drink to the future.'

By the end of the day, the majority of the paths

had been cleaned and cleared away and all the bedding plants were in. Kezzie was really pleased with the result. The gardens looked fabulous, the beds were bursting with colour, the lawn had been cut, and thanks to Tony, the paths were going to be relaid by the Parish Council during the week. It was a vast improvement on the way they had looked. Tony had turned up with a gardening friend, who'd packed all the rubbish which wouldn't fit in the skips, into his van and taken it to the tip for recycling. Kezzie winked at Eileen, who'd come with them. Eileen blushed and looked away.

'You've done a fantastic job,' said Tony. 'All of you. Eileen and I can't thank you enough.'

'No problem,' said Flick. 'It's been great fun.'

'This is the moment in *Ground Force* when they always brought in the champagne,' said Kezzie. 'Sadly, I don't have any, but there is still some beer at mine if anyone can face it. I am, of course, exempting myself from this.'

Kezzie's hangover and sense of paranoia had worsened as the day went on. She knew Troy and Lauren weren't an item, and Lauren had been very clear that she wasn't planning for them to be, but she felt she'd unwittingly strayed into Lauren's territory, and she didn't like it. Neither did she enjoy being secretive. She'd toyed with the idea of what to do all day, before coming to the conclusion that she should go round with a bottle of wine and fess up to Lauren. That way, they could (she hoped) have a good laugh about it, and get it out of the way, before gossip reached Lauren about what had happened. She liked

Lauren, and the last thing she wanted was for there to be secrets between them.

Thus resolved, Kezzie tried to put her worries about Lauren and Troy aside, and enjoy the rest of the weekend with her friends. She was helped in this aim by a nice surprise on her return home. Not only had Troy gone (Kezzie had been worried he might have hung around), but Flo and June had put the time to good use and cleaned up.

'Oh, thanks you two,' said Kezzie. 'You really didn't need to.'

'Nonsense,' said Flo. 'We haven't had such a laugh in ages, have we, June? It was the least we could do.'

Everyone hung around till the late afternoon, before reluctantly packing up their things and clambering into Gavin's minibus, which had always been used for gardening jobs.

'You will come again soon, won't you?' said Kezzie wistfully. 'I've missed you guys.'

'Come back to London,' urged Flick. 'You can't go burying yourself in the countryside forever.'

'Maybe,' said Kezzie, noncommittally. Part of her would love her old life back, but she had to admit she was putting roots down here. Living in Heartsease was doing her soul good. Leaving, if she ever did – Jo having emailed to say that she was having such a great time she was likely to be away for more than a year – would be a wrench.

Sloughing off the end of weekend melancholy feeling that overtook her once everyone had gone, Kezzie grabbed a bottle of wine. She felt she was just about well enough now to tackle the hair of the dog, and went round to Lauren's to confess all.

The sun was setting as she went up the path, and she saw instantly through the window that Lauren wasn't alone. She was with a man. Oh. Troy was round. That was embarrassing. Kezzie hesitated. Maybe Troy had had the same idea. It probably wasn't the best time to call.

Kezzie could see Lauren turn to face Troy, laughing. And then to Kezzie's astonishment, he pulled her towards him and kissed her on the lips.

Oh my God. The sneaky sod. Straight from trying to seduce her, right into Lauren's arms. He really was the worst kind of shit. No wonder Lauren had been so down on him. But what had made her change her mind? Now what to do?

Paralysed by indecision, Kezzie eventually chose retreat as the best option. She'd come back tomorrow and try and find a way of telling Lauren then, when Troy wasn't around. She took a final look up the path, to see Lauren drawing the curtains, still laughing. She looked so happy. How on earth was Kezzie going to be able to tell her the truth now?

Chapter Twenty-Four

The next morning, Kezzie woke up feeling even worse than she had on Sunday. She'd barely slept all night, fretting about what she was going to do. Lauren wouldn't be at all impressed to discover that her newly restored lover had come on so strongly to her friend on Saturday. Thinking about it, she wasn't even sure that Lauren would believe her. Would she if it were the other way round? It would sound like sour grapes, even though it wasn't. She sighed heavily. She couldn't deal with it now. Best she got to work. She had ivy and rosemary bushes to plant.

Kezzie made her way up to Joel's, past Lauren's house. The curtains were still firmly drawn, leading Kezzie to draw her own conclusions. She couldn't possibly tell Lauren what had really happened on Saturday. Luckily everyone else who knew about it had gone home, and she was assuming Troy wouldn't be so stupid as to come clean. Kezzie hated herself for keeping silent – it went against the grain – but she knew it was the only thing she could do right now.

When she got to Joel's the sun was already strong in the sky, despite the early hour. It was shaping up to be a lovely day.

Joel was already strapping Sam into the car when she arrived.

'You're early today,' she said.

'Yup,' said Joel. 'Didn't want to hang about this morning. I think it's best I drop Sam and run, considering what an idiot I made of myself on Saturday.'

'Ah,' said Kezzie. 'I think I should probably warn you–'

'About what?'

'I'm really sorry. It looks as if Lauren had company last night. I saw Troy go round there, and I haven't seen him leave.'

'Well, he's crashed on the sofa before,' said Joel quickly. 'And Lauren's been adamant that they're not getting back together.'

'Maybe,' said Kezzie. 'But they did look pretty friendly.'

'What a sod!' said Joel. 'To be with you one minute, then end up with Lauren the next. That's pretty crap.'

'I know,' said Kezzie. 'I feel so bad about it.'

'Are you going to tell her?'

'How can I?' said Kezzie. 'Oh, by the way, Lauren, I snogged your boyfriend on Saturday night.'

'I can't say anything,' said Joel. 'She'll think I'm making it up.'

'True,' said Kezzie. 'I guess we'll just have to leave it for now.'

'I guess we will.'

They looked at one another gloomily.

'I just hope she sees sense quickly,' said Kezzie.

When Joel had gone, Kezzie set off down the garden with her barrow loaded with plants that Joel had bought at the garden centre. She was still feeling agitated, but an hour or two in the garden was a great tonic, and by lunchtime, when she stopped to survey her handiwork, she was feeling much calmer. The interwoven pattern of box, ivy and rosemary was beginning to take shape, and she could see the patterns clearly. She had filled in the spaces with her chosen plants, and now she was working on the borders, filling them with heartsease and forget me nots and gloxinia. In a few months she'd transformed the place, and she felt rightly proud of her achievements.

Kezzie still felt bad about what had happened with Troy. She would never have even looked at him sober. And at the moment there was no way she could tell Lauren, so it was better to let sleeping dogs lie. Kezzie couldn't see another way round it, even if it meant Lauren had to find out about Troy the hard way.

Joel walked down the path to Lauren's house with a heavy heart. Not only had he blown it with her, he had the sneaking suspicion he might have sent her running straight into Troy's arms. But there was nothing he could do. If he tried to tell Lauren what a two-timing bugger her boyfriend was, she'd never believe him. Besides, she'd evidently got it fixed in her head he was a lothario, and she wouldn't be interested in anything Joel might have to say on the subject of Troy. If she only knew the complete soullessness and misery of the assignations he'd had since Claire died.

He knocked on the door, and after a little while Lauren answered, looking flustered.

'Oh. Er, Joel. You're early.'

'Yes,' he said. 'Early meeting. So I got here sooner. Hope that's OK.'

'Yes, fine,' said Lauren. 'I'm er – running a bit late.'

Lauren was obviously trying to hide the fact that Troy was there, Joel thought. She was blushing in a completely charming manner and never had she seemed more desirable to Joel. She was positively glowing. He cursed himself for an idiot of monumental proportions for having failed to see it before. Faint heart had lost fair lady, and to an undeserving rat at that.

'Hey, babes, who's there?' Troy's voice floated

from the lounge.

'Just Joel,' said Lauren, blushing scarlet.

Joel was at a loss as to what to do. Should he acknowledge Troy's presence, and add to Lauren's discomfort, or ignore him? His heart was churned up. He couldn't bear to think of Lauren being with anyone but him, but it was particularly galling to think of her with Troy. He opened his mouth to try and say something, but no coherent words seemed to want to come out.

'Lauren–' he began.

'Yes?' She looked at him, so flushed and pretty his courage deserted him. What could he say to her when she looked so happy, knowing that it wasn't him who'd made her so?

Cowardice being the easiest option, he thrust Sam into Lauren's arms.

'Got to go,' he gabbled. 'I'll miss my meeting.'

'Your meeting. Of course,' said Lauren, seemingly glad of the excuse. 'Come on, Sam, let's go and find those girls, shall we?'

Joel fled down the path, part relieved and part infuriated. How could she have gone back to Troy after everything she'd said about him? It didn't seem right.

Lauren spent the day in a cloud. She'd been so reluctant to let Troy back into her life, but it seemed he really had changed. He took the girls to school with her, helped her tidy the house and even came to the park with her and Sam before his afternoon shift at the pub. He promised to come round the next evening, when neither of them was working, happy to settle for a takeaway and night in front of the telly. Something the old Troy would never have contemplated. Lauren was trying not to hope for too much, but suddenly the possibility of a proper family life seemed to be within her grasp. It would be foolish of her not to grab the opportunity with both hands.

Lauren was almost skipping as she pushed Sam's buggy down the road to school in the afternoon. The sun was shining, she thought she might truly be in love, and all seemed right in the world. On the way back up the hill as she was chasing after the twins who'd run on ahead, she bumped into Kezzie coming back from work.

'You're finished early, aren't you?' said Lauren.

'I got to a point where I couldn't do any more. I was waiting a delivery of compost, which hasn't come, and I need some more bedding plants, and by the time I waited for Joel to bring them back from Chiverton it would have been time to pack up anyway. Plus I'm still knackered from the weekend, so I thought I'd call it a day.'

'How's the head?' grinned Lauren. 'You seemed pretty out of it on Saturday.'

'Er, I was.' Kezzie looked shifty and a bit embarrassed.

'You didn't make a fool of yourself, did you?' teased Lauren. 'Only I couldn't help noticing that Tom has a bit of a thing going for you.'

'No, no, nothing like that.' Kezzie seemed determined to drop the subject.

'Ooh, you sly dog you,' said Lauren, in delight. 'You did do something with Tom.'

'I didn't, really I didn't,' said Kezzie, looking even more mortified.

'Don't believe you,' said Lauren, grinning. 'You look like you've got a guilty conscience. Go on, who was he?'

'Will you just leave it!' Kezzie snapped. 'Nothing happened.'

'Oh.' Lauren was staggered. Kezzie had never ever spoken to her like that before. 'Sorry, I was just having a laugh.'

'No, I'm sorry.' Kezzie looked embarrassed. 'I'm a bit tired. All that happened on Saturday was I drank too much, smoked too much dope and had the head from hell yesterday. That was quite enough.'

Lauren, sensing it was a sensitive issue, changed the subject.

'Well, you guys did a great job in the Memorial Gardens,' she said. 'It looks fantastic. Everyone's saying so.'

'It does, doesn't it?' said Kezzie. 'Now all we need is to get the war memorial back and we're in business.'

'And you need to finish Joel's garden before the Summer Fest,' reminded Lauren.

'That too,' said Kezzie. She looked as though she were dying for the conversation to end. 'Anyway, gotta go.'

'Are you sure you're all right?' said Lauren. 'Only you seem a bit edgy.'

'Never better,' said Kezzie, but she looked guilt-stricken when she said it. 'I really do have to go though. See you.'

Lauren puzzled over their conversation as she let herself in and sorted the kids' tea out. It wasn't like Kezzie to be so snappy. She only worked it out when Kezzie popped round to borrow some milk, and saw her reaction to Troy sitting in the corner. She tried to hide it, but she was clearly shocked.

'Er, Lauren,' she said, when Lauren walked her back to the front door, 'you can tell me to butt out if you like, but has Troy moved back in?'

'He might have,' said Lauren.

'I thought you weren't ever going to let him back in your life?' Kezzie sounded horrified.

Lauren shrugged, feeling embarrassed. She rather wished she hadn't made the point *quite* so emphatically.

'Things change,' said Lauren.

'Clearly,' said Kezzie, sarcastically, and Lauren flushed with embarrassment.

'Don't be like that,' she said. 'I know I was down on Troy, but I really think we can make a go of it. Please be happy for me.'

'I'm sorry, Lauren, I can't be,' said Kezzie. 'Troy's a louse of the highest order.'

'You don't know him,' protested Lauren.

'I know him well enough,' said Kezzie, with surprising vehemence. 'He'll let you down.'

'He won't,' said Lauren. 'Troy wouldn't do that to me again.'

'If you say so,' said Kezzie, but she looked unconvinced.

Lauren shut the door on Kezzie and sighed. It was going to be hard persuading people that she was doing the right thing, particularly when she'd been so clear that she wasn't getting back together with Troy, but she had to try. Even if it meant losing some of her friends.

Edward and Lily

1918

Lily's diary, November 1918
The joy seems to have gone out of life. I go to the
garden, and I sit brooding, and I can only see pain
and heartache. I keep recalling the babies who never
lived. Edward tells me this is a morbid fancy, and I
dare say he is right, but we have all seen so much
death and sadness over the last few years, I cannot
help but think of them.

It was here in the garden that George proposed to
poor brave Connie. She is away now, in France. She
insisted on becoming a nurse, to do her bit. She writes
that she would like to become engaged to a doctor at
the hospital where she works. We gave our permission,
gladly. I pray she has found happiness at last.

Harry has been in the army now for over a year. I
cannot wait to see him again, and I worry about him
so. He writes as often as he can, and always seems so
cheerful, but the stories from the invalided soldiers
who come from the Front tell such a story. In my
dreams, Harry is always under threat. I fear that I
may never see him again. Edward tells me not to be
foolish, but I am haunted by the idea that he may fall
in battle. And if he does, I know I shall not be as brave
as Connie.

Edward heard the bells pealing out over the village and felt a great weight fall from his shoulders. Lily would know what they meant, too. She was shopping in Heartsease with Tilly, and the pair of them would no doubt be joining the excited crowds as they celebrated the Armistice. At last after four long years, the war was over. Please God, now Harry could come back to them. Lily hadn't been the same since he'd left. She'd been working feverishly at the hospital, and rose every day pale with dark shadows under her eyes, the anxiety about what was happening to their only son too much for her. Well, thank God, she could stop worrying now. Their last letter from Harry had only arrived a week or so ago, and he reported being well and happy, and eager to see them both soon.

Edward was drawing himself a celebratory glass of whisky when he heard the telltale tinkle of a bicycle bell. He frowned, wondering where the telegram boy could be going; there was only one other house further up the hill than they were. Edward felt a clutch of fear as he heard the tentative knock at the door. He opened it with a growing feeling of unreality, remembering the day when they'd received the telegram about George. This was a new boy of course, the other one was long gone, his bones mouldering in a Flanders field along with so many others. Here was a new lad, fresh-faced and chipper, and thankfully for him, young enough to be spared the horror of war. He held out an envelope to Edward, who took it from him without a word. He didn't need to read the telegram to know what it said, but he forced himself to look.

Corporal Harry Handford. Killed in Action. Battle of the Sambre. 4 November 1918

The words swam before his eyes. Harry Handford. Killed in Action. Sambre. 4 November. A week ago. Only a week ago. They hadn't been spared after all.

He let out a great howl of anguish, and the boy looked frightened, and said, 'Sorry sir, I wish it wasn't so.'

'Not your fault,' said Edward, his eyes prickling. He patted the boy on the arm, and found a shilling in his pocket to give him. 'No one's fault.'

He turned the telegram over and over in his hands, trying to work out how he was going to tell Lily. Lily, who spent all her waking time fretting about what would happen to their only son. Lily, whose heart was going to be broken as surely as his was.

He sat in the lounge, watching the sun set over a wintry garden, his coffee untouched where the servant had left it.

Eventually, the door banged open and Lily burst in with Tilly.

'Wonderful news,' she cried, her eyes shining brighter than he'd seen in a long time. 'They say that a peace has been signed. The war is over. Harry can come home.'

Edward stood up with a heavy heart.

'Lily,' he began, but couldn't find the strength to continue. He held out the telegram instead. Lily looked at him as if not quite sure what he was showing her, and then she said, 'Oh,' in a quiet, faraway voice. Guiltily he felt a smidgeon of relief that she hadn't created a scene, but then she let out a scream of anguish so piercing it tore his heart anew.

She slumped down in a chair, weeping and saying, 'Not now. How can it be now?', while Tilly stood looking on in mute shock.

Edward went to her and kneeled down, taking her hands in his.

'I don't know,' he said. 'I don't know. It's too cruel.'

'How can we endure this?' she whispered, her eyes brittle with tears.

'What other choice do we have?' said Edward, drawing her close. 'We aren't the only ones who have suffered. Others have shown great bravery. Now we must too.'

Lily laid her head on his shoulder and wept.

'But what if I can't?' she said.

Part Three

Summer's Promise

Chapter Twenty-Five

It wasn't just Kezzie who was unimpressed by Lauren's news; her mum was none too impressed either. Particularly as she found out about it via Facebook, where Lauren had gleefully changed her relationship status from single to in a relationship with Troy Farrell.

'It will only end in tears,' her mum had warned her. 'Don't say I didn't warn you.'

'I'd never say that,' said Lauren, feeling a little sore. It would be nice if just one person she cared about was slightly happy for her. The girls were, of course, but it wasn't the same. Lauren didn't want to end up in a position where she had to choose between Troy and everyone else, but a small gnawing knot of anxiety growing inside her was warning her that it might be inevitable.

It was a warm May morning as she walked down the hill with Sam, after dropping the girls off at school. The trees were lined with the last of the pink and white apple blossom, which fell at her feet like confetti as she passed. Sam laughed as the petals gently floated into his hands. Lauren smiled as she saw a couple of Summer Fest posters tacked to the trees. Eileen had obviously been out early; she was keen to get what she called a 'buzz' going.

Troy had the afternoon off, and they were going to go shopping later, but for now she and Sam were heading for the playground. Although Lauren was pleased to be back with Troy, she lurched between her anxious feelings that everyone else was right and she was making a mistake, and an insane giddy happiness because Troy made her feel so amazing when they were together. Their relationship was a hundred times better than it had been previously, because now it was a proper adult one, with both of them taking responsibility for it. She wished everyone else could see it.

Humming to herself, she pushed open the iron gate that led into the Memorial Gardens.

'Oh no!' Since the revamp of the gardens, no one had reported any vandalism, and slowly the night patrols had tailed off. Thanks to the campaign in the paper, more parents were using the playground, and Eileen had assured her the Parish Council was looking at allocating some money towards replacing the equipment. 'We'll still have to raise some money via the Summer Fest,' she said, 'but at least it's something.'

The cause of Lauren's dismay was the empty plinth, which once more bore the legend *Daz 4 Zoe,* and was covered with empty bottles. Someone had clearly thought it was fun to pull up some of the bedding plants, too, and there was mud all over the path.

'All that hard work for nothing,' she said, picking up the plants and putting them to one side. If they'd done this here, what on earth had they done to the playground? She pushed Sam towards it with her heart in her mouth.

The damage was not as bad as she feared; there were some broken bottles it was true, and someone had sprayed graffiti on the side of the slide, but it could have been worse. But still. All that effort and people just wanted to destroy it. She could have wept.

Instead, she rang Eileen and Kezzie, who both arrived as quickly as they could, and Rose Carmichael, who promised to get her husband to bring some paint stripper home from work. She had barely seen Kezzie since Troy had moved back in and when they did meet things had felt awkward between them. Kezzie didn't talk about Troy, but Lauren knew what she was thinking. And of late, she'd been getting the idea that Kezzie might be avoiding her.

'I just can't believe it,' said Lauren. 'Bastards.'

'I still think it's bored kids,' said Kezzie.

'They may well be bored,' said Lauren, 'but they need to learn to show some respect for other people's property.'

'Ooh, touchy,' said Kezzie. 'I was just saying.'

'Grow up, Kezzie,' snapped Lauren. 'Even if they are kids, we can't just give them a pat on the back and send them on their way.'

Kezzie looked a little hurt, but said nothing, while Eileen smoothed the way with, 'I guess we'll have to reinstate the patrols. Now the warmer evenings are here, it's more tempting for the vandals.'

'I can do tonight,' said Kezzie. 'I'll see if Joel's available.'

Lauren felt a spasm of envy shoot through her, although she couldn't have explained why. She and Joel had had such a comfortable friendship till Kezzie came along, and over the last few months

Lauren had felt she had been slowly edged out. She had no right to feel like this, she knew, particularly now Troy was back in her life, but she'd got used to being the person Joel relied on, and he seemed to be relying on her less and less. It was no one's fault, Lauren could see that someone as dynamic and dazzling as Kezzie was going to be more attractive to Joel than she was (though why she should care about that, she didn't know), but she missed the easiness of the relationship she'd had with Joel. And worse, Joel had seemed withdrawn in the last few weeks, since she'd been with Troy. They'd never quite recovered from the awkwardness of Joel's declaration of love being so swiftly followed by Troy moving in. And she had no doubt at all that Joel disapproved.

'I can't babysit tonight,' said Lauren, thinking of the evening she had planned with Troy. It was probably good for Joel to know that she wasn't constantly at his beck and call.

'I'm sure Christine's free tonight,' said Eileen. 'I'm not, unfortunately.'

'Hot date is it?' grinned Kezzie, and Eileen blushed.

'I am seeing Tony, as it happens,' she said.

'Good for you,' said Kezzie. 'I'll give Joel a ring, but I'll do it anyway. I'm not having all our hard work going for nothing. In the meantime, I'm going to go and sort those beds out in the Memorial Gardens. There might be something we can salvage.'

She left quickly, barely saying goodbye to Lauren. Damn. It looked as though Kezzie wasn't going to forgive her easily.

As the weeks had gone by, Joel had got used to seeing Lauren with Troy, and even persuaded himself it wasn't like a knife digging into his heart. His feelings for Lauren had crystallized at a point when they could come to nothing. He told himself what he'd never had was no loss, but he knew in his heart it wasn't true. Every time he saw the way Lauren was with Sam, how loving she was with him, how much fun he had with her, he regretted not having been bolder before. He realized with a jolt that, just as Lauren always had, he missed the sense of completion that he would have had from being part of a family. And though he could never have it with Claire again, there had been just the smidgeon of a possibility that he could have had it with Lauren, but he'd cocked it up. By taking her for granted, he'd ensured that Lauren would never show any interest in him. And now that door had been closed to him. With Troy on the scene, Joel felt he had to hang back more, and become more reserved with Lauren, for fear of intruding. Their usual easy intimacy had been replaced with an awkward distance, and Joel regretted that more than anything.

'There's nothing you can do,' Kezzie said to Joel, when they reached the gardens that evening. It hadn't taken him long to agree to come out. He was furious that someone should have tried to destroy their hard work. 'She's completely head over heels in love with the guy. We just have to hope that she sees sense. At the moment she won't hear a word against him.'

Joel sighed, 'I know, it doesn't make it any easier though, does it?

'Nope,' said Kezzie. 'Come on, let's make ourselves comfortable.'

They sat down on the bench, and chatted idly about the Summer Fest, and the gardening celebrities Kezzie had managed to interest in the project. Latest was, that at least one known TV presenter was likely to turn up on the day. 'Wouldn't it be great if he'd endorse my work,' Kezzie was saying, when they heard a rustle in the bushes. Joel flashed his torch.

'Anyone there?' They heard muffled giggles, and a rather obvious, 'Ssshh!'

Kezzie and Joel looked at each other and grinned. They sat waiting for a few minutes, and everything went quiet. This seemed like a good moment to put their plan into action.

'Must have been a fox,' said Kezzie, loudly. 'How about we call it a day now?'

'Good idea,' said Joel. 'I don't think anyone's coming.'

Noisily, they got up and left, clanging the garden gate shut behind them. Then they waited with bated breath. It took five minutes for the giggles to start again, and then there were a few shouts of laughter, and four teenage kids burst out of the hedge.

'Coast's clear,' they said. And one of them ran to the plinth and sprayed something on the side.

'Not so fast.' Joel and Kezzie had crept up quietly behind the kids, who were so intent on what they were doing, they had no idea that anyone was behind them.

Joel grabbed the nearest one, and Kezzie shone the torch in his eyes. The other three stopped in shock, and looked poised to flee, but they were clearly anxious about the fate of their friend.

'Oi, you can't touch me,' said the boy.

'OK, I'm not touching you,' said Joel, letting go. He had no desire to spend the evening in a police cell facing charges of assault on a minor, 'but I am calling the police.'

'No, please don't,' he said, 'my mum will kill me.'

'You should have thought about that,' said Kezzie. 'Have you any idea how much hard work has gone into making these gardens look nice again? And you lot have destroyed it.'

The boys shrugged, and looked embarrassed.

'Why do you do it?' said Kezzie.

'Dunno,' said the tallest one, who was looking particularly sheepish.

'Nuffin' else to do,' another of them said, and kicked a stone away from his feet.

'Why not try and be constructive?' said Kezzie. 'Did you know the council is planning to do up this whole area and have ideas for making it more teenager friendly? If you stopped destroying things, people might be prepared to let you have a proper graffiti area.'

'What? Really?' The boys looked quite hopeful.

'Well, I can't promise anything,' said Kezzie, 'it's not up to me. But they're never going to agree to anything like that if you keep coming here and ruining everyone's hard work. You have to stop doing this, or nothing will change.'

There was a whispered conversation, during

which Kezzie detected a fair amount of swearing, then one of the boys said, 'So if we promise not to do it again, will you let us go?'

'For now,' said Kezzie.

'What do you mean, for now?' The oldest boy eyed her suspiciously.

'I mean, you can go home now, and we'll say nothing more about it, but tomorrow you are going to come back here and clean up your mess.'

'Why should we do that?' said the tallest and cockiest-looking one.

'Because if you don't, we may just change our minds and call the police after all,' said Joel. 'The choice is yours.'

The boys looked at each other and muttered something.

'Right, I want names and numbers,' said Joel. 'And I will be ringing your parents and telling them what's happened.'

The boys looked collectively stricken at that, but when Joel reminded them it was better their parents knew than the police, they gave up their details readily.

'Nick Carmichael,' Joel whistled, as he recognized one of the names given him, 'and your mum and dad have helped out too.'

Nick shifted anxiously from one foot to the other.

'They're going to kill me,' he said. His woebegone manner was so comical, Joel nearly laughed out loud, but he adopted a stern look, and said, 'Well, I hope you've learnt your lesson. We'll see you back here on Saturday morning at nine o' clock.'

Nine a.m. on Saturday found Kezzie and Joel back at the gardens organizing the boys, and some of their mates, whom they sheepishly admitted had helped on previous occasions, to clean up the plinth with paint stripper supplied by Nick's dad. Rose Carmichael had been furious when she'd found out and Nick had been grounded for a month, or so she claimed. 'I might let him off for good behaviour,' she whispered to Kezzie behind his back, 'but he's going to have to work very hard for it.'

With Rose there to oversee things, the boys pretty much got down to work straight away. They clearly regarded her with awe as someone not to be crossed, and in record time they had cleaned all the graffiti off the plinth. Kezzie organized another group to replant the borders with the plants that had been pulled out, and took it upon herself to give them a gardening lesson.

'I do understand about being bored and destructive, you know,' she said, as she showed them how to dig in the roots properly. 'But it's much better to do something constructive.'

The boys didn't look wholly convinced, but they seemed to enjoy her tales of guerrilla gardening, so maybe some of what she'd said wasn't falling on deaf ears.

By lunchtime, the gardens had been restored again, and they were able to send the boys home, but not without Rose issuing dire warnings of what would happen to them if they caused trouble again.

'We certainly won't hesitate to call the police

next time,' Joel said.

'Thanks for not doing it this time,' said Nick, putting his hands in his pockets.

'Did you mean it about having a place to graffiti properly?' said one of his mates.

Kezzie looked at Joel. 'Well, it's certainly something that the council is considering. Could you promise not to vandalize other bits of the village if you had somewhere like that?'

'Yes,' the boys' faces lit up with enthusiasm. 'And if we had a skating park as well, that would be cool,' one said.

'We only did it cos we were bored,' another agreed.

'We've got a meeting coming up for the Summer Fest,' said Kezzie. 'I've mentioned it before, but we could try and do up the old pavilion and have that as a place for you guys to go to.'

'That would be wicked,' said Nick.

'It's conditional on your good behaviour though,' warned Kezzie. 'We won't do it if you continue to mess about.'

'No worries,' said Nick, 'we'll be good as gold from now on.'

'You'd better,' admonished Kezzie, but she grinned. They weren't bad kids; they were like she'd been, bored and idle. If they could be encouraged to more constructive pursuits, it could only be a good thing.

'Do you think we can swing it?' Joel said. 'You know how stuffy some of those Parish Councillors are.'

'I have no idea,' said Kezzie, 'but it's got to be worth a try.'

Chapter Twenty-Six

Joel snuck in to the Summer Fest meeting, late again. It was packed. Thanks to Eileen's amazing efforts with flyers and posters, there probably wasn't a soul left in Heartsease who didn't know about it, and she'd managed to drum up lots more volunteers. Even Joel, who didn't go down into Heartsease that often, was aware that there was a growing enthusiasm about the event. He searched around for somewhere to sit, and, having immediately clocked that there was a spare seat next to Lauren, he tried in vain to look for another one. There wasn't another one. Lauren spotted him scan the room, and waved him over. Damn. He'd have to sit next to her now.

He struggled his way past several other people and slid gratefully into his seat, conscious of Lauren's nearness to him, of how lovely she looked, of how awkward he felt. Apart from brief conversations on her doorstep, he had barely spoken to her for several weeks. Their old easy intimacy seemed to have vanished into the mist since Troy had moved in. He was the unspoken barrier between them.

Lauren gave him a shy smile, and whispered, 'You OK?'

'Fine,' Joel replied. 'You?'

'Great,' said Lauren.

'Good,' said Joel. 'That's good.'

He felt despairing. Was this the best they could do? Making inane comments at one another? He tried again.

'Have I missed anything?' he whispered. Cynthia was in full stride, demanding to know why it was going to be necessary to close the High Street for the day.

'It hasn't really started properly,' said Lauren.

'That's a relief,' said Joel. 'Sam wouldn't settle for Christine and I couldn't get away.'

'Did you give him Snuffles?'

Snuffles was Sam's favourite rabbit, without which he wouldn't go to sleep.

'Unfortunately Snuffles is in the wash, having had a bottle of milk poured all over him,' said Joel. 'I had to prise him out of Sam's grasp.'

'Bet that went down well,' grinned Lauren, and Joel felt a surge of pleasure. That was better. This was the Lauren he knew. Lauren was the only person he could talk to like this about Sam, but over the last few weeks their conversations had become stilted and forced. He had taken her so much for granted, and now he missed her.

'Are you really OK?' Lauren asked.

'Of course, why?' said Joel.

'Only,' Lauren looked embarrassed, 'I thought you might be upset with me.'

'Why should I be upset with you?'

'Because of the party, and what I said,' said Lauren. 'I'm sorry, I didn't mean to offend you.'

It wrenched Joel's heart in two to see her being so kind and thoughtful and wasting all that loveliness on Troy. 'You haven't offended me,' he lied.

'And you don't mind about me and Troy?'

The million dollar question. Of course he minded. But he couldn't say anything, not if he wanted to retain their friendship.

'It's none of my business,' said Joel. 'What you do is up to you.'

'You don't have to pretend,' said Lauren. 'I've had everyone from my mum to Kezzie telling me what an idiot I'm being. Kezzie in particular was most vehement about it, so I'm assuming you agree with them.'

'Look, Lauren,' said Joel, feeling even more awkward, 'what I or anyone else thinks about it is neither here or there, so long as *you're* happy.'

'I am,' said Lauren firmly, and she looked it.

'Then I'm happy for you,' said Joel, wishing he meant it.

Eileen called them to order at that moment, and the meeting got underway.

'Well, we've got less than two months to go,' said Eileen, 'and I think things are coming along a treat. Thanks to all of you who've been working so hard putting flyers up everywhere. And a big thanks to Keith, who I know has been breaking his back in the café doing special promotions designed to get his customers to come back on the day.'

'It all makes great business sense, darling,' gushed Keith, 'I'm not *that* altruistic.'

'I've been on the phone to the people at Radio Chiverton and I'm pleased to announce they are going to spend the whole day here. Joel has done a great job getting us New Horizons who are going to open the proceedings, and they may even play. Tony, how are we getting on with the field, have we got all the relevant permissions to use it yet?'

'Nearly sorted,' said Tony. 'I don't think it will be a problem.'

'Brilliant,' continued Eileen. 'I am also pleased to announce that Sally and Andy from the Labourer's Legs are kindly hosting the Pimms tent, and as you know, George Anderson from the butcher's is providing a hog roast and barbecue all day. I hope you like his minty lamb sausages!'

That raised a laugh; George Anderson's minty lamb sausages were legendary in Heartsease.

Cynthia sniffed. 'Are we to assume that this "Summer Fest" is losing all the traditional elements of our normal fete? I hope there's still going to be a tombola at least.'

'You can be in charge of it,' assured Eileen. 'We're planning to have all the traditional stalls in the field along with fun activities for the children. As you know, the High Street is going to be closed, and there will be plenty of interesting stalls to catch the eye there, and we'll be having the choir singing madrigals at lunchtime.

'In the afternoon, the Mayor of Chiverton is going to re-open the Memorial Gardens, which I think you'll agree look stunning. And we've also got several of our community opening their gardens to the public in the afternoon, including that belonging to our very own Joel. As most of you probably know, Joel's great great grandfather, Edward Handford, created a knot garden at Lovelace Cottage and Kezzie has been helping Joel restore it. It's well worth going to have a look if you've got time.'

'That sounds terrific, Eileen,' said Tony. 'I think the rest of the committee and I all have to thank you for your immense hard work.'

There was a heartfelt round of clapping and Eileen blushed.

'Well, I couldn't do it without all of you,' she said. 'So thank you so much. Now, is there any other business?'

'Have we thought any more about how we're going to use the funds we raise?' Joel asked. 'I know we're planning to upgrade the playground equipment, but as I think some of you may have heard, Kezzie and I managed to confront the lads who've been vandalizing the gardens. Part of the problem is they're bored. So we're hoping that the idea of turning the old pavilion into a drop-in centre for teens is still on the cards. I think it would benefit the village enormously.'

Cynthia sniffed loudly. 'They need a short sharp shock,' she said. 'They shouldn't be rewarded for bad behaviour.'

'They're not bad kids,' said Joel, 'and I think they've learnt their lesson: they just need somewhere to go.'

'I agree,' said Tony, 'and I promise to raise it as a matter of some urgency at the next Parish Council meeting.'

The meeting broke up then, and Lauren got up to go.

'Would you like a lift?' said Joel.

'Thanks,' said Lauren. 'If it's not too much trouble.'

'Nothing would ever be too much trouble for you,' said Joel, and then kicked himself for sounding corny.

Joel drove Lauren home in silence. His emotions were too churned up for him to speak. To be sitting so close to her, and yet knowing how far away from him she was, left him in a state of utter despair.

'You're quiet,' said Lauren, as she got out of the car.

'Got a lot on my mind,' said Joel. 'Work, you know.'

'So long as it's nothing to do with me.'

'No, of course not,' Joel forced a smile. 'I'm pleased you're happy.'

But as he watched her walk up the path to a waiting Troy, he felt like kicking himself. Because he'd been so stupid, and hadn't seen how he felt about Lauren, he'd left her wide open for Troy's return. It should have been him with Lauren, not Troy. He'd blown his chance.

Kezzie was working late on Joel's garden. As the evenings got longer she found it increasingly hard to tear herself away, particularly when the garden was finally beginning to take shape and she was able to see the sort of garden Edward had wanted to create. Well, at least she hoped it was how he'd wanted it. She often thought about Edward when she was out there, patiently working on the garden just as she had done, preparing a wedding present for the woman he loved. She wondered if anyone would love her that much ever again. She'd thought Richard might have done once, but that possibility was gone for good.

She often felt as if Edward Handford were there

316

when she was in the garden, a friendly ghost looking over her shoulder. Sometimes, as the early summer afternoon faded to dusk, she imagined she could see him, standing on the steps of the house, looking towards her, as if approving. She knew it was fanciful, but she liked to think they were connected. She hoped he would have been pleased with her restoration.

As the sun set slowly over the valley, casting golden shadows on the grass, she reluctantly packed her things away, and checked her watch. Damn, she was going to miss the meeting. Joel had called to her an hour before to ask her if she was going, and she'd said yes. Kezzie would have to check with him and Lauren what she'd missed.

Lauren. Kezzie felt really guilty about Lauren. Having failed dismally to confront Lauren with the truth about Troy and then argued with her about him, Kezzie had spent the last few weeks avoiding her. She was going to have to come up with an excuse as to why some time.

It was dusk as Kezzie walked down the path to her house, and she saw to her dismay that Troy was putting out the bins. It was the first time she'd seen him on his own since the party. How awkward. For the first time she wished that Jo had grown a great big hedge between the properties instead of having a white picket fence that looked as though it had come out of an episode of *Little House on the Prairie*.

'Well, hi there, neighbour,' said Troy, coming up rather too close. 'I haven't seen you in a while.'

'I've been busy,' said Kezzie, shortly. She didn't want to talk to Troy. What was there to say to him?

317

'That's not very friendly,' said Troy, 'I was only making polite conversation.'

'Look, Troy, I don't want to be rude,' said Kezzie, 'but I'm tired and it's late, and I don't think it's the best idea if we spend too much time together.'

'I was only talking,' said Troy, lighting a cigarette, 'or don't you trust yourself around me?'

'Puh-lease,' said Kezzie, 'don't flatter yourself. I am not interested in you.'

'That's what they all say,' said Troy, winking.

He reeked of booze and fags. Kezzie was no angel and not that hot on responsibility, but even she wouldn't have done that if she was baby-sitting young children.

'Well, must get on,' said Kezzie. 'See you.'

'Not soon enough,' said Troy, lighting a cigarette and blowing smoke, in her direction.

'It is for me,' said Kezzie, and fled inside. Really, he was the pits, and yet Lauren seemed blind to his faults. How on earth could Kezzie let her know the truth?

Lauren got out of Joel's car with a feeling of relief. It had been awkward for the last few weeks. She couldn't blame him for being reticent with her, given what he'd said to her at the party, but she was relieved there were no hard feelings. And at least he wasn't on her case about Troy like everyone else. Kezzie in particular had a real downer on him. Lauren felt bad about it; she'd barely seen Kezzie for weeks. It seemed silly to be arguing over a bloke.

As Joel drove off, Lauren looked at her watch

318

and, deciding it wasn't too late, thought she may as well call in on Kezzie. She texted Troy to say she'd be back soon. He texted back with: *keeping the bed warm, babe.* It gave her a warm glow all over to think of him waiting for her. The long, lonely years of going solo seemed to be over. She loved having someone at home to wait up for her.

Kezzie looked surprised to see Lauren at the door.

'Sorry, I haven't brought anything,' she said. 'I just wondered if you'd like to know how the meeting went.'

'Oh yes, sure,' said Kezzie. 'Come on in.'

Lauren came in and accepted the glass of wine that Kezzie offered her, and they chatted for a few moments about the Summer Fest, and laughed about Cynthia's general outrage at the world in general. When she'd been there for ten minutes or so, Lauren plucked up her courage and said, 'I'm sorry, Kezzie. I'm kind of here under false pretences. I was a bit worried that I might have offended you somehow.'

'You? Offended me?' Kezzie looked stricken. 'Of course you haven't.'

'Oh, it seemed as though you were avoiding me,' said Lauren.

'No, not at all,' said Kezzie. 'I've been busy with Joel's garden and the Memorial Gardens.'

'So you're OK with me and Troy then?' said Lauren.

'Well...' Kezzie looked awkward – almost guilty.

'Look, I know what you're thinking,' said Lauren. 'And if it were the other way round, I'd be inclined to have the same opinion. Hell, I'm still not even quite sure I'm doing the right thing. I know I said I'd never have Troy back, but I do think he's changed. And he's so great with the girls, and he really does make me happy. It's fantastic. Just what I always wanted it to be.'

'Well, you know him best,' said Kezzie. 'So long as he doesn't treat you badly again.'

'Oh, he won't,' said Lauren fervently. 'I know he won't. This time, he's staying for good.'

'Well, that's OK, then,' said Kezzie.

'Yes,' said Lauren with a smile, 'it is.'

Chapter Twenty-Seven

The weeks were speeding by and already June was upon them. There were only a few short weeks until Summer Fest and Lauren was looking forward to it. This year was proving to be hot and sunny, and Lauren couldn't help feeling the weather was reflecting her mood. She was so happy to be with Troy and slowly getting used to her new life with him. They had never had much chance just to *be* together before – when they'd first met, it had been such a whirlwind, exciting, thrilling, but not real. Then it had all gone wrong, and they had barely been living together any time at all, when he walked out on her. But now, she felt they were really establishing themselves as a couple and their relationship was putting down solid roots.

It was great having someone to share the little

things with, like Izzie's first tooth falling out and the girls learning to swim. She'd spent so long on her own with the twins, she appreciated having someone to talk to in the evenings most of all. Of course everything wasn't perfect. Troy was hideously untidy and drank and smoked more than she liked, and he could be moody with the girls sometimes. He also had a habit of forgetting her rule about not smoking inside, which was particularly important in light of Izzie's asthma. But they were quibbles. The children loved him, he made her happy. Life couldn't be better.

True, she saw less of Kezzie and Joel now, but that was inevitable. She was in a full-time relationship; it stood to reason she'd have less time with her friends. She did feel guilty that Kezzie was still working hard at maintaining the Memorial Gardens, and Lauren didn't get much of a chance to help her, but she was sure Kezzie would understand.

Eileen didn't. She dropped in for coffee one day, when Troy was at work, and said, 'Lauren, you are still on board for Summer Fest aren't you? Only I hate to nag, but you've missed the last couple of meetings.'

Lauren felt guilty about that. She and Troy had been out a fair bit recently. Even her mum was getting narky about being asked to babysit so often. 'I do have a life you know,' she said, 'and don't forget I'm going up to Manchester to see your auntie Jan soon. I can't always drop every-thing for you.' With her mum away, and Troy working, Lauren hadn't been able to go to the last meeting.

'I'm sorry,' she said, 'of course I'm still involved. I won't let you down. It's just that I've been a bit busy, what with stuff on at the girls' school and the pub.'

'I know,' said Eileen. 'I appreciate things have changed for you recently. I just hope you're not going to forget everything else. It's easy to do when you're in love.'

'No, no, of course I won't,' said Lauren, feeling even more guilty. She *had* been neglecting her friends.

'I'm sure you won't,' said Eileen. 'But be careful. People can let you down. It would be a shame if you let Troy come between you and your friends.'

'He won't let me down,' predicted Lauren, confidently.

'Hmm, I thought that about Ted,' said Eileen. 'Convinced myself of it for years. And look how that turned out. I just don't want you to get hurt.'

'I won't, don't worry,' said Lauren, 'but I appreciate what you're saying.'

But after Eileen had gone, she did worry. Not about Troy leaving – she really didn't think he would – but about her friends. She shouldn't be feeling guilty all the time about not seeing them, should she? But she did. Lauren realized with a jolt that she hadn't actually spoken to Kezzie beyond saying hello for the last three weeks. She should really do something about that. Maybe arrange to go out for a drink...

An opportunity presented itself sooner than she thought, when Joel came to pick Sam up that evening.

'You like tennis, don't you?' he said.

'Love it,' said Lauren (impressed despite herself that he knew that). 'Why?'

'I've got a couple of tickets for the first week of Wimbledon through work,' said Joel, 'but I can't go, I've got too much on. I thought you and–' he paused, as if uncomfortable saying the name '–Troy might like to go?'

'Oh,' said Lauren in surprise. 'Well, that's really kind. Troy isn't a tennis fan though, he likes football more, but maybe Kezzie could come if you can spare her.'

'I should think so,' said Joel, 'she's doing more of a maintenance job in the garden right now.'

'Right,' said Lauren, 'I'll ask her.'

Kezzie had just finished work for the day and was looking forward to a long soak in the bath. The weather was fantastically hot, which was both a curse and a blessing for gardeners. Kezzie was going a lovely nut brown – she couldn't remember ever having such a great tan – but equally she was bored with lugging watering cans down the garden. She'd finally managed to persuade Joel to reinstate the ancient tap just outside the knot garden, which clearly had been used for that purpose, so at least she could water the plants properly. She was praying that with the heatwave the council wouldn't suddenly introduce a hosepipe ban.

But she was satisfied with her work. She'd completed the planting out of the knot garden, and now it was a question of time for it to take a proper shape. But the basics were there. She'd restored Edward's heart-shaped pattern, with its huge heart at the centre and the interwoven initials of E and L. She'd recreated the gravel path that surrounded the central knot pattern, and dug out the borders around the edges, which were now overflowing with summer bedding: petunias, busy lizzies and lobelia. The pansies had all died back, but she knew they'd come back into their own in the autumn. She was proud of what she'd achieved and Joel had asked her to stay on and work on the main garden, which was in need of a radical overhaul. If she wanted to enter Chelsea, she already had something to show off. She had taken lots of pictures of both the garden and her designs, which she could send in with her entrance form in September. Thanks to working for Joel, she had gained the confidence to feel she had a garden worth entering.

The bath was running downstairs when there was a knock on the door.

Damn. Kezzie had gone upstairs to get undressed. She threw a dressing gown on and leapt back down the stairs.

'Who is it?' she called.

'Only me,' said Lauren's voice. That was unusual. It had been weeks since Lauren had called round. She was so loved up with Troy it was almost as though the rest of the world didn't exist. Despite her misgivings about the relationship, Kezzie had to admit Lauren did look incredibly happy every time she saw her.

'Hi,' said Kezzie. 'Come on in, sorry about the dressing gown, I'm just about to leap in the bath. How are you?'

'Fine,' said Lauren, 'well more than fine, I'm

great actually. And you?'

'Yeah, all good too,' said Kezzie. 'I've nearly finished Joel's garden, and I'm really pleased with it. You should come and see it some time.'

'I should,' said Lauren. She looked slightly tentative, as if she weren't sure about something. 'I was wondering, are you free next Tuesday?'

'I'd have to let Joel know I can't work that day,' said Kezzie, 'but I'm sure he won't mind. Why?'

'I've got tickets for Wimbledon is why,' said Lauren. 'Joel couldn't go, so he gave them to me and Troy hates tennis, so I thought you might like to join me.'

'Oh wow,' said Kezzie. 'I love Wimbledon. That would be fantastic.'

'That's fab,' said Lauren. 'I'm so glad you can come.'

'Who's going to have the girls?' said Kezzie. Unlike her, Lauren couldn't just up and leave things.

'Troy's going to look after them,' said Lauren. 'And Eileen very kindly offered to have Sam as well.'

There was a pause, and then Lauren said in a rush, 'I'm so sorry, Kezzie, I know I've hardly seen you recently but what with Troy and the girls, I don't seem to have much time. You probably think I've been a pretty crap friend lately.'

Kezzie might well have been thinking that, but given what had happened with her and Troy, she didn't feel she was one to talk about being a loyal friend.

'What can I say?' she teased. 'You're a woman in love.'

'Oh, shut up!' said Lauren, blushing. 'So, no hard feelings, then?'

'None at all,' said Kezzie.

'We can have a girlie day out,' said Lauren, 'to make up for it.'

'Sounds good to me,' said Kezzie. 'Thanks. I'd love to come.'

'Thanks for the tickets, Joel,' said Kezzie, next day, when he came home with Sam.

It had been another baking day, and she was exhausted but pleased with the progress she'd made. The garden was going to look fantastic by the time of the Summer Fest. She'd spent the day mainly tidying things up: weeding the flowerbeds, snipping the box, ivy and rosemary and entwining them round one another so they retained their shapes. She'd also planted the symbols that Edward had chosen to represent his children, in the outside patterns of the design: gardenia for the babies who'd died, petunias for Connie, white carnations for Harry and peonies for Tilly. And as the pièce de résistance, she planted a pink rose, as a symbol of married love in the centre of the garden. It was extremely satisfying and rewarding. Kezzie didn't think she'd ever been prouder of a garden she'd worked on.

Joel looked as tuckered out as she did.

'Oh, no problem. Glad they're not going to waste.'

'You look shattered, if you don't mind my saying,' said Kezzie.

'I am,' said Joel, pulling a face. 'Work's pretty stressful right now. With all these government cuts to funding I'm having to ask all the people who run our services to make savings. And every saving they make impinges on someone's actual life. It's pretty dispiriting. If I could only see a way out of it I would.'

'Sounds grim,' said Kezzie. 'I'm so glad I'm doing something for myself now. It's much more satisfying.'

'Sadly, I don't have much choice in the matter, although I do dream about setting up in business restoring old furniture. Maybe one day I will,' said Joel. 'Do you have to rush off? I promised Sammy boy a splash in the paddling pool before bedtime. I was just going to chill on the patio and have a Pimms. Do you fancy joining me?'

'It's so hot, I brought something to change into, but I'm a bit muddy,' said Kezzie. 'I feel like I've had a dust bath with one of your sparrows.'

'Have a shower,' said Joel. 'You know where the bathroom is, don't you? There are spare towels in the cupboard on the landing.'

By the time Kezzie emerged, half an hour later, Joel had made up some Pimms and lit a barbecue, while Sam tottered in and out of the paddling pool, sitting down occasionally. The evening was clear and calm and achingly hot.

Sam was clearly enjoying sitting on the pool seat, tipping buckets of water on his head.

Joel looked up from where he was busy grilling sausages to see Kezzie walk towards him in a flattering but simple halter-neck dress. Joel nearly dropped the sausage he was holding.

'Are you all right? Only you look like you've seen a ghost.'

'Sorry,' Joel swallowed. 'Stupid of me. The dress you're wearing. Claire had one like it. You're not at all like her. It was just suddenly in the light...'

'Shall I go home and change into something else?'

'No, no, you're OK,' said Joel, pulling himself together. 'Come on, tea's ready.'

But he couldn't shake the melancholy feeling that had overcome him from the minute he saw Kezzie in that dress. And when he'd finally put a protesting Sam to bed, he came down and sank heavily into his chair. Gratefully he noticed that Kezzie had cleared up for him. They sat in silence for a few minutes when Kezzie suddenly said, 'You can talk about her you know. Only I noticed you never do.'

Joel ran his hands through his hair.

'You could talk about Richard and you don't,' said Joel.

'Touché,' said Kezzie. 'But that's different. He's not dead.'

'No one wants to hear about my grief,' said Joel. 'People move on. It embarrasses them.'

'Well I do,' said Kezzie. 'For a start it seems to me that you beat yourself up about her unnecessarily. Why?'

'Now that I really don't want to discuss,' said Joel. 'I told you how everyone thinks I was the perfect husband and dad. And nothing could be further from the truth. You wouldn't think much of me if I told you how it really was.'

'Try me,' said Kezzie.

Chapter Twenty-Eight

Joel didn't look at Kezzie, but stared into the gathering darkness. Its warmth gathered him up and enveloped him. Somehow it was easier to talk if he just imagined no one was listening.

'I don't know where to start, really,' he said. 'It's just, what you've done here. It's what I wanted to do for Claire, and she never really got it.'

'Why not?'

'Well, I can see it now of course. This was my dream, not hers.' Joel could see all too clearly now that Claire had never really wanted to come to Lovelace Cottage; she had only done it to keep him happy. If she hadn't died, maybe he would have changed her mind, but for the time she was here, she hated it. 'Plus, she was caught up with a small baby while I was working all hours. And when I was home, I was either doing DIY or digging up the garden. And when we moved in the house was such a mess. It was so dark and gloomy. Claire hated it, and I couldn't persuade her it had potential.'

'And...'

'That's it, really,' said Joel. 'I completely shut her out of what I was trying to do. I thought she didn't care and was being unsupportive. Looking back, I can see it was the other way round. There she was with a tiny baby. She needed me and I let her down.'

'She may not have thought that.'

'Oh, but she did.' Joel looked up at Kezzie, his eyes filled with pain. He remembered the fierce, bitter rows when Claire accused him of caring more about the house than her and the baby, and he – to his shame – had told her that she loved Sam more than she did him. 'We argued about it all the time. And I kept promising to make it up to her. And of course I never did. It seems bloody pathetic now, but I was jealous of her relationship with Sam. I hated coming home. I felt shut out and excluded.

'One night I'd promised I'd be home early from work but I never made it. I ended up going for a drink and got home later than I intended. Claire was furious. She'd cooked me a lovely meal, and I'd gone and ruined everything. We rowed. She went to bed. I drank myself into a stupor. And in the morning...'

'You couldn't have known what would happen,' said Kezzie, holding out her hand to him. 'You shouldn't beat yourself up about it.'

'It was worse than that.' Joel swallowed hard. 'You see there was a girl at work...'

He remembered it all so clearly. Fi Tatton had been a serial flirt. And rumour had it she had shagged nearly every man in the building. Joel was one of the few notches left unmarked on her bedpost, apparently. She'd made no secret of the way she felt about him, and the fact that he was married hadn't seemed to bother her. Normally he avoided her like the plague, but that night, despite having promised Claire he'd be home early, he'd been persuaded to go for a drink after work. 'After all,' Fi had said, putting her arm in his and leaning in too close, 'what harm can one drink do?'

Rewind. If only he could rewind. So that night he'd come home on time, and they'd had the evening Claire wanted. Instead, every time he thought about her, he remembered not the good things: not the way she looked as she laughed, or the smell of her perfume, or the way she flicked her fair hair back, but the disappointment in her eyes and the knowledge that he had let her down.

'So what happened?' prompted Kezzie.

'I went to the pub, and of course I didn't stay for one drink, but several,' said Joel. 'And one thing led to another...'

He'd looked at his watch, seen the time, and gone out to grab a taxi, cursing himself because he'd have to come back for the car the next day. He knew he'd had too much to drink, and he'd spent the evening trying to avoid Fi's less than subtle attempts to make a move on him. And then there she was, standing outside the pub with him while he waited for the cab he'd rung. He burned with shame when he remembered their passionate kisses; the way he'd thrown caution to the wind knowing Claire was going to be cross anyway, and imagining they had a whole lifetime to sort things out.

'Oh God,' said Kezzie, instinctively putting her hands on his. 'Joel, I'm so sorry.'

'So you see,' said Joel, his voice ragged. 'Now you know. I was a lousy husband and a lousy dad.'

'Now stop right there,' said Kezzie. 'That's ridiculous. Yes, you were crap at being a dad at first

– but how old was Sam?'

'Five months,' said Joel.

'And look at the two of you now,' she said. 'One thing you most definitely *aren't* is a lousy dad.'

'But I was a lousy husband. Claire deserved so much more.' Joel put his head in his hands. 'I don't think she guessed what an idiot I'd been, but it haunts me, you know. The last night of her life, when I could have been at home with her, and I spent part of it kissing a stranger. I don't think I'll ever forgive myself.'

'Joel, I think you're being too hard on yourself,' said Kezzie baldly. 'Yes, you were wrong to do what you did, but you loved Claire, right?'

'Of course, with all my heart.'

'What would have happened in the normal course of events?'

'I'd have woken up, felt like a heel, and made it up to her,' said Joel.

'But you never got the chance,' said Kezzie. 'You behaved very badly on one night of your life. You made a hideous mistake. But you couldn't have known that Claire was going to die. If she'd lived, by now that would all have been forgiven and forgotten. I presume she loved you, too?'

'I think so,' said Joel. 'Though God knows I didn't deserve it.'

'Then I'm thinking, if she were still here she wouldn't want you to beat yourself up like this,' said Kezzie. 'You didn't know she was ill. You thought you had all the time in the world. But you didn't. You made a stupid mistake, which you regret, and you never got the chance to kiss and

332

make up. You got a rotten throw of the dice. I think you should cut yourself some slack.'

'Easier said than done,' said Joel, with a sigh. 'I just wish I could take that night back and replay it differently. At least then I'd know she hadn't died hating me.'

'I'm sure she didn't hate you,' said Kezzie, touching his arm gently.

'Are you?' said Joel. 'I'm not. But what's done is done. I can't turn the clock back now, and I'll regret it for the rest of my life.'

Lauren was sipping a glass of wine and contemplating the sunset, waiting for Troy. The girls had gone to bed, neither of them had to work in the pub, and she was looking forward to an evening with just the two of them. It still felt wonderful to even think about it. Lauren had offered to cook a meal, but Troy had suggested a takeaway, 'Save you working so hard, babe.' So here she was, sitting in the evening sunshine, in anticipation of him returning home soon. She felt like a schoolgirl on her first date.

The sun dipped over the horizon, sending lengthening shadows across the garden. In the darkening blue sky above, two bats flitted and flipped above her head. She heard the soft cooing of wood pigeons in the trees, and the cry of baby foxes in the woods at the end of her garden. Bloody things were a menace. She'd tried to persuade Troy not to feed them, but he thought they were cute.

After half an hour, Lauren was getting bored. Troy had been gone ages. She was about to text him when the phone rang. The sounds of busy chat filled her ears, and then she could just make out Troy shouting, 'Loz! Can you hear me?'

'Yes,' said Lauren, 'they can probably hear you in Chiverton.'

'I'm in the pub.'

'I gathered,' Lauren said, between gritted teeth. Try not to lose your rag straight away, she told herself, there might be a reasonable explanation.

'I've got to wait for the takeaway, so I just popped in for one.'

'So long as it is only one.' Lauren was cross, but still prepared to give him the benefit of the doubt.

'It will be, babes. Don't you trust me?'

'Of course I do,' said Lauren, somewhat reluctantly.

'I won't be long, I promise,' said Troy. 'Love you.'

'Love you too,' said Lauren, and put the phone down slowly. She still felt angry. Her plans for the evening hadn't included waiting in for Troy, but maybe she was overreacting. If he had to wait for the takeaway, it did make sense to go and have a beer. So long as it was only one. She was probably making a fuss about nothing. He'd be home soon.

Lauren picked up her wine glass and went inside. She turned the TV on; there was no point sitting in a dark, cooling garden on her own. Being summer, there wasn't anything particularly interesting on TV. Sighing with frustration, she turned to her ancient computer, which sat on a table in the corner of the lounge, and started looking online for cupcake cases for the cake stall she was running at the Summer Fest. She may as well do something useful while she was waiting.

Half an hour later the key turned in the lock. By this time, much to her surprise, Lauren had consumed the best part of a bottle of wine. Oops. She was also very cross and very hungry.

'Just one more?' she said angrily. 'I've never known the Balti House to take so long to prepare a curry.'

'God, I might have known,' said Troy. 'I went to the pub for *one* drink, like I said. They were busy at the Balti, I told you. Christ, it hasn't taken long for the nagging to start.'

'Oh come on, Troy,' said Lauren, incensed by the use of the word nagging. 'I was planning a lovely evening in and you go off to the pub for nearly two hours while I'm sitting here on my own feeling like a lemon. I think I've a right to be cross.'

'Give over will you,' said Troy. 'Here's your bloody curry.' He slammed it on the coffee table, and stormed out into the kitchen and banged open cupboard doors noisily.

Great. That was her romantic evening out of the window. Lauren was aware of the patter of footsteps. Immie was coming sleepily down the stairs sucking her thumb, and holding her favourite teddy.

'Mummy, are you all right?' she said, her little face crumpled in concern, 'only you were shouting.'

Oh lord. Lauren remembered how much she'd hated the arguments between her parents growing up. They'd had a fiery relationship, which ended in divorce when Lauren was seven, and Lauren had always hated to hear them shout at each other. She'd always vowed never to put her children through the same.

'No, everything's fine, sweetie,' she said. 'Daddy and I were just having a little chat that got a bit loud. Everything's fine, isn't it, Daddy?'

She mouthed: 'Say yes,' to Troy, who had just come in with plates and a bottle of wine.

'Of course it is, darling,' said Troy. 'Here, give us a kiss, and then Mummy will take you back to bed.'

Lauren took Immie back upstairs and tucked her in. When she came back downstairs, Troy had opened the wine, put out the takeaway on trays and got a DVD ready for them to watch. He *had* been gone longer than she'd thought he'd be, but at least he was here now.

'Sorry,' she said, reaching for his hand. 'I'm just grumpy and hungry. And I missed you.'

'That's OK,' said Troy. 'Honestly, I really didn't have that much to drink. Come on, let's tuck in. I'm starving.'

Argument swiftly averted, Lauren sat down next to him on the sofa and started to eat her curry. The DVD Troy had chosen from the cheap rack at Macey's, turned out to be a violent thriller, which he assured her was a classic of its genre, before crashing out on the sofa. Sighing, Lauren cleared up after him, poked him till he got moving, and then pushed him up the stairs to bed. Some romantic evening that had turned out to be. Maybe the honeymoon was already over.

Kezzie let herself into her little cottage, thinking about what Joel had told her. Poor Joel. What a lot he had had to contend with. She'd ended up telling him all about what had happened with Richard, to show him he wasn't the only one capable of idiotic behaviour, and by the time she'd left, she thought he seemed a little better. At least it must have done him some good to get that off his chest. What a burden to be carrying around with him.

She went into the kitchen and grabbed a can of lager, before settling down in the lounge to see what was on the telly. Discovering that there wasn't much she wanted to watch, Kezzie decided to have a look at some of the letters and diaries from Edward's trunk. She and Joel were slowly collating material for the exhibition, and Kezzie had been fascinated to read Edward's account of creating the Memorial Gardens, apparently there'd been a huge fete on the day of the opening, which made her smile. Edward and Lily appeared not to have written anything very much after that, too busy bringing up their family she supposed, but the diary and letters had started again from around 1914. Kezzie had cried when she'd read a letter to Connie telling her her fiancé had died, and the last part of the diary she'd read had touched on the death of Harry, right at the end of the war, which struck Kezzie as exceptionally tragic.

She picked up Lily's diary for 1918, and started flicking through. It was filled with references about her worries and concerns for her only son, and then there was a gap with a few pages blank, before Kezzie came across an illegible scribble, *11 November, 1918. Harry is dead. Killed in the last battle of the war. I think my heart might break*. After that there was no more, and Kezzie hadn't unearthed any other diaries for Lily. How incredibly tragic. To lose your son like that, right at the end of the war. Lily must have thought he was safe. She must have thought it would be OK.

Kezzie put her can of lager down, and roamed around her lounge restlessly. Her thoughts were getting all jumbled up. Joel had thought he had the rest of his life with Claire, and lost her swiftly and brutally. Lily had lost so much, those babies, then her only son. Life was a cruel business, and happiness had to be grabbed where it could. She had been extraordinarily happy with Richard in the two short years they were together. Despite their differences, until they'd split up she'd always felt they fitted together like hand and glove. And yet between them they'd thrown it all away. When she'd told Joel about Richard, he'd asked her what was stopping her trying to contact him again, and she'd told him that Richard didn't want her any more.

'Are you sure that's not an excuse?' Joel had said. 'Did you actually ever say sorry to him about what had happened?'

She hadn't, of course, so blinded by fury had she been that he'd taken Emily's part and wasn't prepared to listen to her side of the story. And later on she'd accused him of being an old-fashioned prig who couldn't let his hair down. He had been wrong and overreacted, but then so had she. It took two to make an argument, but maybe it only needed one of them to mend it.

Without stopping to consider what she was

doing, Kezzie sat down and wrote Richard a letter.

12 The Lane
Heartsease
Sussex

Dear Rich,
I know you said you didn't want to hear from me again. And I've tried, really tried to forget you, but I find I can't. If you don't reply I'll try and understand, but I think I know now that a part of me will never be over you. I think we had something good going back there, and I'll regret it to my dying day if I don't try and get you back.

So I'm sorry. I'm sorry that I was stupid enough to have those muffins in the house when Emily came round, and I'm sorry that I didn't realize she'd drunk my vodka. But most of all I'm sorry for having not understood why you were so angry. I was cross with you for not taking my part. I thought you were overreacting and I forgot that you have a duty to Emily first.

It seems silly for us to have fallen out over this. Maybe there's no way we can get back to where we were, but I do know that I miss you with every fibre of my being. If I never see you again, my life will be much the poorer.
Love always,
Kezziexx

She addressed the envelope, sealed it, and put a stamp on it. She went to the post box at the end of the Lane and posted it before she could change her mind. It might not make any difference, but at least she could say she'd tried.

Edward and Lily

1919

Lily continues heartbroken over Harry's death, Edward wrote in his diary in the spring of 1919. *All this long winter she has stayed indoors, no longer working at the hospital, though lord knows they need the help. She shuts herself away, poring over Harry's letters, sitting in his room, touching his clothes, sometimes sleeping in his bed. I cannot reach her. And even now, as the spring returns and the crocuses and daffodils begin to emerge in the garden, I cannot persuade her to come and spend time with me there. The magic healing properties of our garden seem to be no cure for this.*

Even the return of Connie, to whom Lily now clung in a way she had never previously done, did nothing to help. Neither did the news, welcomed by Edward, but barely acknowledged by Lily, that Connie was to marry the doctor she had met in France, a young man called James Chandler, make any difference. In vain Edward tried to lighten Lily's mood, encouraging her to start preparing for the wedding, but she would not be stirred. *It is worse than the terrible time when she lost the babies,* wrote Edward. *I fear she is lost to me forever, locked in a grief so private and painful, even I cannot share it.*

As spring turned into summer, Edward's hopes that Lily's spirits would lift a little faded. He persuaded her sometimes to come and sit in the knot garden with her sketchbook, but more often than not he would come upon her sitting there, staring out across the valley, the paper barely marked. It was as if she had retreated into herself.

James was now a frequent visitor, and a great favourite with all in the house. He was eminently suited to his work as a doctor, with his kindly gentle manner. Having been the head of his own house for some time, his father having died young, he showed great sensitivity towards Lily, admonishing Connie for her frequent impatience with her mother. 'We are not all able to bear the pains of the world as well as you,' he would say, and he would go out of his way to be even more solicitous to Lily. He was the only person who could occasionally make Lily smile, and for that Edward was grateful.

He was pleased, too, that Tilly got on so well with her future brother-in-law. Tilly, whose youth had been blighted by war and suffering, deserved some fun now, Edward felt, and James certainly made her laugh and good naturedly let her join in expeditions with him and Connie. Tilly for her part was very taken with him, stating boldly to Connie when she first brought James home, 'I do declare you've picked a fine one there.' Connie had rebuked her for cheekiness, but Edward had watched with pleasure the way Tilly and James had become such good friends in a relatively short space of time – he hoped that James would

341

in some way replace the much loved older brother that Tilly still grieved for. It eased his aching heart to think that although they had lost Harry, there was still a future for Connie, and in time, Tilly.

But then a day came when the last remaining foundations of his comfortable happy family life fell away. Edward had been out for the afternoon, and come home to find the house deserted. Lily was sleeping in Harry's room, and he didn't like to disturb her. Of his daughters there was no sign. Thinking that they were probably in the knot garden, Edward went down there to find them. He pushed open the garden gate, where he stopped in mute horror. There on the iron seat, where he and Lily had sat so many many times, was James, locked in a passionate embrace with his youngest daughter.

'Tilly!' He had never been angrier with his youngest daughter. How could she betray her sister in this way?

Tilly pulled herself away from James' embrace in horror.

'Father, I–' She blushed scarlet, gathered her skirts up and said, 'Sorry,' before fleeing up the garden.

'I suggest you leave, sir,' Edward told James in icy tones. 'You are no longer welcome in my house.'

'I'm sorry,' said James. 'This is my fault, not Tilly's. We didn't mean it to happen, and we don't want to hurt anyone. But we've fallen in love.'

'I don't wish to hear it,' said Edward, in no mood to thaw, 'please, I want you to leave now.'

As he watched James leave, Edward looked around at the garden he'd created. He'd fashioned it from love, with so much hope for the future. Over the years it had been a place of joy and comfort, through good and bad times. And this was the darkest of times, and now all his foolish hopes lay in ruin and despair. He felt his garden was mocking him. What was he going to tell his beloved Connie? For the second time in her life, she was going to have her heart broken.

Chapter Twenty-Nine

'So, have you been to Wimbledon before?' asked Lauren, as they boarded the Waterloo train at Heartsease.

'Once,' said Kezzie. 'I was fifteen and me and my mates bunked off school and camped out on the pavement. It was fabulous. We got to see Sampras and Henman. What about you?'

'Nope,' said Lauren, 'but I've always wanted to. I can't believe I'm here, or that Troy has agreed to babysit.'

'He *is* their dad,' said Kezzie. 'And they are at school most of the day.'

'I know,' said Lauren, 'but since the children were born, I've never had a whole day away from them up in London. I adore them, but I could really do with a break. I'm so excited about to-day, I feel like I'm on holiday.'

'And so you should,' said Kezzie. 'You're insanely responsible for someone your age.'

'Hmm, well, I have a lot of responsibility,' said Lauren. 'But it is nice to have some time out.'

The journey into London was relatively swift, and they changed at Clapham Junction and were on their way to Wimbledon in record time.

It was a hot June day, and the crowds piling out of the underground at Southfields were clearly going the same way.

'This is fab,' said Kezzie, as they marched up to the gates with their tickets. 'No queuing for hours, *and* we have seats on Centre Court. Brilliant. Last time I was here I spent most of the day on Henman Hill, and only sneaked onto Centre Court at the end.'

They had arrived before play started and spent an hour or so just soaking up the atmosphere, watching some of the lesser-known players slugging it out on the outer courts, before finally taking their places on Centre Court, where Nadal was playing an unknown. They'd missed seeing Murray, who'd got through his match fairly easily the previous day. Kezzie wasn't sure if she was pleased or sorry. At least it cut down on the nerves factor.

The tennis they did see was fast and furious, and she and Lauren were on their feet by the end of a tense four setter, which Nadal won.

'Time for a break,' said Kezzie, in the pause before the next match was due to start. 'Do you need anything?'

'No, I'm OK here for a minute,' said Lauren. 'I'm just going to text Troy to check everything's OK at home.'

'I'll get us ice cream,' said Kezzie, and headed out towards the loos. She was just walking down the corridor underneath Centre Court when she stopped suddenly. There ahead of her in an animated conversation with a pretty young woman was – could it really be? – *Richard*. Oh my God. It couldn't possibly be. Kezzie felt the ground melt beneath her. She'd had no reply from her insanely stupid spur of the moment letter, not that she'd been expecting one, so Richard clearly didn't want to put things right. He was the last person she wanted to see.

Richard looked up and saw her before she could make a bolt for it. She felt as if she was fixed to the ground; trapped like a rabbit in the headlights.

Richard made an excuse to his companion and came towards her.

Kezzie froze to the spot. Her heart was hammering, and her stomach was in knots. Fear made her brazen.

'I see you haven't wasted any time,' she nodded at Richard's companion.

'*Kezzie!*' Richard said in exasperation.

'So, she is the new woman in your life?'

'Don't be daft. She's my new secretary.'

'Oh.' Maybe it was the secretary who'd answered Richard's phone the day she'd rung him. Kezzie's confidence drained away. This wasn't how she wanted things to go. 'So you haven't replaced me then?'

A slight smile played on Richard's lips, and a sudden heartbeat of desire shot through Kezzie. God she missed him. Standing so tantalizingly close to him made her realize just how much.

'As if I could replace you,' he said, and Kezzie melted into a puddle.

'Nor me, you,' whispered Kezzie.

They looked at each other for a long time, and a sense of sadness came over Kezzie. Richard hadn't replied to her letter. The past was the past, what they once had was gone forever.

'How are you?' Richard said eventually.

'Fine,' said Kezzie. 'Brilliant in fact. You?'

'Great,' said Richard, his hearty smile not quite reaching his eyes.

'Well, see you then?' said Kezzie, unable to cope with stringing out the situation any longer.

'How do I get in touch?' he called after her, to her surprise.

'If you'd bothered to read my letter, you'd know,' she said.

'Letter?' Richard sounded puzzled.

'The one I sent you,' she said, and walked away without daring to turn and look back. She thought Richard might have called her name, but she ignored him and carried on walking.

Joel was having a frantically busy day at work. He'd already sat through two difficult meetings in which they'd managed to save the charity plenty of money, but at a huge cost to their service users. Services were definitely having to go, and Joel didn't feel good about it. He was beginning to feel like the Jonah of the organization, whom everyone distrusted. It wasn't a great position to be in. At this rate it was going to be a pleasure to get home, which wasn't always how he felt. He was grateful to Eileen for looking after Sam for him. He stupidly hadn't thought through the implications of giving Lauren a day off, and though she'd offered Troy's help, he wasn't too keen on that idea. In the end, Eileen had volunteered, saying she owed him for getting New Horizons to come and play at the fete.

It was one of those sunny days in the summer, when it felt criminal to be at work. The office fan was working at full stretch, but all it seemed to do was fan hot air around. All the windows were open, but it still felt stuffy, and the room was full of the smell of stale sweat. Joel cursed the workload that meant he had been unable to go out for the day too.

He rang Eileen at lunchtime to see how she was getting on.

'Oh fine,' she said. 'Sam's having a lovely time, particularly as we've got Izzie here.'

'What's Izzie doing there?'

'The school rang,' said Eileen. 'She's got a bit of a cough and they sent her home.'

'Why couldn't Troy have her?' said Joel.

'They couldn't get hold of him or Lauren,' said Eileen, 'and I'm one of Lauren's emergency contact numbers. I don't mind, Izzie's no trouble at all.'

Joel snorted. 'Well, don't let Troy take advantage of you.'

'I'm sure he'll be back soon,' said Eileen, 'he still has to pick Immie up from school.'

Joel put the phone down and wondered if Lauren knew that Izzie was at home. He toyed with ringing her – but what could he say? Your boyfriend seems to have gone AWOL? – and decided not to. It wasn't really any of his business. He turned his attention to what he was supposed to be doing and forgot all about it.

At two thirty, Eileen rang him.

'Joel,' she said, sounding a bit tense, 'do you have Lauren's number? I seem to have lost it. Only I still can't get hold of Troy, and I think Izzie is getting worse. Her chest seems very tight, and she's coughing quite a lot. I'm not even sure if she has a puffer.'

Joel thought for a minute, and then he remembered seeing Lauren administer Ventolin the previous winter.

'I'm pretty sure she does have a puffer,' he said. 'Do you have spare keys to Lauren's place?'

'No, sorry.'

'I guess you'll have to keep trying Troy,' said Joel. 'But call the doctor if Izzie gets worse. Look, why don't I try to finish a bit early? I'll see if I can take some work home with me. At least relieve you of Sam.'

He gave her Lauren's mobile number and then started to clear his desk. Luckily things seemed to be calming down a bit. He called through to his assistant and told her what was happening. He felt a bit guilty about leaving so early in the day, but it wasn't as though he did this often. And this was an emergency. Lauren needed him. Even if she didn't know it yet.

The afternoon had turned sweltering, and Kezzie and Lauren were both wilting in the heat. They'd got to the point they were pouring water on their heads to cool down.

'I can't believe how much water I've drunk today,' said Kezzie. 'And yet I still feel thirsty.'

'We're going to look like lobsters tomorrow,' laughed Lauren, who had spent most of the day covering her fair skin up with Factor 50, but she didn't think it would be enough to stop her burning. 'But it's been worth it.'

'Apart from meeting Richard, it's been a great day,' agreed Kezzie.

'Damn,' Lauren had reached into her bag to check her mobile. 'I forgot to turn my phone back on after the match. Shit. I've missed a couple of calls from school. And Eileen by the looks of it.'

She felt the blood drain from her face. The school never rang. She thought back to this morning when she'd noticed that Izzie had a very slight scratchy cough, which was sometimes, though not always, a precursor to an asthma attack. She got through to the school first. 'She's where? Thank you so much for letting me know.' Lauren turned to Kezzie, who was looking questioningly at her. 'It's Izzie, she's ill.' She rang Eileen. 'You're where? She's what? Oh my God, Eileen, where's Troy? Don't worry, I'm on my way.'

She turned her phone off, feeling a sick panic in her stomach. *Should never have left them. Should never have left them,* pounded in her head. First sign of trouble and no sign of Troy. How could he do this to her? But that anger was wiped out with worry about Izzie. Lauren cursed the fact she was so far away from home.

'What's going on?' said Kezzie.

'Izzie, having an asthma attack,' said Lauren. 'Troy's disappeared and Eileen's with her at the

349

doctor's now. Bloody hell. The only time I've gone so far away and this has to happen.'

She started gathering her things together.

'I'm so sorry, Kezzie, but I'm going to have to go. Please don't feel you have to leave too.'

'Don't be daft,' said Kezzie. 'Of course I'll come with you, you can't go alone.'

They got up and raced to the exit. Suddenly Wimbledon seemed vast, and the crowds, which had excited Lauren on arrival, seemed hostile and threatening. The walk back to Southfields seemed longer than she'd remembered; the wait for a tube train to take them back to Wimbledon, interminable.

Lauren tried not to clock watch, and resisted the urge to ring Eileen every five minutes, but it was difficult. She was trying to stay calm, but her heart was pounding. Izzie's asthma attacks, though not frequent, were swift and sudden, and she could go from being relatively well to going downhill really quickly.

'If only I'd paid more attention to her cough,' said Lauren. 'I should never have come.'

'You weren't to know,' said Kezzie. 'Sod's law would have meant she'd be fine if you had stayed at home.'

'I suppose,' said Lauren, drumming her fingers on the train window, as they limped slowly into Wimbledon station. 'I just feel really guilty.'

'Don't,' said Kezzie. 'Come on, we're getting there as fast as we can.'

They were lucky with their connections at Wimbledon and Clapham Junction, and found themselves approaching Heartsease just over an

350

hour after Eileen had called.

Lauren called Troy again and got no reply. By now she was frantic with worry. Luckily there was a cab in the cab rank and she and Kezzie dived in and asked him to get home as quickly as possible. On hearing it was an emergency the cabbie drove as fast as he could. When Lauren got out, he said, 'I'll wait here for a minute, in case you need me to take you to the hospital.'

Hospital. Lauren hadn't even thought of that.

'Oh, thanks,' she said in surprise.

'I've got two asthmatic kids myself,' said the cabbie, by way of explanation. 'I know what it's like.'

Lauren raced into the house, where she found Troy, and a very pale and breathless Izzie lying forlornly on the sofa. She knew instantly that hospital was where they were heading.

Troy got up, looking panicked and helpless.

'You took your time,' he said. 'Doc says she's got to go to hospital if she gets worse.'

'Well, why on earth didn't you take her?' said Lauren. 'You can't muck around with a kid having an asthma attack. You should have taken her straight there!'

'I thought she'd be better with you,' said Troy. 'When Eileen called me, I just didn't know what to do. I panicked, I'm sorry.'

'Right,' said Lauren, 'she needs a bag. And her puffer. You get the car ready. We'll be in the hospital in no time.'

'Woah,' said Troy, 'I don't do hospitals.'

'Troy! She's your daughter,' said Lauren, 'it goes with the territory. You could at least drop us off and stay with Immie.'

She looked around. 'Hang on, where is Immie?'

'Eileen's got her,' said Troy. 'I couldn't cope with two of them. You know.'

'No,' said Lauren, 'I don't know. You have to get Immie, while I sort Izzie out.'

'This is just too much,' said Troy. 'I'm sorry, I just can't do this.'

And with that he walked out of the house.

'What?' Lauren was stunned, but she didn't have time to react to Troy's betrayal; concern for Izzie overrode any other feeling. 'Shit, I can't leave Immie with Eileen forever. I don't know what to do.'

'If you give me your house keys, I'll go and get Immie from Eileen's, if you like,' said Kezzie.

'Oh, would you?' Lauren was so grateful. 'Thanks. And could you run out and tell that cabbie I do need him, while I grab the things for Izzie.'

Lauren went into default emergency mode, picking up stuff she thought Izzie might need, and carrying her child to the taxi.

As the taxi sped off, she saw Troy walking down to the pub. He'd let her down again. But she hadn't got time to think about that right now. All that really mattered was Izzie.

Chapter Thirty

Kezzie flew round to Eileen's house.

'What the hell's been going on?' she said.

She was surprised to find Joel there with Sam. Immie was sitting watching TV, while Joel and Eileen were talking in quiet anxious tones in the kitchen.

'Troy's been going on,' said Eileen. 'Honestly, I thought my ex husband was useless in a crisis. But Troy's been worse than hopeless. He picked Immie up from school, but said he couldn't manage both of them and took Izzie home. I told him that the doctor said if she hadn't improved after having her puffer he should take her to hospital. I feel really bad now, I wish I'd taken her there myself.'

'Lauren's just gone in a cab,' said Kezzie. 'Troy didn't even go with her.'

'Damn,' said Joel. 'I'd have happily taken her. I don't like the thought of her being there on her own.'

'I'd go,' said Eileen, 'But I'm really sorry I've already promised to babysit for Niall.'

'And someone needs to stay and look after Immie,' said Kezzie. 'I said I would. I've got Lauren's house keys.'

'Great,' said Joel. 'Come on. Why don't we give Eileen a break and get these two over to Lauren's house while we work out what to do next?'

Immie was quiet as they crossed the road and she put her hand in Kezzie's. Kezzie was touched. She lacked experience with small children, but she had grown very fond of the twins since she'd been living in Heartsease.

'Izzie is going to be all right, isn't she?' said Immie.

Kezzie felt a bit helpless. What did you say to a four-year-old? She had only the vaguest notion of what asthma did to people, so she had no idea how seriously ill Izzie was. It must be so frightening for Immie, not knowing or understanding what was happening to her sister.

Joel came to the rescue. He squatted down, Sam in his arms, next to Immie and said, 'She'll be fine, sweetie. Mummy's taken her to the hospital, and the doctors there will help her get all better again. She'll soon be home, you'll see.'

That seemed to do the trick and within minutes of being inside, Izzie was busy playing with her dolls, while simultaneously making Sam laugh.

'They haven't had tea yet,' said Joel. 'I guess we'd better sort that out first.'

Kezzie was impressed by the speed at which Joel organized the tea. He was much better at this dad thing than he let on.

By now it was heading for seven, and there had been no word from Lauren.

'I really think someone should see if she's all right; I don't like the idea of her being alone,' said Joel. 'If I get Sam settled in the travel cot he sleeps in when he's here, would you be all right looking after him and Immie for a bit?'

Kezzie gulped. Apart from babysitting the twins

once, she hadn't looked after any children since the fiasco with Emily. Immie she felt she could cope with, but Sam? What if he didn't settle?

'Are you sure you trust me?' she said.

'Of course I am,' said Joel firmly. 'I presume you're not planning to spend the next few hours getting high as a kite?'

'No, of course not,' said Kezzie. She felt a wave of gratitude towards Joel. It felt good to be trusted again. 'Thanks. That means a lot to me.'

Lauren felt as though she'd been sitting in Casualty for hours. They'd been seen speedily by the triage nurse, who'd swiftly got them into the children's department, where Izzie was given a nebulizer to help open her airways.

'If she doesn't improve, we might have to keep her in,' said the nurse.

Lauren nodded. She knew the score. Izzie had been admitted to hospital twice previously – but she'd been smaller then. This time she was more aware of her surroundings and frantic when given the nebulizer. Lauren sweated buckets trying to keep her calm, and ensure the mask stayed on so she actually benefited from the Ventolin.

Once the nebulizer had finished, Izzie immediately perked up and became very lively. She wasn't at all happy to have to sit still while her vital signs were being monitored. The trouble was, every time they took the oxygen mask away her oxygen levels dropped, so in the end she had to have it on permanently, much to Izzie's disgust. She wriggled crossly on Lauren's lap, refusing point blank to lie down on the bed, while Lauren sat waiting for someone to come and pronounce sentence. The early evening had brought a rash of new patients, and Lauren was getting to the point when she thought she might have to call someone, when eventually a young doctor came in.

'Hello there,' he said, 'and who's this?'

'Izzie,' said Izzie crossly.

'And how are you feeling, Izzie?'

'Can't breathe,' said Izzie.

'Oh dear,' said the doctor, 'we'll have to do something about that.'

He did a swift but thorough examination of Izzie, managing to make her laugh in the process.

'Well,' he said, 'it looks like the nebulizer's helped a bit. I suggest we give her another one in about an hour, and with luck she might be able to get home.'

'That would be wonderful,' said Lauren, who'd been dreading the chaos of an overnight stay. The last time Izzie had been admitted her mum was around, but Mum had just gone off to see Auntie Jan, and Lauren didn't want to trouble her unnecessarily. There was nothing she could do from Manchester. For the first time she let herself think about Troy. How could he have done that to Izzie? That was what hurt the most, that he had been unable to help their daughter when she really needed it. Lauren wasn't sure she would ever be able to forgive him.

As she gave Immie the second nebulizer, a familiar face appeared round the cubicle.

'Hi, Lauren,' said Joel. 'I thought you could do with some company.'

'You thought right,' said Lauren. 'But where's

Sam? And what's happening with Izzie? I feel awful. I haven't even seen her.'

'Kezzie's got them both; they've been fed and they're now in bed,' said Joel. 'Please don't worry. Everything's under control. Do you want a coffee?'

'A coffee would be wonderful,' said Lauren. 'Thank you.'

Izzie's breathing seemed to get better after the nebulizer, so after another hour the doctor pronounced her ready to go home. He sent them home with a huge spacer, more puffers, and a course of steroids, which Lauren knew from past experience, would help enormously.

'Well, that's a huge relief,' said Lauren. She was carrying Izzie, who'd half dozed off in her arms in Joel's car. 'Thanks so much for the lift and everything.'

'No problem,' said Joel. 'I'm happy to do it.'

'Which is more than her dad was,' said Lauren. Bloody hell. She'd always thought Joel was a bit useless in a crisis, but he'd turned up trumps. Troy had done the opposite. He'd let her down again, but this was the last time.

Joel brought Lauren back into the house, and insisted he stay for a while after Kezzie had gone.

'You've had a shock,' he said, after Lauren put Izzie to bed, 'and I bet you haven't eaten. Sit down and have a drink, and I'll knock you up something.'

Joel spent a happy half an hour cooking up a stir fry. Although Lauren's kitchen was smaller than his, it felt so much more homely and comfortable than his huge, sterile one. As they

357

sat down to eat, he sensed Lauren was beginning to relax.

'Thanks so much for this, Joel,' she said. 'I can't tell you how much it's meant to me the way you've all rallied round.'

'My pleasure,' said Joel. 'Besides, I owe you so much the way you've looked after Sam for me. I couldn't have managed without you.'

Lauren blushed.

'Don't be silly,' she said. 'I'm sure you would have been fine. Sam's got a great dad.'

'I doubt it,' said Joel. 'I was such a mess after Claire died, and I didn't have the first idea of how to look after Sam. You taught me how to be a proper dad, and I'm really grateful.'

'Claire did say you were struggling with it, at first,' said Lauren.

'Did she?' Joel felt a sharp pang. He knew he deserved that assessment, but it still hurt to hear how much he'd let Claire down. She'd been right of course. She always was.

'But she also said that you'd get there in time,' said Lauren. 'She was always telling me how kind you were. And you know she was right. I felt so cross with you on her behalf, I couldn't see it before. I misjudged you, and I'm sorry.'

'I'm not sure you did misjudge me,' said Joel. It was on the tip of his tongue to tell Lauren about Claire's last night, but he couldn't bear to shatter her newfound admiration of him. It meant so much that she thought better of him now.

Just then the key turned in the door.

'I'd better be going,' said Joel, tactfully. 'I'll get Sam up and I'll be out of your hair. But if you need me tomorrow, just ask. I'll be there.'

'I will,' said Lauren. 'Thanks.'

Troy wandered into the kitchen looking sheepish.

'I'm sorry for earlier,' he said. 'I stuffed up. And I panicked. I didn't know what to do.'

'Luckily for Izzie, that I do then,' said Lauren drily.

'How's Izzie?' Troy said, awkwardly.

'Better,' said Lauren. 'She'll be OK now.'

'I'll be off,' said Joel hastily, carrying a sleepy Sam out of the cot and towards the front door.

'Will you be OK?' Joel asked, as Lauren saw him to the door.

'I expect so,' said Lauren, her smile bleak. 'I feel so stupid. Everyone told me Troy would let me down and he has.'

'Don't beat yourself up,' said Joel, 'you only wanted the best for everyone.'

'And look what's happened,' said Lauren. 'Izzie was lucky not to be seriously ill.'

She looked so devastated, Joel put one arm round her and kissed the top of her head.

'If there's anything I can do?'

'You've done more than enough,' said Lauren. 'I don't know how to thank you.'

'You don't have to,' said Joel. 'What are friends for?'

He carried Sam to the car and strapped him in, waving at Lauren before speeding off in the darkness.

His last view of Lauren showed her framed in the porch light, looking lost and lonely. He wished there was something he could do about that.

Chapter Thirty-One

Lauren woke up with a headache. She hadn't slept well. To Troy's evident disgust, she'd insisted on taking Izzie in with them when she went to bed. Although Izzie seemed much better, there was a little residue of worry lodged in Lauren's brain, and she had a sleepless night fretting every time Izzie coughed. It was like going back to when the girls were babies. She'd sent Troy to sleep on the couch, too exhausted to deal with what she knew she must. Lauren woke to a grey, steely dawn while Izzie tossed and turned and coughed, but by sunrise, Lauren was relieved to see Izzie's breathing had improved.

Troy was still asleep when she came downstairs. She ignored him while she got Immie ready for school. She hadn't quite worked out how she was going to get Immie there, as there was no way she was leaving Izzie with Troy, when there was a knock on the door. It was Joel.

'Hi,' she said, feeling absurdly shy all of a sudden. 'Sorry, I'm running a bit late, I'd forgotten all about Sam.'

'Don't worry, that's all sorted,' said Joel. 'It occurred to me you might need someone to take Immie to school.'

'What about work?'

'I've arranged to go in late, and Eileen kindly said she'd have Sam for me again this morning.

Kezzie's offered to have him for the afternoon and she will pick up Immie for you.'

'That's really kind.' Tears prickled Lauren's eyes. She felt truly grateful to have thoughtful friends who supported her, even if the person who was meant to didn't.

She got Immie ready and waved them goodbye. Now Immie had seen her sister was better, she seemed happy enough to trot off to school, holding on to Sam's buggy, and chattering nineteen to the dozen with Joel.

He was a natural with her, Lauren realized with a jolt. Why had she never noticed that before?

She sighed and went to the kitchen and started to sort out laundry. Izzie, who'd been as lively as a cricket first thing, thanks to a dose of Ventolin, was now fast asleep upstairs, and Troy had yet to emerge from the lounge. It was going to be a long morning.

Izzie eventually woke up and came downstairs, trailing her teddy and demanding a boiled egg. She was just finishing it when Troy came into the kitchen.

He looked a wreck: his eyes were bloodshot, and his breath reeked of booze and fags.

'How's my little munchkin today?' said Troy, going over and tickling Izzie under the chin.

'Better,' said Lauren. She bit her lip, not wanting to say anything that might provoke an argument when Izzie was still in the room. She waited till Troy had cleared his junk from the lounge, and Izzie was settled in front of the TV curled under a duvet, before saying, 'It's a shame you weren't more concerned yesterday.'

'I'm sorry, I panicked,' said Troy. 'You know I hate hospitals and doctors.'

'But you were in charge,' said Lauren. 'She needed you. *I* needed you. You let us both down.'

Lauren spoke in a low, urgent whisper so as not to upset Izzie.

'Look, babe, you know I'm a free spirit,' said Troy. 'I've never pretended otherwise.'

'But I thought you'd changed,' said Lauren. 'I really believed you wanted to be different for the kids' sake. But at the first sign of trouble, you run out on me. You can't do that. You need to take responsibility.'

'I won't let you down again,' said Troy. 'I promise.'

'Till the next time,' said Lauren. 'I've heard it all before. I can't trust you.'

'You can, babes, really you can,' said Troy, pleadingly. 'Yesterday I know I cocked up, but I panicked. I didn't know what to do. I hate hospitals, you know I do, ever since Mum...'

'I know all that,' said Lauren, 'but Izzie needed you. Couldn't you rise above your problems for her? Being a parent isn't just about the fun things, it's about putting the needs of your children above yourself, and I'm sorry, Troy, I just don't think you can do that.'

She was sorry, too. Lauren had really wanted this to work.

'So what are you saying?' said Troy.

'I'm saying it's over,' said Lauren. 'I want you to leave.'

'Where will I go?' Troy looked pretty woebegone, and she did feel sorry for him; it wasn't his fault that life had dealt him a bum deal, so he didn't know how to take responsibility, but she wasn't going to carry him any longer.

'I don't really know, and I don't really care,' said Lauren. 'I just want you out of my hair. I won't stop you seeing the girls, but I don't want you living here any more.'

Troy started to protest, but she silenced him with a look.

She knew she'd have a rocky few weeks with the girls. Having introduced their dad back into their lives, it was going to be tough on them losing him again. But it was the right thing to do. For all of them.

'So Troy's gone, has he?' Kezzie was flabbergasted by Lauren's news.

'He will be by the end of the week,' said Lauren, with a sigh. 'You were all right. I should never have got back with him again. What an idiot.'

'We all make mistakes,' said Kezzie. 'And I know you wanted to make it work.'

'I did,' said Lauren, 'probably too much. I should have listened to my head. I think Troy means well, but I don't think he can change.'

Kezzie toyed with telling Lauren what had happened with her and Troy, but decided to let bygones be bygones. Troy was history. Lauren didn't need to know and it was best all round if it were forgotten.

'And Izzie's OK now?' said Kezzie.

'Well, look at her,' said Lauren, as Izzie tore around the garden with her sister, 'what do you think?'

'What a relief,' said Kezzie. 'I hadn't realized till now what a worry it must be to have children. I'm seeing Richard in a whole new light, I can tell you. I wasn't very understanding about Emily. I saw her as a threat to our happiness. Stupid isn't it, being jealous of a fourteen-year-old.'

'Not really,' said Lauren. 'I think it's easy to be jealous of a partner's obsession with their children. Claire always said she thought Joel was a bit jealous of Sam.'

'From what he's told me, I think he probably was,' said Kezzie.

'But she also understood it came from a love of her,' said Lauren. 'I always thought she was too soft on him, and let him get away with murder. But I think I might have misjudged him. He was brilliant yesterday.'

'Well, he's a good man,' said Kezzie. 'He's had an extraordinarily difficult time.'

'I know,' said Lauren. 'I think I've been a bit hard on him.'

Kezzie made her excuses and went home. She was putting together the final touches of the Edward Handford display for Eileen, and though she had been searching, she hadn't found a diary of Lily's dated after 1919. Lily wrote a lot about her grief for Harry, and then nothing. Kezzie decided to see if there was any more information that Joel could give her.

She put away her laptop and poured herself a glass of wine. As she settled down to relax on the sofa, she heard a bleep from her mobile phone to say she had a text.

Kezzie, is this you? Richard.

Richard. Kezzie looked at her phone in stunned silence. How had he got her number? And moreover, why was he texting her? She sat looking at the text for ages. She should ring him back. Nothing ventured, nothing gained and all that. But she'd sent him that letter weeks ago, and he hadn't responded till now. Their relationship couldn't have meant as much to him as it did to her. And she couldn't bear to be hurt again. She deleted the text message and switched off her phone. She wasn't sure she was ready for Richard just yet.

'So what is it you're looking for, exactly?' said Joel.

'I'm not sure,' said Kezzie. 'I've read everything up until the end of the war. Edward and Lily's son died right at the end, and Lily seems to have gone into a decline. Her diary entries are really sad, and then they stop altogether, not long before she died. I'd love to know what happened next. Does your mum know?'

'Mum doesn't seem to know very much about her,' said Joel. 'She says her mother never talked about Lily.'

'There's still one box of letters we haven't been through. Let's see if we can find anything.'

They pored over the letters – some of them from Edward about work-related matters, others from Connie to her fiancé, James, and one slightly cryptic letter from Tilly apologizing to Connie for something.

'Here, look,' said Joel, 'there's a letter from Edward to Connie, dated just before Lily died.'

My darling Connie,
Your mother's progress is still slow. I have hopes that come spring we may see some improvement in her spirits. But now, coming up to the anniversary of Harry's death, she is very low indeed. I wish she had some strength to see beyond her grief, but I fear this has been too much for her.

As to the other matter. Your sister is insisting on marrying James as soon as she can. I'm sorry, darling, if it pains you. But we cannot help where our hearts lead us, and I am sure she did not mean to hurt you. Please come home to us before Christmas. The house is too quiet without you.

Your loving Father

'Crikey, what was all that about?' said Kezzie. 'Who's James?'

'I think that must be my great grandfather,' said Joel. He frowned. 'That would certainly explain the rift between Connie and Tilly. Perhaps James was seeing Connie first. Mum didn't know much about it when I asked her.'

'Poor Lily, what a sad life she had,' said Kezzie. 'I wonder what happened to her.'

'All I know is that no one ever spoke about her death,' said Joel. He had such a lot of fellow feeling for Edward, who'd also lost his wife relatively young, and in tragic circumstances. 'My family seems to have had its fair share of secrets,'

'It certainly does,' said Kezzie. 'It would be nice to find out what really happened, wouldn't it?'

Chapter Thirty-Two

Joel had taken Sam to pick up his mum for lunch at his house, as he was keen to show her how the garden had progressed. He was intrigued by the letters he and Kezzie had found and wondered if his mother could shed more light on them.

'I've never seen any of this before,' his mother said, as she read through them. 'But Connie always kept things close to her chest. I had no idea she'd hidden all this stuff away. I presume it was her; everything's labelled in her writing. And from what I remember of her, she did rather see herself as the guardian of the family honour. Mother always said there were hidden secrets here.'

'I wonder why she didn't destroy all this, then,' said Joel.

'She was very close to her father,' said Mum. 'Perhaps she couldn't bear to.'

'So what actually happened to Lily? How did she die?'

'Well, I know she drowned, but apart from that nothing. There was always some great secret about her death. Everyone referred to her in hushed tones, if at all.'

'What about Edward? What happened to him afterwards?'

'I think he became quite reclusive,' said his mother. 'He locked up the garden and retired from public life. He came to stay with us sometimes and we visited a few times, when Connie was out, because Connie refused to have anything to do with either my mother or my grandparents. She was never keen for us to come.'

'I'm guessing it's because Tilly went off with her fiancé?' said Joel, who'd read it in Edward's diary.

'Is that what happened?' said his mother. 'That would explain so much. Again, it was never discussed. I knew there was a great divide of course, but not why. My mother always tried to make it up to Connie, but Connie wouldn't have it, and hated us coming to see Edward. I remember once almost sneaking in to see him. And Mother insisting on taking him into the garden, because Connie always kept it locked up. I picked a bunch of pansies for him and gave it to him. I was probably three or four years old. I remember it so clearly because he cried, poor man. I suppose he was thinking of Lily.'

'That's sad,' said Kezzie, who had joined them for lunch. 'Do you think he ever got over her death?'

'From what my mother said, no.'

'What about Connie and Tilly? What happened there?'

'Well, they never made up, and then Tilly died not long after the Second World War,' said Joel's mum. 'Connie married Uncle Philip sometime in the twenties, but it wasn't a happy union, and their son Jack was very isolated. My mother saw him only rarely. Connie was quite scary and bitter, from what I remember of her.'

'The plot thickens,' said Kezzie. 'I feel quite sorry for Connie. She lost her first fiancé, then it looks like her sister stole her second. No wonder she was bitter.'

'She softened a little in her old age,' said Joel's mum. 'I think she liked the fact that I'd formed a bond, however small, with her father. And though she was never keen to have Mother in the house, I did visit her here quite often, when she was a very old woman, and I think she almost liked me in the end.'

The sun was streaming through the trees and Joel was keen to show his mother the work Kezzie had done in the garden. The box, ivy and rosemary were thickening nicely, delineating the curve of the heart shapes clearly, and the flowers that Kezzie had planted in each of the corners were blooming beautifully. The smell of the hollyhocks and sweet peas which were an inspired late addition to the design, climbed the wall at the back of the flowerbeds, filling the air with their rich scents, and the roses in the centre bowed slowly in the breeze.

'But it's magnificent,' said Joel's mum, clapping her hands with delight. 'It was still just about being tended to when I was here as a child, but I've never seen it looking as good as this. Well done, Kezzie.'

'Thanks,' said Kezzie shyly.

'I think you've proved you're worthy of entry to Chelsea now,' said Joel.

'Yeah, well, maybe,' said Kezzie, but she looked pleased.

'We'll go to the Memorial Gardens after lunch,'

said Joel, 'and show you how we've got on there.'

They sat out on the patio in the sunshine eating their lunch, with Sam wandering about, looking out over the Downs. Wood pigeons cooed in the trees, and a warm breeze wafted by. It was most idyllic, and Joel sat back and relaxed, feeling pretty content with life.

After lunch they decamped into the car, Joel's mum not being able to walk that far, and again she was full of praise for what Kezzie had done.

'It's wonderful,' she said. 'I'm so impressed with what you've achieved. So when's the great re-opening?'

'At the Summer Fest in two weeks' time,' said Joel. 'There are several other gardens opening up in the area, and someone from the RHS is coming to judge them. I hope you'll be there.'

'I wouldn't miss it for the world,' said his mum.

Lauren had had a lovely, lazy morning with the girls, but they were getting restless, so she decided to take them to the park. They seemed to have adapted pretty quickly to Troy's disappearance from the cottage. He had managed to see them a couple of times, but the girls reported that his rented room smelt 'stinky', and Izzie let slip that he'd smoked when Lauren had been out, and 'we didn't like it, Mummy,' so Lauren concluded they weren't too traumatized by recent events. They clearly missed the fun side of their dad, but his quick, volatile temper, and ability to get bored with them quickly, was enough to worry them; they seemed easier now he wasn't there. Lauren had to admit life was less fraught.

She hadn't realized till Troy had left she had been tiptoeing around him much of the time, fitting in with things the way he wanted them. That was no way to live your life or have a relationship.

'Come on, let's go and play Pooh sticks by the stream,' said Lauren.

'Yeah!' said Izzie.

'Yeah! Yeah!' said Immie, and the three of them set off halfway down the hill into Heartsease, to the bridge which spanned the little brook that ran out of the town and fed into the wider stream that ran at the fields at the bottom of Joel's house.

It was baking hot again – this summer seemed to be endlessly sunny – and the children soon ran out of steam, so Lauren let them have ice creams along the way.

Eventually they got to the bridge over the little stream, which was looking distinctly dry and stagnant. There was a light breeze, but it wasn't enough to affect the sluggish current, so the girls' sticks didn't get far.

'Mine's stuck,' wailed Izzie.

'Mine's not.' Immie gleefully pointed out that hers was moving at a gentle pace under the bridge.

'I won! I won!' said Immie.

'Not fair,' pouted Izzie.

'Come on, don't fight,' said Lauren. 'Let's have another go.'

But the girls had got bored.

'Can we go to the playground?' they said.

'No problem,' said Lauren, though she rather felt as if she might wilt by the time she got there. Lauren followed them as they ran the rest of the way into Heartsease. Troy had been a huge mistake. But the girls hadn't been. They were the one good thing he'd left her with. What would her life be without them?

As she came to the playground she saw Joel and Sam. She stepped forward to say hello, and then paused. Kezzie was there, sitting on a bench with Joel's mum, whom Lauren had met once or twice. They were deep in conversation and Joel came over to them with Sam bouncing on his shoulders. They looked for all the world like a happy family unit.

Lauren felt a sudden pang of – could it be? – jealousy? She thought back to all those weeks ago, when Joel had made his clumsy declaration of love. She'd rejected him then, sure that Troy was what she wanted. But recently she'd revised her opinion of Joel, and come to see him in a different light. He'd been so sweetly supportive of her when Izzie was ill, and she had begun to think of him with something more than affection. Although her feelings were complicated by a sense of guilt about Claire, and she had been wondering if she was right to let herself be attracted to him. He had seemed quite distant to her in the last few weeks, and now she could see why. Who could blame him? Kezzie was attractive, nice and fun. It looked like Lauren had blown her chances.

'Time I was off,' said Kezzie, laughing as Sam careered straight into her legs.

'We'd better get going too,' said Joel. 'I've got to get Mum home before she turns into a pumpkin.'

'It's not quite *that* bad,' said his mother, laughing. 'But you're right; I do need to get back home.'

They gathered up their things and left the gardens in high spirits. It was only as they turned out of the gate, and Kezzie glanced back once more to look at her creation, she thought she caught a glimpse of Lauren. How strange, why hadn't she come to say hello?

If it was Lauren, she was too far away now, and Kezzie had a few things to do at home for the Edward Handford display.

Joel dropped Kezzie off and she went straight on to her laptop, importing images of the gardens Edward had designed for the rich and famous; the Lovelace Cottage knot garden then and now; family pictures, and a couple of photos of the war memorial.

She inputted the text that Eileen had written, with information provided by Kezzie.

Then she went through the latest lot of papers she'd taken from Joel's house to see if there was anything she'd missed. It was then she found it. Picking up a book that had some of Lily's sketches in, a piece of paper fluttered out. It was a letter from Lily to Edward.

Lovelace Cottage
November 11 1919

My darling Edward,
I have loved you for more than half my lifetime, and I love you still. But it is not enough to heal the hole in my heart left by Harry's death. I fear I am a huge burden to you and the girls, and I cannot stand to be

that any longer.
Goodbye my love, and forgive me,
Lily.

Oh *no.* Kezzie felt a rush of horrified sympathy. Lily had committed suicide. *That* was the great family secret. Kezzie sat reading and rereading the letter in total shock. Poor, poor Lily, who had had to deal with so much, and ultimately been unable to cope. And poor Edward, left all alone without her.

She wondered if she should show the letter to Eileen. All the available information about Lily implied she'd drowned by accident, but this letter suggested otherwise. Kezzie frowned. She and Eileen had already decided that some of the more personal letters and diary entries weren't suitable for public display; it wouldn't be right to show this either. If Edward had covered up Lily's suicide, who was she to reveal the truth? Let sleeping dogs lie, and let Lily have drowned in a tragic accident.

She'd just finished for the evening and emailed the document over to Eileen for her to check it over, when an email dropped into her tray.

To: kezziesescape@hotmail.com
From:Rich@yahoo.co.uk
Dear Kezzie,
You're a hard woman to track down. Given what you said in your letter, which incidentally, you didn't address properly, so consequently took ages to arrive, I don't know why you didn't return my text. The last email address you gave me bounced, but Flick kindly

forwarded your details. She told me about the garden you've been working on and I thought I'd come and see it for myself. I'll be at your Summer Fest, if that's OK with you?
  Richard

Richard, here in Heartsease? Why did he suddenly want to see her now, after all this time? Her heart beat wildly. Maybe he was prepared to forgive her after all? But his tone sounded so formal. And businesslike. He probably just wanted to get her to do some work for a friend. But then, why not say so? And why come all the way down here? Her head was in a flat spin. She couldn't have him here. Not on the most important day of her working life.

To: Rich@yahoo.co.uk
From: kezziesescape@hotmail.com
I'll kill Flick. Don't think it's a good idea for you to come. Can send you pics of garden. Then maybe later we can discuss other stuff.
  Kezzie.

Her fingers hovered over the keyboard for a moment. Should she have been a bit more friendly? Decisions, decisions.
  'Take the bull by the horns, Kez,' she said. Then pressed send. Too late to change her mind now.

Edward and Lily

1919

Lily's diary, November 1919
It is nearly a year since we lost our beloved Harry.
Not a day goes by without me thinking of him. Not a
single day, not an hour, not a minute. I thought I
could not bear the pain, all those years ago, when I lost
my precious babies. But then Connie came and Harry
and Tilly. I have been a poor mother and not loved
Connie as I should. Perhaps saving all my fierce pro-
tective love for Harry was a sin, for it led me to neglect
Connie. I see that now. Connie who is so brave, and
strong, and a better person than I am by far. Well, if it
was a sin, I am being punished. I think I will be in
Hell forever.

Edward sat by Lily's bedside, holding her hand.

'I cannot believe it has been a year,' she said. Her eyes were seeped with pain and her face looked gaunt. She had lost so much weight in the last year, but try as he might, Edward couldn't get her to eat.

'Harry wouldn't have wanted us to grieve forever,' he said. 'And we aren't the only family to suffer such a loss. We must look to the future and Tilly's wedding.'

'A wedding without her brother and sister?' said Lily. 'How can we look forward to that? Poor

Connie, I thought she and James would get married. Had I known what Tilly was doing, I would have made sure she was sent away.'

'They're young, they couldn't help it,' said Edward. Faced with the vision of his youngest daughter's evident love for James, Edward had been unable to condemn the young lovers for long. 'I'm sorry, too, for Connie, but there has been so much heartache, I cannot be sorry that James and Tilly have found happiness. In time, Connie will come to see it is better that she was not with someone who didn't love her as she deserved.'

'Do you think so?' said Lily. 'I don't think Connie will ever forgive Tilly.'

Edward sighed. He feared that Lily was right. His eldest daughter was headstrong and stubborn, and she'd been besotted with James. Edward had been so happy that she had found someone after George. Neither he nor Lily had foreseen this. The garden he had built as a monument to love now seemed to be poisoned with despair.

He patted Lily's hand and left her to go downstairs. On this, the eve of the anniversary of Harry's death, he felt the need to stroll to the church and light a candle to his son's memory. He left Lily sleeping, not intending to be long.

When he returned, the house was in darkness. The girl from the village who came to 'do' for them had long gone, Tilly was visiting James' family, and Connie was working in a hospital in London, refusing to come home.

He called to Lily, but there was no reply. He went upstairs to their room and found it empty. Her white coat and galoshes were gone. By the bedside was a note. He read it with a growing sense of horror, and let out a howl of anguish when he realized what she intended.

No. No. *No.* He had often worried she might do something foolish, but never really believed it. Running through the house, calling her name, Edward thought frantically about where she might have gone. Then he realized. It was obvious, she would have gone down to the river, where they had spent so many happy family times. He ran down to the riverbank calling her name in the wind. Then he saw her standing alone on the other side of the river, which was swollen with recent heavy rain.

'Lily!' he called over the wind and rain. 'Lily, no!'

She turned. Had she heard him? Did she give just one last glance in his direction? He could never be sure. All he knew was that she cast herself in the river, and it bore her swiftly away. *There is a willow grows aslant a brook ...* a line from Shakespeare came to him as he frantically tore up and down the riverbank, but of Lily there was no sign.

It was three days before her body was discovered. Edward had walked the length of the riverbank searching for her – until finally he found her – her body finally at rest underneath the willow bank. In her hands she clutched a bunch of violets.

Edward took her body in his arms, and gently loosened the collar of her coat. She looked still and peaceful in death. Her skin was so cold and white, giving her an other-worldly air. Struggling with her body, he realized how heavy her coat was. Not just because it was sodden with water. She'd put heavy stones in her pocket. She'd never intended to come out of the water. It was, as he feared, a deliberate act. Frantically, he emptied her pockets. He could never tell anyone. No one must ever know. Everyone must think it was a tragic accident.

At her funeral Edward nodded, and accepted the gentle offers of condolence, agreed it was a tragedy, and was the image of a bereaved husband bearing his loss with dignity. Yet all the while a torrent swelled within him, as strong as the one that bore Lily away, as he raged at life, at love, at Lily, and the things he'd lost.

Chapter Thirty-Three

'This is looking great,' said Eileen. She had come over to Kezzie's to go through the information for the exhibition. They had a succession of posters, with pictures of Lovelace Cottage and gardens, Edward Handford and his family and pictures of the gardens he'd worked on. 'I think you've done Edward Handford proud.'

'Thanks,' said Kezzie. 'In a way I feel I've got to know him quite well. I think he was an amazing person.'

'I think it was wonderful the way Edward paid for the war memorial,' said Eileen, referring to a piece Kezzie had written about Harry Handford's death.

'From his letters, it looks as though Edward felt it was his duty to put up a memorial for all the other people in the village who'd also lost their sons,' said Kezzie. 'I think it was a lovely gesture. It's a shame we can't have the memorial back in time for the Summer Fest.'

'I know,' said Eileen. 'But I'm hoping we'll be able to get it back in time for this year's Remembrance Day parade.'

'That would be brilliant,' said Kezzie. 'Will your son be back by then?'

Eileen's son was due back from his tour of duty in Afghanistan soon, and everyone knew how worried she was about him.

'I hope so,' said Eileen. 'I try not think more than a day or two ahead. Every time I see a soldier's been killed out there, I think about Jamie. It's enough to send you crazy. I've stopped watching the news.'

'I wish there was something I could do,' said Kezzie.

'What can anyone do?' said Eileen. 'I just have to grit my teeth and get on with it, and hope for the best. Running the Summer Fest has been a great distraction. It's really taken my mind off things.'

The Summer Fest was less than a week away, and already the village was getting ready for it: bunting was going up in the High Street, and a marquee was going to be erected on the field on Friday night. Along with Joel's garden, there were four or five other large gardens in the area opening up to the public. Eileen had arranged for someone from the RHS to come and judge them. And

Anthony Grantham was planning to come down to do a feature on the knot garden on the day itself.

'You never know,' she said to Kezzie, 'this could be your big moment. Someone might talent spot you.'

'Wouldn't that be amazing?' said Kezzie.

However, there was one important person she wasn't sure she wanted to come. Richard hadn't replied to her last email, nor had he tried to ring her again. She felt as though she were in limbo. Part of her was excited by the prospect of potentially seeing him again, and the other half wondered why he had suddenly decided to get in contact now. It had been ten months since they'd split up. Richard had been very clear then about not wanting to have anything to do with her again, and although his email had sounded more conciliatory, she didn't dare hope that he'd changed his mind. Kezzie didn't understand why he wanted to come and see the gardens she'd restored, unless it was to offer her some avenues for work. But why would he do that? All in all, she felt it would be better if he didn't come. She had no idea what he was up to.

Lauren was covered in flour. She was busy baking shortbread and cupcakes for the cake stand she'd offered to run on Saturday, and beginning to think she had bitten off more than she could chew. With Sam in the house she'd been able to get something done, enlisting him to help stir the mixture when he was bored with playing with his toys, though of course more of the mixture had ended up in his mouth than anywhere else. But when the girls came home from school all hell broke loose. Both of them wanted to help, but neither of them was really much help at all. Lauren lost count of the number of eggs that ended up on the floor – at one point she had to prevent an all-out egg war, when Sam put his hands in the egg yolk with delight, and smeared it all over Izzie's face. By the time Joel came to pick Sam up, she was run ragged.

'What's been going on in here?' Joel laughed, as he walked into Lauren's normally pristine kitchen and found it looking as though a bomb had exploded in it. Izzie and Immie were sitting up at the work counter, licking cake mixture out of a bowl. There was flour everywhere, and Sam appeared to have sat on an egg.

'I'm trying to make cakes for the Summer Fest,' said Lauren. 'And I'm getting a little too much help.'

'I can see you are,' said Joel. 'Right, why don't I get my little monster out of your hair and then I'll ask Christine to pop round to babysit for a couple of hours and come and help you bake some cakes.'

'You? Bake cakes?' snorted Lauren. 'Now I've heard everything.'

'I'll have you know my son and I do a fine line in cookies,' Joel said, mock seriously. 'It's a really good way to waste a boring Sunday afternoon. So what do you say?'

'I say, that sounds rather brilliant,' said Lauren. 'Only I'd better just clean Sam up before you take him home, or your car seat will end up covered in egg and flour.'

By the time Joel returned a couple of hours later, Lauren had regained control of her kitchen and the twins were in bed.

'Thanks so much for doing this,' she said. 'Only like an idiot I promised to make lots of cakes, and I just forgot how difficult it was going to be with the kids around. I'm going to be up all night tomorrow at this rate.'

'Well, let's see what we can do,' said Joel. 'I am here to follow your orders.'

'I thought you were the cupcake king,' teased Lauren.

'I do cookies,' said Joel, 'cupcakes are a whole new territory.'

'Watch and learn,' said Lauren.

With Joel helping not only did the time go by fast, but it was much quicker, as Lauren could double up the quantities she was making. There was a slight problem in terms of how many cakes she could actually get in her oven, but luckily Kezzie came to the rescue and offered hers as a back-up. Once they got a system going of making up the mixture, putting it in cases, cooking them for twenty minutes and then leaving them to cool while the next batch went in, things moved along very smoothly. Lauren found to her surprise she was enjoying herself, and felt more relaxed with both Kezzie and Joel than she had done in months. By 10 p.m. they had made one hundred and fifty cakes. Lauren was running out of boxes to put them in, but again, Kezzie helped, producing tons of Tupperware.

'I guess Aunt Jo goes to a lot of Tupperware

parties,' she said. 'I found stacks of these in the cupboard.'

'Ah, I know what that is,' said Lauren. 'She ran the cake stall last year.'

'What are you going to do with this lot now?' said Joel.

'Tomorrow, I decorate,' said Lauren, 'and hope I can get it done before the girls get home. Thanks, guys, I couldn't have done it without you.'

'No worries,' said Joel, getting up to leave, as Kezzie headed back next door. Lauren felt an unexpected stab of jealousy. She had a sneaky feeling something was going on.

Joel spent the Friday night before the Summer Fest clearing the house, making sure it was suitable for the visitors they were hoping for. He looked at Lovelace Cottage with fresh eyes, taking in the brightness of the hallway, now decorated in airy light colours as he'd always intended, the friendliness of the lounge, which felt more like a cosy family room than a barren place to watch TV, and the comforting solidity of the dining room, now about to play host to part of the exhibition. With a jolt of pleasure, he realized that in the past few months his house had finally become a home.

Kezzie and Eileen came over in the early evening to sort out the exhibition. They had decided to use the study, and Edward's newly restored desk to show where he'd worked on his designs. They were going to use the dining room for the rest of the exhibition, as it had space for the impressive-looking displays that Eileen had created. On the centre of the dining room table they carefully laid out Edward's original designs.

'It looks brilliant,' said Joel, when he'd seen their hard work. 'I think people are going to be really fascinated.'

After Eileen had gone, Kezzie went into the garden to sort out a floral display of pots on the patio; Joel mowed the lawn while she worked. The sun was setting as he mowed, and swallows weaved their way in and out of the sky above the garden. The sheep in the field at the bottom of the garden were baaing happily in the distance, lambs gambolling at their mothers' feet, and he could hear faint music coming from a house, where someone was clearly having a party. The smell of barbecues being stoked wafted up from the valley. It was a sweltering evening, so Joel took his shirt off and wiped the sweat off his brow.

'Oi, put it away,' joked Kezzie.

Joel laughed, 'It's really hot work this. I wouldn't be surprised if we had a thunderstorm tonight.'

'Oh God, I hope not,' said Kezzie. 'They did say the weather was about to turn, but it would be a real pity if it changed overnight. That marquee in the field will probably blow away.'

'Yes it would be a shame,' said Joel, 'after everyone's hard work. And I would like to be able to show off Edward's garden at its best.'

He finished what he was doing and went to get a clean shirt.

'Drink?' he said, walking back into the garden with a bottle of champagne and two glasses.

'What's that in aid of?' said Kezzie.

'It's to say thank you,' said Joel. 'You came along and shook me out of my stupor. You made me see that the garden and house were still worth restoring. You've reminded me that life still goes on. I couldn't have got through the last few months without you.'

'Oh, stop it,' said Kezzie, blushing. 'I've been a pain in the arse, mainly.'

'I mean it,' said Joel. He popped the champagne cork, and poured them both a glass. 'You've made such a great difference to my life. I'll always be indebted to you.'

'To the garden and Edward Handford,' said Kezzie, raising her glass.

'And to us,' said Joel, 'survivors of the storm.'

'To us,' said Kezzie, clinking her glass against his, and taking a sip of champagne.

A door slammed shut in the house. Damn, Joel thought. He had been in and out of the front door and must have left it open.

'Better just check I haven't had burglars,' he said.

He went into the kitchen and there on the kitchen table were two little bags full of beautifully decorated cupcakes. There was a note from Lauren, saying *Thanks for your help last night, one's for you and one's for Sam xx,* but no sign of Lauren.

How odd. Why hadn't she come to say hello?

Chapter Thirty-Four

'Right, how are we doing?' Eileen asked, as she arrived at the cake stall, which Lauren was setting up with the girls. Lauren had been up late the night before, tying the cakes and cookies she'd made up in packets of cellophane wrapped up in ribbon. The effect was very impressive. And then she'd woken up early, the image of what she'd seen at Joel's house going over and over in her mind.

The twins had been too hot to sleep, so she decided to take them out for a walk to Joel's, to give him some cakes to say thank you, and to have a look at the garden. She hadn't expected Kezzie to be there – but of course she would be, given that the garden was her project. Joel didn't hear her ring on the doorbell, and so she tentatively pushed the door open and walked through into the kitchen. She was about to go and say hi to Joel when she heard him raise a glass with Kezzie, and say: 'To us.' With that she had simply left the cakes on the kitchen table and fled with the girls, telling them Joel was too busy to see them, and gone home feeling like a fool. She had suspected it before, of course, but it was a whole other thing to be presented with the reality of Joel and Kezzie together. She couldn't face either of them today.

'Not too bad,' said Lauren. 'I'm expecting Rose Carmichael and Mary Stevens to provide Victoria sponges, and Cynthia's even bringing a Dundee cake.'

'You've certainly worked some magic here,' said Eileen. 'I don't think we've ever had such an enticing cake stand. You should go into business selling cakes.'

'Do you know, I think I might,' said Lauren.

The fete was officially opening at ten, but Lauren had got there at eight to get ready. She looked nervously at the sky. After days of unbroken sunshine, it looked as though the weather might finally break.

'You don't think it's going to rain, do you?' she said.

'Perish the thought, I simply won't entertain it,' said Eileen, before busying on her way.

The High Street was filling up with people setting up stalls, and there was much camaraderie and joking going on.

Lauren was looking forward to the day. After all their hard work, it should be fun. She wondered how Joel and Kezzie were getting on at the house. The gardens of Heartsease were being opened for the afternoon, and Lovelace Cottage, with its Edward Handford exhibition, was going to be the prime attraction. Lauren knew Joel was going to be there most of the afternoon, while Kezzie was planning to flit between there and the Memorial Gardens. Lauren intended to keep her distance from both of them as much as she could. Not that she wanted to; Kezzie had become a good friend to her over the last few months. She had been a breath of fresh air, and Lauren had been reminded that although she was a mother, she was still young and alive. She felt bad about avoiding her, but Lauren wasn't quite ready to deal with the new reality of Kezzie and Joel.

'Ooh, those look good,' said a voice. Talk of the devil. Damn, that was all she needed. Kezzie came up to the stall. 'I can see you've been busy.'

'Well, I've had some help.' Izzie and Immie popped their heads out from under the table, and Lauren had to stop them dragging the tablecloth off. 'Though it's a moot point how helpful they've actually been. Come on, girls, out of there, you'll ruin the display.'

'How about you? What are you up to?' Lauren was trying to be polite, but Kezzie really was the last person she wanted to see at that moment.

'I'm finishing off the Edward Handford display at Joel's and doing some last minute adjustments in the garden, and then I'm waiting up at the house while he fetches his mum, just in case anyone turns up. She really likes what I've done, I'm so pleased.'

'And I'm sure she's very happy for you,' said Lauren.

'I suppose she is,' said Kezzie, looking a bit puzzled. 'I haven't given it much thought.'

This struck Lauren as slightly odd, but her heart had sunk at the mention of Joel's mum. Kezzie was obviously a regular at Joel's Sunday lunches. That said it all.

'I'm happy for you both, too,' said Lauren. 'Come on, girls, we're going to leave the stall for later and go and have breakfast.'

'Happy for who?' said Kezzie, looking bemused.

'You and Joel,' said Lauren, with dogged determination. Might as well get it out of the way sooner rather than later, so they didn't feel they had to pussyfoot around her. 'I think you'll make an excellent couple. See you later.'

Kezzie stood open mouthed, watching Lauren leave.

Oh God, what a mess! That was all she needed to help her jangling nerves. Kezzie had been so worried about Richard turning up today she'd given no thought to anyone else. Joel had thought it odd last night, when Lauren had left the cakes in his kitchen and not said anything. It all made sense now. Somehow she'd got the wrong end of the stick and thought she and Joel were an item.

Kezzie didn't have time to deal with any of this right now though, she had too much to do. She'd have to go and explain to Lauren later. What's more she'd have to point Joel back in the right direction. He hadn't wanted to crowd Lauren since Troy had left, and had been deliberately giving her space. He, too, had totally misread the situation.

Kezzie went to Joel's, where it was clear that Eileen was more than capably dealing with the exhibition, leaving a very enthusiastic Tony (who it transpired had a passion for local history) in charge. A reporter from the local paper had arrived with a photographer who after photo-graphing Joel in the garden, insisted on Kezzie and Eileen having their picture taken in front of the display. After which she did an interview with Anthony Grantham on Joel's newly restored patio. He promised the knot garden would feature heavily on the next episode of *Dig It!* Escaping from the house into the garden, she spent a busy couple of hours weeding and tidying things up, and replacing the odd plant that looked feeble. There was still no sign of Richard. Good. Perhaps he wasn't coming.

'It looks great,' said Joel, as he came down the garden to let her know he was back. 'I think Edward would have been delighted.'

'I hope so,' said Kezzie.

'I'm glad you've spruced up that old bench,' said Joel's mum, who'd limped down with her stick. 'I'm sure if it could speak, that bench could tell us a story. It's where George proposed to Connie, and my grandfather to my grandmother. I always thought that was fearfully romantic.'

Kezzie smiled slyly. Who knows, maybe it was time to inspire some more romance. She nudged Joel. 'Perhaps you should bring Lauren down here.'

Joel blushed. 'She's not interested in me.'

'Oh yes, she is,' said Kezzie. 'The trouble is, she thinks you're not interested in her. In fact she seems to be suffering from the delusion that you're in love with me.'

'What?'

'You heard,' said Kezzie. 'Now's your chance. Go get her!'

Joel was staggered by Kezzie's revelation. He'd been so sure that Lauren wasn't interested in him in that way, and had been keeping his distance to allow her time to get over Troy. It was true, the other night when they were making cakes she'd warmed up a bit and been more like her old self, but he'd put that down to her being grateful. To be honest, he'd been slightly hurt that she'd simply left the cakes last night without saying hello. He'd been certain that she was still getting over Troy, it hadn't occurred to Joel that she might now be interested in *him*. His heart beat with added excitement. Maybe today was the day when everything could change.

'Come on, time to get ready for the grand opening,' said Joel. 'Let's go down and see New Horizons do their stuff.'

They made it down the hill just in time.

A crowd had gathered in the market square, which had been transformed with a huge stage and bunting. New Horizons were greeted by the Mayor of Chiverton, who looked slightly bemused by proceedings, and even more so when the boys sang their latest hit, much to the excitement of all the girls in the audience. There was even more excitement when one of them took his top off and threw it into the crowd of adoring fans, who had pushed their way up to the front of the stage.

'Be still, my beating heart,' said Kezzie, grinning.

'Well, really,' Cynthia snorted behind them, 'I've never seen such a thing. I shall certainly be complaining to the Parish Council about this.'

Kezzie scanned the crowd, searching for Lauren. She spotted her on the other side of the market square.

'Look, Joel. Lauren's over there. Why don't you go and grab her?'

Joel tried to move over towards where Lauren

and the girls had been standing, but they were swept away by the crowds and he lost sight of them.

By now the sun was shining and the Summer Fest was in full flow. Kezzie went off to do her stint at the Memorial Gardens, while Joel, his mum and Sam found the games area suitable for toddlers, where they spent a happy half hour playing Hook the Duck and having a go at the Lucky Dip. Eileen, it seemed, had thought of everything. Heartsease's Summer Fest had something for everybody.

He tried to catch a glimpse of Lauren on the cake stall, but she was doing such a roaring trade he couldn't find a moment; then he had to go and get ready for the garden opening, and suddenly he had run out of time.

'Will I see you later?' he mouthed in her direction, but she didn't appear to have heard him.

Damn, and double damn. Maybe they'd be able to catch up in the afternoon. He certainly hoped so.

Chapter Thirty-Five

Joel was astonished to get back at 11.30 to find several people patiently waiting to see the garden, even though the official opening wasn't until 12. The first in the queue was the RHS judge, who expressed a passion for knot gardens. 'I can't wait to see what you've done,' she said, 'I'd read about

Edward Handford's garden, and am thrilled it's been restored.' The rest were a motley crew: there were the obvious elderly RHS members who were clearly obsessed with gardens and started asking him awkward questions about plant names, but there was also a young couple with a baby, who professed to just love plants, and a middle-aged mum who told him she was doing a course in gardening history and her tutor had told her to come. He let them all in and took them down to the garden and started his spiel about Edward and Lily, and explained how Kezzie had restored the garden to its former glory, the film crew following him all the while. It was going to be strange seeing his house and gardens on TV. Joel's mum, in the meantime, stayed at the top of the house, keeping an eye on Sam and directing people to the knot garden.

The threatened storm held off, but it was a hot and sultry day, so Joel's mum was also doing a roaring trade with the drinks Joel was selling for a small fee. The visitors seemed to enjoy sitting around on the patio admiring the view and talking about what they had seen in the garden.

'If you'd like to know more about Edward, do have a look at our exhibition on the way out,' Joel was explaining to one visitor, who had somehow missed it, when he was conscious of a tall, lanky, blond guy hovering in the background. There had been a considerable amount of press interest, so Joel assumed he was another journalist.

'So was it you who did the redesign?' the bloke said. 'It is very impressive.'

'No, I hired a local garden designer, called

Kezzie Andrews. It's her first big commission, but I think she's done a great job.'

'I should say so,' said the man. 'Is she here? I'd like to congratulate her in person.'

'No, she's in the village. She'll be at the Memorial Gardens, which she's also helped to restore.'

'Ah, yes, the Memorial Gardens,' said the stranger knowledgeably and Joel, who'd been thinking the man was incredibly nosy, suddenly twigged who he was talking to.

'I know who you are!' he said, with certain conviction. 'It's Richard isn't it?' Kezzie had confided in him that Richard had threatened to turn up, and it seemed he had.

'I'm sorry?' The bloke looked confused.

'Kezzie's ex? She's told me all about you.'

'Has she now?' said Richard. 'Do I take it that you're the reason she's been avoiding me?'

He looked so blatantly hostile and jealous, Joel nearly laughed out loud. This was clearly the second case of mistaken love rivalry that day.

'It's all right, I'm not your competition,' he said. 'Kezzie and I are just friends, nothing more.'

Richard didn't look totally convinced.

'She never talks about anyone else but you,' Joel said.

For the first time Richard looked a little hopeful.

'I know this sounds a bit presumptuous, but do you mind me asking why you came?' said Joel. 'From what Kezzie said, you never wanted to see her again.'

Richard looked a trifle embarrassed.

'Ah, yes, that,' he said. 'Let's just say I've got

395

some unfinished business.'

'If she's not at the Memorial Gardens,' said Joel, 'I expect she'll turn up in the Pimms tent sooner or later.'

'Sounds like Kezzie,' said Richard. 'Thanks, mate.'

'Good luck,' said Joel.

Lauren was frantically busy on the cake stall, which was doing a roaring trade. Her mum had taken the girls round to the field to take part in some of the activities there, so she was able to get on with the job in hand with no distractions. But she hadn't figured on quite how busy it was going to be. Nor how greedy people were. There was one woman who pushed her way to the front of the queue and purchased twenty cupcakes for the three piglet-eyed children by her side. Honestly, you'd think they'd never been fed by the way she was grabbing at the cakes. And two elderly women nearly came to blows over the purchase of the Dundee cake.

'Need a hand?' Kezzie pitched up out of the blue. 'This looks manic.'

Despite her resolve to avoid Kezzie for the day, Lauren couldn't help but be pleased to see her. She was regretting having offered to manage the cake stall alone, and it was at least half an hour till someone was going to relieve her.

They were so busy for the next twenty minutes Lauren was able to avoid any awkward conversation, so it wasn't till there was a lull in proceedings that Kezzie suddenly said, 'Lauren, you've got it all wrong.'

'What have I got all wrong?' said Lauren, who was taking advantage of the pause to sort the notes into a cash box, and putting more change into her petty cash tin. She really didn't want to have this conversation.

'About Joel and me of course,' said Kezzie.

'What do you mean I've got it wrong?' said Lauren. 'I can see how good you are together.'

'That's the point, Lauren,' Kezzie said in exasperation. 'We're not together.'

'What do you mean, you're not together? I thought–'

'–wrong,' said Kezzie. 'Honestly, we are not and never have been an item. The guy's obsessed with you, and if you hadn't wasted so much time with that loser Troy, you'd have been tripping the light fantastic with him weeks ago.'

'Say it like it is why don't you?' Lauren said, wincing at Kezzie's directness. She was right of course, but it was quite painful to have your mistakes held up to you *quite* so baldly.

'Yeah, well, we all make mistakes.' Kezzie looked rueful. 'Look, I didn't know how to tell you this at the time, but you were right about my party.'

'What about it?' Now Lauren was really confused.

'I did end up snogging someone,' said Kezzie, who seemed increasingly awkward. 'And I'm really, really sorry. It was a huge mistake.'

'Joel?' said Lauren.

'No, not Joel, you dope,' said Kezzie. 'Although we did accidentally smooch and realize we'd made a mistake. I'm sorry, I was really drunk and stoned, and I ended up snogging Troy. I wanted to tell you, but the next thing I knew he'd moved back in with you and I couldn't. It's why I was so down on Troy the whole time you were with him. Nothing else happened, and at the time I didn't know you were going to get back together. Can you forgive me?'

Lauren sat down on the camping stool she'd brought in deep shock. Kezzie wasn't in love with Joel but *had* snogged Troy? She didn't know whether to laugh or cry.

'Can I have one of those lovely muffins?' A middle-aged woman was standing over the stall, proffering money. As if in slow motion, Lauren handed over the muffin and took the money, still unable to take in Kezzie's revelation.

'I am so sorry, Lauren,' she said. 'It was before you got back together with him, otherwise I'd never have done it, and nothing happened afterwards I swear.'

Lauren let out a breath she didn't know she'd been holding. It wasn't Kezzie's fault that Troy was a useless bastard, and if anything it made her feel better that someone else had been stupid enough to fall for his charms too. Suddenly she began to laugh at the ridiculousness of the situation.

'God, what an idiot I've been,' she said. 'To think I let that lousy two-timer back into my bed, *again*. I tell you what, I have really learnt my lesson as far as Troy is concerned. Never ever again.'

'Good,' said Kezzie. 'So now you need to find Joel, and tell him how you feel.'

'I do, don't I?' said Lauren, with a grin.

Kezzie was practically crowing with excitement

after she left Lauren. At last, Joel and Lauren were going to sort things out properly. It was a huge relief to have finally got the truth out about Troy, too. She was grateful to Lauren for taking it so well. She'd been worried Lauren might never speak to her again.

Kezzie went back to her post at the Memorial Gardens with a lighter heart, and she spent a couple of happy hours talking people through the work they had done to restore the gardens. There was no sign of Richard yet, and she'd had no word from him, so she began to relax. Let's face it, she thought, he wasn't going to come; he'd made the way he felt about her perfectly clear. Now it was time she moved on. At least she could enjoy herself today and bask in the glory of all the compliments people were giving her. As Flick and the others had arrived midway through the afternoon, she soon found she was having fun.

There was a reasonable amount of press interest; a freelance reporter who'd been up at Lovelace Cottage to see Joel had come down specially to interview Kezzie, too, and take pictures of her and the others in front of the empty war memorial.

'I'm hoping to sell the article to one of the week-end sections in the broadsheets, as a summer garden feature,' he explained. 'If you've got a web-site, I can put that in.'

'That would be great, thanks,' said Kezzie, who'd already had several enquiries about work, which was good. There was nothing left to do at Joel's now.

When the hubbub died down a bit, she took a break from her presenting duties, and wandered over to the Pimms tent. She saw to her amusement that the vicar had imbibed too much Pimms, and was earnestly extolling the virtues of moving to the Church of Rome, to a very unimpressed Cynthia.

'Ah, Pimms. The perfect accompaniment to summer,' she said, to no one in particular.

'That's what I always thought,' said a familiar voice.

Kezzie nearly dropped her glass in shock.

'Richard,' she squeaked. 'You came.'

Chapter Thirty-Six

Kezzie stood in disbelief. Richard was actually standing before her, it was only the second time she'd seen him in months. Richard, her lovely Richard, as charming and gorgeous as ever, had come to find her. Maybe she could hope after all. It took all her restraint not to throw her arms around him.

'I told you I was coming,' said Richard.

'And I told you not to,' said Kezzie.

'Since when have I ever listened to anything you've had to say?' said Richard, with a grin. This was true; it had been an annoying feature of their relationship.

'Look,' said Kezzie, 'I know I stuffed up and I'm really sorry. But you don't have to chase me down here to rub my nose in it any more. I came here to get away from all that.'

'Kezzie, will you just shut up for one minute?'

said Richard.

'Why? You made it quite plain last time we saw each other properly how little you wanted me. I'm over you. Why do you have to come down here and ruin everything?' Kezzie tried to brazen it out, but her heart was pumping and she felt weak at the knees.

'Because I did get your letter – eventually – and I'm the one who should say sorry,' said Richard.

'*What?*' Kezzie was reeling with shock now. Richard, apologize to her? In all the time she'd known him, he'd only ever said sorry to her once, when they'd had a stupid argument about politics.

'Really,' said Richard. 'I was so cross with you, I did overreact. I couldn't believe you could have been so irresponsible as to leave the muffins where Emily could get them, and I knew her mother would make my life hell. Which she did, incidentally. It took Emily two months to pluck up courage to tell me that she knew what those muffins were made of, and tried them out of curiosity.'

'She knew? How?'

'She overheard you chatting on the phone to someone. Look, Kezzie. It was daft of you, but it wasn't entirely your fault. Emily's nearly sixteen now. She knows her own mind. And she confessed to me she wanted to split us up, which is why she drank your vodka as well. I was livid when she told me, I can tell you. She is really sorry.'

Kezzie sat down in shock. She couldn't take in what Richard was saying. He was sorry? Emily had done it on purpose? She felt as if her world had just shifted crazily to one side. All these months blaming herself and it wasn't her fault.

Or at least, not entirely.

'So I'm sorry,' she tuned back in to what Richard was saying, 'I said some unforgivable things to you. Can you forgive me?'

'You did say some terrible things,' she said.

'And I regretted them quite quickly,' he said. 'But you'd disappeared, and no one seemed to know where you were. I've spent the last few months trying to find you.'

'But when I emailed you, you said you didn't want any contact,' said Kezzie.

'I was still angry then,' said Richard. 'It took me far too long to get over that. And by that time it was too late. I tried to email you again and it bounced back.'

'I changed my email address,' admitted Kezzie, 'so you couldn't get in touch.'

'Why?' said Richard.

'Self-preservation,' said Kezzie. 'I didn't like the clingy pathetic person I'd become. I thought if I just cut all ties with you I would get over you quicker.'

'And did you?'

Kezzie didn't answer, so Richard continued, 'I couldn't believe it when I saw you at Wimbledon. I did try to talk to you, but you ran off again. If I hadn't pestered Flick to death, I'd have never got your number off her.'

All these months, she'd been so sure Richard was never going to forgive her, and now it appeared he'd been trying to find her the whole time.

'Nice garden, by the way.'

'What?'

'Your knot garden. I went there first, hoping to

find you, and your client said you'd be here.'

'Did he now?' said Kezzie, not sure whether she should thump Joel or kiss him next time she saw him.

'Only there's something missing,' said Richard.

'Which is?'

'An arch designed by me,' said Richard. 'I think we should recreate it and enter it for next year's Chelsea Flower Show. What do you think?'

'Sounds ... amazing,' said Kezzie.

'Good,' said Richard. 'And I've been waiting to do this all day.'

And he took her hands, pulled her close to him, leant over and gently kissed her on the mouth.

Lauren finished her stint on the cake stall, found her mum and the girls and they all went to have a burger. She was desperate to go and find Joel at the first opportunity but she knew he'd still be busy with his visitors, and the girls were still keen to go on some of the attractions: there was a small fairground in the market square with a merry go round and teacups. She was standing waving at the girls as they had a go on the merry go round when Troy wandered up to her. He had the girls once or twice a week, but he and Lauren had had little or no other contact since the day she'd thrown him out.

'Hi,' he said.

'Hi,' said Lauren.

'They look like they're having fun,' said Troy, nodding to the children.

'They are,' said Lauren, feeling very thankful that her mum had called it a day and gone home.

Her views on Troy had become even more entrenched since she'd found out how he'd let her beloved granddaughter down.

'Loz,' Troy seemed a little hesitant. 'I don't suppose–'

'What?'

'That we have any chance of getting back together? Only you know I've got a proper job now, don't you? I'm going to be the Youth Leader at the new teen drop-in centre, which Tony's persuaded the Parish Council Heartsease needs. And I'm moving out of that grotty bedsit into a flat above the café.'

'I didn't know, no,' said Lauren. 'But that doesn't change anything.'

'Loz, I know I let you down, but I want to prove to you I can change.'

'Troy, I'm sorry,' said Lauren, and she was genuinely surprised to realize she was sorry, 'but it's over. We gave it another go, but I don't think it will work. We have too much history. Too much baggage. I don't think I'll ever be able to trust you properly.'

'Is there nothing I can do to make it up to you?' Troy looked genuinely heartbroken, and for the first time Lauren felt sorry for him.

'No,' she gently touched him on the arm, 'or rather, yes. You can be the best possible dad to them,' she said, nodding at the girls, 'and you can learn from the mistakes you made with me. Make sure the next girl you meet is one you stay with and commit yourself to properly.'

'I'll try,' said Troy, his voice thick with tears. The girls came running over to him, excitedly telling him about their day, and he pulled himself together and gave them both a hug. 'I guess I'll see you around,' he said to Lauren.

'I guess you will,' she said, and gave him a hug. She watched him go and felt a lightening of her heart.

'Can we go and see Sam and Joel?' the girls wanted to know.

'Yes,' said Lauren, 'I think we can.'

The film crew had finally departed, the RHS judge had been back to let Joel know the knot garden had won, and there would be a presentation in the field later that evening, and the last guests were making their way up the garden at Lovelace Cottage. It had been a wonderful and satisfying day. Joel's mum had done a grand job pouring tea and telling anecdotes about Edward; some from memory, some he suspected, embellished somewhat, and Sam had enjoyed toddling around beside her.

Eileen and Tony were busy taking down the exhibition, and Joel thanked them for their hard work. Then he went back and sat down on Edward and Lily's bench in the knot garden for a while to take stock of everything that had happened. It really was the most beautiful spot. No wonder Edward had created the garden here. Joel's heart ached for a bit, thinking of Claire and what they could have had, but sitting here, looking at what Kezzie had achieved, he felt he was coming to terms with losing Claire. The garden would be a fitting memorial to her. Kezzie had blasted in like a breath of fresh air and shaken his life up. She had made him see that he could find love again, with Lauren, if Lauren would let him.

'Mind if I join you?'

Lauren was standing by the garden gate, her golden hair wreathed in sunlight, her light summer dress shimmering in the breeze. He swallowed hard. She looked absolutely stunning.

'No, of course not,' he said. 'Come and sit down.'

'I've left the girls with your mum,' she said. 'Is that OK?'

'Sure, whatever,' Joel swallowed again. He felt absurdly nervous, like a sixteen-year-old on a first date.

Lauren came and sat down.

'So,' she said. 'This is Edward's garden.'

'And Kezzie's,' said Joel.

'She's done a great job.'

'Hasn't she?'

They paused, looking at one another uncertainly.

'Joel—'

'Lauren—'

'You first—'

They both laughed.

'I think I've been mistaken about you,' said Lauren. 'For a long time I was angry with you for the way you treated Claire.'

'And deservedly so,' said Joel. 'I know now I really let her down.'

'I could never understand the way she was so forgiving towards you. Even the night before she died she texted me to say you'd had a row.'

'I know, I really didn't deserve her,' said Joel.

He put his head in his hands. 'I've never forgiven myself for that row, I had no idea she'd told you about it.'

'Well, you should,' said Lauren, 'because Claire did. And I never understood why till recently. Now I know what she saw in you.'

'What do you mean?' Joel was stunned. 'How can you possibly know that?'

'I rang her to see if she was OK,' said Lauren, 'and she was very cross with you. But then she laughed and said you were drunk and being stupid, and she'd gone to bed to punish you, but she knew you'd make it up in the morning.'

Joel's eyes welled up.

'And there wasn't another morning,' he whispered. 'She really said that? I never knew.'

'I'm sorry,' Lauren touched his hand. 'I know you felt bad about Claire, but it never occurred to me that you were beating yourself up so much. All those women... I thought you didn't care.'

'They never made me feel better,' said Joel. 'They were a way of numbing the pain, and trying to fill the black emptiness Claire left. And all the time I was with them, I didn't see what was right under my nose. Namely you.'

He leant over and looked at her deep and hard.

'Lauren,' he said, 'can we start again?'

'I'd like that,' she said shyly.

He leant towards her, and gently cupping her face in his hands, he kissed her. All the pain and heartache fell away, and something new and vibrant took its place. And Joel really understood for the first time that though Claire had gone, he didn't have to stop living, and that she wouldn't have wanted him to. He held Lauren close to him, as if he couldn't bear to let her go.

They walked back up the hill hand in hand as the sun set, and the children ran towards them, a symbol of their bright and shining future.

Epilogue

The band of elderly men, with their poppies and regimental medals proudly displayed on their breasts, marched through the gates of the Memorial Gardens. It was a sharply bright November day, and they were led by a small band of soldiers in full kit. They marched down the newly gravelled path, up to the Heartsease War Memorial, now proudly returned to its place of honour. The flowerbeds to the right and left had been cultivated in the shape of poppies, and the flowerbed behind the memorial was dotted with tiny wooden crosses, each with a poppy attached; one for every man in Heartsease who had given their lives for their country.

Eileen stood proudly watching as Jamie, newly and safely returned from Afghanistan, laid a wreath at the newly restored war memorial. She wiped away a tear, while Tony squeezed her hand.

Kezzie and Richard, now happily sharing two homes between Heartsease and London, waited till the ceremonies were over, and then came forward with their own small wreath, which Kezzie insisted she wanted to lay in Harry Handford's honour.

'I feel I should,' she explained. 'For Edward.'

Joel, Lauren and the children had been standing next to them, and they walked forward with the lilies Joel had felt were appropriate. Together they watched silently as the rest of the crowd came by to either lay a wreath or pay their respects, and they all bowed their heads to the haunting sound of the Last Post.

When the band and the marching soldiers had finally gone, the four of them remained behind, contemplating the war memorial, while the children ran around on the grass.

'Sixty-five men from Heartsease dead in World War One alone,' marvelled Kezzie. 'Every house in the village must have been affected. It doesn't bear thinking about.'

'And look, Harry's name, just there quietly in amongst them,' said Joel. 'Edward could have designed it so Harry's name stood out, but he chose not to. He wrote Connie a letter about it, saying he wanted every family in the village to feel they owned the memorial too, that it wasn't just for Harry.'

'And now it's been restored to the village,' said Richard. 'All thanks to you guys.'

'The war memorial's mainly down to Eileen,' said Kezzie. 'Although I will take some credit for the garden.'

'But it wouldn't have been worth pursuing if you two hadn't restored the garden,' said Lauren. 'I think if Edward Handford's up there somewhere, he'd be really proud.'

'Do you know,' said Kezzie, 'I think he would.'

Edward

1919–1955

'Tis better to have loved and lost, than never to have loved at all.

Alfred, Lord Tennyson
'In Memoriam'

After the funeral, Connie immediately came home to be with Edward, which was some comfort. At first he spent time – too much time – brooding in the garden. He saw Lily constantly there, and it reminded him of what they had had, but it was also too painful, and at times he could almost not bear to leave. In the end Connie took him aside one day, and gently said she was locking the garden up. It gave no more comfort now. Occasionally Edward thought of it, but as the years passed and Connie eventually married, and produced his new grandson, Jack, he thought of it less.

Tilly and her family were rare visitors – Connie was never able to forgive her sister's betrayal, so Edward saw them alone. But as the years passed, and he grew old, his visits to them grew more infrequent, until eventually they stopped altogether.

One day, when Connie was away and he was dozing by the fire, a knock on the door announced a visitor.

'I'm Daisy,' the young woman who stood before him said. 'Tilly's daughter. You remember? Your granddaughter. And this is Lilian, your great granddaughter.'

Edward looked down at the angelic beauty by Daisy's side.

'She looks so like Tilly at that age,' he said.

They stayed for the afternoon, and it being a summer's day, Edward allowed himself to be persuaded to sit in the garden.

'Can we go to the secret garden?' said Daisy. 'I remember cousin Jack hiding in there when I was little.'

'It's locked up now,' said Edward, 'but I believe there's still a key hanging in the scullery.'

Daisy fetched the key, and together they walked to the garden. Edward slowly opened the gate. It had been years since he'd been there, and the sun shone on his neglect.

He could have wept to see what had become of his creation, born out of love for Lily and ruined and destroyed in his despair. Connie had promised to look after it for him, but it had clearly been too painful for her.

He sat down heavily on the ornate bench, carved with the letters E and L, which he'd had made on the occasion of their wedding. It was now rusted after years of damp, cold winters, and Edward stared at the garden with deep sadness. All his labours turned to dust.

Lilian came up to him shyly. 'Look, Grandpa,' she said, 'pretty flowers, just for you.'

She held up a bunch of pansies.

'They're called heartsease,' he said, 'thank you.'

He sat back, holding the flowers and smiling. The garden and all it meant to him had gone, but here was another Lily come along, like a miracle, to ease his aching heart.

Edward

Edward dreams of Lily. She comes to him as he sits on the veranda, looking out at the view they both love so much. She is as young as when he first knew her. His lovely, laughing, joyful Lily, dancing towards him in the sunshine.

'Edward, it's time to come home,' she says. 'Here, take my hand.'

She leads him down the path, towards the sunken garden, and he walks through the gate into a bright sunlit world.

'For your heart's ease,' she says, and presses a bunch of pansies into his hands.

Edward dreams of Lily, still clutching the pansies his great granddaughter brought him. Edward dreams of Lily, and in his sleep he smiles.

Acknowledgements

I'd like to say a huge thank you to my outgoing editor, Kate Bradley, who made many helpful suggestions in the early stages of writing this book, not least by suggesting I made Edward and Lily's story a stronger thread, and also to my incoming editor, Claire Bord, who has made the transition so smooth, and been nothing but helpful and encouraging.

Heartfelt thanks as ever to my fabulous agent, Dot Lumley and to the rest of the Avon team: Charlotte Allen, Sammia Rafique, Helen Bolton, Claire Power and Caroline Ridding.

I'd also like to say thanks to William Dawson for his help on knot gardens, and to Liz Heymoz and Ita Flach for showing me the knot garden he created at Buckden Towers.

My twin sister, Virginia Moffatt is my keenest supporter and critic, and thanks are due to her for giving me such an enthusiastic thumbs up at an early stage.

I'd also like to thank my brother-in-law Nick Williams, for his fantastic detective work in uncovering the story of my family in World War I, which has been hugely influential in the writing of this story.

There were several people who were enormously helpful with last minute queries, so thanks are due too to: Emma Alston, Sarah Duncan, Penny Jordan and Kate Wilstone who generously and swiftly responded to questions which were making me tear my hair out. And a huge thanks to all the lovely people on Twitter, who said, yes, you can buy freesias in September.

And belatedly, I'd like to say a big thank you to you, the reader, for not only buying this, but supporting me in so many ways with my previous books. If you'd like to know more about what I'm up to you can follow me on Twitter @ JCCWilliams or on my blog http;//maniac-mum.blogspot.com

The publishers hope that this book has given you enjoyable reading. Large Print Books are especially designed to be as easy to see and hold as possible. If you wish a complete list of our books please ask at your local library or write directly to:

Magna Large Print Books
Magna House, Long Preston,
Skipton, North Yorkshire.
BD23 4ND

This Large Print Book for the partially sighted, who cannot read normal print, is published under the auspices of

THE ULVERSCROFT FOUNDATION

THE ULVERSCROFT FOUNDATION

... we hope that you have enjoyed this Large Print Book. Please think for a moment about those people who have worse eyesight problems than you ... and are unable to even read or enjoy Large Print, without great difficulty.

You can help them by sending a donation, large or small to:

**The Ulverscroft Foundation,
1, The Green, Bradgate Road,
Anstey, Leicestershire, LE7 7FU,
England.**
or request a copy of our brochure for more details.

The Foundation will use all your help to assist those people who are handicapped by various sight problems and need special attention.

Thank you very much for your help.